W9-APB-868

a
GAME
of
FATE

SCARLETT ST. CLAIR

PUBLISHER'S NOTE: This is a work of fiction. Names, characters, places and incidents are either the product of the author's imagination or are used fictitiously. Any resemblance to actual persons, living or dead, business establishments, events, or locales is entirely coincidental.

ISBN: 978-1-7357719-0-8 (Hardback)
ISBN: 978-1-7357719-1-5 (Paperback)

Copyright © 2020 Scarlett St. Clair

Cover Design by: Emily Wittig Designs

All right reserved. No part of this publication may be reproduced, stored in or introduced into a retrieval system, or transmitted, in any form, or by any means (electronic, mechanical, photocopying, recording, or otherwise) without the prior written permission of the author.

For more information visit www.ScarlettStClair.com

v 1.4

DEDICATION

This book is dedicated to two of the most powerful women I know—Leslie and Regina, my motivators, my mentors, my soul sisters. Thank you for showing me my own power. I love you across lifetimes, I love you forever.

MORE BOOKS BY
SCARLETT ST. CLAIR

A Touch Of Darkness
A Touch Of Ruin
A Touch Of Malice
When Stars Come Out

COMING SOON

King Of Blood And Battle
A Game Of Retribution
A Game Of Gods
A Touch Of Chaos

READING ORDER

CHAPTER I – A GAME OF BALANCE

Hades manifested near the Coast of the Gods.

In the sunlight, the shoreline boasted turquoise water and pristine, white beaches, all set before the backdrop of cliffs, grottoes, and a monastery made of white and green marble that could be accessed after ascending three hundred steps. Mortals flocked here to swim, sail, and snorkel. It was an oasis, up until the sun made its fiery descent in the sky.

After twilight, evil moved in the darkened night, beneath a sky of stars and an ocean of moonlight. It came on ships and moved across New Greece, and Hades was here to neutralize it.

He turned, the gravel crunching beneath his feet, and walked in the direction of The Corinth Company, a fishery that took up an extensive amount of real estate on the coast. The plaster façade of the warehouse blended flawlessly with the ancient architecture adorning the shoreline, appearing worn, bleached, and charming. A simple, black lamp highlighted a sign bearing the company's name, written in a font that boasted prestige and power—admirable characteristics when they belonged to the best of society.

Dangerous when they belonged to the worst.

A mortal moved in the shadow. He had been there since Hades arrived and no doubt thought he was well hidden, which perhaps he was to other mortals, but Hades was a god and he owned the shadows.

As he passed, the man moved and Hades twisted, his hand biting down on the mortal's. A gun was clutched in his fingers. Hades looked at the weapon and then at the man, a wicked smile crossing his lips.

In the next second, sharp spires extended from the tips of Hades' fingers, sinking into the man's flesh. His weapon clattered to the ground and he dropped to his knees with a guttural cry.

"Please spare me, my lord," the man begged. "I did not know."

Hades always found the seconds before a mortal's death intriguing. Especially when he encountered one like this—one who had killed without thought and yet feared his own demise.

Hades tightened his hold, and as the man trembled, the god laughed.

"Your death is not imminent," Hades said, and the mortal looked up. "But I will have words with your employer."

"My employer?"

Hades almost groaned. So the mortal would play dumb.

"Sisyphus de Ephyra."

"H-he's not here."

Lie.

The knowledge coated his tongue like ash, drying his throat.

Hades lifted the man by his arm, spikes still embedded in his skin, until their gazes were level. It was from this angle that Hades noticed a tattoo on the man's wrist. It was a triangle, now spliced by the spears extending from his fingers.

"I do not need your aid to enter that warehouse," Hades said. "What I need from you is an example."

"A-An example?"

Hades decided to use actions to explain, carving two deep fissures in the man's face. As blood coated his skin, neck, and clothes, the god dragged him to the entrance of the warehouse, kicked open the doors, and strolled inside.

What had looked like a building from the shore now appeared to be a wall, because instead of walking into an enclosed space, Hades found himself in a yard open to the inky sky above. The earth was bare, and there were large above-ground pools holding fish. The air smelled like ocean and rot and salt. Hades hated the stench.

Workers dressed in black jumpsuits turned to watch as the god pushed the bleeding mortal forward. The man floundered but caught himself before he hit the ground. Opposite Hades, another man approached, flanked by two large bodyguards. He was dressed in a white suit, and his fingers were fat and suffocated with gold rings. His hair was short and black, his beard manicured and threaded with silver.

"Sis, I-I-It wasn't my fault," the man said as he stumbled forward. "I—"

Sisyphus withdrew a gun and shot the man. He fell, hitting the ground with a loud thud. Hades looked at the still body and then at Sisyphus.

"He was not wrong," Hades said.

"I did not kill him because he let you enter my property. I killed him because he has disrespected a god."

A display like that usually came from a loyal subject. Of those, Hades had few, and he knew Sisyphus was not one.

"Is this your version of a sacrifice?"

"Depends," the man replied, cracking his neck and handing his gun to the bodyguard on the right. "Do you accept?"

"No."

"Then it was business."

Sisyphus straightened the lapels of his jacket and

adjusted his cufflinks, and Hades noted the same triangle tattoo on his wrist.

"Shall we?" The mortal gestured for Hades to walk in front, toward an office on the opposite side of the yard. "Divine first."

"I insist," Hades declined.

Despite his power, he was never eager to have his back turned.

Sisyphus' eyes narrowed slightly. The mortal probably saw Hades' refusal to lead as a form of disrespect, mostly because it showed that Hades did not trust him. Ironic, considering Sisyphus had broken one of the most ancient rules of hospitality—the law of Xenia—by killing his competition after inviting them into his territory.

It was just one of Sisyphus' transgressions Hades was here to address.

"Very well, my lord," The mortal offered a cold smile before starting toward his office, the two bodyguards in tow. Their presence was amusing, as if the two mortal men could protect Sisyphus from him.

Hades found himself considering how he would take them out. He had a number of options—he could call forth the shadows and let them consume the two, or he could subdue them by himself. He supposed the only real consideration was whether he wanted blood on his suit.

The two bodyguards took their places on either side of the door as Sisyphus entered his office. Hades did not look at them as he passed.

Sisyphus' office was small. His desk was solid wood, stained dark, and stacked with paperwork. An old-fashioned telephone sat to one side, and a crystal decanter and two glasses on the other. Behind him, a set of windows overlooked the yard, obstructed by blinds.

It was behind the desk where Sisyphus chose to stand, a strategic move, Hades imagined. It put something physical between them. It was also probably where he kept a store of weapons. Not that they would do any good against him, but Hades had existed for centuries and knew desperate mortals would try anything.

"Bourbon?" Sisyphus asked as he uncorked the decanter.

"No."

The mortal stared at Hades for a moment before pouring himself a glass. He took a sip and asked, "To what do I owe the pleasure?"

Hades looked toward the door. From here, he could see the pools, and he nodded toward them now.

"I know you are hiding drugs in your pools," Hades said. "I also know that you use this company as a front to move them across New Greece and that you kill anyone who gets in the way."

Sisyphus stared at Hades for a moment, and then took a slow sip from his glass before asking, "Have you come to take my life?"

"No."

It was not a lie. Hades did not reap souls—Thanatos did, but the God of the Underworld could see Sisyphus was due for a visit and soon. The vision had come, unbidden, like a memory from long ago. Sisyphus, dressed smartly, would collapse as he left a high-ending dining room.

He would never regain consciousness.

And before that happened, Hades would have balance.

"Then should I assume you want a cut?"

Hades tilted his head to the side. "Of sorts."

Sisyphus chuckled. "Who would have thought, the God of the Dead came to bargain."

Hades gritted his teeth. He did not like the implication of Sisyphus' words, as if the mortal thought he had the upper hand.

"As penance for your crimes, you will donate half your income to the homeless. You are, after all, responsible for many of them."

The drugs Sisyphus trafficked had destroyed lives, eating mortals up from the inside out with addiction and igniting violence in communities, and while he wasn't the only one responsible, it was his ships that brought it into the mainland, his trucks that transported it across New Greece.

"Is penance not served in the afterlife?" Sisyphus asked.

"Consider it a favor. I am allowing you an early start."

Sisyphus used his tongue to pick between his teeth, then he snickered quietly.

"You know they never describe you as a righteous god."

"I am not righteous."

"Forcing crooks like myself to donate to charities is righteous."

"It is balance. A price you pay for the evil you spread."

Hades did not believe in eradicating the world of evil, because he did not believe it was possible. What was evil to one was a fight for freedom to another—The Great War was an example. One side fought for their gods, their religion, the other fought for freedom from their perceived oppressor. The best he could do was offer a touch of redemption so that their sentence in the Underworld might eventually lead to Asphodel.

"But you are not the God of Balance. You are the God of the Dead."

It would do no good to explain the workings of the Fates, the balance they strove to create in the world, and so he remained silent. Sisyphus pulled a metal case from the inside pocket of his jacket and withdrew a cigarette.

"I'll tell you what." He put the cigarette to his lips and lit it. The smell of nicotine filled the small shop—ashy, stale, and chemical. "I'll donate one million, and I won't violate the law of Xenia anymore."

Hades paused a moment and used the silence to quell the rush of anger the mortal's words ignited, his fingers curling into fists. Not so long ago, he would have let the fury overtake him, sending the mortal to Tartarus without a second thought. Instead, he let the darkness do the work for him. Outside Sisyphus' office, Hades called to the shadows and they slithered across the exterior of the building, darkening the windows as they went.

Hades watched as Sisyphus turned, eyes following the shadows until they approached the two bodyguards at the front of the office. In the next second, they slipped into every orifice of their bodies and they collapsed, dead.

Sisyphus' eyes returned to Hades' and he grinned.

"On second thought, you have a deal, Lord Hades," Sisyphus said. "Two hundred and fifty million it is."

"Three," Hades replied.

Defiance flashed in the mortal's eyes. "That is more than half my income."

"A punishment for wasting my time," Hades said. He started to turn and leave the office before pausing. He looked over his shoulder at the mortal. "And I would not worry about breaking the law of Xenia, mortal. You don't have much time left."

Sisyphus was silent after Hades' words. Ribbons of smoke danced from the cigarette poised between his fingers. After a moment, he put it out in his drink.

"Tell me something," he said. "Why do it? Bargain and balance? Have you hope for humanity?"

"Have you none?" Hades countered.

"I live among mortals, Lord Hades. Trust me, when given the choice to tip the scale one way or the other, they'll choose darkness. It's the fastest path with the quickest benefit."

"And the most to lose," Hades said. "Do not educate me on the nature of mortals, Sisyphus. I have judged your kind for a millennium."

Hades paused outside the door, looking down at the two men who lay at his feet. He did not revel in the idea of restoring them to life to spread violence and death themselves, but he knew the Fates would demand a sacrifice—a soul for a soul—and it was likely they would choose souls that were good and pure and innocent.

Balance, Hades thought, and he suddenly hated the word.

"Wake," he commanded.
And as they inhaled sharp breaths, Hades vanished.

CHAPTER II – A GAME OF FATE

Hades appeared in his office at Nevernight, one of his most popular New Athens clubs. It was close to eleven, and at midnight, he would wander through the upstairs lounge, choosing mortals who longed to bargain for their greatest desires and wishes—health, love, and riches. Those were just the things he could grant. It did not include requests like creating life, returning life, or bestowing beauty—desires he would not award.

"You're late."

Minthe's voice was like a whip, shattering his thoughts. He had sensed her the moment he entered the room—all fire and ice—and preferred to ignore her when she was like this.

He focused on adjusting his tie and cufflinks, silently relieved that he had chosen to use shadow magic to take Sisyphus' bodyguards down, so he did not have to hear the nymph demand answers. With his appearance restored, he turned to the flaming-haired nymph. Her lips, a shade darker than her hair, were twisted into a pout. She did not like being ignored.

"How can I be late, Minthe, when I abide by no one's schedule but my own?"

Minthe had been his assistant since the beginning of time, and she went through phases where she would try to exercise rights over him—rights to his time, to his realm, and to his body. Her eagerness for control was not lost on him. He recognized the trait in her because he possessed it himself.

"Tardiness is not attractive, Hades, even from a god," she snapped.

A smile threatened his lips, but he remained composed. His amusement would only anger her further.

"While you were *dallying*," Hades narrowed his eyes at the jab, "*I've* had to entertain your guests."

Hades' brows furrowed and dread crawled up the back of his throat. "Who is waiting for me?"

He knew by Minthe's expression—the way her eyes narrowed, the slight curl of her mouth—that he would not like her answer.

"Lady Aphrodite."

"*Fuck*," Hades muttered.

Minthe did not even try to hide her amusement, her lips coiled into a full smirk.

"You might want to hurry," she said. "When I insisted she wait for you here, she said there was plenty to entertain her downstairs."

Fantastic. The only thing to ever come out of Aphrodite entertaining herself was war.

He sighed. "Thank you, Minthe."

Clearly pleased by Hades' expression of gratitude, Minthe uncrossed her arms, letting them fall at her sides.

"Shall I bring you a drink, my lord?"

"Yes. In fact, I am not to have an empty glass tonight."

Hades vanished and appeared on the floor of his club, where he walked, silent and unseen. As always, it was packed with mortals and humanoids—nymphs, satyrs, chimeras, centaurs, ogres, and cyclopes. Some used glamour, others did not. Some merely wished to experience the thrill of attending the most notorious club in New Athens, others glanced longingly toward the upstairs lounge, hopeful one of Hades' staff would offer the night's password.

A password did not guarantee a game with the God of the Dead, it was just another step in the process. Once mortals passed through the doors of the lounge, fear settled in, and that fear either drew them away or made them desperate. It was the desperate Hades was most interested in—the ones who might change if offered the chance.

It was a delicate process and involved many players. Hades had lost his fair share of bargains, and he could feel those against his skin, a never-ending itch and reminder of failure, but if he could save one life on the path to destruction, he felt it was worth it.

Hades picked up the scent of Aphrodite's magic—sea salt and roses—and found her sitting on the lap of an older, middle-aged man. He had dark, thinning hair. His forehead was greasy and his face chubby, melting into a sweaty neck, around which Aphrodite's arms were laced, her breasts pressed against his chest. Hades noted a gold band on the man's left ring finger. He did not have to look at the mortal's soul to know he was a cheating bastard.

"Why don't we go back to my place, baby?" the man asked as his hands explored Aphrodite's body, moving across her ribs and over her thighs. Hades cringed as he observed the interaction.

"Oh, I really would like to stay just a little longer," Aphrodite was saying. "Don't you want to bargain with Hades?"

The man squeezed her, fingers digging into her bottom. "Not anymore. You're everything I need."

"Really?" Aphrodite said breathlessly, and leaned closer, her pink lips inches from his.

Hades had to admit, the Goddess of Love was a great actress. She hid her loathing for the man and distracted him with her hands as they drifted up his chest. Hades sensed her magic rising and knew she was compelling the man to tell her the truth as she asked her next question.

"What were you missing before?"

Hades knew the answer because he could see it. The mortal's insecurities had grown claws as he had aged, and they twined with his narcissism and need to feel important. He held resentment like his child, close to his heart, and it had poisoned his blood, fueled his lies, and prompted his cheating spree. He had a little bit of humanity left in the guilt that sat upon his shoulders like a leering gargoyle. To numb the ache, he drank, but his tolerance for drinking had grown over the last few years, which meant he needed more to feel detached from what his life had become.

The man had a cracked soul, and Hades had a feeling Aphrodite was about to shatter it.

"I'm insecure. I need to know I am still wanted by other women."

"And it isn't enough to be wanted by your wife?" Aphrodite's pretty lips twisted into a scowl. The man's eyes went wide, his mind at odds with what was coming out of his mouth. Hades had seen it before when he had used the spell.

"I love my wife," he said. "I'm just looking for sex."

"Is that all?" She batted her lashes and then spoke in a voice veiled with darkness and strong with promise. "In that case, when you return to your wife this evening, she will no longer desire you. She will cringe at your touch and gag when your lips touch hers. She will refuse you, she will leave you, and you will never recover."

The man's eyes widened, and he was no longer holding Aphrodite, his hands peeled back from her skin as if she burned.

This was Aphrodite in her true form. The mortal world believed she was nothing more than a sexual being, that she sought entertainment and pleasure from gods and mortals alike, but the truth was she could be a vengeful god, especially toward those who betrayed love.

It was probably time for Hades to make an appearance.

"Aphrodite," he greeted, dropping his glamour.

The goddess turned to meet his gaze and smiled.

"Hades," she purred in a sensual voice, and even though she had just cursed the mortal she was still using as an armchair, his eyes clouded with desire at the sound.

"I think the mortal has had enough excitement for one night. Why don't you let him slither off?"

Aphrodite's face changed at the mention of the cheater, and she turned to glare at him before hopping off his lap. "Run along, snake."

The mortal obeyed and wandered into the crowd, dazed.

"What?" Aphrodite snapped when she looked at Hades again.

His brows rose, surprised by her venom. "Nothing. Although you will hardly help the man's ego by taking away the only love he has ever known."

She dusted off her hands. "He betrayed love, so he will never have it again."

"I don't think your punishment is unfair," Hades explained. "But it has the potential to create a monster."

She smirked, her expression impish. "Then he's all yours. Monsters are your territory, Hades."

Minthe approached just then, balancing a tray of drinks. This was how the nymph spent most of her evenings at Nevernight—taking orders and delivering them, flirting with mortals and immortals alike, and gathering information from Hades' more *elite clients*.

"Lady Aphrodite," Minthe said as she passed the goddess a glass of rosé. "Lord Hades."

She handed off a glass of whiskey, and as she wandered away, he turned to Aphrodite, who raised a pale brow at him.

"Yes?" he inquired at her questioning stare.

"That nymph wants to fuck you," she said.

A mistake I will never make again, he thought.

Hades did not acknowledge her comment and instead said, "You do not often grace my halls with your presence, Aphrodite. What can I do for you?"

She took a sip of wine, her sea-foam eyes locked with

his. "I had hoped you'd be interested in a bargain of our own."

"I do not play gods."

"Just one game, Hades," she said innocently, and then goaded, "Are you afraid?"

"A game played under this roof is never *just* a game." *Not even for me*, he thought. There was always the possibility of losing, and he tended to lose just as much as the mortals who bargained with him, but their requests he could grant. He did not trust what Aphrodite would ask for. "Why request a game? What is it you want, goddess?"

"Why must I want something?" she asked. "Perhaps I am just bored and in need of entertainment."

"There is nothing more dangerous than a bored Aphrodite," Hades mused.

She pouted. "Please, Hades?"

He met her gaze and sipped from his glass before answering.

"No, Aphrodite."

She was after more than entertainment. He could see it in the way she carried herself, rigid and tense. Something had brought her here, and if he had to guess, it had to do with her husband.

"Fine." She lifted her chin in defiance. "You forced my hand."

He glared at her, knowing what she was going to say next.

"I have an unclaimed favor from you, Hades. I wish to use it."

A favor owed between gods was like a blood pact. Once invoked, it could not be taken back.

"You would waste a favor on a game of cards?" he asked. He knew the answer—whatever had brought Aphrodite here, it was worth spending.

Her eyes flashed. "*It is not a waste.*"

He took a drink of his whiskey. It kept him from saying anything he might regret before he gritted out, "One game, Aphrodite, no more."

She brightened like he had given her the stars in the sky. "Thank you, Hades."

Hades snapped his fingers, and the two teleported to the Ruby Suite upstairs. It was one of several rooms Hades used when bargaining with mortals. They were all named after precious stones. He chose this one intentionally, as a bit of a jab at Aphrodite. Ruby was passion—something she lacked these days. The walls were red, and black fabric was draped from floor to ceiling, framing sensual monochrome photos. A pack of unopened cards sat at the center of a table, which was positioned under a pool of muted light.

As Hades took his seat, he offered them to Aphrodite. "Would you like to deal?"

"No." A smile curled her lips. "I'll let you retain some power, Aidoneus."

He glared at her. He did not like that nickname. Mortals used it out of fear. She used it now to taunt him.

"Blackjack, then."

"Five hands," Aphrodite said. "Whoever wins the most, sets stakes."

Hades agreed, dealt the first hand, and lost. His fingers curled into a fist on his thigh.

"What do you see when you look at my soul, Hades?" Aphrodite asked offhand, pursing her lips as he dispensed the cards again.

The question was not all that surprising. It was one he received often, but never from Aphrodite.

"Why do you ask?"

When she met his gaze, he saw she was serious and that she also feared the truth. It was present in her eyes, a shadow that flickered across her expression. She did not look at him long before focusing on her cards.

"Hit me," she said, and Hades gave her another card before revealing their hands—Hades had two aces and a twelve of diamonds, Aphrodite, a bust. She frowned at her loss but continued to speak as Hades dealt a third hand.

"I just wonder if I'm as horrible as Hephaestus seems

to think."

Aphrodite was not horrible, but her union with Hephaestus had hardened her heart and broken her spirit. What was left was a spiteful and cynical shell.

Hades had been bitter once, too, but unlike Aphrodite, who dealt with her anger and loneliness by entertaining herself with mortals and gods, he had isolated himself further and further, until the only thing people could do was make up stories and tales about the elusive God of the Underworld.

"Hephaestus does not think you are horrible, Aphrodite. He's just afraid to love you." She offered a mocking laugh, so Hades challenged, "Have you ever told him you love him?"

"What relevance does that have to my question?"

Everything, Hades wanted to say.

"You were a gift to Hephaestus at a time when you flaunted your lovers. From his perspective, you were a reluctant bride."

It did not matter that Hades knew the truth. Aphrodite had always been enchanted by the God of Fire. In ancient times, on the rare occasions Hades had gone to Mount Olympus, he had caught her watching Hephaestus, mostly frowning because he did not give her the time of day.

But Hades knew Hephaestus well, too. The god was of a different sort. He was not eager to be under the spotlight, less eager to speak. He took pleasure in solitude and innovation, and in his heart, he felt…unworthy, mostly due to his treatment in antiquity. As a god with only one leg, he was often—and wrongly—mocked. Over time, Hephaestus adapted, fashioning prosthetics, and now sported one made of gold.

"I'm not surprised Hephaestus is not interested in forcing you into monogamy."

Aphrodite was silent for a moment, focusing on their game, and as they turned their cards, Hades bit down on his tongue—a bust. He had dealt himself one too many cards.

Aphrodite was in the lead.

Finally, she admitted, "I asked Zeus for a divorce. He will not grant it."

Hades' brows rose. "Does Hephaestus know?"

"I imagine he does now."

"You want Hephaestus' love, why ask for a divorce?"

"I will not pine after him."

"You are sending mixed messages, Aphrodite. You want Hephaestus' love, but you ask for a divorce. Have you even tried talking to him?"

"Have you?" she snapped, glaring at Hades. "He might as well be mute!"

Hades grimaced. He had a feeling Hephaestus kept quiet because her temper was a short fuse.

"You haven't answered my question, Hades."

The god watched her for a moment. He did not particularly like answering questions about the soul. Often, god and mortal alike were not ready to hear what he had to say. Aphrodite was no different. Parts of her soul were a garden, full of roses and lilies and sunshine, dreamy and quiet. Others were a storm, raging over a churning sea— furious and devastating. She was broken, split in two like a cracked mirror, straddling a line. One day, she would choose a side.

"You have a beautiful soul, Aphrodite. Passionate. Determined. Romantic. But you are desperate to be loved and believe yourself unlovable."

He spoke as they played their last hand, and when Aphrodite flipped her cards, a wide smile broke out across her face. Whatever she felt about Hades' comments was lost in her excitement.

"It's time for terms, Hades."

He scowled and sat back in his chair, glaring. Aphrodite threw her head back in laughter.

"Someone does not like to lose."

Her words were like a poker in his side. Hades did not actually mind losing. He lost all the time when he bargained with mortals, but he had not wanted to lose to

Aphrodite.

The goddess pressed a finger to her chin and offered a soft hum, as if she did not know what to ask of him. She was wasting his time. She knew what she wanted, but just as he was about to bark at her, she spoke.

"Fall in love, Hades. Better yet, find a girl who will fall in love with you." Then Aphrodite clapped and exclaimed, "That's it! Make someone fall in love with you!"

Hades' jaw tightened, and Aphrodite stared back as if she wished to see to his soul in turn. Her terms were insulting. If it were that easy to fall in love, he would not be alone now.

"Is this your idea of a joke?" he asked, his voice quiet and calm, despite the anger twisting his insides. He was going to have to torture someone just to release the tension in his body.

"Not a joke," she said, raising a thin blonde brow. "You've offered love advice. Follow it."

Not a joke then, but retribution. She was frustrated with him for offering his opinion on her marriage.

"And if I can't meet those terms?"

Her smile cut across her face wickedly.

"Then you will release Basil from the Underworld."

"Your lover?" Hades could not keep the disgust from his voice. They'd just spent the last few minutes discussing her love for Hephaestus, and here she was asking for a man—her hero, to be exact. Basil had fought and died for her in The Great War. "Why? Don't you want Hephaestus to admit that he loves you?"

She glared at him. "Hephaestus is a lost cause."

"You haven't even tried!"

"*Basil*, Hades. *He* is who I want."

"Because you imagine yourself in love with him?"

"What do you know of love? You've never loved in your lifetime."

Those words did not hurt, so much as embarrass him. He leaned toward the goddess.

"Basil loves you, that is true, but if you don't love him

in return, it is meaningless."

"Better to be loved than not at all," she countered.

You are a fool, Hades wanted to say. Instead, he asked, "Are you sure this is what you want? You have already petitioned Zeus for a divorce, now you have asked me to resurrect your lover in the event I cannot meet the terms of your contract. Hephaestus will know."

Aphrodite was quiet, and he recognized her uncertainty in the way she toyed with her lip.

Finally, she answered.

"Yes. It is what I want." She took a deep breath then and managed a smile. "Six months, Hades. That should be enough time. Thank you for the entertainment. It was... *invigorating.*"

With that, the Goddess of Love vanished.

CHAPTER III – A GAME
OF RESTRAINT

Make someone fall in love with you.

The words were a cruel taunt that echoed in Hades' mind as he prowled the darkness of his club to clear his head.

Perhaps he had gone too far in criticizing Aphrodite's choice to ask Zeus for a divorce, but Hades knew the goddess loved Hephaestus, and rather than admit it, she thought to force the God of Fire into expressing his feelings by goading him. What Aphrodite failed to understand was that not everyone worked like she did, least of all Hephaestus. If she won his love, it would be through patience, kindness, and attention.

It would mean she would have to be vulnerable, something Aphrodite, goddess and warrior, despised.

And if he understood anything, it was that. Aphrodite's challenge forced him to acknowledge his own vulnerabilities, his *weaknesses.* He frowned at the notion of finding someone who wanted to carry his shame, his sins, his malice, but if he failed, the Fates would get involved, and he knew what they would require if he returned Basil to the land of the living.

A soul for a soul.

Someone would have to die, and he would not have a say in the Fates' victim.

The thought made his body tighten, another thread added to the others marring his skin. He hated it, but it was the price of maintaining balance in the world.

A smell brought him out of his thoughts and gave him pause. It was familiar—wildflowers, both bitter and sweet.

Demeter, he thought.

The Goddess of Harvest's name was sour on his tongue. Demeter had few passions in life, but one of them was her hatred for the God of the Dead.

He inhaled again, taking the scent deeper. Something about it was off. Mingled with the familiar aroma was the sweetness of vanilla and a mild, herbal note of lavender. A mortal, perhaps? Someone with the goddess's favor?

The scent drew him out of the darkness in which he had lingered to the edge of the balcony, where he scanned the crowd and found her immediately.

The woman who smelled like vanilla, lavender, and his enemy sat poised on the edge of one of his sofas in a pink dress that left little to the imagination. He liked the way her hair curled, falling in luminous waves down her back. His fingers itched to touch it, to pull it until her head tipped back and she looked him in the eyes.

Look at me, he commanded, desperate to see her face.

She seemed to look everywhere before her gaze halted on him. His hand tightened around his glass, the other gripped the balcony rail.

She was beautiful—lush lips, high cheekbones, and eyes as green as new spring. Her expression was startled at first, eyes widening slightly, transforming into something fierce and passionate as her gaze swept his face and form.

She is yours, a voice echoed in his head, and something inside him snapped. *Claim her.*

The command was feral. He had to grind his teeth to keep from obeying, and he thought he might shatter the glass in his hand from clutching it too tight. The impulse to whisk her away to the Underworld was strong, like a spell. He had never thought himself so weak, but his restraint was a thin, frayed thread.

How could he want this woman so badly? What was this unnatural pull? He stared at her harder, searching for a reason, and became aware that he was not the only one feeling the effects of their connection. She fidgeted beneath his gaze, her chest rising and falling as her breath hitched, her skin turning a pretty pink, and he had the thought that he would like to follow that flush with his lips.

He would give anything to know what she was thinking.

He was so preoccupied by his own salacious thoughts, he had not felt anyone approach until arms snaked around his waist. He reacted quickly, latching onto the hands that held him and twisted to face Minthe.

"Distracted, my lord?" she purred, amused.

"Minthe," he snapped, releasing her arms. "Can I help you?"

He was frustrated by the interruption, but also grateful. If he stared at the woman any longer, he might have left his position on the balcony and gone to her.

"Already zeroing in on your prey?" she asked.

For a moment, Hades did not understand her comment, and then he made the connection. Minthe assumed he was searching for a potential love interest, someone who could help him fulfill Aphrodite's bargain.

"Listening in the shadows again, Minthe?"

The nymph shrugged a shoulder. "It is what I do."

"You gather information *for* me," he said. "Not *on* me."

"How else am I supposed to keep you out of trouble?"

He snorted. "I'm millions of years old. I can take care of myself."

"Is that how you ended up in a bargain with Aphrodite?"

He narrowed his gaze, then lifted his glass. "Did I not tell you I am not to have an empty glass tonight?"

She gave her best *fuck you* smile and bowed. "Right away, my lord."

He made sure Minthe was no longer within sight before returning his gaze to the floor. The woman had turned back to her friends.

Hades studied them in an attempt to discern the kind of company she kept, when he noticed someone he was not particularly fond of—a man named Adonis. He was one of Aphrodite's favored mortals. Why, he had no idea. The mortal was a liar and had a heart as dark as the Styx, but he supposed the Goddess of Love had a hard time looking past his pretty face.

He hoped the woman did not share that quality. He frowned, wondering if she would leave the club with him tonight, and then scolded himself for having these thoughts. His concern should go as far as fearing for her well-being for the mere fact that Aphrodite was fond of punishing anyone who gave her lovers too much attention.

"Your drink, my lord," Ilias said.

Hades glanced at the satyr, relieved that he had sensed his approach.

Ilias could be best described as another assistant. He had worked for Hades almost as long as Minthe, filling roles wherever Hades needed: bartending at Nevernight, managing his restaurants, and enforcing Hades' rule in the Upperworld. He was best at the latter. With an unassuming, pleasant appearance, Hades' enemies were often surprised by his ruthlessness.

Hades did not often employ satyrs. They were wild, prone to drunkenness and seduction, but Ilias was different and not by choice. He had severed ties with his tribe after they betrayed him, raping a woman he loved. She had killed herself and Ilias had killed them.

Hades took the glass, and before he thought too long on the subject, said, "I have a job for you."

"Yes, my lord?"

Hades nodded to the woman who had triggered him with her golden hair and green eyes.

23

"That woman, I want to know if she leaves with anyone."

Silence followed Hades' order, and when the god looked at Ilias, he was staring back, brow raised. "Is she in danger, my lord?"

Yes, he thought, she was in danger of never leaving this place. Something inside him wanted to disregard every civility and *possess* her. Something about her called to him —a thread that pulled at his heart.

He froze as those words surfaced in his mind, eyes narrowing, and thought, *it cannot be.*

Hades peeled back layer after layer of glamour that kept his vision shielded from the ethereal Threads of Fate. They were like shimmering spiderwebs connecting people and things—some were wisps, others were solid, their strength waxed and waned throughout life. The whole floor was like a net, but Hades was only focused on one, fragile cord that ran from his chest to the woman in shimmering pink.

Fucking Fates.

"My lord?" Ilias asked, sensing the sudden change in him.

This cannot be, he thought. The thread and its placement near his heart had significance in a way he was not quite able to wrap his mind around—the Fates had woven this woman into his life.

She was meant to be his lover.

"Lord Hades?"

"Yes," the god finally answered, looking at Ilias as he turned from the floor. "Yes, she is in danger."

He left in a daze, pausing in the shadow to collect his thoughts. His chest felt tight, the thread pulled taut, and he had the thought that if he continued his retreat, it might snap.

This is some sort of game.

It would not be the first time the Fates had dangled a wish in front of him, only to take it away. That was probably their greatest skill—extracting his deepest desires, then weaving them into his life, only to unravel them when they wished.

It was torture.

When he was younger, it had been more fun for the Fates because his reactions were vicious, his retribution violent, but the angrier he became, the more the Fates took. It was like the sisters wanted to see him tear the world to shreds.

For a while, he had obsessed over it, attempting to bargain for love. When that did not work, he decided to defy the Fates. He would find love; he would force it. The results had been a one-night stand with Minthe and a tumultuous relationship with another nymph named Leuce, who had betrayed him.

His wrath had been swift, and his desire to fight Fate on the subject, quashed. He resigned himself to a lonely existence, building walls around his heart and soul. He existed without expectation of happiness or love, and focused instead on bargaining and balance.

Until now.

He would forever remember the vicious reaction his body had when he laid eyes on the woman in pink. His insides still shook. How could the Fates offer him a taste of what it might feel like to have a soulmate, only to take her away?

As easily as I can condemn a soul to Tartarus, he answered, gritting his teeth.

He was still frustrated as he made his way to the lounge. As he approached, Euryale, the gorgon who stood guard at the entrance, nodded at him despite his invisibility.

"My lord," she said.

The god smirked, dropping his glamour.

The gorgon was blind. Centuries ago, her eyes had been gouged out of her face and the venomous snakes that had once graced her head had been chopped to pieces —a punishment for her beauty. Hades had found her in the forest. She lay where she had been attacked, curled into the fetal position, sobbing and shaking. He had gathered her up and brought her to the Underworld, allowing her to heal before employing her.

Despite the horror she had experienced, and her attackers' attempts to take away her power, they had not succeeded, for beneath that blindfold, Euryale's gaze was still potent. After she healed, Hades released her upon her attackers, and the gorgon had turned them all to stone.

"Your sense of smell amazes me, Euryale."

"You make it too easy," the gorgon replied. "Lay off the cologne."

Hades chuckled, pressed a hand to the gorgon's shoulder, and entered the lounge.

The environment here was far more subdued, a mix of mortals and ancient creatures chatting and drinking and playing. Some were relaxed, others on edge, fidgeting as they waited to be summoned to one of the suites in the shadows, ready to bargain for their deepest desires no matter the consequences. Hades wandered among them, assessing and searching, attempting to choose his first contract of the night, when he rounded one of the gaming tables and halted, glimpsing a familiar pink dress and silken hair.

She was a siren, luring him with her scent, her beauty, her very presence.

He should turn around, meld with the darkness, and pretend he never laid eyes upon her, but watching her profile made his chest ache, and there was a part of him that resented the feeling. He had never wanted the Fates to have control over his love life, and yet, it was inevitable.

I could have control, he told himself. *Use this to my advantage to fulfill my bargain with Aphrodite.*

Hades did not often feel guilty, but that thought made his chest sick and heavy.

Make someone fall in love with you.

The bargain was callous and unfair, but Hades wanted to win.

Fucking Fates.

Shoving aside his tumultuous thoughts, he approached

her.

"Do you play?" he asked.

She turned to him, and his breath caught in his throat as he was again, stuck by her beauty. Her eyes were wide and fringed with dark lashes. A dust of freckles kissed the tip of her nose and the apples of her cheeks, fading beneath a flush that colored her creamy skin.

Hades took a sip from his glass to wet his throat, but the movement drew her attention to his mouth, and he repressed a groan as he wondered if she tasted like she smelled—sweet, honeyed, forbidden.

After a moment, she smiled, a playful glint in her gaze. "I'm willing to play if you're willing to teach."

You wouldn't say that if you knew who I was, he thought, taking another drink.

Anyone who entered into a game with him was bound to the rules of Nevernight—a loss meant a contract.

You are a bastard, he told himself as he approached the table and sat beside her. The movement stirred the air, and her scent continued to invade his mind. There was something else in the atmosphere—an electricity that made his heart race and the hair on his arms and neck stand on end.

"It's brave to sit down at a table without knowing the game," he said.

He thought that she might have sensed the warning in his tone, because she arched a brow at him and asked, "How else would I learn?"

"Hmm."

She was right, though Hades would not advise running before learning to walk, especially when it came to bargains with him. Still, her response illustrated her cunning and willingness to try new things, and he found that insanely attractive.

"Clever."

Now that he was close to her, he could not stop staring. He wanted to know why she smelled like wildflowers. What was her connection to Demeter? It felt intrusive and wrong to strip away the barriers that barred her soul from his eyes, but he would be lying if he said he did not want to know who she was beneath that perfect exterior.

She quivered, her lithe shoulders shaking. Was she cold or uncomfortable?

"I have never seen you before," he finally said, hoping that explained his stare.

"Well, I have never been here before," she replied, and then narrowed her eyes. "You must come here often."

He smirked at the tone of her voice, tinged with suspicion.

"I do."

"Why?" She sounded curious rather than disgusted, then blushed and tried to recover by adding, "I mean—you don't have to answer that."

"I will answer it." He met her gaze, challenging. "If you will answer a question for me."

Say yes, he silently begged, though he would never compel her. *Say yes so I can learn all of you.*

A small furrow appeared between her brows as she considered his proposal. *An answer to a question is a small price to pay if she lost*, Hades wanted to say. *Others put their soul on the line.* But he remained quiet.

"Fine," she conceded.

It was a challenge not to smile.

He answered her earlier question, "I come because it is…fun."

It was not a complete lie, and it sounded like something a mortal would say, and for this moment in time, that is what he intended to be—fragile and human.

"Now you—why are you here tonight?"

"My friend Lexa was on the list," she explained, looking at her hands as she twined her fingers together in her lap.

"No," he said. "That is the answer to a different question. Why are *you* here tonight?"

She met his gaze, a mischievous glint in her eyes, and he found himself desperate to chase it—that flicker of defiance, that hint of passion.

"It seemed rebellious at the time," she answered finally.

"And now you aren't so sure?"

"Oh, I am sure it is rebellious," she said as her fingers trailed the felt table. Hades' gaze followed them and he thought he would have liked for those fingers to explore his skin. After a moment, he lifted his gaze to hers.

"I'm just not sure how I'll feel about it tomorrow."

Now he was curious. "Who are you rebelling against?"

Her smile was like an arrow to his chest—devastating, secretive, enticing. "You said one question."

"So I did."

Well played, darling, he thought with a smile.

She shivered again.

"Are you cold?"

"What?" She seemed surprised by his question.

"You've been shivering since you sat down."

She flushed, fidgeted under his gaze again, and then blurted, "Who was that woman with you earlier?"

He frowned but then remembered. "Oh, Minthe. She's always putting her hands where they don't belong."

She paled, and he realized he had said something wrong.

"I…think I should go."

No.

They had not spoken long enough. He did not know her name, and he wanted to teach her—he wanted to teach her so many things. Before he knew what he was doing, his hand was on hers and something volatile sparked between them, eliciting a gasp from her perfect lips. She pulled away quickly.

"No," he said, but it came out as a command, and she glared at him.

"Excuse me?"

"What I mean to say is, I haven't taught you how to play yet." He lowered his voice, forcing away the hysteria that had caused him to reach for her. "Allow me."

Please.

She glanced away from him, and he thought she might bolt. *Trust me*, he wanted to beg, though he knew that was a ridiculous thing to ask. He was the last person she should trust.

Finally, she seemed resolved and relaxed, lowered her lashes as she spoke in the most erotic voice he had ever heard, "Then teach me."

I will. Everything, he thought.

He shuffled the cards and explained the game. "This is poker. We will play five-card draw, and we'll start with a bet."

"But I don't have anything to bet with," she said, glancing down at herself.

I would happily take the dress.

"A question answered, then. If I win, you will answer any question I pose, and if you win, I will answer yours."

She grimaced, but her expression seemed in conflict with her body, because as she spoke, she leaned toward him. The air between them thickened, and Hades found it hard to breathe.

"Deal."

Thrilled, Hades continued to explain the game.

"There are ten rankings in poker. The lowest is the high card and the highest is the royal flush. The goal is to draw a higher rank than the other player..." he expounded. "If you are dealt a bad hand, fold. It is better than the alternative. Checking and calling would apply if we were playing for coin, but since our currency is answers, the point is moot. Perhaps the most important skill in poker is your ability to bluff."

"Bluff?" That seemed to pique her interest.

"Sometimes, poker is just a game of deception... especially when you're losing."

Hades dealt each of them five cards, and they took their time eyeing their hands and then each other. Finally, the goddess laid her cards down, face up, and Hades did the same.

"You have a pair of queens," he said. "And I have a full

house."

"So...you win." She didn't seem upset so much as contemplative, still trying to remember the rules and understand the game. Hades, on the other hand, was impatient, and he jumped at the chance to ask his question.

"Who are you rebelling against?"

She smiled wryly. "My mother."

He raised a brow. "Why?"

"You'll have to win another hand if I'm going to answer."

He was all too eager. When he won a second time, he did not ask the question, just looked at her expectantly.

"Because..." She paused, and her eyes moved away from his, focusing on the table in front of them, brows furrowing. She was searching for an answer. *For a way to avoid telling the truth*, Hades realized. She smiled ruefully as she said, "She made me mad."

There was a hint of darkness to her words, and he wanted to chase that moment. It was the first time he sensed she was holding back. He waited for more of an explanation, but she just smirked.

"You never said the answer had to be detailed."

His grin matched hers. "Noted for the future, I assure you."

"The future?"

"Well, I hope this isn't the last time we'll play poker."

Especially now. She was teaching him how she thought and worked, and he would be more than prepared for their next game. She would not be able to cut corners so easily. The terms would be detailed, the stakes higher.

Her expression turned wary, and he got the sense that she had not planned on seeing him again after tonight.

Something jolted through him—an emotion akin to fear.

I have to see her again. I will go mad.

He pushed those thoughts away. *Finish the game*, he told himself, and dealt another hand and won.

"Why are you angry with your mother?" he asked.

She looked thoughtful for a moment, and then said, "Because…she wants me to be something I can't."

Was that what I sensed beneath the surface? Her true nature, desperate to be free?

Her gaze dropped to the cards. "I don't understand why people do this."

He tilted his head. "You are not enjoying our game?"

"I am. But…I don't understand why people play Hades. Why do they want to sell their soul to him?"

Haven't you ever been desperate for something? he wanted to ask, but he knew the answer. He could feel it burning between them.

"They don't agree to a game because they want to sell their soul," he said. "They do it because they think they can win."

"Do they? Win?"

"Sometimes."

"Does that anger him, you think?"

She had pursed her lips at the question, and dread tightened his chest. This woman had connections to Demeter, which meant she had heard the worst things about him. If he had any hope of deconstructing the myth that had been erected around him, he was going to have to spend time with her, and that meant she needed to know who he was, so he answered her question truthfully.

"Darling, I win either way."

Her eyes went wide, and she stood quickly, almost knocking her chair over. He had never seen anyone so eager to leave his company. His name slipped out of her mouth like a curse.

"*Hades.*"

He shuddered. *Say it again*, he wanted to command, but he kept his mouth shut. His eyes darkened, and he pressed his lips together. The look on her face would haunt him for an eternity. She was shocked, frightened, embarrassed.

She made a mistake. He read it on her face.

"I have to go."

She spun, fleeing from him like he was death himself

come to steal her soul.

He thought about chasing after her but knew it did not matter whether or not he followed. She would be back. She had lost to him, and he had marked her.

He swallowed the rest of his whiskey and smiled.

Perhaps Aphrodite's bargain would not be so impossible after all.

"Fastest path, quickest benefit," he muttered.

CHAPTER IV – FUCKING FATES

"My lord." Minthe's voice brought him out of his reverie. "Your first appointment has arrived."

Fuck. He was definitely in the wrong headspace to entertain another bargain. He frowned and went to drink from his glass, but realized it was empty. When he looked at the nymph, her brow was arched.

"Smitten, my lord?" Her voice dripped with judgment.

"Yes," he said. He saw no reason to lie. "I am."

Minthe's shock registered in her eyes as they widened, then her lips flattened.

"Desperation isn't flattering, Hades."

"Neither is jealousy," he replied, shoving the empty glass into her hands.

She scowled.

"Where is the mortal?"

Her eyes flashed as she answered, "The Diamond Suite."

By the end of the night, Hades had won three contracts. Two men in search of wealth, one young and one old, and a woman in search of love. All now faced the challenge of overcoming what burdened their souls most.

The younger of the two men sought to replace his

college funds, which he had drained to support his cocaine addiction. He would have to kick his habit before Hades would grant his wish. The older man was seeking to pay for his wife's chemotherapy, and the greatest burden on his soul? He had been cheating on her prior to her diagnosis. Hades' terms were that he had to come clean about the affair.

The woman asked for love, or rather, she asked for a specific man to fall in love with her. A co-worker she had been pining after for years.

It was a request Hades heard often, and one he could never grant.

She sat across from Hades, looking desperate and tired, and as he peered at her soul, he saw that it was so twined with the man she loved, she no longer resembled her true self. She was a tangle of vines, marred with thorns, that had grown sharp from years of rejection.

"Change your terms," he advised.

Her eyes narrowed, and she gritted her teeth, daring to raise her voice. "But he is who I want!"

It was the second time he had heard that plea tonight, and both times, it had been a lie.

"I cannot make another mortal love you," Hades said. "You either ask for love or nothing."

She had glared at him for a while, trying to hold back her tears, before agreeing. He supposed she had decided it was better to be loved by someone in the end. Except that she did not win their game, and upon her loss, Hades met her terrified, watery gaze.

"Cease this pointless desire for your co-worker," Hades said.

She glared. "I can't just...*stop* loving him."

"You must find a way," he said. "Perhaps when you do, your eyes will be opened to a new love."

Hades started to rise to his feet.

"Haven't you ever been in love?" she asked, and when he paused, her eyes widened with the realization. "You haven't."

Hades pressed his lips together. "Careful, mortal. This life is fleeting. Your existence in the Underworld lasts an eternity."

He started to rise again, and the woman grabbed his hand. "Please! You don't understand! I cannot help who I love!"

Hades jerked his hand away. "You waste your words and feelings, mortal."

He could have said more. He could have explained that her love for this indifferent man made her resentful, that the moment she decided to release him from her affections, the better her life would be, but he knew she would not hear him, so he did not speak. Instead, he vanished, retiring to the Underworld.

But not to rest.

He teleported to the Library of the Souls, located in the mirrored palace of the Fates. Hades had gifted the three goddesses a portion of his realm—an island that floated in the ether of the Underworld. It was inaccessible to all but him, and the Fates were unable to leave it.

A gilded cage, Lachesis had called it.

A glorified prison, Clotho spouted.

A mirrored cell, Atropos said.

The Fates may have chosen to describe it as a cage, a cell, a prison, but they knew just as well as Hades it was built to their specifications and for their protection.

"Would you prefer to live among the souls and deities of the Underworld?" he asked them every time they complained. "They would stone you, and I would not stop them."

None of them liked his reply, and they had responded by demanding that he change the gardens outside the palace—a request they made often, and one he obliged.

There were no windows in the library, save for a glass dome ceiling that let in a greyish light. The walls were floor to ceiling bookcases, full of tomes bound in black velvet. Each volume detailed the life of every human, creature, and god.

Hades held out his hand and called for Demeter, the Goddess of Harvest. The book came to him, landing in his grasp with a thump. As he opened it, a projection of threads illustrated a timeline from the goddess' birth to the present, which could be read or watched like a film.

Hades chose to watch, following her thread from her battle worn birth to her vengeful existence after Titanomachy, to the creation of her nurturing cult, until her thread branched off, signifying the creation of another life-thread.

"Show me who this thread belongs to," he said, and the gold broke apart until it formed the image of the girl from Nevernight.

As Hades looked at her, his chest tightened.

No wonder she smelled like Demeter—she was her daughter.

"Curious about your future queen?" Lachesis appeared, dressed in white, her face framed with long, dark hair, her head crowned in gold. She was the middle sister, and in her hand, she held a gold rod with which she measured mortal life.

Future queen. The words shuddered through him, and he had to clench his teeth to keep from reacting.

"Her name?" Hades asked.

He did not look away from her shimmering image.

"She is called Persephone," Lachesis replied.

Persephone, he mouthed her name, testing it upon his tongue, surprised by how right it felt, how perfect it sounded.

"The Goddess of Spring."

Hades' gaze snapped to the Fate. Her dark eyes stared back, bottomless, emotionless.

"You wish to taunt me."

Goddess of Spring, Goddess of Rebirth, Goddess of Life. How could a daughter of spring become death's bride?

"Ever suspicious, Hades," Clotho said, appearing out of thin air. The youngest of the three Fates, she looked no different than Lachesis, clothed and crowned in gold. "Perhaps we wish to reward our favorite god."

"You like no gods," Hades replied.

"We dislike you least."

"Flattered," he snapped.

"If you are displeased, we will unweave the thread," Atropos said, appearing before Hades and snatching the book from his hands. She was the oldest and still looked no different than her sisters, dressed in blood-red, a pair of abhorrent, gold shears hung from a chain around her neck.

Hades glared at the three of them.

"I know you well, Morai," he said, addressing all of them at once. "Who are you punishing?"

They exchanged a look. Finally, Clotho answered, "Demeter begged for a daughter."

"A wish that was granted," Lachesis said.

"You are the price she paid," Atropos added.

"I am punishment," Hades stated.

The Fates were aware of Demeter's hatred for Hades. He had been right when he suspected a trick.

"If that is how you prefer to perceive it," Clotho said.

"But we like to think of it differently," Lachesis said.

"It is the price paid for our favor," Atropos explained.

It was how the Fates worked, and the gods were not immune.

"Demeter is aware?" Hades asked.

"Of course. We are not in the habit of keeping secrets, Lord Hades."

Hades grew quiet. If Demeter was aware, no wonder he had never heard about the Goddess of Spring.

"You think to punish Demeter, but you are really punishing Persephone," Hades said.

The irony was not lost on him, because he had done the same thing to her. She was bound via their bargain—the greatest bargain he had ever made, because in the end, she did not have to love him. Thousands of mortals and Divine alike had destinies woven by the Fates. It did not guarantee a love match, and one between him and Demeter's daughter was even less likely.

Lachesis narrowed her eyes. "Are you afraid, Hades?"

The god glared, and the three Fates laughed.

"We may weave the Threads of Fate, my lord, but you retain control over how your future unfolds." Clotho vanished.

"Will you rule your relationship as you rule your kingdom?" Lachesis disappeared.

"Or revel in the chaos?" Atropos faded.

And when he was alone, their merry laughter echoed around him.

Haven't you ever been in love?

The mortal's words returned to him, burrowing under his skin like a parasite.

No, he had never been in love, and now he would always wonder... Would Persephone have chosen him if given the freedom?

***

Hades left the Fates' mansion and found himself outside Hecate's cottage. The Goddess of Witchcraft was a long-time resident of the Underworld. Hades had allowed her to settle wherever she wished, and she had chosen a dark valley to build her vine-covered cottage. After, she spent months cultivating a wealth of poisonous nightshade.

Hades had merely raised a brow when he had discovered what she had done.

"Do not pretend as though my poisons have not been useful, Hades."

"I have had no such thoughts," he had replied.

Hades smirked at the memory. Since then, Hecate had become his confidant, probably his closest friend.

She was outside, standing beneath a patch of moonlight that streamed through an opening in the canopy of trees. Early on, the goddess had praised his ability to create what she referred to as an enchanted night, but it was hardly surprising. Hades was a god born of darkness. It was what he knew best.

"What troubles you, my king?" she asked as he approached. "Is it Minthe? May I suggest lye to remedy the situation? It is quite painful when swallowed."

Hades raised a brow. "Murderous thoughts already, Hecate? It isn't even noon yet."

She smiled. "I am more creative at night."

Hades chuckled, and they fell into a comfortable silence. Hades, lost in his own thoughts. Hecate, staring at the moon. After a moment, she asked him again, "What troubles you?"

"The Fates," he said.

"Oh, the besties. What have they done?"

"They have given me a wife," he said, raising both his brows. "Demeter's daughter."

Hecate laughed and quickly covered her mouth with her hand at Hades' arched glance.

"S-Sorry," she said, and cleared her throat, composing herself. "Is she horrible?"

"No," Hades said. "That's probably the worst part. She is beautiful."

"Then why are you so glum?"

Hades explained the trajectory of his evening in as few words as possible—Aphrodite's bargain, seeing Persephone for the first time, realizing his primal reaction to claim her was unusual, and uncovering the thread that connected them.

"You should have seen how she looked at me when she realized who I was. She was horrified."

"I doubt she was horrified," Hecate said. "Surprised, perhaps—maybe even mortified if her thoughts were anything like yours."

Hecate gave him a knowing look, but Hades was not so sure. Hecate had not been there.

"I have never known you to back down from a challenge, Hades."

"I haven't," he said. He had done the opposite—he had, essentially, bound her to him for the next six months.

Hecate waited for him to explain.

"She played me."

"What?"

"She invited me to her table for a game, and she lost," Hades explained.

By tomorrow morning, his mark would appear on Persephone's skin, and when she returned to him, he would offer her the terms of their contract. If she failed, she would be a resident of the Underworld forever.

"Hades, you didn't."

He just looked at the witch-goddess.

"It is Divine Law," he said.

Hecate glared, knowing that was not true. Hades could have chosen to let her go with no demands upon her time, and he had chosen not to. If the Fates were going to connect them, why not take control?

"Do you not want her love? Why would you force her into a contract?"

After a moment, he admitted aloud, "Because I did not think she would come back."

He did not look at Hecate, but her silence told him she pitied him, and he hated that.

"What will you ask of her?" she inquired.

"What I ask of everyone," he said.

He would challenge the insecurities of her soul. By the end of it, he would create a queen or a monster. Which, he did not know.

"How do you feel when you look at her?" Hecate asked.

Hades did not like that question, or maybe he didn't like his answer, but he spoke truthfully, nonetheless.

"Like I was born from chaos."

Hecate grinned.

"I can already tell I'm going to like her." Then her eyes flashed with amusement. "You must tell Minthe you are to wed when I am present. She will be furious!"

CHAPTER V – A CONTRACT SEALED

Hades found himself in Tartarus.

In the beginning of his reign, he came here more often than any other place in his realm. Post Titanomachy had been a dark time. Born of war, Hades knew nothing else but blood and pain, but he had not spent his time in Tartarus out of a wish to exist with the familiar. He did so out of a wish to punish those responsible for his dark beginning—the Titans.

Over time, he had needed that less and less.

On rare occasions, he still came to channel residual rage.

Tonight was no different.

He stood in his office, a cavernous but modern room at the peak of one of the mountains of Tartarus. It doubled as a chamber of torture, its walls covered with weapons Hades had used on many unfortunate humans and humanoids who found themselves restrained before him, many of them holding secrets, even in the afterlife. Part of the floor was glass, and from this elevated space, Hades looked down upon level after level of torture.

Over the years, the prison had evolved. It had begun underground, with levels spanning miles and miles, all dedicated to punishing the most wicked of crimes and torturing souls in absurd ways—with wind, icy rain, and fire, and the more efficient sentences of choking on tar, eagles and vultures eating livers, and flesh being torn from bodies by razor sharp teeth.

While those forms of torture still existed, Hades evolved with the world above, carving out the mountains and creating isolated cells for various forms of psychological torture. Whatever the variety, Hades only cared that it produced the same result—suffering.

Hades swiped a bottle of whiskey from his desk and took a drink before snapping his fingers, summoning a soul. The man was the one Sisyphus had shot dead in the yard of his fishery.

Isidore Angelos.

His hands were bound behind his back, his legs restrained. His chin rested against his chest. He was asleep.

Souls tended to continue in the Underworld as they did in the Upperworld, meaning they stuck to routine, even though they did not need it.

Sleep was an example of this.

"Well, isn't he handsome," Hermes said, appearing in Hades' office.

The God of Trickery often came and went from his realm, having taken the role of psychopomp—a guide to souls—centuries ago. Hades glanced at him. The god was in his Divine form, gilded and garish. He had great white wings and a pair of short horns that poked out of the side of his head, almost invisible amid his curls. His golden eyes appraised the mortal.

"Do not ogle the prisoners, Hermes," Hades said.

"What? I can appreciate beauty."

"With your track record? No. You tend to forget what is beneath the skin."

"I also tend to have mind-blowing sex," Hermes said, sighing. "It is a sacrifice I'm willing to make."

SCARLETT ST. CLAIR

At that, Hades turned away from the god, rolled his eyes, and swirled the liquid in his bottle before taking another drink.

"Perhaps if you got laid more often, you wouldn't feel the need to torture your subjects," Hermes said.

Hades grinded his teeth, something he had done all day. His jaw would hurt tomorrow. Hermes' words frustrated him for two reasons—that the god felt the need to comment on his sex life at all, and because his thoughts turned to the beautiful Persephone.

He felt a tightening in his groin that almost made him groan.

"Has anyone ever told you, you might need therapy?" Hermes asked. "Because I'm pretty sure torturing people is a sign of psychopathy."

Hades glared at Hermes, who was now holding a cattle prod. Suddenly, it sparked, making a terrible clicking sound. The god yelped and dropped it immediately.

Hades raised a brow. Sometimes, it was hard to remember that Hermes was actually a skilled warrior.

"What?" he challenged. "It scared me!"

Hades swiped the cattle prod from the ground and turned toward the man named Isidore sitting in the center of his office, then said, "Wake."

The man's head lolled, and his eyes opened and closed, heavy with fatigue.

Hades waited while the mortal familiarized himself with his surroundings, only speaking when he saw recognition on his face.

"Welcome to my realm," Hades said.

Isidore's eyes widened. "Am I...am I in Tartarus?"

Hades did not answer. Instead, he said, "You are Impious."

The Impious were mortals, and immortals alike, who rejected the gods when they came to Earth during The Great Descent for a number of reasons—some felt abandoned, some felt the gods were hypocrites, others no longer wished to be ruled. In the end, the two sides went to war, the Impious and the Faithful. Hades had not been eager to join in the fight; after all, it did not matter which side he joined, his realm would grow either way.

"And a loyal member of Triad," Hades added.

Triad was a group of Impious mortals who opposed the gods, demanding fairness, freewill, and freedom. They called themselves activists, the Olympians called them terrorists.

"Tr-Triad? What makes you think I'm a member of Triad?"

He stared at the man for a moment. He did not like answering questions, did not really like speaking at all, but he would answer this, as it might prevent the man from trying to lie further.

"Three reasons," Hades said. "One, you stutter when you lie. Second, even if you did not stutter when you lie, I can sense lies. Yours are bitter and they taste like ash, a mark of your soul. Third, if you do not want to advertise your allegiance, you should not tattoo it upon your skin."

Hades noted how the man's eyes drifted to his right arm where the triangle—the symbol of Triad—was inked.

"So, you will torture me for my allegiance?"

"I will torture you for your crimes," Hades said. "The fact that you are a member of Triad is merely a bonus."

Isidore gave a guttural cry as Hades shoved the cattle prod into his side. The smell of burnt flesh filled his nostrils. After a few seconds, he pulled away. The mortal's back was arched, his breathing harsh.

"Gods, Hades! Do you really have to do this?" Hermes asked, but he made no move to cover his eyes or even look disgusted.

"Don't pretend you haven't tortured a mortal, Hermes. We all know differently," Hades spat. As the cattle prod sparked again, the man glared at Hades and challenged.

"I've been tortured before."

Hades smiled wickedly. "Not by me."

The cattle prod was just the beginning of Isidore's torture. Hades moved from electrocution to fire, setting the ground beneath the man's feet aflame, keeping him alive as the flames licked his skin. He screamed, inhaling smoke, which made him cough until blood spilled from his mouth.

At some point, Hades doused the flames with his magic, and in the quiet aftermath, Hermes spoke.

"You are seriously fucked up, Hades."

"You," Isidore's voice rasped, his chest rose and fell slowly. "You think you are untouchable because you are gods."

"That's exactly why we are untouchable," Hermes said.

Hades held up his hand, silencing the God of Trickery.

"You don't know what is coming," Isidore continued, voice hollow. His head lolled to the side, and he was no longer looking at Hades but the wall. The god gripped the mortal's charred face so he would look at him.

"Um, Hades—" Hermes started to say.

"What's coming?" Hades demanded.

"War," the man answered.

***

It was almost noon, and Hades had yet to sleep. His eyes felt like sandpaper, and Hermes' voice grated in his ears. The god had followed him back to his palace and now walked beside him as he made his way to his bedchamber. Hades took a drink from the bottle he had brought from his office in Tartarus.

"You could have told me you were torturing him for information," Hermes complained.

"Are you saying if I had told you, you would have refrained from telling me how fucked up I am?" Hades asked.

Hermes opened his mouth to reply, but Hades spoke instead—a rare occasion.

"Triad is reorganizing. I need your eyes and ears."

Hermes laughed. "You aren't actually...*afraid* of them, are you?"

"We went to war with Triad, Hermes. It could happen again. Do not underestimate mortals desperate for freedom."

Hermes narrowed his eyes. "It sounds like you sympathize with them."

Hades met the god's gaze and answered as he always did, "What is evil to one is a fight for freedom to another."

He had said it before, and he would say it again. The problem he had with the Triad was the innocent lives they took with them during their fight.

"Do not let your hubris blind you, Hermes."

This time, when Hades started toward his chambers, the god did not follow.

As soon as Hades was inside his room, he sighed, pressing his fingers to his temple. It had been a long time since he had had a headache, but this day was endless. Hades crossed the room to his fireplace and finished off his whiskey. He stared down at the empty bottle, contemplating the day's—yesterday's—events. He had bargained and murdered and tortured.

All things he was certain his future wife would disapprove of.

Future wife.

Fucking Fates.

Hades threw the bottle, and it shattered against the black marble wall.

I am going to have to stop breaking things when she gets here, he thought, and then scolded himself for sounding so... hopeful.

He sighed angrily and started toward his bed, loosening his tie. His eyes had started to burn. He needed sleep. In a matter of hours, he had to be up again. He had another important appointment to make. This one in his own territory, Iniquity, an exclusive club where the worst of society gathered under his protection and rule.

Just as he pulled back the covers, a knock sounded at the door.

"Go away," he said, thinking it had to be Minthe.

Instead, Ilias's voice answered.

"Oh, I think you'll want to hear this, my lord."

Hades sighed. "Yes?"

Ilias entered, arching a dark brow and smiling wryly. "No rest for the wicked. The woman from last night is outside Nevernight fighting with Duncan. He has placed his hands upon her. You had better hurry."

Hades could not describe the feeling that overcame him, but it was like everything inside him had frozen for a second—his blood did not rush, his heart did not pump, his lungs did not expand.

As quick as the ice entered his veins, it was gone, replaced by red-hot fury.

"Why didn't you say something sooner?" he snapped before teleporting to the entrance of Nevernight.

On the other side of the door, a familiar voice threatened, "I am Persephone, Goddess of Spring, and if you would like to keep your fleeting life, then you will obey me!"

Hades threw open the door. He felt frantic until his eyes settled upon the goddess, and then he was stunned.

She stood on the lackluster sidewalk, beneath the too-bright sun, stripped of her human glamour. White kudu horns sprouted from her wild hair, and despite their height, he couldn't help thinking how petite she appeared. He liked seeing her this way. It felt intimate somehow, because he knew he was seeing *her*. This was Persephone, the goddess who would be his queen, and she was *everything*.

She did not meet his gaze, but her eyes were definitely *on* him, trailing his frame with an intensity in her expression he couldn't quite place but wanted to understand.

Despite feeling as if he had no control over his body, his emotions, his magic, he composed himself as best he could and spoke.

"Lady Persephone." Her title felt heavy on his tongue, and at his words, she met his gaze, and again, he was startled by her bright eyes—as wild as the rivers of Tartarus and as green as the Asphodel Valley. Something changed in her composure when she looked at him. She straightened her shoulders and lifted her chin.

"Lord Hades."

She addressed him formally and offered a sharp nod. He was not sure what he did not like about it—the fact that she had used his title, or her ceremonial body language. He frowned but could not think long on the subject, because Duncan drew his attention.

"My lord." The ogre sunk to his knees and hung his head low. "I did not know she was a goddess. I accept punishment for my actions."

"Punishment?" Persephone echoed. She crossed her arms over her chest as if she were uncomfortable with the idea. Hades gritted his teeth, the same fury that had overcome him in the Underworld blazed again.

"I laid my hands upon a goddess," Duncan said.

"And a woman at that," Hades added unhappily.

Duncan had it wrong. His impending punishment had nothing to do with the fact that he had touched someone of Divine blood—it was that he had hurt a woman. Hades was not tolerant of violence against women or children. In fact, he hated it so much, there was a special level in Tartarus for those responsible of such crimes, and their punishments were doled out by the Furies themselves, the three feared Goddesses of Vengeance, Nemesis, the Goddess of Retribution, and Hecate, who took it upon herself to personally punish abusers.

No human or humanoid was excused, whether in Hades' employment or not.

"I will deal with you later," Hades promised. "Now, Lady Persephone."

He stepped aside, making room for her to enter Nevernight. She did not hesitate like he thought she might, entering the darkness of his club like she owned it. He shut the door behind her, and for a moment, they were trapped together and the scent of their magic twined and overwhelmed. Hades recognized the rigidness in Persephone's stance, because he had gone just as still. Her reaction relaxed him, probably because he found hope in the idea that he affected her in the same way.

He considered challenging what was building between them, stepping close and drawing her gleaming hair away from her neck. He could practically hear her shuddering breath as he pressed a kiss to her soft skin. Would she melt in his arms then? Or would she fight?

He drew close. He did not think it was possible, but she became even more rigid, back ramrod straight. She was wound tight, a viper ready to strike. It was a bite he would endure willingly, and he leaned in, his jaw brushing the side of her face, his lips touching her ear.

"You are full of surprises, darling."

He was too arrogant, he realized, unprepared for his body's reaction to her. Her scent sunk into his skin, igniting his blood. He grew heavy and hard at the thought of wrapping his arm around her waist, pulling her against him, consuming her.

Fuck.

An audible breath brought him back to reality, and before she could face him, he was opening the interior door to Nevernight, breaking the strange spell between them.

"After you, goddess."

She blinked, and he noted the confusion in her expression. Maybe she thought what she had just experienced was an illusion. He half-expected her to flee, but again, that spark of defiance entered her eyes. She kept his gaze as she brushed past him—both a challenge and a tease.

He followed behind her and watched as she approached the balcony, eyes scanning the floor below. He wondered what she was looking for but did not ask, just waited until she looked at him and continued down the stairs.

Her heels clicked as she followed him across the floor,

which was how he knew she had stopped moving, because the club grew quiet.

"Where are we going?" she asked. There was suspicion in her voice, and he reminded himself that just because she had entered Nevernight willingly, it was not a show of trust.

Hades paused, turning to look at her.

He should not have looked back. It almost made him question what he was doing, luring this beautiful goddess farther into his realm.

"My office," he said. "I imagine that whatever you have to say to me demands privacy?"

She raised a brow, glancing at the empty space. "This seems pretty private."

"It isn't." He turned and headed upstairs, pleased when he heard the click of her heels following.

At the top of the stairs, he turned toward his office and opened one of the two large doors bearing one of his symbols in gold—a bident—coiled with vines and flowers. When he turned to Persephone, she was still standing a few feet away. Her distance frustrated him.

"Will you hesitate at every turn, Lady Persephone?"

She scowled. "I was just admiring your décor, Lord Hades. I didn't notice this last night."

"The doors to my quarters are often veiled during business hours," he replied, and then indicated to the open door. "Shall we?"

She lifted her chin and breezed past him. He tracked her as she moved across the black marble floor and familiarized herself with his office, eyes settling first on the wall of windows that overlooked the club floor. It was a common feature in most of his offices, a way to observe from above. Despite the heat outside, Hades kept the fire going in his hearth. He liked fire, liked the way the flames danced, liked to watch it from his obsidian desk, but rarely used the sitting area arranged before it. Perhaps he would today, and invite the Goddess of Spring to sit.

But that seemed too civil, and Hades had a feeling that

whatever the goddess had come to say, it was anything but polite.

When he closed the door, she again became rigid. It was then he realized he should have done more to reassure her she was safe with him after her horrific interaction with Duncan. He moved across the floor noisily, not wishing to startle her, and stopped in front of her, eyes searching her face, grazing her lips, before falling to her neck. Her perfect skin was reddened from the ogre's grip.

It took everything in his power to stay where he was and not teleport to the Underworld to torture Duncan.

Anticipation is part of the torment, he reminded himself.

He reached toward her, wanting to heal those marks upon her skin, but her hand fastened upon his arm. Their gazes snapped together.

"Are you hurt?" he asked.

"No," she whispered.

There was something intimate about this exchange. Maybe it was their proximity, inches from one another, skin touching skin. After a moment, he nodded and pulled his arm free from her grasp. He crossed the room, needing the distance so he did not do something stupid. Like kiss her.

The smell of Demeter's magic alerted him that she was about to raise her glamour.

"Oh, it's a little too late to be modest, don't you think?" he asked, leaning against his desk, tugging his tie free from his neck. He did not like the way it felt against his skin, like a restraint, but the movement drew her gaze, and he recognized the hunger in her eyes because he felt it, too. Deep in his gut.

"Did I interrupt something?"

Her tone was almost accusatory, and he considered questioning her jealousy but thought against it. Instead, his lips curled as he explained, "I was just about to go to bed when I heard you demanding entrance to my club. Imagine my surprise when I find the goddess from last night on my doorstep."

She glowered, "Did the gorgon tell you?"

He fought the urge to smile at her frustration. "No, Euryale did not. I recognized your magic as Demeter's, but you are not Demeter." He tilted his head, studying her like he'd studied her image in the Library of Souls. "When you left, I consulted a few texts. I had forgotten Demeter had a daughter. I assumed you were Persephone. Question is, why aren't you using your own magic?"

"Is that why you did this?" she demanded, removing a hideous set of bracelets from her wrist and holding up her arm, where a band of black dots marked her skin.

He noted that she had avoided answering his question. No matter, he would come back to it. Instead, he focused on the mark on her skin, his mark, and smirked.

"No. That is the result of losing against me."

"You were *teaching* me to play!"

"Semantics." He shrugged. "The rules of Nevernight are very clear, goddess."

"They are anything but clear." She threw up her hands and the pointed at him. "And you are an asshole!"

He pushed away from his desk, stalking toward her. There was a part of him that wanted to demand respect, a part of him that wanted to remind her that he was King of the Underworld, God of the Dead, but as he approached her, he remembered who she was—Persephone, Goddess of Spring, his future queen. The thought calmed him, and yet, she must have seen something else flash in his eyes, because she took a step away.

"Don't call me names, Persephone," he said, grasping her wrist gently. He felt a strange energy between them as he reestablished their connection. He traced the shadow marring her skin, and she shivered beneath his hands.

"When you invited me to your table, you entered into an agreement. If you had won, you could have left Nevernight with no demands on your time. But you did not, and now we have a contract."

I could give her freedom. The words entered his head, unbidden, born from his earlier thoughts, and he was suddenly overcome with guilt. It was true that there was no Divine Law, so he could let her go.

But as he watched her, he peered beneath her fair exterior and saw her soul for what it was—a powerful goddess, caged in doubt and fear. This was the reason she used her mother's magic—because hers lay locked away, dormant.

The longer he looked, the deeper he fell. She was intoxicating, and her magic smelled like sweet roses, wisteria, and something completely sinful. His own magic rose within him, wishing to tangle with hers. He wanted to draw it out of her, coax her to release.

Fuck, fuck, fuck.

He was not sure what she saw in his expression, but he noted the way her throat constricted when she swallowed, and he thought he'd like to kiss her there, feel her shudder beneath him.

She spoke, her words dripped with restrained anger. "What does that mean?"

"It means I must choose terms," he said, certain.

Suddenly, this bargain had taken on a whole new meaning to him. He would pry the bars from around her body, free her from this self-constructed cage of hate, and in the end, if she did not love him, at least she would be free.

"I don't want to be in a contract with you," she said between her teeth, her beautiful eyes flashing bright. "Take it off!"

"I can't."

I won't, he thought.

"You put it there, you can remove it."

His lips twitched. He should not find humor in her plight. He knew this was distressing, knew she would not understand why this had to happen. Still, he smirked because she was defiant, because he liked her fire and frustration.

"You think this is funny?" she demanded.

"Oh, darling, you have no idea."

54

"I am a goddess. We are equals."

She said the words, but he knew she did not believe them.

"You think our blood changes the fact that you willingly entered into a contract with me? These things are law, Persephone." She glared at him. "The mark will dissolve when the contract has been fulfilled."

"And what are your terms?"

He considered what he had seen of her soul. She was a woman who equated Divinity with power. It was the core of her insecurity, and it was that he would challenge. At last, he spoke.

"Create life in the Underworld."

Her eyes widened and she paled, the impossibility of the words he had spoken registering quickly. His fingers tightened around her wrist.

"What?"

"Create life in the Underworld," he said again. "You have six months. If you fail or refuse, then you will become a permanent resident of my realm."

"You want me to grow a garden in your realm?"

He grimaced. She had already decided there was only one way to fulfill the bargain, and that was via power she didn't have…yet.

He shrugged. "I suppose that is one way to create life."

It was a clue she did not catch. Instead, she glared at him.

"If you steal me away to the Underworld, you will face my mother's wrath."

"Oh, I am sure," he mused, imagining it now, and yet it was the price Demeter would pay—first for bargaining with the Fates, and second for hiding Persephone from him. When would the Goddess of Harvest come for him, he wondered? "Much like you will feel her wrath when she discovers what you've so recklessly done."

He hated that he spoke those words, and he considered reassuring her that he would protect her from her mother, but then Persephone straightened, met his gaze, and accepted his challenge.

"Fine. When do I start?"

He almost smiled. "Come tomorrow. I'll show you the way to the Underworld."

"It will have to be after class," she said.

His brows drew together. "Class?"

"I'm a student at New Athens University."

It was an example of how much he did not know about this woman, and he found himself curious. What was she studying? How long had she been in college? Where had she been living prior to New Athens? What had Demeter taught her about the Divine?

All things I will learn in time, he reminded himself.

"After...class, then."

They stared at each other for a long moment, still touching, still invading each other's space, and he found he was content with this—the silence, the feel of her energy —because it made his chest feel lighter.

"What about your bouncer?" she asked suddenly.

Hades frowned, brows lowering. "What about him?"

"I'd prefer he not remember me in this form." She lifted her hand to her horns, and Hades eyes followed. They were beautiful horns, gracefully twisted into sharpened points, but as he looked at them, they disappeared from his view, covered by the glamour Persephone had called up. His eyes, again, fell to hers.

"I'll erase his memory...*after* he is punished for his treatment of you," he promised.

"He didn't know I was a goddess," she said.

Do not come to his aid, he wanted to say. *He does not deserve your kindness.*

"But he knew you were a woman, and he let his anger get the best of him. So he will be punished."

And I will enjoy the process thoroughly.

"What will it cost me?"

He focused upon her again, on her thick lashes, mesmerizing eyes, and sensuous mouth.

"Clever, darling. You know how this works. The

punishment? Nothing. His memory? A favor."

"Don't call me darling," she snapped, and he raised a brow at her sudden frustration. Perhaps she thought he was growing too comfortable too fast. "What kind of favor?"

"Whatever I want," he said. "To be used at a future time."

She narrowed her eyes, skeptical of his request, and she should be. The most dangerous favors were those unspecified, and if she agreed, it would give him an idea of just how much she truly knew about what it meant to be Divine.

"Deal."

Nothing, he thought. *She knows nothing at all.* It made him more than curious. How could Demeter let her daughter enter a world run by the Divine and know nothing of them? She had to know that sooner or later, Persephone would find her way into this world.

Despite his worrying thoughts, Hades smiled at her. "I will have my driver take you home."

"That's not necessary."

"It is," he insisted.

Hades was not in the habit of trusting the world. He knew too much about what lingered beneath its surface.

"Fine," she snapped.

He frowned. She was probably more than ready to leave, except that he was not quite ready to see her go. Not on the heels of his last thought.

Keep her safe, he thought as he grasped her shoulders, sealing the space between them. He had thrown her off-balance, and her fingers clenched the front of his shirt, nails scraping his chest. He pressed his lips to her forehead, and the heat from her skin rushed to the bottom of his stomach, making his cock throb and his thoughts turned chaotic. He wanted to tilt her head toward his, to kiss her mouth and taste her tongue.

Focus on the task, he told himself angrily, and bestowed his favor upon her. In ancient times, Greek heroes were favored by the gods, given special weapons and aid during battle, and on rare occasions, even a second chance at life. In modernity, favor could mean anything—access to exclusive clubs, insurmountable wealth, or protection from harm.

Hades offered Persephone the latter, along with access to his realm. He released her from the kiss. Inches apart, she looked up at him.

"What was that for?" she whispered.

Hades smiled, brushing a finger across her heated cheek.

"For your benefit. Next time, the door will open for you. I would rather you not piss Duncan off. If he hurts you again, I will have to kill him, and it's hard to find a good ogre."

"Lord Hades," Minthe's voice interrupted. "Thanatos is looking for you—Oh!"

The nymph's presence frustrated him, because it meant Persephone was no longer looking at him. She tried to pull away, but Hades held her tighter, refusing to let go.

"I did not know you had company," Minthe said, her voice dripped with judgement. Perhaps Hecate had been right when she had suggested he tell Minthe about his future bride.

"A minute, Minthe," Hades gritted out without looking at her.

When she was gone, Persephone's gaze returned to his, and he studied her, lips pressed together.

"You haven't answered my question. Why are you using your mother's magic?"

He wanted to see if she would admit what he already knew—that she had no magic of her own. Instead, she surprised him by smiling.

"Lord Hades," she said, her voice breathy and sensual. She drew a finger down his chest, and the movement stirred his desire for her once again. He was going to have to find release by his own hand after this. He could not stand it. Did she know her power? "The only way you are getting answers from me is if I decide to enter into another gamble with you, and at the moment, it's not likely."

Then she took the lapels of his jacket and straightened them before leaning in, much like he had done earlier in the foyer, and whispered, "I think you will regret this, Hades."

Her eyes fell to the red polyanthus flower in the pocket of his suit jacket, and as she brushed it with her fingers, the petals wilted.

CHAPTER VI – A SOUL FOR
A SOUL

Hades escorted Persephone downstairs. He wanted to ensure she accepted the ride home he had offered and introduce her to Antoni, his driver.

The cyclops waited patiently, dressed in a black suit and tie. When he saw Persephone, he smiled, his eyes alight.

"Lady Persephone," he said. "This is Antoni. He will ensure you make it home safely."

While he knew the cyclops would take care of her, he felt the need to make his point by holding Antoni's gaze as he spoke.

She is important.

"Am I in danger, my lord?"

Her question drew his attention, and he found her looking up at him. Despite the sarcastic tone in her voice, he sensed her unease.

No one will harm you, he wanted to say, but those words would only inflame her fear. In truth, Hades was being overly protective. Perhaps it had something to do with the mortal he had tortured last night—the man who had threatened war from Triad.

"Just a precaution," he assured her. "I would not want your mother banging down my door before she has a reason to."

They stared at one another for a long moment before Antoni cleared his throat and opened the rear car door. They both looked at Antoni, who gestured toward the cabin of the car.

"My lady," he offered.

"My lord." Persephone spoke his title in that quiet, breathy voice. It made him think of other things, like how she might say his name as she found release beneath him.

She turned and slid into the back of the car. As Antoni shut the door behind her, he glanced at Hades. He knew that look. It was the *you'll thank me later* look, but Hades wasn't so certain. If Antoni had not opened his mouth, he might have kissed the goddess again the way he had wanted to in his office.

But maybe that was what the cyclops was saving him from, because Hades was not certain he would have let Persephone go a second time.

He watched as his black Lexus departed down the street.

"I hope you know what you're doing," Minthe said, leaning in the doorway behind him. She had been eavesdropping in the foyer while he saw Persephone off.

Hades kept his eyes on the car; it was in a turning lane, almost out of sight. "What do you think I am doing?"

"Encouraging her," Minthe said. "If you aren't careful, she'll fall in love with you."

He was glad he was not looking at the nymph, because a smile curled his lips.

The Lexus finally moved out of view, and Hades turned to face Minthe. Her features were pinched and slanted, partly due to the brightness of the sun, and partly from her seething judgement.

"Was Thanatos looking for me, or were you spying?" he asked, referring to her earlier intrusion into his office.

"Why is it that every time I catch you doing something

you shouldn't, I'm suddenly a spy?"

Hades did not like her words. The nymph pretended her role as assistant somehow meant she was his keeper.

"And what should I not be doing, Minthe?"

The nymph folded her arms over her chest. "Tell me, Hades. Would you have kissed her had I not shown up?"

"I did kiss her," he replied. The nymph's eyes widened and then narrowed as he continued, "If you saw something you disliked, Minthe, I suggest you knock in the future."

"Thanatos is waiting for you in the throne room," she said, before spinning on her heels and slamming the door behind her.

He sighed and teleported to the Underworld, where he met Thanatos. The God of Death was tall and slender, sporting white-blond hair and two black gayal horns. Hades liked Thanatos and trusted him as much as Hecate. He was a kind god, and he cared for the souls. He had been one of their greatest advocates, more of a king to them than Hades had ever been.

He bowed when Hades appeared, his large, black wings sweeping behind him like a silken cape.

"My lord," he said, and as he straightened, bright blue eyes met his. "We have a problem."

"What is it?"

"The Fates are in an uproar," he explained. "Atropos's shears have broken."

Hades raised a brow. "Broken?"

Thanatos nodded. "You had better come."

Dread pooled in Hades' stomach, but he agreed and followed Thanatos to the Fates' island. He found the three sisters in their weaving room.

At the center of the room was a shiny black globe where millions of threads had been woven into the surface like a tapestry. Each thread represented a person—a fate— that the Moirai had spun into existence. Usually, the three sisters sat in an arc around the globe. Clotho would start the Thread of Life, weaving it into the surface of the map, and when it was long enough, Lachesis would begin her work, weaving into it a destiny, while Atropos plucked and unraveled threads, determining the deaths of all souls, cutting their lifelines with her shears.

Except when Hades appeared, Clotho and Lachesis were consoling Atropos, who wailed and sobbed into her hands.

"You must fix this, Hades!" Lachesis demanded when she noticed him.

"Yes, you must!" Clotho cried.

"My shears! My beautiful shears!" Atropos cried.

"I cannot help if I do not know what happened," Hades said, already frustrated with the three.

"Did you not hear?" Lachesis spat.

"Atropos' shears have broken!" Clotho seethed.

"How?" Hades asked through his teeth, fingers tightening into fists. He was losing his patience, a dangerous quality when it came to the Fates. Hades knew he would have to handle this carefully, or he would find himself at their mercy.

"Atropos?" Hades asked.

It took a moment for the Fate to calm herself. Then, she spoke, her dark eyes red from crying.

"I picked a thread from the globe, chose and wove a death, and when I went to cut the thread, it would not sever. I tried again, and again, and again, and again, until my shears broke apart."

Her voice quivered, and she began howling again, a horrible keening that pierced Hades' ears and made him feel violent. He took a breath and held it until he felt a little less murderous.

"Whose thread?" Hades asked next.

Breathing hard and sniveling, Atropos looked at Hades again, gaze fierce and wild. He recognized the feral look—it was the look of a goddess, ready for vengeance.

"It is a mortal who seeks to cheat death!" she fumed. "Sisyphus de Ephyra."

Hades scowled at the name, and a dark feeling crept

into his chest. The mortal from the fish yard. It was not completely surprising that the man had somehow managed to find a way to defy the Fates. He had connections in the criminal underworld of New Greece, as well as to Triad. He probably tried a number of options—magical potions and spells cast by Magi, mortals who practiced dark magic, even relics—until he found something that worked.

"Fix this, Hades!" Clotho exclaimed.

"Find him!" Lachesis shrieked.

"Fix this, find him, Hades," said Atropos. "Or we will unweave the Goddess of Spring from your life!"

"Yes," they all hissed in unison. "Or we will unweave the Goddess of Spring from your life!"

Then you will invite a war.

Hades eyes flashed, and he almost verbalized the threat —the promise—he was now making, when the sisters began to scream.

It took Hades a moment to discover why, but he finally spotted the source of their agony. A thread had risen to the surface of the globe between them and disintegrated— and it was not due to the Fates' will.

A soul for a soul, Hades thought. The universe would have balance, even against the will of the gods.

"Thanatos," Hades said, turning to the God of Death. It was an order—*take us to that dying soul.*

The god obeyed, and the two found themselves in the upperworld outside a dilapidated apartment in the Macedonia District.

Hades recognized the smell of death immediately— sharp and foul and tangible. It was an odor he never got used to, one that seized his mind and sent him back to his early and ancient days on the bloody battlefield, where he had come to know the varying scents of decay.

He exchanged a glance with Thanatos. They had come too late.

Hades touched the door, and it opened. Inside, lay a man. He was sprawled on the floor, face down with his arms fanned out. It was as if he had just entered his home and collapsed, lifeless.

"He wasn't due to die for another year," Thanatos said. While it was not uncommon for mortals to die unexpectedly, those deaths were still orchestrated by Atropos.

And someone had denied her that right.

Hades stared down at the lifeless corpse for a long moment. The man was young, but his face was scarred and scabbed, and there were track marks and bruises in the crook of his arm.

Evangeline, the god thought grimly.

"Name?" Hades asked.

"Alexander Sotir," Thanatos said. "Thirty-three."

Hades frowned. A pang in his chest caught him off-guard, but he recognized it for what it was—sadness. He would have liked to help this man overcome his addiction.

"Hades," Thanatos said. "Look."

His gaze shifted from the body to Thanatos to the black scratches on the floor; they were wet and looked like drag marks. Hades followed them, and what he found in the corner of the room enraged him.

It was Alexander's soul, and it lay at Hades' feet in a fetal position, broken and beaten. It looked more skeletal than human. The skin around it was like a membrane, blackened and tar-like. The state of the soul told Hades two things about how the mortal had died; that the death had been traumatic and unnatural.

Hades had seen few souls in this state, and he knew there was no hope. This soul had no chance of healing, no chance of reincarnating.

This was the end.

"Contact Ilias," Hades instructed Thanatos. "I want to know Sisyphus' connection to this man."

"Yes, my lord," Thanatos said. "Shall I…"

"I'll take care of him," Hades said quickly.

"Very well." He nodded and vanished, leaving Hades alone with the soul.

The god stood there for a moment, unable to move.

He had no doubt this would keep happening. Would every death break a soul? Would every death fray another thread connecting him to his future queen?

He was certain of only one thing—he would find Sisyphus and reap his soul himself.

Hades knelt and gathered the soul into his arms, teleporting to the Elysium Fields. Despite the heaviness of the day, there was peace here in the silence, in the way the wind moved the golden grass. It was a space reserved for healing, and though Hades knew Alexander's soul would never recover from its horrific end, he would give him the best end.

Beneath the brightness of the blue sky, Hades settled the soul beneath the leaves of a pomegranate tree, heavy with crimson fruit.

"Rest well," he said, and in the next second, the shade transformed into a swath of red poppies.

***

Hades traded the peace of Elysium for the horror of Tartarus, teleporting to the part of his realm affectionately known as The Cavern. It was the oldest part of his realm, boasting towering stone formations, shimmering draperies, and crystal pools of icy water. The natural beauty was marred by the desperate pleas of the souls who were tortured here; part of the misery was the echoing cries that carried through the vast ceilings.

Hades approached one of the stone slabs, where Duncan was stretched out, wrists and ankles chained. He had been stripped down, and a cloth covered his groin. His chest rose and fell quickly, a mark of his fear. His textured skin was coated in sweat. He turned his head and met Hades' gaze, beady eyes desperate.

"My lord, I'm sorry. Please—"

"You put your hands on a woman," Hades said, cutting him off. "One who caused no harm, save for a few biting words."

"It will never happen again!" The ogre began to struggle against his restraints, panting as hysteria settled in.

Hades' lips curved into a fiendish smile.

"Oh, of that I am certain," he replied as a black blade manifested in his hand. The King of the Underworld leaned over the ogre, pressing the blade to his bulbous stomach. "You see, the goddess you touched, the one you attempted to choke, the one you left a mark upon, will be my wife."

Just as Duncan bellowed his final rebuff, Hades plunged the knife into the ogre's stomach.

"I did not know!" Duncan cried.

Hades dragged the knife down, cutting deep with the intention of exposing the creature's liver and summoning vultures to feast upon it, but the more Duncan repeated himself—*I did not know, I did not know*—the angrier Hades became. The more he thought of Persephone, lithe and powerless, suspended by the throat from the ogre's very hand, the more his rage blossomed. He plunged the blade into the ogre's stomach once, twice, then over and over, until he no longer spoke, until blood pooled from his mouth. Until he was dead.

Last, Hades cut off his hands, and when he was finished, he stood back, breathing hard, face splattered with blood.

This had not been torture.

It was a slaying.

Hades dropped the blade as if it burned and drew his hands behind his head. He closed his eyes and took deep breaths until he felt calm again. He was insane, sick, and violent. How could he possibly think he might one day be worthy of love?

The thought was laughable, and his hope was selfish.

And he knew then that the only way he would ever keep Persephone was if she never discovered this side of him. The one that craved brutality and bloodshed.

***

Later that evening, Thanatos found Hades in his office and offered a bundle wrapped in white cloth.

"Atropos's shears," he said.

Hades would take them to Hephaestus so the God of Fire could restore them.

The two were quiet, each lost in their own thoughts.

After a moment, the God of Death spoke. "What sort of power would destroy the Fates' magic?"

"Their own," Hades replied.

Which meant more than likely, Sisyphus de Ephyra had found a relic.

After The Great War, scavengers collected items from the battlefield—pieces of broken shields, swords, spears, fabrics. They were items that contained residual magic, items that could still pose a threat if they fell into the wrong hands. Hades had worked for years to extract relics from circulating in the black market, but there were thousands and sometimes it took a disaster to figure out who was in possession of one.

A disaster like Sisyphus de Ephyra.

Hades would be damned if he let a mortal like him cheat him out of love.

Ilias had delivered a file earlier. It confirmed what Hades had suspected—Alexander Sotir was addicted to Evangeline and in debt to his dealer, Sisyphus, but making the connection did no good until Hades located the mortal.

"What will you do?" Thanatos asked.

"Visit Olympus," Hades replied, shuddering.

CHAPTER VII – MOUNT OLYMPUS

Olympus was a marble city upon a mountain. It was bright, beautiful, and vast. Several narrow passages branched off from a courtyard rimmed with statues of the Olympians, leading to homes and shops where demi-gods and their servants lived.

Like the gods and the world below, Olympus had also evolved. Zeus had ordered the installation of a stadium and theater in addition to the existing gymnasium, where gods trained and mortals fought or performed for them. It was one of Zeus's favorite pastimes and a practice that had not changed, even though the God of Thunder now lived on Earth.

Hades did not often venture to Olympus. Even before The Great Descent, it was a place he preferred to avoid, much like he preferred to avoid Olympia, the new Olympus, but there were a few gods who still resided in the clouds, among them Athena, Hestia, Artemis, and Helios.

It was Helios Hades wanted to see now—Helios, God of the Sun, one of few Titans who did not dwell in Tartarus.

Hades found Helios resting in the Tower of the Sun, a

sanctuary made of white marble and gold that rose over the other buildings on Olympus, a pillar cutting through the clouds. The surface gleamed with its own internal light, like the sun shining on water. It was the tower from which he launched his four-horsed golden chariot across the sky and where he returned at night.

The Titan lounged upon a gold throne, his head resting on his fist as if he were bored, not exhausted from his work. He was dressed in purple robes, and his white-blond hair fell in waves past his shoulders, his head crowned with the aureole of the sun.

Helios blinked slowly at Hades, his hooded eyes the color of amber.

"Hades," he spoke, acknowledging him with a lazy nod, his voice deep and resonate.

"Helios." Hades inclined his head.

"You wish to know where the mortal Sisyphus is hiding."

Hades said nothing. He was not surprised that Helios knew why he had come, it was the reason Hades was here. Helios was all-seeing, which meant he witnessed everything that occurred on Earth. The question was, had he chosen to pay attention and would he choose to share with Hades now?

Helios was a notorious asshole.

"He is not hiding. I see him now," the god answered.

"*Where*, Helios?" Hades said between his teeth.

"On Earth," the Titan replied.

Since Helios had fought on the side of the Olympians during Titanomachy, the God of the Sun felt that any aid he offered after their victory was a favor, one he did not have to bestow if he did not want to.

"I am in no mood for your games," Hades said darkly.

"And I am in no mood for visitors, but we must all make sacrifices."

A spike of anger rushed through him, manifesting in a set of black spikes ejecting from his hand. Helios's eyes drifted there, and he smiled.

"Still struggling with anger, I see. How will you conceal your true nature from Demeter's daughter? Will you find more souls to torture?"

"Perhaps I will begin with your son."

Helios' mouth tightened. His son, Phaethon, had been in the Underworld for a long time. The naïve boy had attempted to drive his father's chariot and lost control of the horses. He was struck down by Zeus after causing great destruction on Earth.

"He was a stupid boy who did a stupid thing," Helios said, dismissing Hades' threat.

"This mortal is a murderer, Helios," Hades said, trying again.

"Aren't we all?"

Hades glared. He should have known that appeal would not work. Helios had no real sense of injustice, having helped his granddaughter, Medea, escape to Corinth after she had killed her own children.

"Is it a bargain you want?" Hades asked.

"What I want is to be left alone," Helios snapped with more vigor behind his words than anything he had said since Hades arrived. "If I had wanted to get involved in mortal affairs, I would have descended with the rest of you."

"And yet you use their land for your cattle," Hades pointed out, noting the shadow that passed over Helios' amber eyes.

He had found the Titan's weakness.

"Perhaps I was wrong to set my sights on your son when you care more for your animals."

Helios' hands tightened on the arms of his throne. For the first time since Hades had arrived, the god straightened.

Helios coveted his cattle—also called the Oxen of the Sun. They were immortal, and he kept them on the island of Sicily, guarded by two of his daughters. Anyone who harmed them would incur his wrath. Odysseus and his men had learned that the hard way.

But Hades did not fear Helios' wrath, not when it came to a mortal who dared to cheat death and not when it came to facing the unraveling of his fate with Persephone.

"You ask for blood, Hades."

"If you are asking me if I will slaughter a few heads of cattle to get what I want, then yes, I ask for blood," Hades replied. "I will revel in the thought of your agony as I sit upon my throne with fifty of your cattle in the Underworld."

Tense silence followed Hades' threat, and he could see and sense Helios' anger. It burned his eyes and raged between them, as hot as the sun's rays.

"The man you seek is being protected by your brother."

Hades already knew that was not Zeus; the God of Thunder would never protect a mortal who had broken one of his most coveted laws.

"Poseidon," Hades hissed.

He did not get along with either of his brothers, but if he had to choose one to sacrifice, it would be Poseidon. The God of the Sea was jealous, power-hungry, and violent. He did not like sharing power over the Upperworld with Hades or Zeus and had tried more than once to overthrow the King of the Gods, but all attempts had failed.

"You will not disturb my cattle," Helios said. "Are we clear, Hades?"

Hades narrowed his eyes but said nothing. As he turned on his heels and left the Tower of the Sun, he heard Helios call.

"Hades!"

***

Hades returned to his office at Nevernight. He considered going straight to Atlantis, his brother's island and home, and demanding to know where he was hiding Sisyphus, but he knew his brother, knew the violence that swirled inside him was greater than the anger Hades attempted to keep at bay. Any accusation leveled at his brother, even if it held truth, would infuriate the god. By the end of the encounter, thousands would be dead.

Hades could not help thinking of Alexander's soul, broken beyond repair. One soul taken before its time was too many, and the god knew there would be more like him if he did not act fast. He had to come up with an alternative plan, something that would gain Hades the truth he needed and prevent destruction. His eyes fell to the white bundle he had left on his desk—Atropos' shears.

Perhaps Hephaestus would have a solution. He gathered the bundle in his hands and started to teleport, when Minthe knocked at his door and threw it open, strolling into his office.

"Entering before being invited defeats the purpose of knocking," Hades said tightly, frustrated by the interruption. "I'm busy."

"Tell your side piece," Minthe countered. "She's downstairs."

Hades brows furrowed. "Persephone is here?"

She was not due to arrive until this evening for her tour of the Underworld. A strange feeling unfurled within his chest. It felt exciting, almost like hope, but as he moved to the windows that overlooked the floor of Nevernight, those feelings darkened. Persephone had brought a companion, a man he recognized immediately as Adonis, Aphrodite's favored mortal.

His eyes darkened.

"I told you this would happen," Minthe was saying. "You encouraged her, and now she thinks she can demand an audience with you. I will tell her you are…indisposed."

"You will do no such thing," Hades stopped her. "Bring her to me."

Minthe raised a brow. "The man, too?"

She was trying to goad him, and it worked because Hades could not help answering with a bitter hiss.

"Yes."

Minthe made a strange sound in the back of her throat,

something akin to a laugh, and then left. Hades' gaze returned to the floor below.

Persephone stood apart from Adonis, arms folded over her chest. Despite her audacity, he wanted to see her, especially on the heels of the Fates' threat. He would just be punishing himself if he sent her away. Besides, he wanted to know why she had come and brought a mortal with her.

When Minthe walked into view below, he turned away from the window, sat Lachesis' bundle aside, and poured himself a drink. If he did not have something to distract him, he would pace, and he'd rather not illustrate the chaos of his mind right now.

By the time Minthe returned with Persephone and Adonis in tow, Hades had positioned himself near the windows again. He barely registered Minthe's approach, because his eyes had locked on his goddess the moment she entered the room.

"Persephone, my lord," Minthe said.

She was determined. He could see it in her expression —the way her head was tilted, her lips pressed into a hard line. She had come here for something, and Hades found himself eager for a time when she would approach him with a smile, with no reservations or hesitations because she wanted him and nothing else.

"And…her *friend*, Adonis," Minthe continued.

At the mention of the mortal's name, Hades' mood darkened, and he looked at Adonis, whose eyes widened under his scrutiny. He found it strange that Aphrodite would take this man as a lover, given her attraction to Hephaestus. They were complete opposites—this mortal, untouched by the sufferings of the world. His skin was smooth, his hair glossy and not singed by the forge, his face free of stubble, as if growing a beard would be a hardship for him. And then there was his soul.

Manipulative, deceptive, and abusive.

Hades glanced at Minthe, nodding. "You are dismissed, Minthe. Thank you."

With her exit, Hades downed the remainder of his drink and crossed the room for a refill. He did not offer a glass to either of his two visitors or invite them to sit. It was not polite, but he was not interested appearing pleasant.

He spoke once his glass was full, leaning against his desk.

"To what do I owe this...*intrusion?*"

Persephone's eyes narrowed at his words and tone, and she lifted her head. He was not the only one fighting to be amicable.

"Lord Hades," she said, taking a notebook out of her purse. "Adonis and I are from *New Athens News*. We have been investigating several complaints about you and wondered if you might comment."

Another thing he did not know about his future bride —her occupation.

A journalist.

Hades hated the media. He had spent a lot of money to ensure he was never photographed and denied all interview requests. He did not refuse because he had things to hide, though there was plenty he preferred to keep to himself. He simply felt that they focused on the wrong things—like his relationship status—when Hades would rather give the spotlight to organizations that helped dogs and children and the homeless.

He lifted the glass to his lips and sipped; it was drink or show his anger in a worse way.

"*Persephone* is investigating," Adonis said with a nervous laugh. "I'm just...here for moral support."

Coward, Hades thought before focusing on the notebook Persephone had pulled from her purse. He nodded to it.

"Is that a list of my offenses?"

He would be lying if he said he had not expected this. She was the daughter of Demeter; she had been told only the worst about him. He knew because she had looked at him with such loathing when she had discovered who he was the night of their card game.

She read a few of the names on the list—*Cicero Sava, Damen Elias, Tyrone Liakos, Chloe Bella.* She couldn't know what hearing these names meant to him or how it made him feel. It reminded him of his failures. Each one was a mortal who had entered into a bargain with him, each one had been given terms in hopes that they would overcome the vice that burden their soul, and each one had been unsuccessful, resulting in their death.

He was relieved when she stopped reading from the list, but then she looked up and asked, "Do you remember these people?"

Every detail of their face and every worry on their soul.

Again, he sipped his drink.

"I remember every soul."

"And every bargain?"

This was not a conversation he wanted to revisit, and he could not help the frustration in his voice as he spoke, angry that she was bringing this up.

"The point, Persephone. Get to the point. You've had no trouble of it in the past, why now?"

Her cheeks flushed, the tension between them building —a solid thing he would destroy if he could. It made his lungs hurt and his chest feel tight.

"You agree to offer mortals whatever they desire if they gamble with you and win."

She made it sound like he was the aggressor, as if mortals did not beg him for the chance to play.

"Not all mortals and not all desires," he said.

"Oh, forgive me, you are selective in the lives you destroy."

"I do not destroy lives," he said tightly. He offered a way for mortals to better their lives, once they left his office, he had no control over their choices.

"You only make the terms of your contract known after you've won! That is deception."

"The terms are *clear*, the details are mine to determine. It is not deception, as you call it. It is a gamble."

"You challenge their vice. You lay their darkest secrets bare—"

"I challenge what is destroying their life," he corrected her. "It is their choice to conquer or succumb."

"And how to do you know their vice?" she asked.

A wicked smile crossed Hades' face, and suddenly, he thought he understood why she was here, why she was leveling these accusations at him—because she was now one of his gamblers.

"I see to the soul," he said. "What burdens it, what corrupts it, what destroys it, and I challenge it."

"You are the worst sort of god!"

Hades flinched.

"Persephone—" Adonis spoke her name, but his warning was lost over Hades' reaction.

"I am helping these mortals," he argued, taking a deliberate step toward her. It was not his fault she did not like his answer.

She leaned toward him, demanding. "How? By offering an impossible bargain? Abstain from addiction or lose your life? That's absolutely ridiculous, Hades!"

Her eyes had brightened, and he noted that her hold on her mother's glamour had faltered the angrier she became.

"I have had success."

She would know that if she was not so eager to only see the bad in him. Wasn't that the mark of a good journalist? Understand and interview both sides?

"Oh? And what is your success? I suppose it doesn't matter to you as you win either way, right? All souls come to you at some point."

He moved to close the distance between them, his frustration boiling over. As he did, Adonis stepped between him and Persephone, and Hades did what he had wanted to do since the mortal stepped into his office—he paralyzed him, sending him to the floor, unconscious.

"*What did you do?*" Persephone demanded and started to reach for him, but Hades took her wrists and drew her flush against him. His words were rough and rushed.

"I'm assuming you don't want him to hear what I have to say to you. Don't worry, I won't request a favor when I erase his memory."

She scowled at him.

"Oh, how kind of you," she mocked, her chest rising and falling with each angry breath. It made him aware of their proximity, reminded him of the kiss he had pressed to her skin the day before. Heat curled in the bottom of his stomach, and his eyes dropped to her lips.

"What liberties you take with my favor, Lady Persephone." His voice was controlled, but he felt anything but composed on the inside. Inside, he felt raw and primal.

"You never specified how I had to use your favor."

"I didn't, though I expected you to know better than to drag *this* mortal into my realm," Hades glanced at Adonis.

Her eyes widened slightly. "Do you know him?"

Hades ignored that question; he would come back to it later. For now, he would challenge her reason for coming to Nevernight to begin with.

"You plan to write a story about me?" He felt himself leaning in, bending her backward and holding her tighter, sealing their bodies together. He was certain the only way he could get closer to her was if he was inside her, a thought that made his stomach feel hollow and his cock hard. "Tell me, Lady Persephone, will you detail your experiences with me? How you recklessly invited me to your table, begged me to teach you cards—"

"I did not beg!"

"Will you speak of how you flush from your pretty head to your toes in my presence and how I make you lose your breath—"

"*Shut up!*"

It amused him that she did not want to hear this—all the ways she communicated her desire for him, all the ways her body betrayed the words that came out of her mouth. Her body was supple beneath his hands, and he knew if he trailed his hand between her thighs, she would be hot and wet.

"Will you speak of the favor I have given you, or are you too ashamed?"

"*Stop!*"

She pulled away, and he released her. She stumbled back, breathing hard, her pretty skin flushed. Though he did not show it, he felt the same.

"You may blame me for the choices you made, but it changes nothing," Hades said, and felt he was challenging the real reason she came here—to tell him his bargain with her was unfair, for retribution. "You are *mine* for six months, and that means if you write about me, I will ensure there are consequences."

"It is true what they say about you," she said. "You heed no prayer. You offer no mercy."

Yes, darling, he thought, angrily. *Believe what everyone says about me.*

"No one prays to the God of the Dead, my lady, and when they do, it is already too late."

He was finished with this conversation. He had things to do, and she had wasted his time with her accusations.

Hades waved his hand, and Adonis woke with a sharp inhale. He sat up quickly, looking dumbfounded. Hades found everything about him annoying, and when the mortal met his gaze, he scrambled to his feet, apologizing as he did and hanging his head.

"I will answer no more of your questions," Hades said, looking at Persephone. "Minthe will show you out."

He knew the nymph waited in the shadows. She had never truly left them alone, and he hated the smug look on her face as she came into his office from the Underworld entrance. Perhaps that was what made him call out to his goddess before she left.

"Persephone." He waited until she faced him. "I shall add your name to my guest list this evening."

Her brows came together in confusion. She probably thought her invitation to tour his realm would be revoked after her behavior, but it was important, now more than ever. It was the only way she would see him for who he was.

A god desperate for peace.

CHAPTER VIII– AT THE ISLAND OF LEMNOS

Hades found Aphrodite waiting for him on the steps of her mansion on the island of Lemnos. It was a beautiful home, built by Hephaestus himself, a mix of modern lines, intricate filigree, and walls of windows that offered a view of each glorious sunrise and enchanting sunset.

This island was a sacred place for Hephaestus. It was where he landed when Hera cast him off Olympus. As a result of the fall, he'd broken his leg, and the people of Lemnos cared for him. Even after he was invited to return, the god preferred to stay, as he had built a forge, taught the people ironwork, and gained worshippers. Hades always considered the fact that the God of Fire was willing to share this island with Aphrodite a sign of his love for her, but he had never told her his thoughts—she probably would not listen, anyway.

"Come to surrender?" Aphrodite asked. She wore a dress that looked like the inside of a seashell and a seafoam robe rimmed with flowing feathers. Her golden hair gleamed, cresting like waves down her back.

"I have come to speak to your husband," Hades

replied.

"Do not call him that," she snapped, her eyes flashed with anger.

"Why? Has Zeus granted your divorce?"

"He refused," she said, and looked away toward the ocean, where the sun hung low in the sky. She paused a moment, and Hades recognized the silence for what it was —time for her to compose herself. Whatever she was about to share was difficult for her. "Even after Hephaestus agreed it was best."

Fucking Hephaestus, Hades thought to himself. The God of Fire was worse than him at saying the wrong things.

"He expressed not a *shred* of anger when I told him what I'd done," Aphrodite continued, looking at Hades again. "He works a forge all day and has not an ounce of fire within."

"Have you considered that he wasn't angry because he expected it?"

Aphrodite glared, and Hades explained.

"You admitted yourself you've never had a marriage, Aphrodite. Why would you expect Hephaestus to mourn what he never had?"

"What do you know, Hades? You've never had a marriage, either."

Hades suppressed the urge to roll his eyes. All of his conversations with Aphrodite ended with her flippantly rejecting his opinion or advice and throwing his own loneliness back in his face.

Why did I try?

"Hephaestus is in his lab," Aphrodite said. She turned, bare feet moving over the marble steps.

Hades trailed behind her. She did not enter her home, but instead, turned down a walkway that cut through a garden full of bright, tropical flowers and swaths of ornamental grasses. The path lead to a glass bridge that connected the mansion to a volcanic island where Hephaestus kept his shop, carved from the largest mountain.

The workshop contained a forge on the lower level and a lab on the upper level, where he experimented with technology and enchantments. Over the years, the God of Fire had created armor and weapons, palaces and thrones, chains and chariots—and people, among the most famous being Pandora, who he molded and sculpted from clay. She would later be used as a scapegoat, a way for Zeus to punish mankind. Hades had never asked Hephaestus about her fate, but he had a feeling it haunted the god to this day.

"He's been working on a project. Bees," Aphrodite said as she walked, and there was a note of admiration in her voice. "They are mechanical, disease resistant."

Bees were dying at an alarming rate for various reasons —parasites and pesticides, poor nutrition, and environment. The latter had more to do with Demeter than anything, as the Earth tended to suffer when her mood was dark. Hades felt it was a strategic move on the part of the goddess, as a loss of bees meant less food production, which resulted in a reliance on the Goddess of Harvest for healthy crops.

Hephaestus' creations would ensure mortals—and bees —were not at the mercy of a goddess. Conversely, his creations could be seen as an act of war against the goddess.

"Did Hephaestus tell you this?" Hades asked, curious, because if so, that meant they were communicating.

"No," Aphrodite said, hesitating for a moment, as if she wanted to say something but stayed quiet.

"So, you were spying?" Hades questioned, raising a knowing brow.

Aphrodite pursed her lips. "How else am I supposed to learn what my husband is up to?"

"You could...*ask*," Hades suggested.

"And receive a one-word reply? No, thank you."

"What did you expect to learn while spying?" Hades asked.

A heavy silence followed his question. Finally, she answered, "I guess I thought he might be cheating."

Hades could not help it, he paused to laugh. Aphrodite whirled to face him.

"It isn't funny!" she snapped. "If he isn't fucking me, he's fucking someone."

Hades raised a brow. "Is that what you discovered while you spied?"

Aphrodite's shoulders fell, and she looked away. "No."

She seemed disappointed. Like she might have felt better if Hephaestus was distracted by women rather than things.

"Hmm," Hades hummed, and Aphrodite gave him a bruising look before they continued to the entrance of Hephaestus' lab.

"The cyborgs will take you to him," she said.

Hades narrowed his eyes, suspicious of her quick exit. "You're not going to leave just to spy, are you?"

Aphrodite rolled her eyes and crossed her arms over her chest. "I have better things to do, Hades."

He considered challenging her reply, but decided against it, stepping around her and entering Hephaestus' lab alone.

Inside, he found a cavernous room full of Hephaestus' inventions—shields, spears, armor, helms, pieces of detailed ironwork, unfinished thrones, robotic humans and horses. At the center of it all, working with his back bent over a wooden table, was the God of Fire. Despite Hephaestus' modern inventions, his work area and overall aesthetic paid homage to his ancient roots. His blond beard was long, his matching hair pulled back with a leather strap. He worked shirtless, exposing the scars on his skin, and wore a set of trousers that came to mid-calf.

"Lord Hades," Hephaestus said as he approached, though the god continued to work, soldering a circuit board. Hephaestus was probably the only god who used titles with other gods out of respect instead of disdain.

After a few more minutes of work, Hephaestus put his tools down and pushed a set of clear glasses back on his head. He stood and looked at Hades with a pair of deep-set grey eyes. Hephaestus was huge, his physique chiseled like a marble statue. After landing on Lemnos and breaking his leg, it had been amputated. In its place was a prosthetic of his own design. It was gold but minimalistic, made of geometric shapes. Even not being able-bodied, he was probably the strongest physically, and definitely the smartest, of the gods.

"Hephaestus," Hades nodded, looking at the metal and wires scattered across his table. Despite already knowing what these pieces were for, he asked, "What are you working on?"

"Nothing," the god said quickly.

It did not surprise Hades that Hephaestus would keep quiet about his work. He had never been chatty, but after his exile and the scrutiny he had faced from other gods due to his scarred face and disability, he had become even more quiet.

"It cannot be nothing," Hades said. "It does not look like nothing."

Hephaestus blinked at the god and then answered, "A project." He cleared his throat. "What can I do for you?"

Hades averted his eyes, looking around the room as he spoke. "I need your expertise. I need a weapon. One that will subdue violence and encourage truth."

Hephaestus offered a hint of a smile. "Sounds like a riddle," he said.

"You haven't heard the last part," Hades said. "It's for an Olympian."

Hephaestus raised a brow, but just as Hades suspected, the God of Fire did not ask questions.

"I can create something," he said. "Come back in a day."

There was silence for a moment, and then Hades said, "You know Aphrodite spies on you."

Hades felt like a gossip. He was not sure why he was telling Hephaestus about Aphrodite's secret. Maybe he felt like it was revenge for her bargain. Maybe he was hopeful it would encourage conversation between them, except that Hephaestus did not react to the news, his expression passive, disinterested.

"She is suspicious," he said.

"Or curious," Hades countered, because it was true.

"I suppose she can be both," he replied, turning his back on Hades and focusing again on his work. Hades waited despite the silence, and finally, Hephaestus spoke in a quiet, coarse voice.

"She asked Zeus for a divorce. He will not grant it."

"Is that what you want?" Hades asked. "A divorce?"

He watched the god's profile—the way his jaw clenched and his fingers curled at the sound of the word. The God of Fire looked at Hades then, his brows drawn together, and there was a sincerity within his eyes Hades had never perceived before.

"I want her to be happy."

***

Hades appeared at the center of a perfectly green meadow on the island of Sicily, where fifty pure-white cows grazed. A few feet away, Helios's daughters, Phaethusa and Lampetie, slept beneath a fig tree, their wheezing breaths disrupting the silence of the night.

Hades had to admit, he felt a little guilty that these two would incur Helios' wrath come morning, but not enough to leave their father unpunished for his vitriol.

Just as Hades began to select the best of Helios' cattle to take with him to the Underworld, his phone rang.

It never rang.

Something is wrong.

"Yes?" he answered quickly, despite the chance he would wake the two sisters.

It was Ilias.

"My lord," he said. "Lady Persephone is missing."

He had never felt such a terrifying sense of dread. A thousand emotions converged upon him at once—rage and fear and alarm. He wanted to demand to know why

Ilias had not watched her better, wanted to know where he had looked, wanted to threaten to end his life if he found her in any condition other than pristine.

But he knew Ilias, and by now, he knew Persephone.

Beautiful, defiant Persephone.

She was not one to obey, especially when told.

"I will be there in seconds," Hades replied and hung up.

There was a beat of silence where Hades wrestled with every demon inside him. This fear was irrational, but it told him something important.

If the Fates did take her away, the world would not survive.

After a moment, he looked up, observing the white cows and spoke.

"I had hoped to take my time selecting only the best of you to join me in my realm, but it seems I am out of time."

When Hades vanished, so did every cow in the meadow.

CHAPTER IX – A GAME OF
FEAR & FURY

As soon as Hades' feet touched Underworld soil, he could sense Persephone. Her presence in his realm was like an extension of himself. It weighted on his chest just as heavily as the thread that connected them.

He teleported again and appeared in the Fields of Mourning, where shoots of white gladioli and orchids grew. The Fields were once reserved for those who had wasted their lives on unrequited love. It had been one of the decisions Hades had made early in his reign and was born from his anger toward the Fates. If he was not destined to love, then he would punish those who had died because of it. He had since sent the souls who once resided here to other parts of the Underworld, letting the field remain beautifully landscaped, as it was the view the souls were treated to on their way to the Field of Judgement.

A few feet from where he had appeared, lying on the bank of the Styx, was Persephone. He attempted to absorb the scene through his rage—Persephone was on her back, her hair was wet, and she was covered with Hermes' gold cloak, the thin, metallic material clinging to her damp body. Hermes knelt over her; his lips curled in a smile. He was clearly interested in Persephone, and he watched as the god tapped his lips, spoke, and made Persephone laugh.

That was when Hades decided to separate them.

He sent a burst of power barreling toward the god, who went flying halfway across the Underworld. Still, Hades frowned when Hermes did not land as far away as he had hoped, but the impact of his body hitting the ground was satisfying enough.

Hades strolled toward Persephone, who rose and turned, craning her neck to meet his gaze. She shifted Hermes' cloak so that it draped over her shoulders, revealing the dress she had worn to his club—a thin, silver number with a neckline that teased the curve of her breasts. Now that it was wet, it clung to them, accentuating the peaks of her hard nipples.

Fucking Fates, Hades thought as a fire burned a path down his chest straight to his groin.

"Why did you do that?" Persephone demanded.

The god frowned, clenching his jaw. He could not tell if it was to suppress his reaction to her body or the fact that she was angry about Hermes.

"Your try my patience, goddess, and my favor," he replied.

"So you are a goddess!" Hermes shouted enthusiastically, despite crawling from the pit his body had made upon impact.

Persephone narrowed her eyes, and Hades realized that he had only succeeded in making her more frustrated by outing her.

"He will keep your secret, or he will find himself in Tartarus," Hades promised, driving his point home by glaring at the God of Mischief, who approached now, brushing dirt and grime from his person. Hades found it amusing to see the god in disarray, as he prided himself on his appearance like many gods.

"You know, Hades, not everything has to be a threat.

You could try asking once in a while. Just like you could have asked me to step away from your goddess here instead of throwing me *halfway across the Underworld.*"

"I'm not his goddess! And you!" Persephone's tone was full of disdain as she made her way to her feet. Hades narrowed his eyes, unable to put into words how much he hated being spoken to in this manner before another Olympian, especially Hermes. "You could be nicer to him. He did save me from *your* river!"

"You wouldn't have had to be saved from *my* river if you had waited for me!"

"Right, because you were *otherwise engaged.* Whatever that means."

She rolled her eyes. *Was she…jealous?* Hades wondered.

"Shall I get you a dictionary?"

When Hades heard Hermes' gleeful laugh, he turned on the god. "Why are you still here?"

Just as the words fell from his mouth, Persephone swayed. Without thought, he reached for her, catching her around the waist, and was surprised when a sharp moan escaped from somewhere deep in her throat.

Pain. She's in pain.

"What's wrong?" He was not used to the hysteria rising within him; it felt like a foreign thing splitting open his skin.

"I fell on the stairs. I think I…" He watched her take a deliberate breath, wincing. "I think I bruised my ribs."

Hades could best describe how he felt as angry, but it was more than that. He *hated* that she had been hurt in his realm. It made him sick, frustrated, made him feel like he had lost control. He was surprised to notice Persephone's gaze soften, and after a moment, she whispered, "It's okay. I'm okay."

Except that she wasn't. She had fainted in his arms.

"She has a pretty nasty gash on her shoulder, too," Hermes added.

That same feeling of losing control consumed him, and it was heavy, like he had been dropped into a tarpit. He felt his jaw tighten to the point that his teeth might split, then he lifted her into his arms as gently as he could, despite the chaos inside him.

"Where are we going?"

"To my palace," he said.

If he could heal her, at least he could regain some sort of power over the situation and she would be safe.

He transported them to his bedchamber, and when he looked down at her, she opened her eyes. For a moment, she seemed unfocused.

"Are you well?" Hades asked, and she met his gaze.

When she nodded, he strolled to his bed and settled her on the edge, kneeling on the floor in front of her.

"What are you doing?" she asked.

He did not answer but reached to peel Hermes' cloak from about her shoulders. She stilled at his touch, and he thought about telling her to breathe but decided that maybe she was reacting to pain and not his presence. He was not prepared for what the cloak was hiding—her shoulder was torn to the bone.

Nasty gash? Hermes had grossly misrepresented this wound.

Hades sat back on his heels, studying the damage. He would need to clean it before he healed it, or there was a chance infection would set in. Though it was rare for a god to become ill; it was not impossible, and he would not take any chances. Not with her.

He let his gaze wander the length of her, searching for other wounds. The dead who inhabited the Styx were vicious, their claws and teeth sharp, and they shredded their victims. Persephone was lucky to have gotten out of the river with a shoulder wound.

It could have been worse.

His horror was real and painful, like hitting a brick wall. He had crafted his realm to discourage curious exploration, and yet here was Persephone, inquisitive and unfazed.

It was not until Persephone drew an arm over her chest

that Hades lifted his gaze to her eyes; he hadn't realized that he'd been staring. He scolded himself and came to his knees, bracing his hands on either side of her thighs. The movement brought him within an inch of her face. Even having almost drowned in the Styx, she still smelled like vanilla—sweet and warm.

"Which side?" he asked quietly.

She held his gaze for a moment, and he noted how she swallowed before covering his hand with her own and guiding it to her side. Something gathered in the back of his throat, and he wanted desperately to clear it, but couldn't.

He wasn't breathing now, either.

He focused instead on her side, sending a wave of power from deep inside his body to his hand, letting the magic soak into her skin.

She moaned and leaned into him, his head resting against her shoulder, and something akin to fire ignited in his stomach.

Fuck.

He took deep breaths through his nose and out his mouth, trying to concentrate on his magic and not his growing erection.

When he was certain she was healed, he moved his head a fraction, their lips level as he spoke.

"Better?"

"Yes," she whispered, and he noted how her eyes fell to his mouth.

"Your shoulder is next." He stood and when she started to look, he stopped her with a hand on her cheek.

"No. It's best if you don't look."

It would hurt worse if she did.

Hades stepped into the bathroom and wetted a cloth. He was not gone long, but when he returned, he found Persephone had shifted to her side and lay on his bed with her eyes closed.

He frowned as he watched her.

While he understood why she would be exhausted, he

did not like it. It made him worry that perhaps he had taken too long to heal her, or maybe she had been injured worse than he knew?

He approached and leaned toward her.

"Wake, my darling."

As she stirred, he knelt beside her again, relieved to see that her eyes were clear and bright.

"Sorry." Her voice was a hushed whisper, and it shivered through him.

"Do not apologize."

He should be apologizing. He had intended to advise her of the dangers of the Underworld on their tour tonight, but he hadn't had the chance.

He began cleaning her shoulder, infusing the damp cloth with his magic so she felt less pain.

"I can do this," she offered, and started to rise, but Hades held her in place.

"Allow me this." He wanted this—to take care of her, to heal her, to ensure she was well. He could not explain why, but the part of him that desired this, it was primal.

She nodded, and he resumed his work. After a moment, she asked in a sleepy voice, "Why are there dead people in your river?"

A ghost of a smile touched his lips. "They are the souls who were not buried with coins."

He felt her gaze upon him as she asked, appalled, "You still do that?"

His smile widened. "No. Those dead are ancient."

"And what do they do? Besides drown the living."

"That's all they do."

Their life in the Styx had initially been a punishment, a place souls were sentenced for not possessing coin to cross the river. Coin was a sign that a soul had been properly buried, and back then, Hades had no time for souls who were not being cared for in the Upperworld.

It was a painful memory, one that he had decided to rectify long ago. He had The Judges evaluate all of them, and those who deserved respite were given water from the

Lethe and sent to Elysium or Asphodel. Those who would have been sent to Tartarus were left in the deep.

Hades was not sure what Persephone thought of his explanation, but she fell silent after that and he was glad. Her questions had drudged up memories he preferred to keep isolated in the back of his mind forever.

This was the second time her presence had unearthed something painful from his past. Would this be a common occurrence? Was this the Fates' form of torture?

Once he finished cleaning her wound, he focused on the healing. It took longer than her bruised ribs, as he had to cure tendon and muscle and skin, but once he was finished, there was no sign that she had been hurt. He released a short breath, relieved, and then placed his finger against her chin so that she would look at him, partly so he could ensure she was well and also because he wanted to see her expression.

"Change," he advised.

"I…don't have anything to change into."

"I have something," he said, and helped her to her feet. He didn't know if she felt dizzy, but he preferred to keep a tight grip on her hand in case that changed. Plus, he liked to feel her warmth. It reminded him that she was real.

He directed her behind a changing screen and handed her a black robe, noting the look of surprise on her face as she registered what she was holding.

She arched a brow. "I'm guessing this isn't yours?"

"The Underworld is prepared for all manner of guests," he answered. It was the truth, but he also could not remember who the robe belonged to.

"Thank you." Her response was curt. "But I don't think I want to wear something one of your lovers has also worn."

Her comment might have been amusing, but instead, he found that he was frustrated by her anger. Would he encounter this every time they discussed past loves? If so, the conversation would get old very fast.

"It's either this or nothing at all, Persephone."

Her mouth fell open. "You wouldn't."

He narrowed his eyes, and a thrill shot through him at the challenge. "What? Undress you? Happily, and with far more enthusiasm than you realize, my lady."

She used her remaining energy to glare at him before her shoulders fell.

"Fine."

While she changed, Hades poured himself a glass of whiskey, managing to take a sip before she stepped out from behind the partition. He almost choked on his drink. He had thought the silver dress she'd been wearing left little to the imagination, but he was wrong. The robe accentuated her small waist, the flare of her hips, and her shapely legs. *Giving her that scrap of fabric was a mistake*, he thought as he approached and took her wet dress, hanging it over the screen.

"What now?" she asked.

For a moment, he wondered if she could sense his sinful thoughts.

"You rest."

He lifted her into his arms, expecting her to protest, but he was relieved when she didn't. He would not be able to explain why he needed this closeness, didn't fully understand it himself, he just wanted to touch her, to know that she was full of life and heat.

He lowered her to the bed and pulled the blankets over her. She looked pale and fragile, lost in a sea of black silk.

"Thank you," she said quietly, looking up at him with heavy lids. She frowned and touched the space between his brows with her finger, tracing his cheek, ending at the corner of his lips. "You're angry."

It took everything inside him to remain where he was, to not lean into her touch, to not press his lips to hers. If he kissed her, he would not stop.

After a moment, her hand fell away, and she closed her eyes.

"Persephone," she said.

"What?"

"I want to be called Persephone. Not *lady*."

Another faint smile touched his lips. Lady was a title she would have to get used to; he had ordered his staff to address her as such.

"Rest," he said instead. "I will be here when you wake."

He sensed her breath evening, and when he was sure she was asleep, he teleported back to the Styx, appearing on the bank of the river. His magic flared, a combination of the anger and lust and fear.

"Bring me those who smell of Persephone's blood!" he commanded, and as he lifted his arms, four of the dead burst forth from the Styx, the water rushing after them like the tail of a comet. The corpses shrieked, sounding and appearing more like monsters than the bodies of once flesh-and-blood mortals. "You have tasted the blood of my queen and therefore shall cease existing."

As he closed his fists, the wailing increased to an almost impossible shrill, and the corpses turned to dust that was swept away into the mountains of Tartarus.

In the aftermath, Hades' ears rang and his breathing was harsh, but the release was euphoric.

Behind him, he heard Hermes' familiar chuckle. He whirled to face the God of Mischief.

"I knew you would return," he said. He nodded toward the mountains of Tartarus. "Feeling better?"

"No. Why are you still here?"

"So rude. You have yet to thank me for saving your... what should we call her? Lover?"

"She is not my lover," Hades snapped.

Hermes was unamused, raising a pale brow.

"So you just threw me halfway across your realm for nothing?"

"It's a sport," he replied.

"Have your fun, and I'll have mine."

"What's that supposed to mean?"

Hermes might be the messenger of the gods, but he was also trickery and mischief. He liked fuckery, and he had been responsible for many battles between gods.

"Only that I will enjoy watching your balls get bluer by the hour."

Hades offered a small smile, and after a beat, he looked at Hermes.

"Thank you, Hermes, for saving Persephone."

He vanished before the god could grin.

CHAPTER X – MIND GAMES

Hades sat in a chair before his fireplace, drinking and watching Persephone sleep. The slow rise and fall of her body as she breathed soothed his nerves. His head swarmed with the events of the last few days—discovering his connection with the beautiful goddess, their subsequent bargain, her anger toward him for merely being the God of the Dead.

She might hate him, but she had let him get close to her today, and he was not sure he would ever be the same. He had hoped to maintain a modicum of control over this situation the Fates had woven for him, but he felt like he was losing that battle each time he looked at the woman in his bed.

He had lost his composure twice in the span of an hour—first with Hermes, and then with the dead in the river—because this goddess was curious, because seeing her bleed had ignited rage in him so hot, he'd had no other place to expel it except at those who had injured her.

Perhaps you should meditate, he heard Hecate's voice echoing in his head.

"Fuck meditation," he said aloud.

Then Persephone stirred, and he stilled. She sat up

quickly and then paused to close her eyes.

Dizzy, he thought, frowning.

When she opened her eyes again, they were bottle-green and seemed to glow like pale light streaming through a muted window. She stared at him with those eyes for what seemed like an eternity. His body tensed beneath her gaze, his grip tightened around his glass, and the fingers of his other hand pressed into the supple leather of his chair. His cock grew hard, pinned against his leg and trousers.

"How long have I been here?" she asked. Her voice was husky, and he wanted to groan. Instead, he managed a one-word reply.

"Hours."

Her eyes grew wide. "What time is it?"

He shrugged because he did not know. "Late."

"I have to go."

Hades expected her to be angry or react with a sense of hysteria, but she didn't. She just sat there in a pool of black silk looking beautiful and rosy and warm.

"You have come all this way. Allow me to offer you a tour of my world."

He stood and downed the last of his whiskey. Her eyes did not waiver from his as he approached and drew the covers from her, revealing a sliver of skin between her breasts where her robe had parted in her sleep. It took everything in his power to avert his eyes as she clasped the robe closed. After a moment, he extended his hand. Her fingers slipped into his, and he found himself wondering when he would stop being surprised by her willingness to touch him. He guided her to her feet and waited for her to look up at him before asking, "Are you well?"

"Better," she answered quietly.

He traced the curve of her cheek. "Trust that I am devastated that you were hurt in my realm."

Her gaze told him she was surprised by his words, or perhaps their sincerity.

"I'm okay," she whispered, but okay was not good enough.

"It will never happen again. Come."

He guided her to the balcony outside his room, where the Forest of Ash stretched for miles, meeting a wall of obsidian mountains. She wandered ahead of him, her fingers twined with his as she peered over the balcony.

"Do you like it?" he asked.

"It's beautiful," she breathed as her gaze wandered over the landscape. "You created all of this?"

He nodded. "The Underworld evolves just as the world above."

He tugged on her hand, and she followed him down the stairs into the garden below. He felt a thrill of excitement as he brought her to the edge where lavender wisteria wept, where inky roses and pink peonies bloomed, and purple and red slavia twisted like serpents from darkness. Would she find this just as astounding?

His answer came as soon as her feet touched the dark stone path leading into the garden. She wrenched her hand from his and turned on him.

"You bastard!"

Hades suddenly felt completely ridiculous. His mouth tightened. "Names, Persephone."

"Don't you dare! This—this is beautiful!"

So she was impressed, but why the anger?

"It is," he agreed.

"Why would you ask me to create life here?" She sounded...devastated, as if seeing his realm and the flora that grew here drained her hope. Did she grieve for what she felt she had no power to create?

With a wave of his hand, he dismantled the illusion. Revealing the truth of his realm felt like revealing the truth of his soul. The Underworld was desolate—a wasteland of ash.

"It is illusion," he explained. "If it is a garden you wish to create, then it will truly be the only life here."

Hades called the glamour back and walked ahead. Persephone followed, and he wondered what she was thinking. Was she appalled by what he had shown her? Did she think less of the Underworld just because its beauty was a creation of his own magic? He had not intended to give her a tour of the Underworld to make her feel powerless…but he could feel her doubt and anger flare. As much as he hated being the reason for these feelings, he knew it was the only way she could reach her potential. One day, Persephone would tire of feeling defenseless, and his queen would rise from the ashes. A goddess.

Hades stopped near a retaining wall at the back of his garden. On the other side were the Asphodel Fields. At his feet, the earth was barren and black.

"You may work here," Hades said.

If Persephone wanted to grow a garden, if that was her way of creating life in the Underworld, then she would have to do it in the ashy soil of the Underworld.

"I still don't understand," Persephone said. "Illusion or not, you have all of this beauty. Why demand this of me?"

Because it is the will of your soul, he thought.

"If you do not wish to fulfill the terms of our contract, you have only to say so, Lady Persephone. I can have a suite prepared for you in less than an hour."

"We do not get along well enough to be housemates, Hades."

Her comment inspired a few salacious images—bare skin and breathy moans.

He disagreed.

"How often am I allowed to come here and work?"

"As often as you want," he said, because after today, he would ensure she never took that portal again. "I know you are eager to complete your task."

Her gaze fell to the ground, and she bent to scoop up a handful of sand. It was not meant to nurture life, the texture like ground bone. She rose to her feet again.

"And…how shall I enter the Underworld?" she asked. "I'm assuming you don't want me to return the way I came?"

"Hmm." It was the question he had been waiting for, and his answer made his body tight with anticipation. He tilted his head to the side, and she stared back, lips parting.

It was enough of an invitation.

He gripped her shoulders and pulled her flush against him, bringing his mouth to hers. He could have offered her favor without laying so much as a finger on her, but it was an excuse to touch her. Given that, he should have been gentle, but he found he was anything but tame. His body reacted like it was on fire and desperate to be smothered. He felt ridiculous; he had kissed and fucked, but he had never felt *this*...whatever it was. This burning desire, this desperate wish to claim and protect and to *love*.

Then again, he had never kissed or fucked a woman destined to be his lover. Was the thread the reason he felt so...uncontrolled?

He urged her lips apart, his tongue gliding against hers, his teeth grazing her lips. She tasted like wine and salt, and smelled like a bed of sweet roses. Her body trembled, and he held her tighter so that there was no space between them, feeling all her soft curves against the hard contours of his own body. She was just as enthusiastic, kissing him with unabashed abandon. He got the sense that she would not have appreciated gentle, that she craved passion, rough and raw.

Her arms wound around his neck, and he groaned, the sound coming from somewhere deep and long asleep. He moved, directing her until she was pressed into the stone. His hands drifted down her waist and over her round bottom, where he gripped and lifted her from the ground. With her legs planted around his waist, her heels digging into his back, his erection grinding into her most sensitive place, he let his lips wander, trailing her jaw, nipping her ear, kissing down her neck. Now and then he would pause and taste her skin, salty from the river. She arched beneath him, gasping until she took control, driving her hands through his hair, loosening the strands until it fell in layers around his face. It was his hair she used to control him, because as his hands slipped beneath her robe, grazing the hot and tender skin between her thighs, she gripped it harder, and it was that sharp pull that brought him back to reality.

He had gone too far. He broke their kiss, breathing hard, struggling to contain his lust. He had meant to tease her to gauge her desire, but it had turned into something more. Even now he continued to hold her, fighting the urge to begin where they ended. All he had to do was shift his hand ever so slightly, part her damp flesh with his fingers, and he would be inside her.

But this was not how it should be. She had no reason to trust him with her body, no reason to trust him at all. He would not let her regret their time together, and when he made love to her, it would not be against a garden wall.

That would come later.

He lowered her to the ground but did not release her.

"Once you enter Nevernight, you have only to snap your fingers, and you will be brought here."

He knew he had said something wrong when the color drained from her face and she attempted to shoved him away, demanding, "Can't you offer favor another way?"

"You didn't seem to mind," he pointed out, liking the flush that touched her cheeks and elegant neck. He wanted to tell her she should not be embarrassed, but when she touched her lips with shaking fingers, he lost his train of thought.

"I should go," she said.

Hades nodded in agreement. If she did not leave now, he would rescind his earlier statement.

Fuck waiting to love her elsewhere, the garden is perfect.

"What are you doing?" she demanded as his arm tightened around her waist.

He was silent, snapping his fingers and teleporting. When they appeared in Persephone's room, she was gripping his arms like a cat who had been frightened. He waited for her to adjust, her head turning slowly, and as she recognized her surroundings, she pried her fingers from his skin one by one.

"Persephone." There was one more thing she needed

to know before he left her for the night. "Never bring a mortal to my realm again, especially Adonis. Stay away from him."

Her eyes narrowed, glinting with defiance. "How do you know him?"

"That is not relevant."

He felt her attempt to pull away, but he held her in place. This was important. He had not saved her from Underworld monsters just to have her hurt by mortal ones.

"I work with him, Hades."

He ignored the pleasure he got from the sound of his name on her lips.

"Besides, you can't give me orders."

"I'm not giving you orders. I am asking."

"Asking implies there's a choice."

His grip increased, and he leaned over her, nearly bending her backward so their faces were inches apart. Again, Hades thought of her lips, her taste, her touch, and he knew she was having similar thoughts because she closed her eyes and swallowed.

He spoke in the silence between them.

"You have a choice, but if you choose him, I will fetch you and I might not let you leave the Underworld."

Her eyes flew open. "You wouldn't," she hissed.

Hades chuckled, his breath caressing her lips as he spoke. "Oh, darling. You don't know what I'm capable of."

Then he vanished like smoke fading into the sky.

CHAPTER XI – A GAME FOR
A GOD

"I asked for a weapon, Hephaestus."

Hades stared at the small, octagon-shaped box the God of Fire held out to him. It was beautiful—obsidian and inlaid with jade and gold—but it did not look like something that could restrain a god.

When Hades met Hephaestus' grey eyes, he knew he had missed something. The corner of his mouth lifted, and he dropped the box at Hades' feet. In the next second, heavy manacles clamped down upon his wrists, their weight keeping his arms fastened at his sides, and when he tried to lift them, he found it was impossible.

"And so I have granted you chains," the god replied.

Hades tried to lift his arms again, and his muscles tightened, veins rising to the surface of his skin, but it seemed like the more force he exerted, the more the chains oppressed.

"Tell me what you think of them," Hephaestus said.

"Brilliant," Hades answered, the word falling out his mouth before he even had a chance to think—and he remembered what he'd requested of the God of Fire—a weapon that could subdue violence and encourage truth. Hades smiled despite feeling like a lab rat. Hephaestus' ability to create and innovate never ceased to impress.

"This is a dangerous weapon," Hades said, but when he looked at Hephaestus, he knew something else was on the god's mind. His eyes were steely and menacing. Hades stiffened; he knew this look, he had seen it in the eyes of every mortal and immortal who had wished death upon him.

"Have you fucked my wife?" The question did not match Hephaestus' cool composure or dispassionate tone, but Hades recognized himself in the God of Fire and knew that beneath his calm exterior, he was raging inside.

"No."

"Eleftherose ton," Hephaestus said, turning his scarred back to Hades as he was released from the restraints, the chains returning to the black box. Hades rubbed his wrists as the full weight of Hephaestus' question settled upon him. He had thought Hades was sleeping with Aphrodite, and he had believed it so thoroughly, he felt he needed magic to get the truth.

Hades scooped up the box and straightened, staring at Hephaestus' back.

"Why ask me about Aphrodite?" He could not help the frustration in his voice. He knew why Hephaestus had asked—because, despite his feigned indifference, he cared about his wife and who she chose to sleep with. He loved her, and yet he chose to be miserable, chose to be passive.

"Have I not revealed enough of my shame?" Hephaestus asked.

"It is not shameful to love your wife."

Hephaestus said nothing.

"If you feared her infidelity, why did you release her from the bonds of marriage to begin with?"

The god tensed. Clearly, he did not know what Aphrodite had shared with him. That on the eve of his marriage to the Goddess of Love, Hephaestus had released her from all obligations of that marriage.

"She was forced to marry me," Hephaestus said, as if that explained everything. Though, it was true. Zeus had arranged their marriage to keep peace among those who wanted Aphrodite for a wife.

"You didn't have to agree," Hades said.

Hephaestus' muscles rippled, and the God of the Dead knew he had angered him. Yet when he spoke, his voice was calm, void of emotion.

"Who am I to reject a gift from Zeus?"

It was a simple comment, but it spoke volumes about how Hephaestus viewed himself—unworthy of happiness, of favor, of love.

Hades sighed. In truth, it was not his place to get involved in Hephaestus and Aphrodite's relationship. He had enough to worry about as it was with the Fates, Sisyphus, and Persephone.

"Thank you, Hephaestus," Hades said, lifting the box. "For your time."

He teleported from the cavernous lab, appearing in the sky over the ocean, and let himself fall through billowing clouds. Hades landed on Earth, on the island of Atlantis. The impact shook the ground and marred the marble at his feet. Around him, Poseidon's people—mortals who called themselves Atlanteans—screamed. It took seconds for his brother to appear, bare chested and wearing a *pteruges*, a decorative skirt made of leather strips. Gold cuffed his forearms, his wavy and blond hair was crowned with gold spears, and two large spiral markahor horns jutted from the top of his head.

The God of the Sea looked like he was prepared for battle, which was fair. Hades only ever visited when he had a score to settle, and this time was no different.

"Brother." Poseidon offered a curt nod.

"Poseidon," Hades said.

There was a moment of tense silence before Hades asked, "Where is Sisyphus?"

Poseidon smirked. "Not one for pleasantries, are you, Hades?"

Hades tilted his head to the side, and as he did, a great marble statue of Poseidon cracked and split. As the pieces crashed to the ground, more of Poseidon's cult, who had stopped to stare, ran for cover, screaming.

"Stop destroying my island!" Poseidon commanded.

"Where is Sisyphus?" Hades demanded again.

His brother's eyes narrowed, and he chuckled. "What did he do? Tell me it was good."

Hades' anger was acute, and for the first time since he had asked Hephaestus for a weapon to contain Poseidon's fury, he realized it was just as much meant for him as it was his brother. Tired of wasting time, Hades tossed the box at Poseidon's feet. In the next second, the God of the Sea found himself ensnared in chains. For a few seconds, Poseidon blinked in shock at the metal around his wrists. He pulled at them, trying to snap them with his strength, muscles bulging, veins popping, but no matter how hard he tried, they remained.

"What the fuck, Hades?" he snarled.

"Tell me where Sisyphus is hiding!" Hades' voice was brutal and rough.

"I don't know where your fucking mortal is," Poseidon spat. "Release me!"

Hades could sense Poseidon's power rising with his rage. The sea around the island churned violently, lapping at the edges of the landmass. Hades only hoped he could get the answers he was looking for before his brother's violence was unleashed. Poseidon would not grieve the loss of his people if it meant revenge against him.

"Careful, brother. Your rage may add worshippers to my realm."

It was the one thing he could say that would at least give Poseidon pause.

The god glared, his chest rising and falling with his anger, but Hades felt his magic ebb. Given his frustration, Hades had forgotten that the chains drew truth from their captor, which meant that Poseidon truly did not know where Sisyphus was.

He needed to ask a different question.

"How do you know Sisyphus de Ephyra?" Hades asked.

Poseidon roared, clearly trying to fight the words the magic pulled from his throat. "He saved my granddaughter from Zeus."

Ah. Now they were getting somewhere.

"And did you reward him?"

"Yes," Poseidon hissed.

"Did you grant him favor?"

"No."

"*What did you grant him?*"

"A spindle."

A spindle—a relic—just as Hades suspected. It explained how Sisyphus had been able to steal lives from another mortal.

"You gave a mortal a *fucking* spindle?" Hades snarled. "Why?"

For the first time since Hades had begun interrogating Poseidon, he seemed to speak with ease as he said, "To fuck with you, Hades. Why else?"

It was a petty reason, but a very Poseidon reason, nonetheless.

"I tell you what, though. I'll make a deal with you," Poseidon said. "A bargain, as you call it."

"Those are brave words coming from someone who has no power to fight the magic holding them captive," Hades observed.

"I'll help you find Sisyphus. Hell, I'll lure him here myself. If…"

Hades waited, hating how slow Poseidon spoke, how much *time* he wasted.

"*If* you release my monsters from Tartarus."

"No."

Hades' did not even need to think. He would not relinquish any of the creatures who lived in the depths of Tartarus. They did not have a place in the modern world and definitely did not have a place in Poseidon's hands.

The ground began to quake, and the ocean rose up on all sides of the island, welling in the cracks Hades had created in Poseidon's marble. He had pushed too hard. Hades cast his magic like a net, enveloping the landmass in shadow to keep his brother at bay.

"You lost your monsters because you tried to overthrow Zeus," Hades said through gritted teeth. Poseidon's magic was heavy, and he felt like he was being buried alive as it battled against his wall of shadow. "Now you are angry because there were consequences for your actions. How childish."

The disgust Hades felt for his brother in this moment fueled the strength of his magic, though Poseidon's display was not surprising. His life had been a sequence of childish outbursts that had dire consequences for those involved.

"You claim to be a king and yet follow the rule of Zeus," Poseidon spat.

"I follow my own rule," Hades said. "It just doesn't align with your will."

Hades didn't often agree with Zeus, but at least the God of the Sky believed in the existence of a free society. He believed that all gods had their role in the world, and that they should keep order within their specialty and nothing more.

Poseidon was not of the same mind, and if he could rule supreme, he would.

The problem was he had two equally powerful brothers who could—and would, and had—stopped him.

Hades closed his eyes and reached into his darkness, into the part of himself that had been born to war and chaos and destruction. To the part of himself that was desperate for control and order and power. He drew upon that desperation, that will, that strength, coaxing it to the surface until the power that welled deep in his chest exploded in a stream of shadow. It tore through Poseidon and his wall of water, and the god went to his knees, the ground shaking beneath him.

The two gods breathed hard and glared at one another, and as the water settled around them, Hades spoke.

"I have saved your people and your island. I am due a favor."

There was a chance Poseidon would not agree, that he would go to the same dark place Hades had to retrieve power, but Hades hoped the God of the Sea would realize what was at stake—more than just monsters. If he fought, it would mean the end of Atlantis, his people, and perhaps his freedom.

Zeus had taken that before. Nothing would stop him from doing it again.

"Think, Poseidon. Do you really want your empire to end over this mortal?"

He could see the indecision warring in Poseidon's eyes. At this point, it wasn't about a mortal anymore, it was about Hades and the fact that he had challenged—and overpowered—Poseidon in front of his own people.

"Poseidon." A musical, feminine voice called the god's name.

Hades' gaze shifted to Amphitrite, Poseidon's wife. Her eyes were large and round and the color of peridot. They were eerie to behold and set in a delicate face. Long ginger hair shrouded her curvy body like a cape. She was beautiful and deeply in love with her husband, despite his infidelity.

In her presence, Poseidon's anger evaporated and his body slumped. Hades watched as Amphitrite hurried to him, and the God of the Sea grasped her, chains rattling as he did. They held one another close before pulling apart and staring into each other's eyes. Something passed between them, a wordless communication born from years of partnership. After a moment, Poseidon looked at Hades.

"A favor, then," he agreed.

"You will help me capture Sisyphus," Hades said. "Since you are responsible for this blight upon the world."

It was like asking for Poseidon's help and Hades hated it, but it was probably the easiest way to get Sisyphus off the streets and the spindle out of circulation.

"Iniquity," Hades said. "Tomorrow at midnight."

"Sisyphus will not come within a mile of your territory," Poseidon said. "And not that quickly, especially after your...*gross* display of power. It will be a few days, and it will be in my territory."

Hades did not like the idea of meeting on Poseidon's turf. It meant that he had more at his disposal, both in power and people, but the God of the Sea was right. It was best to meet in a place that would not draw suspicion from Sisyphus.

"Fine," Hades said. "Eleftherose ton."

As Hades spoke the words, Poseidon was released from his chains. Amphitrite helped the burly god to his feet, which was almost comical, considering she was half his size. Poseidon drew her close, his large hands nearly spanning her waist, and kissed her. Hades averted his eyes, confused by their display of affection. If his brother loved his wife so much, why did he pursue other women? They seemed lost in one another for a moment, Poseidon's anger toward his brother momentarily forgotten.

Hades used his magic to reclaim the small, black box Hephaestus had given him. There was no way he would let something so useful and so powerful slip through his hands. As the box came to land in Hades' palm, Amphitrite looked at him. She might be his sister-in-law, but he knew very little about her, save that she could calm the seas and Poseidon.

But right now, Hades felt her fury.

"I think it is time you left, Lord Hades," she said.

The corner of his mouth tipped, and he nodded before vanishing.

CHAPTER XII – A GAME WITH A GODDESS

Hades returned to the Underworld and summoned Ilias. He was exhausted after expending so much energy keeping Poseidon's magic at bay, but he had a plan to locate Sisyphus. It was the first time he had felt any kind of success since the beginning of this ordeal.

He poured a glass of whiskey and drank quickly, approaching the window to look out upon his realm, spotting Hecate walking with Persephone. The two goddesses talked and smiled and laughed, and Hades could not help thinking how perfect Persephone looked in his realm, like she belonged there, like she should have always been there.

"My lord?" Ilias asked.

Hades turned his head and found the satyr beside him, brow raised.

"Enjoying the view?" he asked, amused.

Hades would have liked it better if he had realized Ilias had arrived.

"I have a job for you," he said. "Poseidon gave Sisyphus a relic. A spindle, to be exact."

The satyr's eyes widened. "A spindle? Where did he get that?"

"That is your job," Hades said. "Trace it."

"And what would you like me to do when I find it?"

Usually, Hades gave Ilias free rein over how he dealt with illegal dealers. The satyr would organize raids, burn shops, destroy merchandise. On rare occasions, he found someone worthy of joining Iniquity.

"I want their name," he replied. He would be visiting them personally.

"Consider it done," Ilias bowed, but he did not leave Hades' side. Looking outside, nodding toward Persephone and Hecate.

"She is curious about you," he said.

"She is eager to examine my flaws," Hades corrected.

The satyr chuckled. "I like her."

"I am not seeking your approval, Ilias."

"Of course not, my lord."

With that, the satyr departed, and Hades watched until Persephone was no longer in view, but he could feel her presence in his realm, a torch that scorched a path across his skin. He considered seeking her out but thought against it. As much as he hoped to change Persephone's opinion of himself, he also needed her to find solace and friendship in his realm.

Not needed.

Wanted.

He wanted her to find solace in his gardens, to walk the paths of the Underworld with Hecate, to celebrate with the souls. He wanted her to, one day, think of the Underworld as her home.

A strange feeling overcame him, one he was familiar with and hated—embarrassment. If anyone could hear his thoughts, they would laugh. The God of the Dead, hopeful for love, and yet he could not help it. When he had taken Persephone into his arms in the garden, when he had kissed her, he had suddenly understood what their life could be—passionate and powerful. He wanted that desperately.

And despite her dislike for him and his bargains, she could not deny her desire. He had felt it in the pull of her fingers through his hair, the mold of her soft body to his, and the desperation in her kiss.

His head started to rush, and a warmth spread through him that went straight to his cock. He groaned; he was going to have to expel some of this energy.

He shed his jacket and shirt and headed for the Asphodel Fields.

"Cerberus, Typhon, Orthrus, come!" he called, and turned in the direction of his approaching Dobermans. They charged through the grass, determined in their stride.

"Halt," Hades commanded when they drew near, and the three obeyed and sat. Cerberus sat in the middle, Typhon on the right and Orthrus on the left. They were handsome dogs with glistening black coats, pointed ears, and wedge-shaped heads.

The three were never apart, always traveling in a pack, guarding the Underworld from intruders or unwelcomed deities who lived outside the gates of his realm. Sometimes, Hecate recruited them for various punishments, commanding them to feast upon innards or maul a deserving soul.

Hades preferred playtime.

"How are my boys, huh?" he asked, roughing up their ears. Their demeanor changed from fierce to playful. The dogs' tails wagged, and their tongues lolled out of their mouths. "Punished a lot of souls today?"

He took some time to scratch behind their ears.

"Good boys, good, good boys."

He summoned a red ball from thin air. When the dogs saw it, they sat straight, panting with anticipation. Hades grinned, tossing the ball into the air, once, twice, the dogs eyes following with rapt attention.

"Which one of you is fastest, huh? Cerberus? Typhon? Orthrus?"

As he called each Doberman's name, they offered a

growling bark, impatient for the chase.

Hades smirked, feeling a little devilish.

"Stay," he commanded, and then threw the ball.

Fetch with Cerberus, Typhon, and Orthrus was not like fetch with normal dogs. Hades' strength was great, and when he threw the ball, it went on for miles, but his Dobermans were unnaturally fast, able to travel across the Underworld in minutes.

Hades waited until the ball disappeared, before turning to the dogs. "Fetch."

At his order, the dogs took off, muscles working powerfully. Hades laughed as the three raced to find the ball. They returned in no time, running in sync, the red ball clutched in Cerberus' mouth, who brought it obediently to Hades and dropped it at his feet. He continued playing with his dogs, running in circles through the meadow, working off his frustration and lust until he felt breathless and sweaty.

He tossed the ball once more, free from the burden of his feelings, when he turned and found Persephone standing in the clearing, watching him with wide eyes.

Fuck.

She was beautiful, and his eyes traveled the length of her, unashamed. She had flowers in her hair—camellia, if he had to guess—and they threaded through long strands of curly blonde locks. She wore a blue tank that was cut in a low V at the neck, drawing attention to her breasts. Her shorts were white, revealing her long legs—legs he had fastened around his waist just days ago. As his eyes traveled back up her body, he found that her gaze had made the same descent, and he smirked.

He might have challenged her to deny her attraction, except the Goddess of Witchcraft was here and marching straight for him.

"You know they never behave for me after you spoil them!" she was saying, casting her arms out in the direction where Cerberus, Typhon, and Orthrus had disappeared. Her complaint was playful, mostly because the three were quick to listen, especially if instructed to return to their work.

He grinned. "They grow lazy under your care, Hecate."

And fat. She liked to feed them.

Hades' eyes slid to Persephone. "I see you have met the Goddess of Spring."

He did not miss how she stiffened at the title.

"Yes, and she is quite lucky I did," Hecate said, eyes flashing. "How dare you not warn her to stay away from the Lethe!"

His eyes snapped to Persephone, who was trying hard not to smile. It seemed she enjoyed hearing Hecate scold him, but Hecate was right, he should have warned her not to approach any of the rivers in the Underworld. The Lethe, in particular, was powerful, drawing memories from souls like air.

What would he have done if she had touched it? Drank from it? He shoved the thoughts away.

"It seems I owe you an apology, Lady Persephone."

She was surprised. Perhaps she had not expected him to apologize, but she stared at him with those fiery emerald eyes and parted lips, and he found his desire for her renewed.

Then, the Horn of Tartarus sounded, and he and Hecate turned in its direction.

"I am being summoned," Hecate said.

"Summoned?" Persephone asked.

"The judges are in need of my advice."

The Judges, Minos, Rhadamanthus, and Aeacus, often summoned Hecate to sentence certain souls to eternal punishment, mostly those who had committed crimes against women.

"My dear," Hecate said to Persephone, "call the next time you are in the Underworld. We'll return to Asphodel."

"I would love that," Persephone said with a smile, and it made Hades' heart beat harder.

She enjoyed her time with the souls. Good.

When they were alone, Persephone turned to Hades.

"Why would the judges need Hecate's advice?"

He cocked his head to the side, curious at her demanding tone, and answered, "Hecate is the Lady of Tartarus and particularly good at deciding punishments for the wicked."

"Where is Tartarus?"

"I would tell you if I thought you would use the knowledge to avoid it."

But given her history, he did not trust her.

"You think I want to visit your torture chamber?"

"I think you are curious and eager to prove I am as the world assumes—a deity to be feared."

All things that would probably be confirmed if she found her way to his eternal torture chamber.

She gave him a challenging stare. "You're afraid I'll write about what I see."

That made him laugh. "*Fear* is not the word, darling."

He feared for her safety. He *dreaded* her assumptions.

She rolled her eyes. "Of course you fear nothing."

Oh darling, you know *nothing*, he thought as he reached to pluck a flower from her hair. He twirled the stem between his fingers and asked, "Did you enjoy Asphodel?"

She smiled, and the honesty of it left him breathless. "I did. Your souls... They seem so happy."

"You are surprised?"

"Well, you aren't exactly known for your kindness."

Hades lips flattened. "I'm not known for my kindness to mortals. There is a difference."

"Is that why you play games with their lives?"

He studied her, frustrated by her question and the way she asked it—like she forgot that mortals came to him to bargain, not the other way around.

"I seem to recall advising that I would answer no more of your questions."

Persephone's inviting lips parted. "You can't be serious."

"As the dead."

"But...how will I get to know you?"

The corner of his mouth lifted. "You want to get to know me?"

She looked away, glaring. "I'm being forced to spend time here, right? Shouldn't I get to know my jailer better?"

"So dramatic," he muttered, and fell quiet, considering. He wanted to answer her questions because he wanted her to understand his perspective, but he wanted control. He wanted the ability to limit, to explain until understanding was achieved, he wanted to be able to ask her questions, too.

"Oh, no."

Persephone's voice drew his attention, and he raised a brow. "What?"

"I know that look."

"What look?"

"You get this...look," she explained, and paused, like she did not quite know how to explain. He liked watching her search for the right words, brows knitted together over her pretty eyes. "When you know what you want."

"Do I?" he asked, and couldn't help teasing her. "Can you guess what I want?"

"I'm not a mind reader!" His question flustered her, her cheeks turning crimson. She might be more of a mind reader than she thought.

"Pity," he said. "If you would like to ask questions, then I propose a game."

"No," she said flatly. "I'm not falling for that again."

"No contract," he promised. "No favors owed, just questions answered. Like you want."

She lifted her chin and narrowed those lovely eyes, and he had the fleeting thought that he would like for her to look at him like that while she rode his cock, hard and fast.

Fuck me, he thought.

"Fine," she agreed at last. "But I get to pick the game."

His instinct was to reject her offer, and the words were on the tip of his tongue. *No, I hold the cards*. But as he considered the consequences, he thought it might be a chance to show her he could be flexible.

Finally, he grinned. "Very well, goddess."

He led Persephone to his office, where he had watched her walk with Hecate earlier. He left her alone for a few minutes, long enough to change, and when he returned, she was standing near the windows. At his appearance, she looked at him over her shoulder.

His steps faltered, and he paused in the doorway, staring.

She was beautiful, wreathed in the landscape of the Underworld.

"This is a beautiful view," she said.

"Very," he breathed, and then cleared his throat. "Tell me about this game."

She grinned and turned fully toward him. "It's called rock, paper, scissors."

She explained the game, demonstrating the various shapes—rock, paper, and scissors—with her hands. Despite her enthusiasm, Hades was not impressed.

"This game sounds horrible."

"You're just mad because you haven't played," she countered. "What's wrong? Afraid you'll lose?"

Hades laughed the question off. "No. It sounds simple enough. Rock beats scissors, scissors beats paper, and paper beats rock. How exactly does paper beat rock?"

"Paper covers rock," Persephone said.

"That doesn't make sense. Rock is clearly stronger."

Persephone shrugged. "Why is an ace a wild card?"

"Because it's the rules."

"Well, it's a rule that paper covers rock," she said.

Hades smiled at her retort. He had smiled more in the last hour than he had in his lifetime.

"Ready?" she asked, lifting her hand, and forming a fist. Hades mimicked her movements, and she giggled. Clearly, this was amusing for her, and he groaned internally. The things he did for her already.

"Rock, paper, scissors, shoot!" She spoke the words with fervor. She was definitely having fun, and for that, Hades was glad.

"Yes!" she shrieked, arms flying into the air. "Rock beats scissors!"

Hades frowned. "Damn. I thought you'd choose paper."

"Why?"

"Because you just sang paper's praises!" he explained.

She giggled some more. "Only because you asked why paper covers rock. This isn't poker, Hades. It's not about deception."

"Isn't it?" he disagreed. He was certain if he played this game long enough, he would learn her tendency to choose one of the three options over the others. It was an algorithm, and most people had a pattern, even if they did not realize it.

Silence stretched between them for a moment, Persephone's earlier excitement subsiding. The atmosphere was changing, and Hades did not like it. He wanted to recapture their earlier reverie, not explore darker secrets.

Suddenly, he wondered if he could distract her, close the distance between them and press his lips to hers, but she looked away, took a breath, and asked, "You said you had successes before with your contracts. Tell me about them."

Hades pinched his lips together before retreating to the bar across the room to pour himself a drink. The alcohol would help him loosen up and hopefully prevent him from saying something he regretted.

I wanted a chance to explain, he reminded himself.

He took a seat on his black leather sofa before answering.

"What is there to tell? I have offered many mortals the same contract over the years. In exchange for money, fame, love, they must give up their vice. Some mortals are stronger than others and conquer their habit."

It was a little more complicated than that, and as he spoke, he could feel the threads that covered his skin burn from every failed bargain he had made with the Fates.

"Conquering a disease is not about strength, Hades,"

she said as she sat opposite to him, folding her leg beneath her.

"No one said anything about disease."

"Addiction is a disease," she said. "It cannot be cured. It must be managed."

"It is managed," he argued.

He managed it by holding mortals to their agreements, reminding them of what they would lose if they failed—their life.

"How? With more contracts?"

"That is another question," he snapped, but she seemed unfazed and lifted her hands, signaling she was ready for another round. Hades sat his drink aside and mirrored her stance. When she landed on rock and he scissors, she demanded, "How, Hades?"

"I do not ask them to give everything up at once. It is a slow process."

He did not want to admit that he had given no way for mortals to manage their addictions. It was up to them to find ways to come clean. When he did not elaborate, they played another round.

This time, to Hades' relief, he won. "What would you do?" he asked, because he was curious, and he had no answers.

She blinked, brows furrowing. "What?"

"What would you change? To help them?"

Again, he felt a prick of frustration when her mouth parted in surprise at his question, but her expression quickly changed, becoming determined. "First, I wouldn't allow a mortal to gamble their soul away."

He grumbled at her critique, but she continued.

"Second, if you're going to request a bargain, challenge them to go to rehab if they're an addict, and do one better, pay for it. If I had all the money you have, I'd spend it helping people."

She had no idea of his influence or how he maintained balance by bargaining with the world's worst to feed the world's deprived.

"And if they relapse?"

"Then what?" she asked, as if it were nothing. "Life is hard out there, Hades, and sometimes living it is penance enough. Mortals need hope, not the threat of punishment."

Hades considered her words. He knew life was hard, but he knew that because he could see the burden upon souls when they arrived on his doorstep, not because he actually understood what it was to be mortal and to exist in the Upperworld.

After a moment, he lifted his hands as she had done before to signal another game. When he won, he took her wrist and turned her hand over, laying her palm flat, fingers brushing the bandage tied there.

"What happened?"

Her laugh was breathy, like she thought he was silly for asking.

"Just a scrape. It's nothing compared to bruised ribs, I promise."

Hades jaw tightened. Perhaps there was no comparison, but he did not like that he could not keep her from being hurt in his realm. In truth, this was a small part of a greater fear—that he could not protect her from those who would wish to harm *him*.

After a moment, he pressed a kiss to her palm, sending a shock of magic into her skin to heal the wound. When he pulled away, he met her heated stare.

"Why does it bother you so much?" she whispered.

Because you are mine, he wanted to say, but those words froze in this throat. He could not say them. They had known each other for a week, and she had no knowledge of the thread that bound them together, only the bargain that forced her to be here. So instead, he touched her face. He wanted to kiss her, to somehow communicate this desperate need he had to keep her safe in every way, but just as he started to lean forward, the door to his study opened and Minthe entered the room. She stopped short, her eyes narrowing into slits.

Had he not commanded her to knock?

"Yes, Minthe?" he asked, his jaw clenched. She had better have a good reason for this interruption...but he doubted that was the case.

"My lord," she said tightly. "Charon has requested your presence in the throne room."

"Has he said why?" He did not try to hide the irritation in his voice.

"He has caught an intruder."

"An intruder?" Persephone asked, her curious eyes falling to Hades" .'How? Would they not drown in the Styx?"

"If Charon caught an intruder, it's likely they attempted to sneak onto his ferry," he replied, standing and extending his hand for her to take. "Come, you will join me."

If she was curious about him and his realm, she would want to be present for this anyway. Perhaps she would see the demand mortals placed upon him.

She pressed her fingers into his palm, and he led her down the halls of his palace to his cavernous throne room, with Minthe leading the way.

In the beginning of his reign, Hades had used this room more often than any other part of his palace. It had been the one place souls had feared more than Tartarus, because it was a place of judgement. He would sit upon his obsidian throne, flanked by black flags bearing golden narcissus, and cast souls into a bleak eternity without a second thought. Then, he had been ruthless and angry and bitter, but now, this was his least favorite place in his realm.

Charon waited for them, his brown skin ignited against his white robes. He was a daimon—a divine creature that ferried souls across the River Styx. He met Hades' gaze before it slipped to Persephone, his dark eyes sparking with curiosity. Beneath his gaze, Persephone started to withdraw her hand from his, but Hades' grip tightened. He guided her toward his throne, manifesting a smaller one beside it, composed of the same jagged edges but in ivory and gold.

He gestured for her to sit and knew she was about to protest.

"You are a goddess. You will sit on a throne."

Those words were similar to what he was really thinking. *You will be my wife and queen. You will sit on a throne.*

She did not protest. After she took her seat, Hades did too, turning his attention to the daimon.

"Charon, to what do I owe the interruption?" he asked.

"*You're* Charon?"

Hades jaw tightened, not only at the goddess' interruption, but at the evident admiration in her expression and tone. It was true that Charon did not look as the Upperworld depicted. He was regal, a son of gods —not a skeleton or an old man—and he was about to face a stint in Tartarus if he did not wipe that grin off his face.

"I am, indeed, my lady."

"Please call me Persephone," she offered, her smile matching his.

"My lady will do," Hades interrupted. His people would not call her by her given name. "I am growing impatient, Charon."

The ferryman bowed his head, probably to hide his laughter and not out of respect, but when he looked at Hades again, his expression was serious.

"My lord, a man named Orpheus was caught sneaking onto my ferry. He wishes for an audience with you."

Of course, he thought. *Another soul eager to beg for life—if not their own, then another's.*

"Show him in. I am eager to return to my conversation with Lady Persephone."

Charon summoned the mortal with a snap of his fingers. Orpheus appeared on his knees before the throne, his hands tied behind his back. Hades had never seen the man before, and there was nothing particularly remarkable about him. He had curly hair that stuck to his face, dripping with water from the Styx. His eyes were dull, gray, and lifeless. It was not his appearance Hades was interested in anyway, it was his soul, burdened with guilt. Now that interested him, but before he peered deeper, he heard Persephone's audible inhale.

"Is he dangerous?" she asked.

She had posed the question to Charon, but the daimon looked to him for an answer.

"You can see to his soul. Is he dangerous?" Persephone asked, looking at Hades now. He was not sure what had him so frustrated about her question. Perhaps it was her compassion?

"No."

"Then release him from those bindings."

His instinct was to fight her, to scold her for defying him in front of a soul, Charon, and Minthe. But looking into her eyes, seeing to *her* soul, how desperate she was to see compassion from *him*, he relented and released the man from his bonds. The mortal was unprepared and hit the floor with what Hades felt was a gratifying clap. As he picked himself up from the floor, he thanked Persephone.

Hades grinded his teeth. *Where is my thanks?*

"Why have you come to the Underworld?" Hades' question was more of a bark. He was finding it hard to contain his impatience.

The mortal stared into Hades' eyes, unafraid. *Impressive...or arrogant.* Hades could not decide.

"I have come for my wife. I wish to propose a contract —my soul in exchange for hers."

"I do not trade in souls, mortal," Hades answered.

The fact that his wife had died was an act of the Fates. The three had deemed her death necessary, and Hades would not interfere.

"My lord, please—"

He held up his hand to silence the man's pleas. No amount of explaining Divine balance would help, and so Hades would not try. The mortal looked to Persephone.

"Do not look upon her for aid, mortal. She cannot help you."

He might have given her free rein over his world, but she could not make these decisions.

"Tell me of your wife," Persephone said.

Hades' brows knitted together at her question. He knew she was challenging him, but what was her aim?

"What was her name?"

"Eurydice," he said. "She died the day after we were married."

"I am sorry. How did she die?"

Hades should discourage this line of conversation. It would only give the man hope.

"She just went to sleep and never woke up."

Hades swallowed. He could feel the man's pain, and yet there was still guilt weighing heavily upon his soul. What had he done to his wife? Why did he feel such guilt at her passing?

"You lost her so suddenly." Persephone sounded so sad, so forlorn for the man.

"The Fates cut her life-thread," Hades interjected. "I cannot return her to the living, and I will not bargain to return souls."

He noted the curl of Persephone's delicate fingers into a fist. Would she attempt to strike him? The thought amused him.

"Lord Hades, please—" Orpheus choked. "I love her."

His eyes narrowed, and he laughed. He loved her, yes, he could sense that, but the guilt told him the mortal was hiding something.

"You may have loved her, mortal, but you did not come here for her. You came for yourself. I will not grant your request. Charon."

Hades leaned back in his throne as Charon obeyed his command, vanishing with Orpheus. He would return the man to the Upperworld where he belonged, where he would mourn like other mortals for his loss.

In the silence, Persephone seethed. He felt her anger, billowing. After a moment, he spoke.

"You wish to tell me to make an exception."

"You wish to tell me why it's not possible," she snapped, and Hades' lips twitched.

"I cannot make an exception for one person, Persephone. Do you know how often I am petitioned to return souls from the Underworld?"

Constantly.

"You barely offered him a voice. They were only married for a day, Hades."

"Tragic," he said, and it was, but Orpheus was not the only one with this kind of story. He could not spend time *feeling* for every mortal whose life did not turn out the way they expected.

"Are you so heartless?"

The question frustrated him. "They are not the first to have a sad love story, Persephone, nor will they be the last, I imagine."

"You've brought back mortals for less."

Her statement took him aback. To what did she refer?

"Love is a selfish reason to bring the dead back," he replied. She had not yet learned that the dead were truly favored.

"And war isn't?"

Hades felt his gaze turn dark. The anger her words inspired burned through him. "You speak of what you do not know, goddess."

The bargains he had struck to return wartime heroes weighed heavily upon him, but the decision was not made lightly, and he had not been swayed by gods or goddesses. He had peered into the future and saw what lay ahead if he did not agree. The sacrifice was the same—a soul for a soul—burdens he would carry forever. Burdens that were etched into his skin.

"Tell me how you picked sides, Hades," she said.

"I didn't," he gritted out.

"Just like you didn't offer Orpheus another option. Would it have been relinquishing your control to offer him even a glimpse of his wife, safe and happy in the Underworld?"

He had not thought of that, and he did not have long to think on it in the moment, either, because Minthe spoke.

He had forgotten the nymph was still in the room.

"How dare you speak to Lord Hades—"

"Enough!" Hades cut her off and stood. Persephone followed. "We are done here."

"Shall I show Persephone out?" Minthe asked.

"You may call her *Lady Persephone*," he snapped. "And no. *We* are not finished."

He registered her shock for only a moment before turning to face Persephone. She wasn't looking at him, but watching Minthe leave. He drew her attention, his fingers touching her chin.

"It seems you have a lot of opinions on how I manage my realm."

"You showed him no compassion," she said, and her voice trembled.

Compassion? Did she not remember their time in the garden? When he had showed her the truth of the Underworld? Was it not compassionate to use his magic so that his souls may live a more peaceful existence?

"Worse, you mocked the love he had for his wife."

"I questioned his love. I did not mock it."

"Who are you to question love?"

"A god, Persephone."

That man's guilt was not for nothing.

Her eyes narrowed. "All of your power, and you do nothing with it but hurt."

Hades flinched. He could not help it; her words were like knives.

"How can you be so passionate and not believe in love?"

He laughed bitterly and said, "Because passion doesn't need love, darling."

He had said the wrong thing. He knew it before the words left his mouth, but he was angry and her assumptions made him want to hurt her in the only way he could—with words, and it worked. Her eyes widened, and she took a step away as if she could not stand being so close.

"You are a ruthless god!"

She vanished, and he let her go. If she had not accused him of only hurting others, he might have tried to help her understand his side of things, he might have even told her of the guilt he perceived upon Orpheus's soul, but he could not bring himself to do it.

Let her think the worst.

CHAPTER XIII – REDEMPTION

Hades stood before the desolate plot he had gifted Persephone. There had been no changes in the soil, still dry as bone, still no signs of life.

She had not been here in four days. She had not returned to visit Hecate or Asphodel or water her garden.

She had not returned to *him*.

You are a ruthless god.

Her words echoed in his head, bitter and angry and… truthful. She was right.

He was ruthless.

The evidence was all around him, and he saw it now, standing in his palace garden, surrounded by beautiful flowers and lush trees. It was in the illusion of beauty he maintained, in the charities he supported, in the bargains he made. It was his attempt to erase the shame he had felt at who he once was—merciless, heartless, suspicious.

"Why are you moping?" Hecate's voice came from behind him.

"I am not moping," Hades said, turning to face the goddess. Cerberus, Typhon, and Orthrus sat obediently at her feet. She wore sleeveless robes, crimson in color, and she had wrangled her long, thick hair into a braid.

Hecate arched her brow. "It looks like you are moping."

"I am thinking," he said.

"About Persephone?"

Hades did not respond immediately. Finally, he said, "She thinks I am cruel."

He explained what had transpired in the throne room, recognizing his tendency toward bargaining—this for that —not compromise. Persephone had been right—he could have offered Orpheus a glimpse of Eurydice in the Underworld. Perhaps he would have learned, then, why the mortal felt such guilt at her passing.

"She did not say you were ruthless for the reasons you think," Hecate said.

The god met her dark-eyed gaze. "What do you mean?"

"Persephone has hope for love, just as you, Hades, and instead of confirming that, you mocked her. Passion does not require love? What were you thinking?"

Hades' face felt warm, and he scowled. He hated *feeling*, especially embarrassment.

"She's…frustrating!"

"You're no walk in the park, either." Hecate leveled her stare.

"Says the witch who uses poison to solve all her problems," Hades grumbled.

"It's far more effective than moping."

"I am not moping!" Hades snapped and then sighed, pinching the bridge of his nose. "I'm sorry, Hecate."

She offered him a half-smile. "Tell me what you fear, Hades."

It took him a moment to find the words, because he did not really know himself.

"That she is right," he said. "That she will see no more within me than her mother."

"Well, lucky for you, Persephone is not her mother. A truth that is just as important for you to remember."

He supposed it was just as unfair to keep comparing her to Demeter as it was for Persephone to compare him to Demeter's words, but there was a part of him that wondered why he agonized. It was just a matter of time before the Fates took their scissors to these threads that held them entwined.

"If you want her to understand, you must share more."

"And give her more fodder for the articles she wants to write? I think not."

He was still frustrated by her visit to Nevernight, only to discover she was there to accuse him of destroying mortal lives.

Hecate raised a brow. "I have never known you to care what other people think, Hades."

And now he knew why he never bothered before—because caring was a nuisance.

"She is to be my wife," Hades said.

"And does that not give her a right to know you differently than anyone else?" Hecate asked. "Over time, she will learn you—how you think, how you feel, how you love—but she cannot if you do not communicate. Start with Orpheus."

***

When Hades returned to the castle, he found Thanatos waiting for him in his office. The God of Death appeared paler than usual, his vibrant eyes dull, his red lips drained of color. Normally, he had a calming presence, but Hades could feel his unease, and he shared it.

"We've had another," Thanatos said.

Somehow, Hades knew what the god would say, even before he opened his mouth. It was as Hades anticipated —Sisyphus had not been content with merely avoiding imminent death. He wanted to avoid death altogether.

"Who this time?" Hades asked.

"His name was Aeolus Galani."

Hades was quiet for a moment, crossing the room to his desk. It was an attempt to walk off some of the fury he felt toward the mortal who was defying death and harming others.

"His soul?"

Thanatos shook his head.

Hades slammed his fists on the desk. A fissure appeared down the center of the perfect, shining obsidian. The two gods stood in silence for a moment as each of them processed how to move forward.

"What connection does he have to Sisyphus?"

"There is only one. They were both members of Triad," Thanatos replied. "Our sources say Aeolus was an elevated member of the organization."

Hades brows lowered. He understood Sisyphus' motives for killing Alexander. He had been an underling, someone whose addiction had led to a debt. Sisyphus had seen him as disposable, but a high-ranking member of Triad was different. His death was like declaring war. What had motivated Sisyphus? Had he learned about Hades' encounter with Poseidon? Was he hoping to send a message? Did he think himself invincible now that he was in possession of the relic?

"The Fates?" Hades asked after a moment.

"Furious."

He was not sure why he asked, he knew they were in an uproar. He had not visited their island since he had returned Atropos' scissors, and even that had been an ordeal. As soon as he had entered, the three began lecturing and threatening. He could only imagine how they sounded now, wailing in a horrible refrain, threatening Hades in the only way they knew how—to unravel what he had always wanted.

He was already doing a fine job of that on his own.

"What will we do?" Thanatos asked, and his voice was quiet, full of a melancholy Hades felt in his chest.

He turned, straightened his tie, and buttoned his jacket.

"Summon Hermes," Hades answered.

Thanatos' pale brows furrowed. "Hermes? Why?"

"Because I have a message to send," Hades said.

Lucky for Hermes, it would not even require words.

***

Hades left the Underworld and teleported to Nevernight. He had expected to go about his usual rounds, wandering unseen among the mortals and humanoids crowding the floor below, sending his staff to deliver passwords to the lounge above, before ascending to bargain, except when he arrived, he was summoned to the balcony by Ilias.

"My lord," the satyr said as Hades approached.

"Yes, Ilias?"

He nodded to something in the distance, and Hades' eyes narrowed as he followed.

"That nymph. I believe she's one of Demeter's, here to spy on Persephone."

Demeter had all types of nymphs in her employment—alseids, daphnaie, meliae, naiads, and crinaeae—but this one was a dryad, an oak nymph. She wore a glamour, probably hoping that she would go unnoticed, but Hades could see her green skin beneath the magic. Even if her nature was not apparent, it was obvious she was up to something. Her eyes roamed the crowd, seeking and suspicious. She was clearly looking for someone.

"Has Lady Persephone arrived?" Hades asked, keeping his tone neutral, and yet after the embarrassing conversation he'd had with Hecate in his garden, he could not help being hopeful.

"Yes," Ilias responded, and Hades felt a mix of relief and tension build inside him all at once, a push and pull that made him eager to see her. "The nymph followed her in. I didn't prevent her from entering in the event that you wish to speak to her."

"Thank you, Ilias," Hades said. "Have her removed from the floor."

At Hades' request, Ilias spoke into his mic. In seconds, two ogres emerged from the shadows. The nymph's eyes widened at their approach, one on either side. There was a short exchange, but she gave no fight and allowed the two creatures to escort her into the darkness of the club. They would leave her in a small, windowless room to wait until Hades was ready to confront her.

"You know what to do," Hades said. "I'll be there shortly."

Ilias would conduct a background check on the nymph, learn her name, her associates, and her family. It was an arsenal of sorts, a way to weaponize words so Hades could obtain what he wanted from the nymph—for her to defy her mistress.

"Oh, and Ilias—make an appointment with Katerina when you are finished."

Katerina was the director of The Cypress Foundation, Hades' non-profit organization. If he was going to help mortals the way Persephone desired, he was going to have to create something special, and he knew just when to unveil the project—at the upcoming Olympian Gala.

He left the balcony and called up his glamour, moving unseen across the floor of Nevernight in search of Persephone. She had to be in the club, because he had sealed the entrances to the Underworld to keep her from coming and going without his knowledge.

As he searched the shadows, he came upon Minthe, who was engaged in an argument with Mekonnen. Hades rolled his eyes; there was nothing unusual about this. The nymph fought with everyone in his employment.

"We are not a charity!" Minthe was saying.

"She is not asking for charity." Despite Minthe's anger, Mekonnen remained calm. It was a trait Hades admired in the ogre, who he had appointed to Duncan's position.

"She is asking for the impossible. Hades does not waste his time on grieving mortals."

There was truth to that, and yet hearing the words out loud, hearing them spoken in a tone so careless and so crass, sent a spear right through his heart. Is that what he had sounded like when he had dismissed Orpheus? No wonder Persephone had been appalled.

He was suddenly at odds with the way Minthe and

Persephone perceived him, as it struck him that they thought similarly. Minthe expected him to refuse a mortal in distress, and Persephone assumed the same.

"Since when do you decide what Hades considers worthy, Minthe?" Mekonnen asked, and Hades felt true appreciation for the ogre.

"A question I'd very much like to hear the answer to," Hades said, stepping from the shadow.

Minthe whirled to face Hades, the surprise on her face evident in her raised brows and parted lips. Clearly, she did not have as much confidence speaking on his behalf when he was present.

"My lord," Mekonnen said, bowing his head.

"Did I hear right, Mekonnen? There is a mortal here to see me?"

"Yes, my lord. She is a mother. Her daughter is in the ICU at Asclepius Children's Hospital."

Hades' mouth was set in a grim line. The Asclepius Foundation was one of his charities. There were elements of being the God of the Dead he did not like, and one of those was the death of children. As much as he understood the balance of life, he would never quite accept that the deaths of children were necessary.

"The child isn't gone yet, my lord."

"Show her to my office," Hades instructed. He started to walk away, but paused. "And Minthe, I am your king, and you shall address me as such. My given name is not for you to speak."

Hades crossed the floor of his club with Minthe on his heels. The nymph grabbed his arm, and Hades whirled to face her.

"You forget your place," he hissed.

She did not even flinch, just stared at him with furious eyes. She was undaunted by his anger, fearless of his wrath.

"Any other time, you would have agreed with me!" she snapped.

"I have never *agreed* with you," he said. "You have

assumed you understand how I think. Clearly, you do not."

He turned from her and headed upstairs, but the nymph continued to follow.

"I know how you think," the nymph said. "The only thing that's changed is Per—"

Hades turned on her again and lifted his hand. He was not sure what he had intended to do, but he ended up clenching his fist.

"*Do not say her name.*" The words slipped between his teeth, and he spun, throwing open the door to his office.

He sensed Persephone and Hermes inside, but did not see them. Years of existing in battle kept him from hesitating in the doorway, but he was on edge and he could not deny that the thought of them hiding in this room together sent him spiraling.

Why are they in here together to begin with? Is this why he did not locate her on the floor earlier?

He gritted his teeth harder than necessary.

"You are wasting your time!" Minthe bit out, pulling him from his thoughts and redirecting his frustration. He wondered what she was referring to—the mortal or Persephone?

"It's not like I'm running out," Hades snapped.

Minthe's lips flattened. "This is a club. Mortals bargain for their desires; they do not make requests of the God of the Underworld."

"This club is what I say it is."

The nymph glared. "You think this will sway the goddess to think better of you?"

His eyes narrowed, and he snarled as he spoke. "I do not care what others think of me, and that includes you, Minthe. I will hear her offer."

Her severe expression relaxed, eyes widening, and she stood in stunned silence for a moment before leaving without another sound.

Hades was glad he had a few seconds to get a grip on his anger, and it was even more important because he was aware that he had an audience. Persephone's and Hermes' magic brushed the edges of his own, igniting his blood in a way that made him want to rage, but before he could spiral, the doors to his office opened and a mortal woman entered.

She was disheveled, like she had dressed hastily. The neckline of her sweater draped off one shoulder, and she wore a long coat that made her body look like a balloon. Despite her haphazard appearance, she held her head high and he sensed determination beneath her broken spirit.

Still, she froze when she saw him, and he hated the way it made his chest feel. He knew why he was the enemy of the world above—because he was shouldered with the blame for taking all loved ones away, because he had done nothing to contradict those ancient beliefs about his hellish realm, but that never bothered him until tonight.

"You have nothing to fear."

Her voice shook as she laughed. "I told myself I wouldn't hesitate. I wouldn't let fear get the best of me."

Hades tilted his head to the side. There were very few moments in his life when he felt true compassion for a mortal, but he felt it now for this woman. The core of her soul was good and kind and…simple. She wanted for nothing but peace, and yet she had the opposite.

Hades spoke in a quiet voice. "But you have been afraid. For a very long time."

The woman nodded, and tears spilled down her face. She brushed at them fiercely, hands shaking, and offered that nervous laugh again. "I told myself I wouldn't cry, either."

"Why?"

"The Divine are not moved by my pain."

She was right, he was not moved by her pain, but he was moved by her strength.

"I suppose I cannot blame you," she continued. "I am one in a million pleading for myself."

She was one of a million who had made the same request, and yet, this one was still different.

"But you are not pleading for yourself, are you?"

The woman's mouth quivered, and she answered in a whisper, "No."

"Tell me."

"My daughter." The words were a sob, and she covered her mouth with her hand to quell her emotion. After a moment, she continued, brushing at her face. "She's sick. Pineoblastoma. It's an aggressive cancer."

He studied the woman; the hurt dwelled within her broken soul. She had struggled to conceive. After several devastating miscarriages and painful treatments, she finally had what she wanted—a perfect baby girl. But at two years old, she started having trouble walking and standing, and all the elation the woman had felt turned to despair.

Still, beneath that horrific sorrow, he could sense the hope she still had for her daughter, the dreams she still dreamed for her. The woman had fought to have this child, and she would fight to keep her on Earth, even if it killed her.

And it would.

Hades' fists tightened at the thought.

"I wager my life for hers."

Many mortals had offered up the same, the life of one they loved for another, and no one meant it more than the mothers who begged at his feet. Still, he would not accept.

"My wagers are not for souls like you."

"Please," the woman whispered. "I will give you anything. Whatever you want."

A humorless laugh escaped him. *What do you know about what I want?* he wanted to say as his thoughts turning to Persephone.

"You could not give me what I want."

The woman blinked, and she seemed to come to some sort of unspoken conclusion, because she hung her head in her hands and her shoulders shook as she sobbed.

"You were my last hope. My last hope."

Hades approached her, placed his fingers under her chin, and brushed her tears away. "I will not enter into a contract with you, because I do not wish to take from you.

That does not mean I will not help you."

The woman inhaled sharply, her eyes widening with shock at Hades' words.

"Your daughter has my favor. She will be well and just as brave as her mother, I think."

"Oh, thank you! Thank you!" The woman threw her arms around him. He stiffened, not expecting her to react physically, but after a moment, his grip on her tightened before he pulled her away. "Go. See to your daughter."

The woman took a few steps away. "You are the most generous god."

Hades' lips twitched as he chuckled. "I will amend my previous statement. In exchange for my favor, you will tell no one I have aided you."

The woman's brows rose. "But—"

He held up his hand to silence her. He had his reasons for asking for anonymity, among them that this offer could be misinterpreted. He could offer her reassurance that her daughter would be okay because she was not dead yet, just in limbo. It was not the same as Orpheus asking for Eurydice's return to the Upperworld.

Hades had more control over souls in limbo because they were like wildcards, their fate was undetermined. There were various reasons for this—sometimes the original destiny needed to change and the Fates used limbo as a mechanism to alter lives, sometimes the soul themselves did not know if they wish to live or die and limbo was used as a way to give them time to decide.

Finally, she nodded and then broke into a smile, tears still streaming down her face.

"Thank you." She turned on her heels. "Thank you!"

Hades watched the door after she left, the satisfaction he felt at helping the mortal dissolving into something unpleasant once he was alone, with Hermes and Persephone still hiding in his office. He turned, his magic surging, and forced the two out of the mirror over his fireplace. Hermes, having been in these situations numerous times, was prepared and landed on his feet.

Persephone wasn't so lucky. She landed on her hands and knees with a loud thud.

"Rude," Hermes said.

"I could say the same," Hades replied, his eyes quickly shifting to Persephone as she got to her feet, dusting off her hands and knees. She looked different, but he assumed that was because of the way she was dressed. She wore a white tank top and black pants, and her hair was piled in a bun on top of her head, exposing her angled jaw and graceful neck. He liked her like this. She seemed... comfortable.

"Hear everything you wanted?" he asked her.

She glared at him. "I wanted to go to the Underworld, but *someone* revoked my favor."

He had not revoked her favor; he'd just kept her from entering the Underworld before he had a chance to talk to her. Unfortunately, he now needed to talk to Hermes, and without an audience.

He turned to the God of Mischief. "I have a job for you, messenger."

Hades snapped his fingers and sent Persephone to the Underworld. Hermes raised a brow, looking particularly judgmental.

"What?" Hades snapped.

"You could have handled that better."

"I did not ask for your opinion."

"It isn't opinion, it's fact. Even Hecate would agree with me."

"Hermes—" Hades warned.

"I can summon her to make my point."

"You are in my territory, Hermes, lest you forget."

"And I am your messenger, lest you forget."

They glared at one another. Taking relationship advice from Hermes was like asking Zeus for the same—pointless.

"Lucky for me, it isn't your messenger skills I am after, God of Thieves."

CHAPTER XIV – A BATTLE OF WILLS

As Hades made his way to the Underworld, guilt pressed in on his chest. It was akin to having stones stacked upon his body, and he thought of Hermes' words. *You could have handled that better.* But as he considered his actions, he saw no other way. He was asking Hermes to steal, and he would rather not explain himself to Persephone, even if he felt he had good reasons.

But he agonized. Was this a time when he should have communicated? Should he have told her the whole history behind the mission he had assigned Hermes? That he wanted the God of Mischief to intercept all of Sisyphus' shipments? In effect, Hades was dismantling his empire. Or would it have merely sufficed to ask her to give them a moment of privacy?

And at that thought, he suddenly understood why he had not extended such an offer—she had essentially spied on him, and he had reacted with anger instead of calm rational.

He groaned.

He was a fucking disaster at this.

Still, he went in search of her and found her in the library. She stood on the tips of her toes, hands braced on the side of a basin in which was contained a map of the Underworld. She bent closer and closer to the watery surface, and the movement made Hades anxious because the basin doubled as a portal. One touch, and she would be transported to another location in the Underworld. Normally, it would not worry him so much because he could quickly retrieve her, except he knew how her mind worked and chances were that she would end up dropping herself into the flaming waters of the Phlegethon.

He chose that moment to make himself known.

"Curiosity is a dangerous quality, my lady."

Dangerous. Infuriating. Exciting. It was multifaceted and had its place, but he'd rather she was curious about other things, like him.

She whirled to face him, her pretty, green eyes growing wide. Her hand went to her heart, and Hades' eyes dropped to her perfect breasts. For a moment, all he could focus on was the hardening of her nipples, straining against her white top.

"Don't call me my lady," she snapped, and then glanced back at the basin. "I... This map of your world is not complete."

Hades advanced. He liked the way she had to tip her head back just to keep his gaze. He paused inches from her, wishing to close the distance even more, wishing to lift her into his arms and make love to her against this basin. Perhaps they would fall in and find themselves among the flora of the Underworld. Gods, how he ached to take her beneath his sky.

Her sharp breath drew him from his carnal thoughts, and his gaze moved to the water. She turned to face it, her back to him now. This position was no better. From here, he could draw his arm around her waist and seal her back to his chest, press kisses to her neck while his other hand explored, roving her breasts, down her stomach, and between her thighs.

He shook those thoughts from his head.

"What do you see?"

"Your palace, Asphodel, the River Styx and the Lethe… That's it. Where is Elysium? Tartarus?"

He smiled at her eagerness to understand the Underworld, even if a part of him felt uneasy. If he had it his way, she would never explore the mountains and caverns of Tartarus. That part of his realm was a manifestation of his soul—dark and harrowing.

"The map will reveal them when you've earned the right to know."

"What do you mean *earned*?"

"Only those I trust most may view this map in its entirety." The map was a true weapon, and Hades let few have access to it, among them, Thanatos and Hecate.

"Who can see the whole map?" Then her voice tightened, and her eyes narrowed suspiciously. "Can Minthe see it?"

Her jealousy interested him, and he could not help goading her. "Would that bother you, Lady Persephone?"

"No," she said quickly, and let her eyes fall to where her hands rested on the basin.

She was lying. He could hear it in the inflection of her voice, see it in the language of her body, taste it in the air between them. He should challenge her, much as he'd done the day she'd come to Nevernight to demand answers for his bargains. *Will you speak of how you flush from your pretty head to your toes in my presence and how I make you lose your breath?* He could point out that she had not put space between them since he approached, that she had been leaning closer to him the longer they spoke, arching her back in a way that drew attention to her curves.

It made him want her even more, and he knew if he kissed her now, she would let him take her. Their coupling would be hard and fast and desperate, and it would be full of regret.

He could not love her and have her lie, so he turned, needing distance, and retreated into the stacks, but she followed him, suffocating him with her heat and her smell.

She struggled to match his stride, panting out, "Why did you revoke my favor?"

"To teach you a lesson," he replied, not looking at her.

"To not bring mortals into your realm?" He thought it was odd that her thoughts went to Adonis and not Orpheus. He was not sure what to make of that.

"To not leave when you are angry with me," he said.

"Excuse me?"

She halted, setting aside the books she carried, and Hades turned to face her. His heart raced, and he questioned whether he could have this conversation.

"You strike me as someone who has a lot of emotions and has never quite been taught how to deal with it all, but I can assure you, running away is not the solution."

I'm really one to talk, he thought. He was giving this speech for his own sake as much as hers.

"I had nothing more to say to you."

"It's not about words," he said, frustrated, and then paused to take a few breaths before explaining, "I'd rather help you understand my motivations than have you spy on me."

"It was not my intention to spy," she said. "Hermes—"

"I know it was Hermes who pulled you into that mirror," he said gently. This was not about the mirror at all. It was about changing her opinion of him. "I do not wish for you to leave and be angry with me."

She shook her head slightly, brows furrowing, and asked, "Why?"

"Because…" He felt stupid. In all his lifetimes, he had never had to explain himself. "It is important to me. I would rather explore your anger. I would hear your advice. I wish to understand your perspective."

She started to speak again, and he knew what she would ask. *Why?* So, he answered, "Because you have lived among mortals. You understand them better than I. Because you are compassionate."

She looked away, a faint color in her cheeks. After a

moment, she asked in a quiet tone, "Why did you help the mother tonight?"

"Because I wished to," he said, and he could practically feel Hecate's eyes rolling. *You can do better than that. I said communicate!*

"And Orpheus?"

Hades offered a raspy sigh, rubbing his eyes with his forefinger and thumb. Hecate was right—he had to do better with his explanations.

"It isn't so simple. Yes, I have the ability to resurrect the dead, but it does not work with everyone, especially where the Fates are involved. Eurydice's life was cut short by the Fates for a reason. I cannot touch her."

"But the girl?"

"She wasn't dead, just in limbo. I can bargain with the Fates for lives in limbo."

"What do you mean, bargain with the Fates?"

"It is a fragile thing," he said. "If I ask the Fates to spare one soul, I do not get a say in the life of another."

It meant that another life in limbo would be taken, something Hades tried hard not to think about in this moment.

"But…you are the God of the Underworld!"

He was, but that did not mean he would overrule decisions. Even if he could, he'd learned long ago there are consequences for such actions, and some burdens he was unwilling to bear. There was always a greater purpose at work, and for him to interfere would mean ruin.

"And the Fates are Divine," he said. "I must respect their existence as they respect mine."

"That doesn't seem fair."

"Doesn't it? Or is it that it doesn't sound fair to mortals?"

Persephone's eyes flashed, a hint of her glamour reeling beneath her skin. "So mortals have to suffer for the sake of your game?"

"It is not a game, Persephone. Least of all mine," he shot back, frustrated. Had he not done a good enough job explaining the balance of the Underworld? Or was it that she really wanted to think the worst of him?

"So, you've offered an explanation for part of your behavior, but what of the other bargains?"

Hades slanted his head, his brows slamming down over his eyes, and he took a step forward. He did not like her question. He had answered this, was she still not satisfied with his answer? Or was she angry about her own bargain? He expected her to backdown at his approach, but she did not, remaining where she was and lifting her chin in defiance.

"Are you asking for yourself or the mortals you claim to defend?"

"*Claim?*" Again, that light in her eyes stirred, and Hades wanted to smile at it.

Yes, my queen. Let me feed that fire, awaken your power.

"You only became interested in my business ventures after you entered into a contract with me," Hades pointed out. It was true. Would she have started this witch hunt had he let her leave his club unattached?

"Business ventures? Is that what you call willfully misleading me?"

"So this *is* about you."

"What you have done is unjust. Not just to me, but to all the mortals—"

"I do not want to talk about mortals. I would like to talk about you." Hades leaned in closer, guiding Persephone toward the bookcase. His hands caged her, one on either side of her face. "Why did you invite me to your table?"

Persephone looked away, and Hades' eyes lowered to her neck as she swallowed. "You said you'd teach me."

She whispered the words, and they skittered down his spine, making him shiver, making him want to press into her, to cradle her softness between his thighs.

"Teach you what, goddess?" His lips dropped to her skin, and he brushed the column of her neck. He felt her shiver as he whispered words against her skin. "What did you truly desire to learn then?"

"Cards."

The word was breathy, and the air between them was thick, a tangible weight full of erotic thoughts and fantasies. Her head fell back, supported by the bookcase, and her hands gripped the shelves as if she were fighting her own instincts and the voice in her head that commanded she touch him too.

His lips explored, and as he pressed a kiss against her breastbone, he looked up. "What else?"

She met his stare then, eyes fire-bright and searching. Their lips grazed each other's as they shared breath.

"Tell me," Hades begged.

Tell me you want me, he thought, *and I will take you now*. He would lift her into his arms, part her legs, and settle between them. The friction would release their passion, shake the earth and reverse rivers. It would end worlds and begin them.

It would change everything.

He waited, and her eyes fluttered closed as her lips parted, inviting his own. She took a breath, her chest rising and falling against his own. He leaned in, ready to capture her mouth when she admitted the truth. *Tell me you desire me.*

"Just cards."

He drew away lightning fast, despite his raging desire, and attempted to mask his frustration at her response. It took some effort, and his fingers curled into fists, nails piercing his palms. The pain made it easier, helped him focus on something other than his hard-as-steel cock.

Fuck me, he thought.

If she would not own up to her lust, he would not continue to make a fool of himself.

"You must wish to return home," he said, turning from her and leaving the stacks, pausing to look back. "You may borrow those books, if you wish."

She blinked, as if she were under some sort of spell, before gathering the books and following him into the main part of the library.

"How? You withdrew my favor."

"Trust me, Lady Persephone," he said, keep his tone void of emotion. "If I stripped you of my favor, you would know."

It would be painful, like skin stripped from bones.

"So I'm Lady Persephone again?" Her voice held contempt, and he wondered at her response. Was she angry with him?

"You have always been Lady Persephone, whether you choose to embrace your blood or not."

"What is there to embrace?" she asked and did not meet his gaze. "I'm an unknown goddess at best, and a minor one at that."

Hades frowned; those beliefs were the bars that kept her true nature caged.

"If that is how you think of yourself, you will never know your power."

Hades had nothing more to say. He had a nymph to interrogate, energy to expend, and Persephone had made it clear she wished to leave. He started to gather his magic and teleport to Nevernight, when her sharp command stopped him.

"*Don't.* You asked that I not leave when I'm angry, and I'm asking you not to send me away when you're angry."

He dropped his hand. "I am not angry."

"Then why did you drop me in the Underworld earlier?" she asked. "Why send me away at all?"

"I needed to speak with Hermes," he said.

"And you couldn't say that?"

He hesitated.

"Don't request things of me you cannot deliver yourself, Hades."

He stared at her. Her line of questioning helped him understand a few things about her. He had hurt her feelings when he dropped her in the Underworld earlier. She felt ignored and discarded.

We are equals, she'd said on their second encounter.

When she had come to ask that his mark be removed. She was making the same plea now.

After a moment, he nodded. "I will grant you that courtesy."

She exhaled, and Hades wondered if she had expected him to say no. The thought made his chest tighten.

"Thank you."

Her words relaxed him, and he extended his hand. "Come, we can return to Nevernight together. I have... unfinished business there."

She shifted the books in her arms and took his hand, and they returned to his office. Her gaze fell on the mirror over the fireplace and then wandered to his.

"How did you know we were in there? Hermes said we couldn't be seen."

"I knew you were here, because I could feel you."

She shivered visibly and withdrew her hand from his. Hades mourned the absence of her warmth. She picked up her backpack where she had left it and heaved it onto her shoulder. On the way out the door, she paused and glanced back. She looked so young, so beautiful, framed by his gilded doors, and he wondered what the fuck he was doing.

"You said the map is only visible to those you trust. What does it take to gain the trust of the God of the Dead?"

"Time."

***

Hades saw Persephone out, despite her protests. He knew she feared being seen with him, and really, he could not blame her. The media was ruthless and obsessive, and they tracked gods like prey, hoping for a shot that would perpetuate sensationalism and gossip. Some of his fellow Olympians loved the attention, but Hades had made it a goal to avoid them completely, going so far as to post guards up and down his street, on roofs, and in buildings around his club to keep his privacy.

"Antoni will take you home," Hades said, having already summoned the cyclops. He stood outside Hades' black Lexus. He expected Persephone to protest, but she looked up at him, a gentle expression on her face.

"Thank you."

She climbed into the back of the car, meeting his gaze through the window as Antoni closed the door.

Watching her leave felt different this time, like they had found common ground. Like they were closer to understanding one another...and he felt hopeful.

As soon as his car was out of sight, Ilias approached, handing him a file he had created on the dryad who had followed Persephone into his club. He glanced over the content and handed it back to the satyr.

"Thank you, Ilias," he said and vanished, appearing in the small room where the dryad had been held. She screamed when she saw Hades and shrunk against the wall, shaking.

"Rosalva Lykaios. Assistant to Demeter. Funny that your résumé does not also include *spy*."

She spoke softly, voice quaking. "P-Please, my lord—"

"I will be brief," he said, cutting her off. "You have two choices before you. Either you lie to your mistress and tell her Persephone was not here tonight, or you tell the truth."

He moved toward her as he spoke, and the girl cowered.

"If the first, you risk the wrath of Demeter," he said. "If the second, you risk my wrath."

"You are asking me to do the impossible."

"No," he said. "I am asking you, which of us do you fear more?"

CHAPTER XV - A GAME
OF TRICKERY

It was early when Hades made his way to the Underworld stables. They were located at the back of his estate and just as grand as his castle. Marble floors lined a wide aisle flanked by stalls with glossy black doors. Hades had four sable-black horses, Orphnaeus, Aethon, Nycteus, and Alastor, who occupied each pen, and as he came into view, they neighed, pawing the ground with their hoofed feet.

"Yes, yes, I know. You are wasting away in these stables, and you want to go for a run," he said as they complained noisily. "I'll bargain with the lot of you. Be good while I brush your coats and trim your hooves, and I'll let you roam the realm."

They snorted in response—an agreement. "Who wants to go first?"

They were quiet.

They were fire and brimstone, and they had seen battle as Hades had seen battle. Despite how he tried to care for them, their spirits were wild, their dreams haunted. They were tortured like he was tortured.

"Come now. The longer you wait, the further you are from freedom."

That got their attention, and they all responded at once, knocking against their stall doors.

Hades grinned and laughed. "One of you will just have to charm me."

He sidled along the marble walkway, pausing at each stall.

"Alastor?" he questioned, and the horse mewled. Of all his horses, Alastor was the most gentle, an irony considering in battle, he was known as the tormentor. His memory was long, and he never forgot an enemy.

"Orphnaeus?" The beast whined.

"Aethon?" The stallion blew a harsh breath from his nose and knocked against his gate, the most aggressive of the four.

"Nycteus?" The youngest of the four snorted.

Hades chuckled and then approached Aethon's stall. "Alright, since you were so vocal."

He opened the gate, leading the beast to the wash station in the stables. He did not need to secure him to keep him from running off. Despite their wish to roam, they would not disobey their master. Hades began the process by cleaning Aethon's hooves, prying dirt and mud free from the soles of his feet. After, he curried the coat, loosening mud and grit and dirt. As he worked, he spoke.

"Hecate tells me you four have been grazing in her mushroom grove again."

They snorted in denial at the accusation.

"Are you sure?"

They shook their heads, neighing.

"Because Hecate said she called to each of you, and you fled like shadow, eyes aflame."

They were all quiet.

Then, Alastor brayed, and Hades laughed.

"Are you suggesting Hecate *hallucinated* the whole thing?"

The four snorted in agreement.

"While I don't doubt Hecate's use of hallucinogenic mushrooms, I also do not doubt *your* use," he said.

Hades moved on, working the knots free from Aethon's mane and tail. He brushed his coat two more times, with a stiffer brush and a finishing brush. Last, he used a damp cloth to clean around Aethon's eyes, muzzle, and ears.

"Off you go," he said, and Aethon hurried from the stable into the early morning of the Underworld.

Hades moved onto Orphnaeus, then Nycteus, and last Alastor, repeating the same steps of cleaning hooves, coat, and mane.

As he wiped around Alastor's eyes, he asked in a quiet voice. "Are you well, my friend?"

The horse stared at Hades with dark eyes, and within them, he saw the depth of his torture. Of the four, Alastor was the most haunted. He often separated from the others to wander alone, needing the isolation to fight his own demons.

Hades understood.

The horse exhaled quietly, and Hades brushed his snout.

"I would mourn the loss of you," he said. "But if you need to drink from the Lethe...I will grant your wish."

Alastor offered a snort, and shook his head, declining the offer.

Hades grinned. "It is just an offer," he said. "On the table...if ever you grow too weary."

He finished cleaning Alastor's ears and stepped away.

"Alright, my friend. Off you go."

As Alastor raced from the stables, he passed Minthe, who approached Hades with a smug expression on her face. He wasn't sure why, but dread pooled in his stomach at her approach.

"My lord," she said. "I have news."

Hades focused on cleaning up, not meeting her gaze.

"And what news is that, Minthe?"

"It's something you'll want to see, my lord."

He hung the last of the brushes on a post near the wash station before turning to look at her. The nymph held up a paper, a copy of *New Athens News*. His eyes were immediately drawn to the cover story, which included his name.

Hades, God of the Game
by Persephone Rosi

Hades snatched the paper from her hands, staring at those bold, black letters until they blurred across the page.

"It seems your precious Persephone has betrayed you," Minthe was saying, but her voice sounded far away. He was too focused on the words his goddess had written to pay attention.

In my short encounter with the God of the Underworld, he can best be described as tense. He is cold and boorish, his eyes colorless chasms of judgement set within a callous face. He lurks in the shadows of his club, preying upon the vulnerable.

Hades felt a rush of embarrassment and shame and anger, and for a moment, all he could think was, *So this is what she truly thinks of me?* And yet he could not reconcile how she had acted in the library the night before, the way she had leaned into him, the way she had parted her lips, ready for his own. He had felt her passion just as acutely as he felt his own.

Could these really be her thoughts? Her words? Was she trying to cage her heart?

He continued reading.

Hades says the rules of Nevernight are clear. Lose against him, and you are obligated to fulfill a contract, one that exposes his debtors to shame, and while he has claimed success, he has yet to name a single soul who has benefited from his so-called charity.

So-called charity.

He gritted his teeth; he was *plenty* charitable.

How is she supposed to know? I haven't told her, he countered.

"I will visit Demetri today. Persephone will never write

again," Minthe said.

It was the usual avenue. Anyone who photographed or wrote about Hades usually found themselves out of a job and unable to be hired. No one wanted to incur the wrath of Hades, and despite how this article made him feel, he could not take away Persephone's dream.

"No," Hades said, and the word was harsh, a mix of alarm and frustration.

Minthe's eyes widened. "But...this is defamation!"

"Persephone is mine to punish, Minthe."

The nymph's brows narrowed harshly over her burning eyes. "And what is your idea of punishment? Fucking her until she begs for release?"

"Fuck you, Minthe."

"This isn't you," she argued. "If it were any other mortal, you would let me do my job!"

"She is no mortal," Hades snapped. "She is to be my wife, and you will treat her as such."

Silence followed, and after a moment, Minthe spoke, her voice shaking.

"Your wife?"

"Your queen," Hades said.

Minthe's jaw tensed. "When were you going to tell me?"

"You act as if I owe you an explanation."

"Don't you? We were lovers!"

"For a night, Minthe, nothing more."

She stared at him, eyes glistening. "Is it because she is a goddess?"

"If you are asking me why not you, it was never you, Minthe."

The words were harsh but they were true, and he hoped they hit home. He would see that she respected Persephone as her queen, or he would dismiss her.

The nymph lingered for a few seconds longer before turning on her heels and running from the stables.

***

"I'm disappointed in you," Hecate said.

The two stood in the shadows outside Dolphin & Co. Shipbuilding. It was a company owned by Poseidon, and because it was owned by a god, it had the monopoly on ship and boat building in New Greece. It helped that Poseidon claimed his ships were unsinkable, a promise many believed because he was God of the Sea. His dockyard spanned for miles, employing thousands of mortals and immortals who built yachts, cargo ships, and wartime vessels, the latter being a type of ship Zeus has ordered Poseidon to cease building after The Great War. Hades doubted Poseidon had listened.

It was here where Sisyphus had agreed to meet Poseidon under the guise that the god would help him escape Hades' wrath, a ruse that was not implausible. Hades did not trust Poseidon. He was well-aware that the god had fulfilled his part of the bargain—luring Sisyphus. Beyond that, he was not obligated to help Hades capture the mortal.

"Why this time?" he asked, responding to Hecate's earlier comment.

"I told you I wanted to be present when you told Minthe you were to be married."

Hades glanced at the goddess, raising a brow. She was cloaked in black velvet, as was her nature when she came to the Upperworld. She preferred to blend with the darkness. He had asked her to accompany him on this trip to handle the spindle. Ilias had not been able to track how Poseidon had come into possession of it, so Hecate would have to perform a trace on the object.

That was the problem with relics—there was so much to clean up in their aftermath.

"How do you know I told her?"

"Because she has vented to half the staff about it," Hecate said. "Though, it has not had the effect she desired."

"What does that mean?"

"She hoped they would be just as affronted, but I think

the staff are hopeful."

"Hopeful?"

"They want Persephone much as you do, Hades," Hecate said, a little mischievously.

"Hmm," Hades grunted. It was true that he wanted her, but after the article she had written, he was not certain she wanted him, or ever would. Still, he knew she had made an impression on his souls. After she watered her garden, she spent hours with them. She had learned many of their names and spent time with them, going for walks or taking tea, even cleaning. She played with the children and brought them gifts, even his dogs tended to follow her, even if he promised playtime.

She had won their favor in no time, and he had yet to win hers.

Hades focused on the smell of Poseidon's magic—salt and sand and hot sun—as his brother appeared before them. He was fully dressed this time in a pink suit with black lapels and a white pocket square. Despite using a mortal glamour, he had kept his crown, the gold spires losing their luster amid his honeyed hair. Hades wondered if he wore it as a show of power, to remind him that they were in his territory.

"I see you brought your witch," Poseidon said, aqua eyes sliding to Hecate.

It was not Hecate Poseidon disliked, so much as her relationship with Zeus. Hecate, on the other hand, hated Poseidon merely for being arrogant. As soon as the god spoke, Hecate's eyes narrowed, and the leg of his's trousers caught fire.

"Motherfucker!" he roared as he hopped about, trying to put out Hecate's mystic fire.

Hades smirked at his brother's pain.

"Hecate is far older than us, Poseidon," Hades called over his brother's screams. "We must respect our elders."

"Careful, Hades. I am not above setting you aflame," the Goddess of Magic replied.

"And I am not above incinerating your nightshade."

They smiled at each other.

"If you two are finished flirting," Poseidon shouted. "I should remind you that my *fucking leg is on fire!*"

"Oh, I haven't forgotten." Hecate's eyes flashed as she returned her gaze to Poseidon, which caused the god to go still. Whatever he saw in her eyes caused him more fear than the fire claiming his leg. Finally, she dismissed the magic. Poseidon brushed at his pant leg, hands shaking as he assessed the damage. The cloth was blackened and curled, parts of it melted into his bubbling skin. He glared at Hecate, and she shrugged a shoulder.

"You called me a witch," she said.

"You are a witch," Hades reminded her.

"It was the *way* he said it, like it was an insult. Perhaps next time, he'll remember the power behind the word."

Poseidon straightened, fists curled at his sides. Hades sensed his rage churning beneath the surface, fierce like a deadly storm. He was not sure what the god intended to do next. Perhaps he wished to war with Hecate, which would spell disaster for him, his business, and the goal of this meeting.

"Where is the mortal?" Hades asked.

Poseidon's eyes shifted to his, and Hades felt his hate. Usually, his brother's intense emotion left him smiling, but today, he felt dread. Poseidon had a number of reasons to fuck this up. Favor or not, Hades had embarrassed him in front of his people and his wife, and while Poseidon had earned Hecate's wrath, there was only so much the God of the Sea would endure before he took his revenge. Everyone had a breaking point, and Poseidon had done well to stay composed this long. He wondered what sort of magic Amphitrite had worked upon him.

"He will arrive soon." Poseidon indicted to a watchtower that overlooked his shipyard. "Wait there."

The two did as he instructed and teleported to the lookout. The box was small, and Hades and Hecate stood shoulder to shoulder as they peered out over the yard. This particular security station overlooked the entrance and the main office. In the distance, a series of lights illuminated hundreds of ships in various states of construction. Hades thought the view was beautiful in its own way.

"He is even more unpleasant than I remember," Hecate muttered.

"You know he can hear you?" Hades reminded her.

"I hope so."

Hades smirked, and then his gaze shifted to the entrance of the shipyard. Something rippled in the air—magic, but not Poseidon's or Hecate's. He tensed and saw Sisyphus walk into view. The mortal's thick, broad frame was unmistakable. As he approached Poseidon's office, the god walked out to meet him.

"That is not a mortal," Hecate said.

It was at that moment that Thanatos appeared in a billow of black smoke, his great wings spread wide, and he wielded a long blade he used to slide through Sisyphus' body, but the mortal disintegrated into bits of rock and clay.

"*Poseidon,*" Hades growled.

Sisyphus' laugh echoed from every direction, and Hades looked at Hecate.

"Someone has given the mortal magic," the goddess said.

"You might be all-powerful, but I can guess your tricks, *Lord Hades.*"

Hades ground his teeth and called upon his magic, sending his shadows searching for the mortal in the darkness. He would draw the man out like poison from a wound.

"Ah!"

As soon as Sisyphus screamed, Hades teleported, finding him atop the yard's wide, stone wall.

"Hello, mortal."

His foot shot out, kicking Sisyphus in the stomach. He fell from the wall onto his back in the middle of the yard. Hades followed, landing on his feet and took a few deliberate strides toward him, spires protruding from his fingertips. He would sink them so far into Sisyphus' chest, he'd puncture his heart.

The mortal groaned and rolled onto his back, eyes widening as Hades approached. He pushed himself onto his elbows, his feet sliding against the dirt as he tried to crawl away.

Again, Hades felt that same shift in the air. It was magic of some kind, but it was not Divine.

"Hades! Down!" Hecate commanded, her voice was near, but he could not see her.

He obeyed, hitting the ground just as the wall behind him exploded. Debris flew, hitting Hades' back as he crouched on the ground. The impact was harsh, and he groaned. He might heal easily, but that did not mean he could not feel pain.

Somewhere in the distance, Poseidon laughed. "You had better run, mortal, unless you wish to find yourself at the end of Hades' claws."

Hades looked up, and through the curling smoke, he saw Sisyphus climb to his feet. He was covered in dust, and his head was bleeding.

"No!" Hades growled. With his magic working to heal him fast, he had no time to teleport. Instead, he withdrew the small box Hephaestus had made and tossed it after the mortal. As he did, Thanatos moved to chase Sisyphus, the god blocking Hades' aim. The box fell at Thanatos' feet, and the chains unfurled, trapping the God of Death in heavy manacles.

Sisyphus raced toward the gaping opening in Poseidon's wall, and Hades growled as he got to his feet and followed, but when he made it outside, the mortal was gone and the street quiet.

A mortal could not have fled that fast; he'd had help.

"Magic," Hecate said, appearing beside him. "The air smells of it. If I had to guess, a portal."

Hades stood for a few moments in silence, glaring at the space where Sisyphus once stood before returning to the yard. Poseidon stood near his office, large arms crossed over his chest, a smug expression on his face.

"What's the matter, brother? Evening not go quite as planned?"

Hades cast his arm out, and the spires that protruded from the tips of his fingers shot toward Poseidon like bullets. The god summoned a wall of magic, and the spikes halted inches from his face.

Hades turned his attention to Thanatos, whose lithe body bowed beneath the weight of Hephaestus' chains. Hecate stood aside, studying him, the corners of her lips turned up.

"Chains of Truth, Hades?" she asked, raising a brow. "Thanatos, what do you think of Hades' hair?"

The God of Death's eyes widened in fear, and when he spoke, it was like the words had been torn from his throat.

"It's a mess. A complete contradiction to his pristine appearance."

Hecate's smile widened, and Hades glared at the two.

"Eleftherose ton," he said, and as the Thanatos was released from the chains, he collapsed to his knees. Hecate helped him to his feet.

"I'm...so sorry, my lord."

Hades said nothing, his hand clenched around the box, edges digging into his palm. He looked at Hecate.

"What was the creature that came in place of Sisyphus?" he asked.

"It was a golem," Hecate said.

A golem was a creation made of clay and animated with magic. It could take on any form, so long as the potion included a piece of the person it was to imitate.

"Sisyphus had help creating that creature," Hades said. "Can you trace the magic?"

"Of course I can trace the magic," Hecate said. She seemed offended he would even ask. "Can you ask nicely?"

At that moment, his phone rang. Before Persephone, he had hardly used it, but it was that thought that had him drawing it out of his pocket to answer before he responded to Hecate.

"Yes?" he hissed as he answered his phone.

"Hades?" Aphrodite purred his name.

Hades sighed, frustrated. "What do you want, Aphrodite?"

If she was calling to goad him, he would torture Basil tonight. He swore it.

"I just thought you might like to know your goddess has come to my club for a visit."

Something possessive reared its head at the mention of his goddess. It was a dark feeling, and it came out of his chest, a monster ready to fight, to protect, to claim.

"A visit?"

"Yes." Aphrodite's voice was breathy. "She arrived with Adonis."

Forget fighting and protecting and claiming. That monster in his chest wanted blood.

"I hope you hurry," she said. "He seems smitten."

CHAPTER XVI – A BATTLE FOR CONTROL

Hades appeared outside La Rose. Like all clubs owned by gods, Aphrodite's was a popular hangout in New Athens. While many mortals came to him looking for love, just as many flocked here, believing that a sip of her drinks or a spray from her infamous pink mist would mean an end to their search for a soulmate.

There was no such thing, of course. No drink or mist that could lead another to their soulmate. That was up to the Fates.

Aphrodite was waiting for him. She wore a silky, light pink dress with a cowl neckline. She looked pale in the light outside her club, her cheeks and lips flushed.

"Do not cause a scene, Hades," Aphrodite said.

"Says the goddess who started a war over an apple," Hades snapped. "Where is she?"

The Goddess of Love glared, her frustration with Hades palpable.

"*Persephone*, Aphrodite."

"She is dancing."

Dancing, he thought. *With Adonis?*

His jaw tightened, and he bared his teeth as he stepped past the goddess, summoning two ogres, Adrian and Ezio, to flank him.

"Hades!" Aphrodite's voice was sharp, the tone of a woman who had fought and killed on the battlefield.

Hades paused, did not turn to look at the goddess.

"You will *not* hurt him." Her voice shook as she spoke.

He said nothing and stepped into the darkness of the club, straightening his jacket and smoothing his hair.

I'm an idiot, he scolded himself. He called up his glamour so that he would be invisible as he came to the edge the dance floor, where people moved in a hypnotic tangled of limbs. Overhead, lights flashed, and pink mist hung heavy in the air. The smell of roses and sweat clung to his skin, and somewhere in this chaos, was Persephone.

With Adonis.

He gritted his teeth.

Had he not warned her to stay away from the mortal?

Hades glanced at Adrian and Ezio, and the ogres branched off to the left and right while he took the middle. Mortals made space for him, unaware he walked among them. He scanned faces, searching for Persephone's familiar features. His chest felt tight and his breaths grew shallow as he looked for her, thinking of all the sin he had seen upon Adonis's soul. He was a predator and a liar.

Were they somewhere in the shadows together? Was he touching her the way Hades longed to touch her? The thought made him feel violent.

And then he found her in Adonis's arms, and everything seemed to move in slow motion. He realized he had never really known rage. This was primal. It jolted his whole body and made him quiver. He wanted to roar, to strike fear in each and every person in this room, just so they would cease their unabashed revelry.

Adonis' hand cupped her head, fingers twining in her glossy hair, and his lips were pressed against hers so hard, his nose was bent. But it was Persephone's body language he watched—the way she pushed against the mortal's chest the closer he tried to bring her, the way she clamped her lips together, refusing to partake of his, the tear that slipped down her cheek the longer he held her there.

This is torture, Hades thought.

All of a sudden, everything resumed its usual speed. Adrian and Ezio appeared, each fixing a hand on Adonis' shoulder, and yanked him away from Persephone. Hades moved toward her, unsure of what he intended to do, but wanting to be near her, to comfort her.

The goddess turned toward him as she wiped her mouth, her eyes meeting his.

"Hades." She breathed his name, and the sound made him shiver. He was further surprised when she threw her arms around his waist and buried her head in his chest. For a moment, he was frozen. Had he not just wished to offer her comfort? Why was he suddenly unable to move? Slowly, he pressed a hand to her back, the other twining with her hair, hating that Adonis's fingers had experienced the feel of her.

He held her for a moment and wanted to hold her longer, but they needed to leave this place, so he drew his finger beneath her chin, tilting her head until her eyes met his.

"Are you well?"

She shook her head.

Hades gritted his teeth, quashing the urge to find Adonis and grind him into ash.

"Let's go."

He drew her against him and guided her toward the exit. Like before, the crowd parted, but this time, it was because they could see him. He had dropped his invisibility when he approached Persephone and had not bothered to glamour up again. They stilled and stared while the music blared.

"Hades—"

"They will not remember this," Hades assured, knowing her anxiety would rise at the thought of being seen together like this in public. The media would descend, the headlines would speculate. She would become the story, not the storyteller.

As much as she did not want that to happen, Hades did not either, and as they came to the edge of the crowd, his magic rippled out, stealing memories and returning the floor to its blissful chaos.

Then Persephone tried to bolt.

"Lexa!"

She moved too fast and swayed. Hades wasn't certain if she tripped or if she had too much to drink. Either way, he bent to gather her into his arms, unwilling to risk having to chase after her.

"I will ensure she gets home safe," he promised.

He watched her face, seeing her close her eyes tight and frowned.

"Persephone?"

"Hmm?" Her voice vibrated, her breath teased his lips, carrying the scent of wine and something metallic he could not quite place.

"What's wrong?"

"Dizzy," she whispered.

He didn't speak but left the building. If he stayed any longer, he would burn it to the ground and incur the wrath of Aphrodite, something he might welcome to free himself of this rage. Outside, the air was cool, and Persephone started to shiver, burrowing closer to his chest. She took a deep breath.

"You smell good."

Her small hands curled into his jacket, and he chuckled at her lack of inhibition, holding her tighter as he ducked into the back of his limo. He considered keeping her cradled against him until they arrived at Nevernight, but decided against it. She had been accosted on the floor of La Rose, and probably wanted distance. Plus, she was cold. He helped her into the seat beside him and adjusted the controls so the heat would warm her.

"What are you doing here?" she asked, her voice quiet,

and Hades looked at her as he sat back in his seat.

"You don't listen to orders."

She offered a breathy laugh. "I don't take orders from you, Hades."

They sat close, shoulders and arms and legs touching, heads inclined, sharing breath and heat and space, and he knew he was in trouble because his whole body had gone rigid, including his cock.

"Trust me, darling. I'm aware."

"I'm not yours, and I'm not your darling."

Hades watched her, searching her meadow-green eyes, glassy from alcohol and simmering with oppressed passion. When he spoke, his voice was gruff, heavy with arousal.

"We've been through this, haven't we? You are mine. I think you know that just as well as I do."

She crossed her arms, accentuating her breasts, and lifted her chin in challenge. "Have you ever thought that maybe you're mine, instead?"

Her words ignited a fire low in his belly, and the corners of his mouth lifted, eyes falling to her wrist. "It is my mark upon your skin."

There was a beat of silence, and it burned the air between them. Then she straddled him, her hands on his shoulders, her shapely legs gripping his thighs. Her softness pressed against all his hard edges, and he grit his teeth, fingers curling into fists at his sides. He wanted to touch her, press her closer, feel her harder, but she had been drinking and it did not seem right.

A smile curled her lips, and he felt like his eyes were on fire, burning into her soul. She knew what she was doing, teasing him, challenging him. She leaned close, the tips of her breasts grazing his chest.

"Should I leave a mark?" she asked, her voice hushed.

"Careful, goddess," Hades cautioned. She was playing with darkness, and he would consume her.

She rolled her eyes. "Another order."

"A warning." The words grated between his teeth.

Finally, he could take it no longer. His hands fastened on her bare thighs, and he was rewarded with the sound of Persephone's breath catching in her throat. He tilted his head a little so that their lips were level. Her hands had moved, fingers tangling with his hair at the base of his neck. "But we both know you don't listen, even when it's good for you."

"You think you know what's good for me?" Her lips brushed his as she spoke. "You think you know what I need?"

He chuckled, and his hands traveled beneath her dress, seeking her heat. Persephone gasped.

"I don't think, goddess, I know. I could make you worship me."

The air around them felt heavy and charged, potent with their hunger. Hades found it impossible to concentrate on anything but her—every part of her body that touched his, the smell of vanilla in her hair, the way she bit down on her lush lip as she stared at his own.

Then she kissed him, and he opened for her, their tongues sliding together, tasting, exploring, demanding. His hands moved to her back and he pressed her close, his arousal fitting between her thighs, growing harder as she became more frenzied, fingers coiling into his hair, forcing his head back, kissing him deeper and harder than he had ever imagined. He couldn't help wondering... Was this the reaction of a woman who believed he was tense and cold and boorish?

When she pulled away, it was with his lip between her teeth. She leaned in, her tongue touching his earlobe, then her teeth.

"You will worship me," she said, grinding against his cock. "And I won't even have to order you."

Oh, darling, he thought. *If you only knew how I worship you now.*

His hands dropped to her thighs again, gripping her tight. Something primal was unfurling inside him, and he wanted to know what it would feel to be inside her. He could have her like this, seated in the back of this car. He would take pleasure in the way she moved up and down his shaft, her breasts bouncing as she found release.

And despite his vivid imagination and his desperate wish to have her in any and every way, he found himself shifting her so that she was cradled against him and lowering her dress. He managed to shimmy out of his jacket and covered her with it. He had to remove the temptation or at least restrain it. He would not let her regret him.

And yet, as their passion dissolved into an awkward and abrupt silence, he could not shake the feeling that maybe she already did. He glared out the window, though he felt her gaze on him. After a moment, she spoke, her words heated and whispered.

"You're just afraid."

She was not wrong.

He was afraid that even by some miracle she decided she did not hate him, the Fates would take her from him. It was an all too real possibility, especially after the disaster that was this evening. Sisyphus had slipped through his hands again.

When they arrived at Nevernight, Antoni helped Persephone out of the cabin of the limo. Hades took over from there, leading her into the club, nodding to Mekonnen as they passed. Before they entered the main part of the club, Hades used his glamour so that they moved unseen across the packed floor, up the stairs, and to his office. He was too nervous to teleport with her at the moment and did not want to make her sick, fearing she had too much to drink.

Once they were inside his office, he dropped his glamour and crossed the floor to his bar, pouring her a glass of water.

When he looked up, he was struck by her beauty. Why did it hit him differently every time he looked at her? Tonight, she wore teal, and it made her skin look bronzed and her hair look like spun gold.

He pushed the glass across the table. "Drink."

She approached as he poured himself a drink. As he finished, she swiped it from the table.

"Persephone," Hades growled, and she smiled, his glass raised to her lips.

"Yes, Hades?"

Her voice was husky and made him grip the edge of the table hard. She sipped the whiskey and then turned, strolling across the floor. Her hips swayed, drawing his attention.

"I think you should stop drinking," he said.

"You are bossy."

"I am not bossy. I'm…advising."

"Isn't someone supposed to ask for your advice before you offer it?" she asked as she turned and leaned against his desk.

"The same could be said for your opinion."

She glared at him.

"Why did you bring me here?"

Hades came out from behind the bar and approached.

"Because I wanted you safe." He took the glass from her and held her gaze as he downed the remainder before setting it aside.

"I don't think I'm safe with you," she whispered when he looked at her again.

Hades did not know what those words meant, but he felt compelled to say, "I would never hurt you."

"You don't know that."

They stared at one another, before he lifted his hand. "Come."

He led her toward the wall behind his desk, and he noted her hesitation in the way she pulled away from his touch.

"Why don't we just teleport?"

"It makes you dizzy," he said. "And I'd rather not contribute to that given your…state."

Persephone's eyes narrowed, and her lips pressed flat. "I'm not in a *state*."

He sighed inwardly and tugged on her hand, and she followed him through the wall, which was really a portal, or gate, into the Underworld. Those who entered here would find themselves in a cavernous entrance called Cape Tenaron. There, they would be met by the River Styx, a body of water they would likely not survive.

Hades could use this entrance to go anywhere in the Underworld he wished, and when they stepped through, they found themselves in his chambers.

He indicated the bed. "Rest. When you wake, we will talk."

He had questions, about Adonis and about her article in *New Athens News*.

"I don't want to rest," she said.

Hades just stared at her.

"Ask me what I want, Hades."

He wanted to groan. This was torture, and worse, he indulged her.

"What do you want?"

"To finish what we started in the limo."

It was significant to him that she had not responded with *'you.'* And only solidified his wish to ensure they go no further than they had.

"No, Persephone."

She scowled. "You want me."

He said nothing; he could not deny it and would not admit it.

She pushed away from him and walked toward the bed, slipping the straps of her dress off her shoulders.

"Persephone—"

"What?"

She turned toward him, and her dress fell in a puddle at her feet. She stood bare before him, all golden skin and glorious curves.

"Tell me you don't want me."

He swallowed hard, clenching his hands at his sides. So many emotions swirled inside him, a carnal need to claim her and protect her. He could not do both. He reached for the robe she had worn the last time she was here; it hung in the same place, on the screen behind where she'd changed. He held it out so that she could slip her arms inside.

"Get dressed, Persephone."

She glared at him and snatched the robe from his hands, but she did not put it on. Instead, she stared at him.

"You didn't answer my question."

He hadn't because if he said he did not want her, that would be a lie, and admitting it would be inviting her to his bed.

She touched him, her hands sliding down his arms, pausing at his fists.

"Let go," she coaxed, stepping into him and placing his hands on her hips, his fingers splayed, digging into her skin. Was this some sort of trial? Had this woman been sent to test his control? He studied her hard, expecting her to vanish into smoke, but she did not. She remained there, solid and warm and soft beneath him. Her hands twined behind his neck, her bare breasts pressed against his chest.

"Hades?" She whispered his name, breath caressing his lips. "Hold me."

Her mouth closed over his, and his arms tightened around her waist. He drew her against him tight, one hand breaking free to glide up her back to the nape of her neck, where he held her head, lips pressing hard against hers, urging her mouth open wide, tasting and taking. Persephone's hands moved from around his neck, down his chest, to his crotch. She grasped his cock through the fabric of his slacks, and he groaned, tearing free from her mouth.

"Persephone."

"I want to touch you," she said, and suddenly, Hades found himself being guided back toward his bed. She pushed him, guiding him to lie flat on the silken sheets, and as she climbed on top of him, straddling him, naked and rosy and beautiful, he thought he might come then. She leaned over him, her hot and soft center rocking against his hard length, the tips of her breasts barely touching his chest.

"Let me please you," she whispered, and kissed him again.

His hands landed on her sides, and he rolled, pinning her beneath him. He took her wrists and guided them over her head.

"You please me," he said, kissing her swollen lips a final time, reveling in the way her body arched against his, warmed with need. It was a reminder of why he had to stop this. "Sleep."

The command came with a rush of magic that instantly sent Persephone into a deep slumber. Hades paused there a moment, suspended over her, before rolling off onto his back.

He sighed, full of frustration and rage, and growled.

"Fucking Fates."

CHAPTER XVII – BREAKING POINT

Hades watched Persephone sleep while he tried to reconcile the contradiction of her words and actions. He reminded himself that she had been under the influence, not just of alcohol but of some sort of drug. He had tasted it upon her tongue—metallic, salty, *wrong*. She had not been herself, not in the limo or his office or his bedroom, which meant her words—the ones she'd written in her article—won his thoughts, and he turned them over and over again in his head until he seethed.

He sensed when she woke because her breathing changed. She bolted upright, holding his silk sheets to her chest, eyes bright and cheeks flushed. He would have liked to see her this way after a night of love making. Instead, he was watching her after a night of rejecting her drunken advances. He took a sip from his glass, holding her gaze, bright eyes trained on him, wary.

"Why am I naked?" she asked.

"Because you insisted on it," he said, keeping his voice as devoid of emotion as possible. It took effort, because every other thought was a remembrance from last night—

a memory of her desperation to hear him say he wanted her, the phantom press of her body against his, the heat of her lips urging his apart. "You were very determined to seduce me."

Her already-flushed cheeks turned crimson. "Did we —"

His laugh sounded more like a bark. He wasn't sure what he was reacting to, maybe it was the fact that she would assume he would take advantage of her in her inebriated state, or that he had spent the better part of her slumber agonizing over the words she'd used to describe him.

"No, Lady Persephone. Trust me, when we fuck, you'll remember."

Her features hardened, and her lips pressed into a thin line. "Your arrogance is alarming."

"Is that a challenge?"

"Just tell me what happened, Hades!" she snapped.

He met her ferocious stare with just as much venom before answering, "You were drugged at La Rose. You're lucky you are immortal. Your body burned through the poison fast."

She was quiet for a moment, processing the information he had shared. Her gaze left his, as if searching the middle distance for answers to her questions.

"Adonis," she said suddenly, eyes narrowing in accusation. "What did you do to him?"

Hades ground his teeth and focused on the remaining liquor in his glass rather than her gaze. He downed the last bit before setting it aside. "He is alive, but that is only because he was in his goddess's territory."

"You knew!" She pushed off the bed, the sheets rustling around her. He wanted to take them from her, challenge her to stand bare and confident before him as she had last night. "Is that why you warned me to stay away from him?"

"I assure you, there are more reasons to stay away from

177

that mortal than the favor Aphrodite has bestowed upon him."

"Like what?" she asked, taking a step toward him. "You can't expect me to understand if you don't explain anything."

What need have I to explain? He kissed you when you did not want him to, Hades wanted to say, but it was possible she did not remember.

"I expect that you will trust me." He stood, swiping his glass off the table and refilling it at the bar. "And if not me, then my power."

He was more than aware she knew of his ability to see what mortals tried to hide with charms and lies. It was a power she condemned in her article, claiming he used it to prey upon their darkest secrets.

"I thought you were jealous!"

The laugh that ruptured from the back of Hades' throat sounded harsh, even to his ears. He was not sure why he mocked her either, but maybe it was because he just now realized his jealousy, now that he was beyond the anger and the challenge last night had posed to his sense of control.

"Don't pretend you don't get jealous, Hades. Adonis kissed me last night."

Hades slammed his glass on the table, betraying himself, and twisted toward her. "Keep reminding me, goddess, and I'll reduce him to ash."

"So, you are jealous!" she cried.

"Jealous?" he hissed, stalking toward her. He watched as the excitement of her triumph melted from her face, replaced by an expression he could not discern. He only knew it was not fear. "That...leech touched you after you told him not to. I have sent souls to Tartarus for less."

He paused a few inches from her, his anger acute, radiating off him like the heat from Helios' sun.

Until she uttered an apology.

The words fell from her mouth, quiet and breathy. "I'm...sorry."

He was not sure why she was apologizing, but those words seemed misplaced on the heels of his speech about Adonis.

His brows knitted together, and he cupped her face, stepping closer, sealing the space between them. "Don't you dare apologize. Not for him. Never for him."

She covered his hands with her own, and as he searched her eyes, full of kindness and compassion, he felt a little of that fury dissipate and couldn't help asking, "Why are you so desperate to hate me?"

"I don't hate you," she said quietly.

He could not sense the lie, but he could not reconcile why she would write that article about him, not when she did not hate him. He tore away from her.

"No? Shall I remind you? Hades, Lord of the Underworld, rich one, and arguably the most hated god among mortals, exhibits a clear disregard for mortal life."

As he spoke, she seemed to cower, shoulders rising, growing smaller and smaller beneath her own viscous words.

"This is what you think of me?" he challenged.

"I was angry—"

"Oh, that is more than obvious," he barked.

"I didn't know they would publish it!"

"A scathing letter illustrating all of my faults?" He paused to laugh bitterly. "You didn't think the media would publish it?"

She had used the article as a threat, knowing Hades valued his privacy. She was well-aware that it would be a coveted piece to the media, and yet, there was something troubling about her defense, and that was that he sensed no lie. Still, if she truly meant for it not to go live, why did she write it? And how had it gotten published?

His sarcasm did not win him any compassion from the goddess. Her eyes flashed, and her words slipped from between barred teeth.

"I warned you."

"You warned me?" Hades raised his brows and offered

179

a breathy laugh. "You warned me about what, goddess?"

"I warned you that you would regret our contract."

They were words he remembered, spoken as she had straightened the lapels of his jacket and killed the flower in his breast pocket. He had no doubt then, and he had no doubt now.

"And I warned you not to write about me." He dared to close the distance between them again, knowing it was the wrong thing to do, knowing that their anger only had one outlet.

"Perhaps in my next article, I'll write about how bossy you are," she threatened.

"Next article?"

"You didn't know?" she asked smugly. "I've been asked to write a series on you."

"No."

"You can't say no. You're not in control here."

He would show her control, he thought, bending into her body, feeling the way she arched with him. She was a viper, responding to his call, and when she struck, it would be venomous.

"And you think you are?"

"I'll write the articles, Hades, and the only way I'll stop is if you let me out of this godsdamned contract!"

So that was her game?

"You think to bargain with me, goddess?" he asked. "You've forgotten one important thing, Lady Persephone. To bargain, you need to have something I want."

Her eyes sparked, and her cheeks turned rosy again.

"You asked me if I believed what I wrote!" she argued. "You care!"

"It's called a bluff, darling."

"Bastard," she hissed.

It was the word that broke his restraint. He dragged her against him, burying his hand in her hair, and his lips closed over hers. She was soft and sweet, and she smelled like him. He wanted all of her, and yet, he pulled away, separating by mere inches.

"Let me be clear," he said fiercely. "You bargained, and you lost. There is no way out of our contract unless you fulfill its terms. Otherwise, you remain here. With me."

She stared up at him, eyes raging, lips raw. "If you make me your prisoner, I will spend the rest of my life hating you."

"You already do."

He noted how she seemed to recoil at his words, staring up at him as if his comment hurt. "Do you really believe that?"

He did not answer, just offered a mocking laugh, and then pressed a hot kiss to her mouth before tearing away viciously. "I will erase the memory of him from your skin."

He yanked the sheet from her hands, and she was naked before him as she was last night, her eyes full of desire, and all he could think was that he fucking wanted this—her passion and her body and her soul.

He grasped her bottom, lifting her from the ground, and her body molded to his without his guidance. It was silent surrender, a sign that she wanted this just as much as he did. His lips crushed hers, and heat blossomed low in his belly, filling his groin until he was hard and desperate to be inside her. He felt frantic, and his body vibrated with need, urged by Persephone's vicious hands, scraping his scalp, yanking on his hair. He growled low in his throat, pressing her into the bedpost, grinding his lengthen into her softness. He reveled in the way her mouth broke from his so that she could gasp for breath as he moved against her, pressing kisses down her neck and shoulder, tongue tasting. He was senseless, and she was a spell, a contract he would fulfill endlessly if it meant having her like this every day for the rest of his life.

My lover, he thought. *My wife, my queen.*

He froze, almost saying those words aloud, and then shifted, dropping her on the bed. He stood over her, breathing hard, and she looked up at him, surprised but as beautiful and as sensual as ever, legs parted, breasts firm and full. He had two choices before him, he could take her or leave her, and on the heels of her article, he felt it was best to leave because the only thing that would wait for them on the other side of this was sorrow.

After a moment, he managed a savage smile. "Well, you would probably enjoy fucking me, but you definitely don't like me."

He barely registered the horror on her face before he vanished.

She was right—he was a bastard.

CHAPTER XVIII – THE THREE MOONS

Hades stood outside an occult shop known as The Three Moons. It was where Hecate had traced the scent of magic used at Poseidon's shipyard. Beside him was Hecate, who looked like a member of a cult, dressed in a black silken cloak and hood. They were both gazing at the imagery on the shop window—a full moon framed by two half-moons. It was Hecate's symbol, and it had multiple meanings, none of which were represented by the man who ran the shop—Vasilis Remes, a Magi.

Magi were mortals who tended to practice black magic and poorly, often creating chaos Hecate had to quell.

"Tell me you have brought me here to curse this mortal," Hecate said, hopeful, glancing at Hades.

Hades lips quirked. "Only if you are very good."

He stepped past her and entered the shop. As he did, a bell sounded overhead, and a voice snapped from somewhere in the dark, "Be with you in a minute!"

Hades and Hecate exchanged a look.

"Excellent customer service," she commented and began to explore the shop, wrinkling her nose as she went.

"This place stinks of dark magic."

Hades could smell it, too. It reeked of burnt flesh and something...metallic. The shop was dark. The large window bearing Hecate's symbol had been covered with dark paint. The only light source came from black candles, all varying heights. Hades did not know much about witchcraft, but he knew those candles were typically used for protection, which made him wonder exactly what Vasilis Remes needed protecting from...well, other than them.

Then again, perhaps the Magi kept the shop dark to hide the chaos. It was a wreck, crowded with cases of stones and crystals of all shapes and sizes, books that were unorganized and shoved into every open nook. There were hexing poppets and athames, vials of oils and dust, and—

"Dove's blood," Hecate said.

Hades looked at the goddess, who had been across the room moments ago. They had a competition going for a few years. The first to sneak up on the other wins, the prize to be claimed on the day of victory.

He raised a brow. "I know you were trying to scare me."

"Did it work?" she asked.

Hades leaned in a little more, offering a deliberate, "No," before turning back to the line of vials, nodding toward the one with the red-black blood.

"What is it used for?"

"Mostly love spells," she replied.

Hades should have guessed. The dove was Aphrodite's symbol and love her wheelhouse. This was an example of why Magi were so dangerous—they attempted to obtain the power of the gods, usually for nefarious purposes and disastrous implications.

"It is also used to seal pacts and promises," she said. "Too bad they cannot extract favors."

"Hmm," Hades agreed, when he noticed Hecate stiffen. Something had caught her attention. "What is it?"

The goddess crossed the room, approaching the clerk's

counter. Hades followed, curious at first and then horrified by what he saw. A set of shelves were mounted upon the wall behind the counter and, displayed like prized possessions, were a set of shriveled hands. Each one had a candle clutched between their fingers.

"Hecate." Hades said her name quietly. "What are those?"

"Hands of Glory," she said. "Traditionally, they are the hands of hanging victims."

The two exchanged a look; people were no longer hanged in New Greece. If Hades had to guess, those hands came from graves.

"It is said that those in possession of one may render anyone else immobile."

It was a blasphemous weapon that could do a lot of harm if given to the wrong person.

Just then, a rotund man stumbled from a shrouded doorway behind the clerk's counter. He did not look in their direction as he rubbed his palms over his black robes, which Hades found unsettling.

"Can I help you?" His voice was a high-pitched whine, and Hades had the thought that he would be annoying to torture.

"You can start by telling us where Sisyphus de Ephyra is hiding," Hades said.

The Magi's head snapped toward them, small eyes widening in his chubby, sallow face. He stumbled clumsily and fell over something hidden in the shadows behind his desk. After a moment, he popped back up, struggling to reach one of the hands shelved on the wall. When he finally swiped it from its place, he held it aloft, shaking.

"Stay back!"

Hades and Hecate exchanged a look.

"I possess the power of the gods!" His voice wavered, and he spit as he spoke. "Pagoma!"

There was silence for a moment as the Magi realized he was not at all as powerful as the two gods in front of him.

"Oh, precious mortal," Hecate said, and the sweet tone

of her voice contradicted her

narrowing eyes. The shriveled hand he held aloft disintegrated, then the others on his shelf followed. "You would threaten me when it is my symbol you bear upon your shop?"

Hecate's voice changed in that moment, taking on a distorted edge, and Vasilis cowered, shrinking against the wall and shaking. It was not often Hades got to witness Hecate's wrath, and he had to say, he enjoyed seeing the fire in her eyes.

"You will never know the power of the gods."

The air stirred with Hecate's magic, extinguishing the flaming candles, and while Hades would have liked to see the goddess' rage climax, he also needed the Magi alive and able to talk.

"Are you finished scaring the mortal?" Hades asked.

"Wait your turn," she said.

"It *is* my turn." Hades gave her a meaningful look that said, *remember why we came here.*

"If you are arguing over my impending punishment," the Magi said. "Then I'd really rather stick with Lady Hecate."

"You don't get to choose who punishes you, mortal," Hades snapped. "You have a lot of nerve, threatening gods. Not to mention this blasphemous business you run."

"I panicked," he said.

Hades' lips flattened. "Sisyphus de Ephyra. Where is he?"

Hades saw recognition in the mortal's eyes.

"Tell me!" Hades commanded.

"Sis-Sisyphus de Ephyra, you say?" Vasilis stuttered. "N-No. I think you are mistaken, my lord. I don't know anyone by that name."

Hades hates lies. They had a taste and a scent, bitter and pungent. His brows slammed down over his eyes, and as he advanced upon the Magi, he changed his tune.

"I mean, did you say Sisyphus de Ephyra? I thought you said Sisphus de Phyra," he continued, his laugh awkward while sliding along the wall, away from the two gods. "Yes, yes... Sisyphus was here just yesterday."

There was a beat of silence, and then Hades spoke, words slipping between his teeth. "*Where is he now?*"

"I-I don't know."

Hades' patience was a thin thread, and it snapped. He snapped. Claws protruded from the tips of his fingers. As he stepped toward the man, there was a crashing sound that came from the back room where the mortal had been. Hades glared at the mortal before changing course and making his way toward the back room.

"Wait—"

"Are you asking for Hades, God of the Underworld, to slice your face to bits?" Hecate asked. "Because I will gladly watch."

"You're looking for Sisyphus? I'll tell you where he is! Come...come back!" he called as Hades disappeared behind the curtain.

He found himself in a dark hallway that emptied into a larger room. The air was cold and stale, smelling faintly of decay, wax, and something akin to burnt hair. It was cleaner than the storefront and full of sleek glass cases, under which were a variety of carefully displayed items. It was clear why Vasilis had not wanted Hades to venture here. He was selling relics—tattered fabric and bits of jewelry, shattered spear tips and slivers of shields, bones and broken pottery. These were things that had been scavenged from the battlefields after The Great War. He wasn't sure why, but seeing the remnants of war was never easy for him. It reminded him of the trauma of Titanomachy, of bloody battlefields and broken corpses.

Still, Hades searched the darkness for the source of the noise and found it. A set of books had been knocked from a shelf. Hades bent to pick them up, and as he straightened, his gaze met that of a black cat with yellow eyes. The creature hissed at him, and he hissed back. The cat yowled and hopped from its place, disappearing into the darkness.

"We have ourselves a black market dealer," Hades called to Hecate.

Vasilis shuffled into the room first, his hand stretched into the air as if he were surrendering. It was then Hades noticed a familiar image etched on the pale skin of his wrist—a triangle. Hades' eyes narrowed.

"So, you are a member of Triad?"

The Magi froze. "Not by choice."

It was the fastest answer he had given, and it rang of truth.

"Then why is their mark upon your skin?"

The question left Hades feeling uneasy. He could not help thinking of Persephone and the mark upon her wrist. The one he had placed there against her will.

"What did they do?" It was Hecate who asked the question, her tone gentle, seeing something within the mortal Hades had not, apparently.

"They burned her," Vasilis replied, lowering his hands.

"Who?" Hades asked.

"My cat."

"Your cat?" Hades was not impressed.

"They burned her right in front of me," he said, his voice thick with emotion. "I thought she was gone forever, but their leader...he kept her collar. He said he would return it if I joined them. They...needed magic."

"A golem?" Hades asked.

Vasilis nodded.

Hades understood now. The Magi had agreed to serve Triad in exchange for the collar. It was the only item left that belonged to his cat, but he had not wanted it because he was sentimental. He'd wanted it for a purpose—the collar could be used to resurrect her, which by the looks of it, had been successful.

"So, you traded your freedom for a collar?"

"What would you trade for something you loved?" the Magi countered.

The world, Hades thought.

"Oh!" Hecate exclaimed suddenly, bending to scoop up

the cat that had hissed at Hades earlier. "Is this her? What a sweet baby! What is her name?"

"S-Serena."

"Serena," Hecate said, lifting the cat as she would a child. "I have a polecat named Gale—"

Hades sighed. "Hecate, can you not?"

"This is being human, Hades," the goddess said. "You should be taking notes. Don't you want to impress Persephone?"

"Who is Persephone?" the magi asked.

"Not your concern," Hades snapped, then he glared at Hecate and hated himself for his next question. "What does a cat have to do with being human?"

"It has everything to do with the cat," Hecate said, then she sighed. "The cat is humanity. It's what makes this," she gestured toward the Magi, "unfortunate, sad, and pitiful mortal worth saving."

"You haven't seen his soul," Hades muttered.

Hecate glared.

"I am teaching you a lesson, Hades! Learn it."

Hades was about to snap that she was a horrible teacher, when he felt the air shift behind him. He turned and shadows split from his essence, racing toward the retreating form of the Magi, who was attempting to escape down the hall.

The shadows enveloped him and sent him flying backward. The Magi crashed into one of his immaculate glass displays and was still.

Hecate grimaced.

"You didn't have to throw him so hard. He isn't a god."

"He wanted to act like one."

Hecate arched a brow. "Is that the response of a compassionate god?"

"Is that what you were trying to teach?"

Hades took a step toward the mortal and waved his hand. The Magi opened his eyes, blinking, and then groaned as the pain from his landing set in.

"Listen here, mortal, and listen well. You will tell me

who requested your services, or I will spend eternity cutting out your tongue and feeding it to your cat. *Do you understand?*"

The man nodded, breathing hard, and answered, "His name is Theseus."

Theseus.

It was a name Hades knew well, as it was the name of Poseidon's son, his nephew.

"The golem was Sisyphus' idea," Vasilis explained. "He was a client of mine. It was after he came to visit that Theseus arrived, demanding to know Sisyphus' plans. He made me summon a portal to the warehouse. He left from here with Sisyphus. I don't know where they went."

So Sisyphus had been deceived just as much as Hades had. The question was, what did Theseus want with Sisyphus? Had he sought revenge for the murder of Aeolus Galani, or was there something more to his actions?

After a moment, the Magi spoke.

"Please…please don't take my cat."

"Hecate," Hades called to the goddess, who had made her way toward the dark hallway with the cat still in her arms. "Bring the cat."

"W-wait. I said please!"

"Oh, you're coming, too, mortal," he said, and Vasilis' eyes grew wide.

"But I told you the truth! I—"

The Magi was silenced, vanishing with a wave of Hades' hand. He would spend time imprisoned, but not in Tartarus—he would go to a Phantom Site, a prison that could only be seen by those who were favored. It was a special place for mortals like him—Magi who broke the law or held secrets—and on rare occasions, might be used as bait.

Hades turned to Hecate. "See, I can be compassionate."

***

Before leaving The Three Moons, Hades summoned Ilias to the shop so the satyr could dispose of the contents —which meant burning it to the ground. He and Hecate parted, Hades had business with Aphrodite, while Hecate intended to return to the Underworld.

"The souls are celebrating you tonight," she reminded him. "They would be overjoyed to see you."

Guilt slammed into him, as it always did when his people set aside time to worship him.

"Persephone will be there. I believe they plan to honor her as well."

That was not unexpected. She deserved their worship. She was more of a god than he had ever been to them. Besides, they would have to get used to celebrating her. She was to be their queen.

"Perhaps I will make it this time," he said before departing, but doubted his words.

The Goddess of Witchcraft meant well, but there were some demons Hades did not wish to face, and his people —his past treatment of them—was one.

Hades found Aphrodite at her seaside mansion, reclining on a blush chaise in her marbled home, floor to ceiling windows overlooking the ocean and Hephaestus' island. When he appeared, she yawned, placing the back of her hand over her mouth.

"I expected you to return last night," she said, fanning herself with what looked like a bundle of feathers. "You must have had quite the distraction on your hands."

"Your mortal drugged Persephone," Hades said, getting to the point of his visit. He did not normally mind Aphrodite's badgering, but he was not in the mood for it today.

The goddess did not react, but her hand continued to move, the feathered fan beating in a steady rhythm.

"Where is your proof?" she asked, bored.

"I tasted the poison on her tongue, Aphrodite," Hades said tightly.

"Tasted?" Aphrodite sat up, eyes widened slightly as she set her fan aside. "So you kissed her, then?"

Hades' jaw tightened, and he did not respond.

"Are you in love?" she asked, and there was a note of alarm in her voice Hades did not understand. Did Aphrodite fear that he would win their bargain and she would lose her chance to see Basil returned from the Underworld? Or did she even care about Basil? Did she fear more that she would no longer see him as she saw herself—alone?

He glared at her, and her eyes sparkled, a smile curling her lips. "You are! Oh, this is news, indeed."

"Enough, Aphrodite."

She glared, folding her arms over her chest. "I suppose you have come here to threaten Adonis?"

"I have come to ask why you let it happen."

Aphrodite's eyes widened, and she blinked, clearly not expecting Hades to ask that question. Then her eyes narrowed. "What are you accusing me of, Hades?"

"You keep your lovers on a short leash, and yet you let Adonis go and summoned me when things got out of hand. Were you hoping to see me rage?"

"I think you are accusing me of setting up last night's debacle."

Aphrodite might be the Goddess of Love, but she did not believe in it and often made obtaining it difficult for mortals. She saw it as a game and played them like pawns, introducing distractions, challenging the bond she could never establish with another.

He knew what she was doing, and he was here to stop it.

"Persephone is not a plaything, Aphrodite. You do not get to fuck with this."

Her lips thinned, and her sea green eyes darkened.

"There are no rules to the bargain, Hades. I can challenge your choice as much as I wish."

"Let me be clear, Aphrodite. This bargain has no bearing on whether or not Persephone will be my queen, as that is a future woven by the Fates. If you fuck with her, you fuck with me."

"If she does not love you, you cannot prevent her eye from wandering."

"Is that what you were attempting to prove last night? Because all I saw was my future wife in distress. A crime that will not go unpunished."

"Unless?"

Her question made Hades chuckle, and the sound stole Aphrodite's smug expression.

"Oh, there is no bargaining when it comes to my queen," Hades replied. "Adonis' existence in the Underworld will be horror."

As he spoke, the Goddess of Love's eyes widened, and anger clouded her face.

"Hades—" His name slipped from between her lips like a warning.

"*Nothing* will keep me from shredding Adonis' soul. Rest well in the knowledge that you have decided his fate, Aphrodite."

The last thing he heard before he left was Aphrodite screaming his name.

***

Hades returned to his office in the Underworld. It overlooked Asphodel, and he watched his people's merrymaking from afar, illuminated by lantern light. From this distance, he could not see Persephone, but he knew she was here. Her presence unearthed more memories from the previous night, and along with it, the guilt of leaving her on his bed, naked, skin flushed with desire. At least he had proven one thing to himself—she wanted him sober.

He sighed and downed a glass of whiskey before loosening his tie and heading for the baths. He needed a shower. He felt unclean, the stench of dark magic and Vasilis' shop clinging to his skin.

He paused at the entry to his private baths where he could hear the splash of water and smell Persephone's scent. The thought of seeing her naked again filled him with lust, his cock thickening at the thought of being inside her.

But would she reject him? Or invite him to explore every facet of her body?

He was about to find out.

He stepped out of the shadow, making his way down the steps, ensuring he made enough noise so that he would not startle her. When he came into view, he found her at the center of the oval pool, flanked on either side by marble columns. Her eyes were wide, her cheeks flushed, her hair was wet and suctioned to her body like vines curling around porcelain. The water lapped at her breasts, coming just to her rosy nipples, and it was so clear, he could make out the curve of her hips and the dark curls at the apex of her thighs. His thoughts turned to how it would feel to part that satin flesh and explore the evidence of her desire for him. He was sure she would be slick and hot, ready for his fingers and his mouth, and he would drink from her until she came apart in his arms.

Then his eyes fell to his feet, where her clothes were piled. On top, sat a beautiful gold crown. He recognized the craftsmanship as Ian Kovac's, a talented blacksmith who had resided in the Underworld for centuries.

Hades bent and picked it up for a closer examination. It was a beautiful gem and floral crown, a perfect balance of flora that represented him and Persephone alike.

"This is beautiful."

She stared, her eyes burning like a forge. Hades wondered what thoughts accompanied that gaze. Were they just as salacious as his own? Was she wondering what his cock would feel like in her hands, how he would taste in her mouth, the sound he would make as he came?

She cleared her throat, breaking his thoughts. "It is. Ian made it for me."

"He is a talented craftsman. It is what led to his death."

Her brows drew together over her forehead. "What do you mean?"

"He was favored by Artemis, and she blessed him with the ability to create weapons that ensured their wearer could not be defeated in battle. He was killed for it."

Favor could be a dangerous thing to bestow. It made targets of mortals in antiquity and today. Sometimes, the results were positive and the receiver was granted celebrity and status, then other times, they were killed.

Hades stared at the crown a moment longer. It was significant that she had accepted such an ornament from his people, even if she had done so to please them. It was a sign of her dedication to them, a quality in a true queen. He set it down atop her clothes and then rose to his feet, meeting Persephone's gaze again. It was also significant that she had not moved to hide herself from him.

"Why didn't you go?" she asked. "To the celebration in Asphodel. It was for you."

"And you. They celebrated *you*," he said. "As they should."

"I am not their queen."

"And I am not worthy of their celebration."

"If they feel you're worthy of celebration, don't you think that's enough?"

Hades did not respond. He did not wish to speak on this topic. In fact, the only words he wanted to share with her were erotic pleas and breathy moans. His cock throbbed, desperate for freedom and pleasure, which made his blood rush to his head and kept him from focusing on anything but sex.

"May I join you?"

He noted the way her throat constricted as she swallowed, nodding. Her invitation only encouraged the fire. He held her gaze as he stripped, almost groaning as he freed his jutting sex from the confines of his trousers. It felt swollen and taut to the point of pain. He needed release, and he was even more desperate for it as Persephone's gaze traveled the length of his body, just as hungry as he felt.

He stepped into the pool and spoke as he approached. "I believe I owe you an apology."

"For what, specifically?"

A smile touched his lips. He was aware she felt he owed her an apology for more than just the way he had left her yesterday. The problem was, an apology was offered when someone truly felt sorry for what they had done, and Hades didn't think he'd ever be sorry for tricking her into their contract. It would mean her freedom, whether she realized that now or not.

He moved closer, towering over her, and touched her face, brushing his finger across her cheek.

"Last time we saw each other, I was unfair to you."

She averted her eyes, and Hades' hand fell from her face as she said in a quiet voice, "We were unfair to each other."

She was talking about the article she had written, and the fact that she was acknowledging its unfairness made his breath catch in his chest. Was it too much to hope that she was changing her mind about him?

"You like your life in the mortal realm?" He had to ask, needed to assess her attachment to the Upperworld. Would she leave it to be his queen?

"Yes." She pushed away from him, swimming backward, her breasts lifting above the water. Hades followed as if she were pulling him on a string. "I like my life. I have an apartment and friends and an internship. I'm going to graduate from university soon."

"But you are Divine."

He did not understand. Why was she building this mundane life in the Upperworld, when she could have anything? Everything?

She stopped wading away, and they stood centimeters apart. He could feel the brush of her nipples against his skin as she breathed.

"I have never lived that way, and you know it," she replied, and she looked almost frustrated with him, a line appearing between her brows.

"You have no desire to understand what it is to be a goddess?"

"No."

"I think you're lying," he said. He could taste it immediately, that bitter, metallic tang at the back of his mouth. The question was, why? If he were to guess, he would think it had something to do with her dormant power.

"You don't know me."

Her eyes ignited like souls ascending into the night sky.

Yes, he thought, *build that fire*.

He wanted her angry, wanted to feel her passion radiate from her body and vibrate through his own.

He narrowed his eyes, challenging. "I know you."

He moved so that he was behind her, touching her only with the tips of his fingers, trailing along her collarbone and shoulder.

"I know the way your breath hitches when I touch you. I know how your skin flushes when you're thinking about me. I know there is something beneath this pretty façade."

He pressed a kiss to her shoulder, before his hand moved lower, grazing her breast. Persephone offered a sharp inhale as her body arched into his, and Hades almost groaned.

"There is rage. There is passion. There is darkness." He punctuated his words with the swirl of his tongue against her neck.

"And I want to taste it."

His hand drifted across her belly before hooking around her waist, then he drew her tighter against him, leaving her in no doubt of his desire for her. His cock fit perfectly against her shapely bottom, her back against his chest.

"Hades." She breathed his name, and it made him ravenous.

He dropped his head in the crook of her shoulder and he begged, "Let me show you what it is to hold power in your hands. Let me coax the darkness from you. I will help you shape it."

While he held her against him, his other hand sought her center. His fingers threaded through coarse, dark curls until he cupped her sex, feeling its heat wet his hand. Persephone's head flew back, resting on his shoulder, and her gasp encouraged him.

"Hades, I've never—"

"Let me be your first."

It was a plea, but also a question. He wanted this desperately, could feel how much she wanted this, too. But there was a difference between wanting and being ready, and he would not push her if she needed time.

Except that she nodded, inviting his hand to part her flesh. His thumb brushed lightly over her clit, teasing along the entrance of her delicate and delicious flesh. She rose onto the tips of her toes, body growing rigid beneath his touch.

"Breathe," he whispered, and when she did, his fingers sank deeper, eliciting a cry from Persephone and a groan from Hades. His head was clouded with lust. He wanted so much from this one instance, to explore her with his hand and his mouth and his cock. He wanted to take her in a million different erotic ways, and yet she was new to all of this, her body unfamiliar with this…invasion. He bit his lip hard to bring himself back to this moment, to focus on pleasuring Persephone, not his throbbing need for release.

This should be about her.

"You're so wet." The words came out like a hiss, his face buried deep in her hair. The smell of vanilla and lavender clouded his senses. When he felt her nails bite into his skin, he guided her hand down to where his was buried deep.

"Touch yourself. Here."

He showed her how to work her clit, lightly brushing the bundle of nerves that sat just above her moist heat, where he was still moving. He reveled in watching the erotic way she moved against him, rocking her hips, desperate to feel him deeper, and he was happy to oblige. He loved the way she moaned, the way her breath caught in her throat, the way her head lolled against his shoulder. He continued moving inside her while his other hand moved to her breasts, squeezing and kneading her nipples, and then he withdrew from her.

Persephone's shocked cry made him smile, and she whirled on him. He was not sure what she had intended to do, but he didn't give her a chance to follow through. He drew her to him, and his mouth descended upon hers, parting lips, tongues moving against each other with a desperation he had never felt before. It was the result of weeks of pent up need, and he would unleash it now, worship her until she was red and raw.

He broke their kiss and rested his forehead against hers, and he had the thought that he would treasure this moment—the pause between passion where they had shared so much and would share more.

"Do you trust me?"

"Yes."

He studied her a moment longer, memorizing the honesty etched across her face, before kissing her and lifting her from the pool. He sat her on the edge and wedged himself between her thighs, hands anchored to her waist. He would stay here forever if it meant she always looked at him with those heavy-lidded eyes.

"Tell me you have never been naked with a man. Tell me I am the only one."

It was a primal question, a strange need he felt deep in his stomach that vibrated through the thread that connected them. He wanted to be the first to explore her body, the only one to know its truth and bring her pleasure.

Her expression softened, and he felt her hand cup his face. "You are."

Again, he kissed her and snaked his arms beneath her knees. He drew her forward until she barely rested on the side of the pool. His kisses dropped from her mouth to her jaw, to her chest and stomach, chin brushing the wet curls at her center, urged on by Persephone, whose hands threaded through his hair, pulling and scraping as sharp gasps and sensual moans escaped her mouth. It was an erotic symphony he could listen to for the rest of his immortal life.

As he covered her skin in kisses, tongue tasting, he found something he did not expect—a blemish on her perfect skin. Discolored patches of healing yellow-green, bruises splayed across her thighs.

He looked up at her. "Was this me?"

"It's okay."

Still he frowned, hating that he had hurt her and kissed each bruise, healing them completely as he neared her entrance. There was no waiting once he felt her heat. He had thought to tease her more, to illicit gasps of frustration and demands for his tongue, but he was weak, his restraint shredded. He descended upon her as if she were a feast and he starved. Her cry of pleasure shuddered through him, straight to his cock, reminding him that they had hours of pleasure to come.

He began with light strokes, brushing her clit and sliding over her damp entrance, but as her hands tightened in his hair and her cries became guttural, he pulled her closer, tongue reaching deeper, tasting sweet slick skin. She writhed beneath him, and he used one hand to keep her in place while the other teased that bundle of sensitive nerves. She grew taut beneath him, a dam ready to burst, and when she finally found release, he drank.

When he was finished, he rose to his full height and kissed her, his mouth still wet from her sex. She welcomed him, wrapping her arms and legs around him. She sat just above his cock, her entrance teasing his tip, and he grit his teeth to keep from impaling himself upon her. When he pulled away, his eyes bore into hers.

Let me have you, he thought. He watched as she pulled her lip between her teeth, another wordless invitation, but just as he moved to guide his throbbing member into her, he heard Minthe's voice.

"Lord Hades?"

His teeth felt as if they would shatter. He had never hated a sound so much in his life, but this was one he would curse for the rest of his existence. He noted the way Persephone stiffened, and he held her in place as he pushed away from the edge of the pool, turning so that her back was to the nymph as she entered the baths. It was an attempt to preserve some of her modesty, even with her legs still around his waist.

Except Persephone surprised him by wrapping her hand around his cock.

They stared at each other, and if gazes could start fires, they would incinerate.

"Ha—"

Minthe stood at the top of the steps that lead into the baths. Her jaw had tightened, and her features grew rigid at the sight she had stumbled upon.

"Yes, Minthe?" Hades voice was strained, his anger and desire warring for dominance in his mind. Persephone's hand stroked down his shaft, her thumb rubbing light circles over the crown of his cock.

"We…missed you at dinner," Minthe was saying.

All Hades could think was, *Why is she still talking?*

"But I see that you are busy."

Persephone's hand moved down to the very root.

"Very," he said between his teeth.

"I will let the cook know you have been thoroughly sated."

Up to the tip.

"Quite," he gritted out.

Minthe lingered there a moment longer, as if she wished to say something further, but—smartly—thought against it. She turned and left, and Hades reached for Persephone. They would pick up where they had left off. She had teased him enough, and now he would know what it felt like to be inside her, to be consumed by that mesmerizing heat.

Except she pushed away from him.

"Where are you going?" He followed after her.

"How often does Minthe come to you in the baths?" she asked as she stepped out of the pool.

"Persephone."

Do not do this. Do not go there, he wanted to say, but she was not looking at him and she had covered herself with a towel.

"Look at me, Persephone."

He was still in the pool, but he had moved forward enough so that the water came to his thighs. In some way, he felt just as exposed, his hard flesh on full display, so she could be left in no doubt of his want for her.

"Minthe is my assistant."

"Then she can assist you with your need." She dared to pin his cock with her vicious stare. His brows slammed down, and he left the water, arm sliding around her waist. He drew her to him.

"I don't want Minthe," he growled.

"I don't want *you*."

He wanted to snarl at the bitter taste in the back of his mouth as he tasted her lie.

"You don't...want me?" he asked.

"No," she said, but her voice was a hoarse whisper.

Hades' eyes dropped to her kiss-swollen lips before lifting to her eyes once again. After a moment, he asked, "Do you know all of my powers, Persephone?"

He noted the way her throat constricted as she swallowed. He wondered why, after what they had shared in the pool, she was nervous. Perhaps she did not trust herself to maintain this façade of indifference.

"Some of them," she answered.

He tilted his head, inching close. "Enlighten me."

"Illusion," she said, and as she spoke, his lips brushed along the column of her neck.

"Yes," he whispered, continuing to explore and taste her skin.

"Invisibility?"

"Very valuable."

"Charm?" she breathed as his lips moved toward the sensitive skin of her breasts.

"Hmm." He paused and looked up at her. "But it doesn't work on you, does it?"

"No." She shivered as she answered, and a smile threatened Hades' serious composure. He drew a finger down the center of her chest, hooking around the towel and exposing her breasts.

"You seem to not have heard of one of my most valuable talents." He took one tight bud into his mouth and sucked, enjoying the way Persephone's breath caught loudly in her throat. He pulled away and leveled his gaze with hers.

"I can taste lies, Persephone. And yours are as sweet as your skin."

She planted her hands on his chest and pushed him away.

"This was a mistake."

That was not a lie, and the truth of it shattered his soul.

Persephone gathered the remainder of her clothes and the crown Ian had made. She held them to her chest like they were a shield, as if she were ashamed of what she had let happen. Hades stared as she retreated up the stairs.

"You might believe this was a mistake," Hades called, and Persephone halted, her head turning only slightly so he could see her profile. "But you want me. I was inside you. I tasted you. That is a truth you will never escape."

And it was that truth that gave him hope, because Hades knew he could build affection with fire.

He watched as Persephone shivered and ran.

CHAPTER XIX – THE HALCYON PROJECT

Hades teleported to his chambers, naked, cock straining, desperate for release.

She left me, he thought as he took a long pull straight from the whiskey bottle he had swiped from his bar. He paced, body rigid. The more he moved, the more he was reminded of his need.

Fucking Fates. Fucking Minthe.

This is a taste of my own medicine, he thought. *I left her, too. Is this how she felt?*

The thought was both pleasing and agonizing at the same time.

He paused, drank once more from the bottle, and threw it into the roaring fire. It shattered, and for a moment, the flames raged, the perfect representation of how he felt on the inside. As the blaze died down, he braced himself against the table and wrapped his fingers around his swollen length, gritting his teeth and closing his eyes.

In the darkness of his mind, he teleported to Persephone, finding her splayed on her bed, legs apart, fingers buried inside her, giving pleasure just as he had taught her in the baths. Her heels dug into the bed, her back arched, her breathing grew heavy. She was beautiful, exposed skin bathed in moonlight—a silvery goddess in the throes of passion.

Then she moved onto her knees and rocked back and forth, rolling her hips as she rode her hand.

"Tell me you're thinking about me," Hades said, and his hand gripped his cock, stroking lightly, savoring the pleasure that rushed to his head.

Persephone turned, her wide green eyes meeting his in the dark. Even in this light, he could see her cheeks were flushed. Her hair fell in disarray around her face, and her nipples strained against her nightshirt.

"Well?" he prompted.

"Yes," she breathed. "I was thinking about you."

He growled low in his throat. "Don't stop on my account."

She rose onto her knees and pulled her shirt over her head. His eyes roved her beautiful body, full breasts and dark nipples. A small waist he wanted to hold as she rode him to release, and wide hips that would cling to him as he drove into her.

The goddess began again, parting her flesh to pleasure herself. For a while, they maintained eye contact, and as she moved up and down, Hades stroked himself, increasing in urgency the more he witnessed her passion, head rolling back, breasts bouncing, teeth biting down on her bottom lip. Soon his hips moved, thrusting into his hand.

"Come for me," he commanded. "Come, my darling."

Her cries gave way to his own as his body jerked, hand filling with hot release. He collapsed against the table, breathing hard. Despite his need to catch his breath, he laughed.

He laughed because he had just had one of the hottest sexual encounters of his long life. Because his goddess— his future wife—had pleasured herself—and she had thought of him.

***

"Tell me why you are taking Minthe to the Olympian Gala tonight and not Persephone?"

The question came from Hecate, who stood behind Hades as he adjusted his tie in the mirror. The Goddess of Witchcraft did not look pleased, looming in her purple robes, arms crossed over her chest.

The Olympian Gala occurred every year and was hosted at the Museum of Ancient Arts. It was an extravagant affair and an excuse for the gods to flaunt their wealth. The only reason Hades went was because the event doubled as a fundraiser. This year, the gala was themed after the Underworld, which meant that Hades and his foundation had a hand in choosing the charity.

"I am not taking Minthe," Hades said. "She is my assistant."

And he had not asked Persephone because she was going as an assignment for work, and taking Lexa.

"You do realize the only thing Persephone will see is you arriving at the gala with Minthe?"

Hades thought about the other night in the baths, when Minthe had interrupted them. Persephone had looked pointedly at his groin, his cock and balls heavy. He heard her words in his head. *Then Minthe can assist you with your need.*

Hades ground his teeth and turned to the goddess.

"I do not intend to arrive with her on my arm," Hades said. "She is there to introduce the Halcyon Project."

It was something his staff has been working on at The Cypress Foundation—a non-profit that would provide rehabilitation care to mortals for free. It was inspired by Persephone, whose words he could still hear clear as day. *If you are going to request a bargain, challenge them to go to rehab if they're an addict, and do one better, pay for it.*

He had not been doing enough. If his true goal was to ensure that life in the Underworld was a better existence

206

for souls, they had to have hope while alive. In the last few weeks, Hades had come to know more and more about hope than he ever imagined.

Hecate was staring, brow raised. "Does Minthe know that?"

"I have given her no reason to think otherwise," Hades said.

The goddess shook her head. "You do not understand women," Hecate said. "Unless you have made it explicitly clear, meaning unless you have said the words, *Minthe, you are not my date*, she will think exactly that."

"And what makes you an expert suddenly?"

"I may not be interested in relationships, Hades, but I have lived longer than you and have seen these emotions destroy humanity. Besides," she lifted her chin, "I overheard Minthe telling her minions she had a date with you this evening."

"Her *minions*?" he asked.

"She has a group of nymphs she complains to about everything. You should hear the way she talks about Persephone."

Hades' eyes narrowed, and suddenly, he was full of curiosity.

"How *does* she talk about Persephone?"

Hecate's eyes glittered menacingly as she described in detail the horrible things Minthe had said about the Goddess of Spring, including calling her a *favor fuck*—a derogatory term mortals used when describing someone who sleeps with a god in exchange for their favor. When Hecate was finished speaking, Hades only had one question.

"Why am I just now hearing about this?"

"I was gathering evidence," she said defensively. "And if you think I let them get away with calling Persephone names, you're mistaken."

Hades waited, and Hecate finally explained.

"I...might have sent an army of poisonous centipedes to crash their picnic. The second time I sent blister beetles."

"Second time? This has happened more than once?"

"What can I say? Minthe's out of control," Hecate said, ignoring the true nature of Hades' question, which was why hadn't she come to him earlier?

Hades turned from Hecate, swiping his mask off the table behind him.

"So," Hecate hedged. "What are you going to do?"

"I will speak with Minthe," Hades answered.

"Speak," Hecate repeated. "You aren't going to use this as an opportunity to...I don't know...*ban* her from the Underworld?"

"Perhaps I haven't made myself clear enough," Hades said, and leveled his gaze with Hecate's. "As you so...*aptly* pointed out in the beginning of this conversation. Trust, goddess, after I'm finished with Minthe, there will be no doubt in her mind of how she should treat Persephone."

Hades moved to open the door, finding the nymph on the other side. Her hand was raised, as if he had caught her just before she was about to knock. She was dressed in emerald, and jewels hung heavy on her ears and neck.

"Oh," she said, smiling wide, her eyes darting to Hecate, who still lingered in the background. They narrowed slightly before refocusing on Hades. "I...came to see if you were ready."

"More than," Hades replied, and before the nymph could react, he gathered his magic and teleported. They appeared in the Museum of Ancient Arts, just outside the ballroom where the dinner would take place.

"Favor fuck," Hades said, as he secured his mask.

Minthe looked at him, a mixture of apprehension and fear on her face. "Excuse me?"

"Do you claim to not recognize those words?" Hades asked.

Minthe had nothing to say.

"The next time I hear that you have spoken ill of Persephone will be the last time you assist me," Hades said. "*Do I make myself clear?*"

The nymph lifted her chin, eyes glistening with anger, but she remained silent, more than likely embarrassed and angry that she had been called out for her malicious behavior. Hades left the hall and entered the ballroom. He was greeted immediately by the sight of Persephone descending the stairs crowned with gold and dressed in fire.

He stared openly and hungrily. Her gown hugged her body, reminding him that he had seen her naked, touched her in the most intimate way, heard her breathe his name. He knew she thought similarly as her bottle-green eyes trailed his body, igniting him from the inside out, and then his thoughts became chaos and he wondered if she wore anything beneath that dress.

But as she stared, her eyes darkened. Hades stiffened as Minthe walked up beside him, and the rustle of her dress grated against his ears like a steel blade being sharpened.

He did not acknowledge the nymph, but it did not matter. He understood the expression on Persephone's face. She had assumed what Hecate had predicted, that they had come together. Hades could hear Hecate's smug voice.

I told you so.

Persephone downed her wine and then disappeared into the crowd, Lexa following close behind.

"I think you were just snubbed," Minthe commented.

Hades' mood darkened, and he skirted the crowd in an attempt to keep Persephone within sight. He wanted to explain before it was too late, but he found his way blocked by Poseidon. The god wore a flashy suit, and his hair appeared to have been gelled into something that resembled an ocean wave. Hades thought he looked ridiculous and wondered what Thanatos would think of his hair.

"Brother," Poseidon said, and glanced over his shoulder to where Persephone stood with Hermes. "Am I keeping you from someone?"

Hades did not respond.

"She is beautiful," he said. "I can tell even with the mask. Perhaps you'll share when you tire of her."

Hades narrowed his gaze, tilting his head as he took a step closer to his brother. They were equal in height, but not in size. Poseidon was bulkier, but Hades was stronger. If Poseidon needed a reminder, Hades was happy to oblige.

"If you so much as glance in her direction again, I will tear you limb from limb and feed your carcass to the Titans," Hades said. "Do you doubt me?"

Poseidon had the gall to look amused, his aqua eyes sparkling, and he raised a blond brow. "Territorial much, brother?"

"That's nothing. You should have seen what he did when I rescued her from drowning," Hermes said, sauntering around them, wings dragging the ground. Hades took a step back.

"Did he piss in a circle around her?" Poseidon asked.

Hades' jaw grew taut, and he turned his dark gaze upon Hermes, who had just started to open his mouth, when he looked at Hades and shut it. He had a feeling he knew what Hermes was about to say, that he had marked Persephone in another way via a bargain.

"What's the matter, brother? Afraid her eye will wander?"

Hades felt the darkness rise in him. He would show Poseidon what it was to have wandering eyes when his were removed from his skull and tossed across this room.

But Poseidon was saved by Minthe, who appeared behind him. She slid her arm through his and offered a charming smile.

"Poseidon," she said in a sultry voice. "It's been a while."

The God of the Sea gazed down at her, offering a wide, predatory smile.

"Minthe. You look ravishing."

She pulled on Poseidon's arm. "Have you found your table?" she was asking. "I would be more than happy to help."

As she turned, she glared at Hades as if to say *don't start a scene*.

When they were gone, Hermes spoke.

"If you don't want Poseidon to be an asshat, you shouldn't provoke him."

Hades looked at the God of Mischief. "What did Persephone say to you?"

Hermes raised a brow. "Lover's quarrel?"

He glared.

"I called her out for eye fucking you and she tried to deny it, but we all saw it—from both of you, I might add —and we all felt uncomfortable. Did you know she thinks you don't believe in love?"

"What?"

"She seems rather bitter about it, too," Hermes added, eyes wandering around the room. "Oh! Cherries!"

He started to take off but paused and looked at Hades.

"If you want my advice…"

Hades didn't, but he also didn't feel like talking.

"Tell her."

"Tell her what?"

"That you love her, you idiot." Hermes rolled his eyes. "All these years lived, and you are not the least bit self-aware."

Hermes left then, and when Hades started to find Persephone again, she was no longer there. He gave a frustrated sigh, and his fingers curled into fists at his sides. There were so many words whirling in his head—words from Hecate and Minthe and Poseidon and Hermes. Strangely, it was something Hecate had said long ago that echoed in his mind now.

Persephone has hope for love, and instead of confirming that, you mocked her. Passion does not require love? What were you thinking?

He hadn't been, that had been the problem.

Why did I let her think something so false? he thought, and then answered himself. *Because I feared exposing the truth of my heart—that I have always desired to love and be loved.*

He'd been hoping to guard his heart, build a cage around it so thick that nothing—not even Persephone and her compassion—would find its way through. Except now, she was the only person he wanted close to his heart. It was her compassion he sought. It was her love he wanted.

Because it was her he loved.

Those words impaled his chest and twisted there like a blade. He felt the ache all over his body, in the bottom of his feet and the ends of his fingers. He was left feeling shaky, raw, and exposed. He looked out over the crowd at the mortals and immortals gathered, who were oblivious to the fact that he had been utterly changed in this very moment, in the most bizarre place.

Why could he not have had this realization elsewhere? In the Underworld, perhaps? Poised over Persephone with his cock teasing her entrance?

"Fucking Fates," he muttered.

"What was that?" Minthe asked, appearing at his side.

Hades glanced at her. "I trust Poseidon found your assistance pleasurable."

"Jealous, Hades?"

"Hardly," he replied.

"Don't insult me," Minthe snapped. "I did that for you. Everything I do is for you."

They stared at one another. Hades was not sure what he should say. He was not ignorant to Minthe's feelings for him, and he had to admit that he had never handled them well.

"Minthe—"

"I came to tell you it's time for your announcement," she said, interrupting him. "You should take your place."

She gathered her dress in her hands and turned, strolling toward the stage. Hades followed behind, keeping to the shadows, his presence ignored as Minthe was introduced and took the spotlight. She looked almost gleeful as she spoke, no hint of her earlier frustration present, but she could not hide her heartbreak from him. He could see it in subtle ways—eyes that were not bright enough, a smile that was not wide enough, shoulders that were not tall enough.

"Welcome," she said. "Lord Hades is honored to reveal this year's charity, The Halcyon Project."

The lights dimmed, and a screen lowered, playing a short video about the project. Hades was not sentimental, but this was a project that felt like his whole heart. Maybe that was because it was inspired by Persephone, or that he had been heavily involved in the design of the building, choosing the technology, and the services the facility would provide. Each time Katerina, the director of his foundation, would ask him questions, he answered them thinking of Persephone. It was his hope that she would be proud of this, that she would see how much her words meant to him.

Hades made his way on stage in the dark, and when the lights came up, he stood before a crowd that cheered at the sight of him. As they quieted, he spoke.

"Days ago, an article was published in *New Athens News*. It was a scathing critique of my performance as a god, but among those angry words were suggestions on how I could be better. I don't imagine the woman who wrote it expected me to take those ideas to heart, but in spending time with her, I started to see things her way." He smirked, chuckling, thinking of how fierce she could be when defending mortals. "I've never met anyone who was so passionate about how I was wrong, so I took her advice and initiated The Halcyon Project. As you move though the exhibit, it is my hope that Halcyon will serve as a flame in the dark for the lost."

Gods and mortals alike shot to their feet, clapping, and Hades retreated, uncomfortable with the spotlight. He wanted to dematerialize into darkness for the rest of the evening, but he also wanted to know what Persephone thought of the project. He stood aside as a line of people made their way into the exhibit, eyes catching Aphrodite's, who glared at him, probably having not forgiven him for the threat he had leveled at Adonis.

He averted his gaze and searched for Persephone, finding her at her table. He recognized the look on her face, as he had seen it the first time she had arrived at Nevernight.

She was hesitating.

She did not approach until almost everyone had gone inside, and as she did, Hades followed, calling up his glamour to walk beside her. It felt intrusive to observe her this way, but also intimate, and he marveled at the serene expression on her face as she took her time wandering through the exhibit, stopping at each poster to look at concept drawings of the building and gardens, statistics about the current state of addiction and mental health in New Greece, and how those numbers had only increased since The Great War.

She lingered the longest at a 3D printed model of the actual building and expansive grounds, full of trees and gardens and secret pathways. He thought about approaching her, but there was something beautiful about the look on her face—something contemplative and gentle —and he did not want to disturb her, so he left.

Outside the exhibit, Hades found his brother, Zeus. The God of Thunder grinned, looking more like the ancient King of the Gods than the modern man he usually attempted to embody, standing half-dressed beside Hera.

"Well played, brother." He clapped Hades on the back, and the god curled his fingers into a fist to keep from punching him. "You have the entire world swooning over your *compassion*."

"Well done," Hera said, sounding bored. She met Hades' eyes only briefly before craning her neck, looking elsewhere across the room, her arm still looped through her husband's.

"What are you talking about, Zeus?" Hades asked.

"The mortal!" he cried. "Using her slander to your advantage. Genius, really."

Hades glared. He had not seen this as an opportunity to make himself look better and he hated that his brother was corrupting his intentions, but it was not surprising.

"I desire no such praise or attention," Hades said. Persephone had valid points, and he listened.

"Of course you didn't," Zeus quipped, nudging Hades in the side, as if they were sharing some sort of secret. "I must admit, I kept my expectations low when I heard the Gala would be themed after your realm, but this…this is nice."

"What praise," Hades commented blandly. "If you'll excuse me, I need a drink."

Hades sidestepped his brother and Hera, and headed straight for the bar. He ordered a whiskey and downed it quickly, wondering how much longer he needed to stay here. It was not as if these people came for him or even the charity. It was about the fashion, the drinking, the dancing, the fun, except this was not Hades' idea of fun. He had wanted to spend the night between Persephone's legs, giving and receiving pleasure.

At that thought, he turned, and found the object of his scandalous thoughts a few steps away. His eyes were immediately drawn to her bare back, and he thought of how she had arched against him in the pool, desperate for pleasure. He approached, and he knew she felt him because she straightened and turned her head so that he could see the side of her face—delicate nose and pretty lips.

"Anything to critique, Lady Persephone?" he asked.

"No," she said quietly, thoughtfully. "How long have you been planning The Halcyon Project?"

"Not long."

"It will be beautiful."

He leaned close, fingers skimming her shoulder, tracing the edges of the black appliqué that snaked down her back. She was warm, her skin soft, and she shivered each time they touched skin to skin.

"A touch of darkness," he murmured, fingers trailing down the inside of her arm until they tangled with her own. "Dance with me."

She turned to face him, head tilted so that their gazes met. He could see clear to her bright soul, and his darkness was drawn to it.

"All right."

He drew her hand to his lips, kissing her knuckles before leading her to the floor. He pulled her close, their hips touching, and he growled low in his throat. His cock grew taut, reminding him of the baths and how much he wanted to be inside her. He wondered what sort of headlines would splash across the media if he kissed her now and took her to the Underworld.

Hades abducts Persephone, he thought, fingers tightening around hers and her hip as he guided her through a dance, their gazes unwavering, the heat between them building, an inferno that became as cold as ice when she spoke.

"You should be dancing with Minthe."

He gritted his teeth. "Would you prefer that I dance with her?"

"She's your date."

"She is not my date." He had to work to control his frustration. "She is my assistant, as I have told you."

"Your assistant doesn't arrive on your arm to a gala."

He recognized Hecate's words as she spoke and seethed.

"You are jealous," Hades said, smirking.

"I'm not jealous!" Her eyes flashed. "I will not be used, Hades."

He frowned. "When have I used you?"

She stayed silent, her frustration palpable.

"Answer, goddess."

"Have you slept with her?"

He froze, and so did everyone else who shared the floor.

"It sounds like you are requesting a game, goddess."

"You want to play a game?" She jerked her hands away from his. "Now?"

It was the only way he would answer her question, and she knew it. He held out his hand for her to take, eyes

216

alight, begging her to reestablish their connection.

Come with me to the Underworld, he thought. *You will not come back the same.*

He knew when she had made her decision, because her gaze became fierce and determined—she would have what she wanted. Then, her fingers curled into his, and he smiled, teleporting to the Underworld.

CHAPTER XX – A GAME
OF PASSION

Hades appeared in his office, hand still twined with Persephone's. His body was tight with anticipation, and his mind whirled with the possibilities of this night. Why had she been so eager to know about his relationship with Minthe? If he answered, would she succumb to him?

They stared at one another for a moment, and Hades released her hand, fingers trailing her palm. He reached to untie her mask. The movement felt intimate but right, and he had never felt so much longing. It curled in the bottom of his stomach and made his throat feel tight.

"Wine?" he asked as he approached the bar, removing his own cumbersome mask.

"Please." She spoke quietly, and his chest felt heavy as he imagined that word poised upon her tongue as she begged him to fill her.

He poured her a glass and slid it toward her. She took it, her graceful fingers curling around the stem as she sipped. Hades watched her a moment, distracted by her mouth and the way her tongue snuck out to moisten her lips. Her gaze burned his skin, eyes starved.

"Hungry?" he asked. "You barely ate at the gala."

Her eyes narrowed. "You were watching me?"

"Darling, don't pretend you weren't watching me. I know your gaze upon me like I know the weight of my horns."

She averted her eyes, blushing. "No, I'm not hungry."

Pity, he thought, pouring himself a glass of whiskey.

They found themselves on opposite ends of a table before the fireplace, a deck of cards sat at the center.

"The game?" she asked as Hades reached for the cards.

"Poker," he replied, opening the box and shuffling the cards.

She took a breath. "The stakes?"

At her question, the air thickened, and Hades offered a smile. "My favorite part. Tell me what you want."

"If I win, you answer my questions."

He knew it was the bet she would make.

"Deal," he said as he finished shuffling the cards. "If I win, I want your clothes."

If she was shocked, she did not show it. "You want to undress me?"

"Darling, that's only the start of what I want to do to you."

Had he imagined the quirk of her lips? "Is one win equal to a piece of clothing?"

"Yes," he said, eyeing her dress—that glorious piece of satin fabric. He hoped it was the only thing she wore. Then her hand drew his attention, brushing the chain of her necklace where it dipped between her breasts.

"And...what about jewelry? Do you consider that undressing?"

He sipped his drink. "That depends."

"On?"

"I might decide I want to fuck you with that crown on."

There was no guessing at her smirk now; it curved across her beautiful face, full of mischief. "No one said anything about fucking, Lord Hades."

"No? Pity."

She leaned over the table, offering him a full view of her breasts. He groaned inwardly. "I'll accept your bargain."

His brows rose. "Confident in your ability to win?"

"I'm not afraid of you, Hades."

Never, he thought. He would never want her to fear him, even in his darkest moments. The problem was, she had never seen him that way—angry and aggressive and violent. The truth of that statement remained to be seen.

Persephone shivered.

"Cold?" he asked, dealing the first hand.

"Hot," she rasped and smiled, eyes full of passion.

Hades laid his cards down—a pair of kings.

It was the set of her lips that told him she had lost, and he had confirmation when she laid her cards down. He smiled, and lust ran through his veins, straight to his cock. He assessed her, taking his time scanning her body, deciding what he would take.

"I suppose I will have the necklace."

When she reached to unfasten it, he stopped her. "No, let me."

She dropped her hands into her lap as Hades approached. His fingers tingled as he gathered her thick hair in his hands, sweeping it over her shoulder. He unclasped the chain, letting the metal fall between her breasts, liking the way she inhaled as he kissed along her collarbone.

"Still hot?" he asked against her skin.

"An inferno."

He could practically smell her sex.

"I could free you from this hell." His lips trailed up the column of her neck.

"We're just getting started," she whispered.

His disappointment was heavy, and yet not as burdensome as the pressure building in his cock. He managed a laugh and pulled away, ready for another hand, already thinking of what he would request next.

Except that Persephone won.

She smirked as she placed the cards on the table.

Hades was not pleased, more impatient than anything. He wanted her naked, spread before him. He wanted to be balls-deep inside her. "Ask your question, goddess. I am eager to play another hand."

He knew what she would say, and he wanted to get it out of the way.

"Have you slept with her?"

He hated this question because it reminded him of a different version of himself. One that felt hopeless and dispassionate. One that sought to rekindle any sense of belonging and need, and he had turned to Minthe. He was not proud, but he knew she would be willing.

It was a decision he regretted, not only because of his insincerity but because he had been unfair to her. He had given her hope when he had no intention of establishing a relationship with her, and that was exactly what she had expected and in the aftermath of their coupling, then he had told her she would never sit beside him as queen.

So he answered the question, a bitter taste on his tongue.

"Once."

She paled visibly and Hades suddenly understood the emotion Persephone had invested in this question. It meant something to her that he had been with this woman, but would it mean she would deny him?

"How long ago?"

"A very long time ago, Persephone."

He could not ask her to wait another round for the answer. It did not seem fair when it was so important to her.

At hearing this, she looked away.

"Are you...angry?" he asked.

"Yes." He was surprised by her honesty, surprised when she met his gaze and expressed her confusion. "But...I don't know why exactly."

He tried to imagine what must be going through her

head, but when he found himself thinking of her fucking another man, he decided it was the wrong course of action. The thought only served to call up his violence. So he focused on the cards instead, dealing another hand.

This time, he won, and he reclined in his chair, considering the goddess before him. There was not much to commandeer, but it was not so much the taking he enjoyed. It was the tension that ignited the air between them as he considered, and she waited. Finally, he stood and Persephone straightened as he approached, neck straining to hold his gaze.

"I will take the earrings, my darling."

She was not breathing. He knew because as he leaned toward her, her chest did not move, so as his lips brushed her ear, he whispered, "Breathe."

And he was rewarded with her sharp exhale. He proceeded to wrap his lips around her earrings and pry them from her ears, catching the backs in his hand. Once they were out, he drew his tongue over the spot, and grazed it with his teeth, noting that her hands gripped the edge of the table.

As he returned to his seat for the next round, he prayed to the Fates who had gifted this woman, and could take her away, that this was the last round. *Let me have her.* Here, now, on this very table where they had agreed to bargain for clothing and answers and the rest of their lives.

Except the Fates granted no such prayer—or relief for Hades' raging hard-on—because Persephone won.

"Your power of invisibility," she began, eyeing him as if she expected him to be surprised that she knew. "Have you ever used it…to spy on me?"

Hades considered her question carefully, particularly the word *spy*. It was a word that, in this context, sounded like an accusation, and he had a feeling it didn't come from this evening when he had lingered beside her as she explored the exhibit. That was a different sort of intimacy.

This question had its roots in the night when Hades had watched Persephone masturbate—when he, too, had pleasured himself at the sight.

In truth, he had not been using invisibility, but a different power that involved projecting the soul. Besides, could it really be called spying if she knew he was there?

"No," he finally answered.

"And will you promise to never use invisibility to spy on me?"

It was not the only method he could use to keep tabs on her, and if he had to give one up, it might as well be invisibility. He hoped that soon, wherever she went, she would want his presence.

"I promise."

His hands flexed over the cards as Persephone asked another question. "Why do you let people think such horrible things about you?"

As he shuffled the cards, he considered not answering, but decided he would entertain her...and distract himself from the source of his discomfort growing between his legs.

"I do not control what people think of me."

"But you do nothing to contradict what they say about you." She seemed irritated about this, which intrigued Hades.

He raised a brow. "You think words have meaning?"

A line appeared between her brows, and he dealt another hand.

"They are just that—words. Words are used to spin stories and craft lies, and occasionally, they are strung together to tell the truth."

The world was built on words—the words of gods, the words of enemies, the words of lovers.

"If words hold no weight for you, what does?"

When he met her gaze, he felt the whole world shift and approached her. She held his gaze, the air between them morphing into something hot and heavy. Hades let his eyes fall to his cards as he spread them on the table before her—a royal flush.

"Action, Lady Persephone." His voice rasped, a match

igniting. "Action holds weight for me."

She rose to meet him, their lips colliding, arms and tongues entangling. Their movements were frenzied, like they could not come together fast enough or hard enough. Finally, Hades gripped her hips and turned to sit, dragging her into his lap so that she straddled him. He had the fleeting thought that this dress she wore was made for sex as he drew the straps down her arms, exposing her breasts, kneading them until her nipples were taut. Persephone gasped, biting down on his lip, eliciting a growl from deep in his throat. Her hips rolled against his, and for a brief moment, he helped her move, enjoying the friction the movement elicited. But her breasts pressed against him, and he found himself drawn there, taking each perfect globe in his hand and devouring them with his mouth. Persephone offered a satisfying moan, her head lolling back and forth, her fingers running recklessly through his hair until it hung loose around his face. Soon, the only thing he could hear was her heavy breathing, her precious moans, her frustrated growls, and he moved, hauling her onto the table, hands on her knees spreading them as wide as they would go.

They stared at one another, Persephone elevated on her elbows, Hades bent over her.

"I have thought of you every night since you left me in the baths," he said, pressing his erection into her heat, and his voice dipped, clouded with the desire he felt. "You left me desperate, swollen with need only for you." He paused and pressed a kiss to her knee. "But I will be a generous lover."

He trailed kisses down the inner part of her thigh, following with his tongue until he reached her center. There, he pried her apart, exposing her sensitive pink flesh and her aching clit, and touched it with his tongue, circling it, before licking down her slit. She writhed beneath him, and reached for him, but he clasped her wrists and held them at her sides, looking up at her from his place between her legs.

"I said I would be a generous lover, not a kind one."

He returned to her sex, skimming with his tongue, lapping at her heat, sinking inside her, all the while he held her hips in place, pressing into her, spurred on by her wicked moans. Soon, his fingers joined his tongue, sinking deep into her heat. She was a furnace, and her muscles clenched around him as he worked, moving in and out while he took her clit into his mouth until she came apart, calling his name.

He wasted no time dragging her to his mouth. He wanted her to taste her need on his lips. As their mouths collided, her hands went to the buttons on his shirt, but before she could work them free, he stopped her, drawing away and fixing her dress.

"What are you doing?"

For a moment, he saw fear flash in her eyes, as if she thought he might leave.

He was far too selfish.

"Patience, darling,"

He gathered her into his arms and strolled out of his study, into the palace halls.

"Where are we going?" she asked.

"To my chambers," he said.

"And you can't teleport?"

"I'd prefer the whole palace know we aren't meant to be disturbed."

It was a ridiculous display of masculinity, a primal show of his claim to her, but he wanted the whole castle in an uproar over this night, wanted to leave no doubt in the minds of his people that Persephone was untouchable

Once they were inside his chambers, he lowered her to the floor, keeping her close. He studied her, eyes searching, looking for any sign of hesitation. His greatest fear was her regret, and so he gave her an out.

"We don't have to do this," he said.

Her hands flattened on his chest, smoothing over his shoulder until his jacket slid down his arm. It took some maneuvering to tug it over his biceps. Once it was off, she met his gaze.

"I want you. Be my first, be my everything."

He kissed her, sweetly at first, savoring the feel of her lips against his, but Persephone's hands roamed, over his stomach and straight to his cock. She held him, and he kissed her harder, hand gripping the back of her head, prying her mouth open as far as it would go, until he could no longer stand being clothed.

He pulled away and spun her around, unzipping her dress and easing it down her shapely hips until she stood naked before him, wearing only her crown and heels.

He wasn't sure it was possible, but his cock thickened, and his groan was audible. He walked a circle around her, his muscles clenched, fingers flexing. He could not wait to be inside her.

"You are beautiful, my darling."

His hand cupped her neck, and he kissed her while her fingers fumbled with the buttons of his shirt. He took over when she gave a cry of frustration and yanked at the cloth, chuckling as he shrugged out of his shirt.

A hollow hunger erupted in the pit of his stomach, and he reached for her, but she stepped away. Hades halted, jaw tightening, mind jumping to conclusions. Had she decided she did not want this? But how could she look at him like that and still deny him?

"Drop your glamour," she said.

He tilted his head, curious.

She shrugged her bare shoulder. "You want to fuck me with this crown; I want to fuck a god."

Who was he to deny a queen? "As you wish."

His glamour fell away like shadow, revealing his Divine form, a form he did not often take. It wasn't that he disliked his true nature, it was that it seemed to make others uncomfortable. He was not ignorant to his size, and with his spiraling horns, he seemed even bigger. His eyes went from black to an electric blue that had been described as uncanny and unsettling, but that wasn't how he felt when Persephone looked at him. When she looked at him, he felt powerful.

He lifted her from the floor and lowered her to the bed, covering her body with his. He kissed her, lips trailing her neck, her breasts, licking each hard peak as Persephone wiggled beneath him, hands seeking the button of his pants. He chuckled.

"Eager for me, goddess?" he asked as he kissed down her stomach and her thighs until he stood, removing each of her shoes and the rest of his clothes.

When he was naked before her, the air in the room changed, growing thick and hot. Persephone's eyes looked like embers ignited among ash, and they burned his skin as they passed over his body, lingering on his swollen cock. She rose to her knees, fingers wrapping around his shaft. He inhaled sharply between his teeth, and she looked up at him as if to ask *is this okay?*

His hand tangled into her hair as she stroked him, her thumb playing with the moisture that gathered at the tip. Then she kissed him there and took him into her mouth. His fingers tightened in her hair.

"Fuck."

His cock was sheathed in warmth that sent a rush to his head. Her tongue slid against his shaft, teasing and tasting, putting pressure in the right places. For a while, she paid close attention to the very tip, rolling her tongue there, and he gripped her head harder, his other braced against her shoulder. He had the fleeting thought that he hoped he tasted good for her, but she gave no indication otherwise as she moved him in and out of her mouth, teeth faintly grazing his girth. Soon, his hips moved, and he was pumping into her mouth, gripping her head and holding her gaze until he could take it no longer and pulled her away, keeping a hold on her neck.

"Did I do something wrong?" she asked.

He chuckled darkly, staring into her eyes. "No."

She was perfect. She was everything, and he kissed her again, tongue reaching deep before he pulled away.

"Tell me you want me."

He needed to hear her say it, because he had not completely told the truth. Words did matter, and the only ones he had heard since the night before were the ones she'd spoken on the steps of the baths. *I don't want you.*

"I want you."

He guided her to her back and stretched out over her, her thighs cradling him, his erection pressing into her stomach. He searched her eyes, his fingers brushing her lips as he whispered. "Tell me you lied."

"I thought words meant nothing."

His mouth closed over hers, and as he kissed her, he pressed into her until his shaft ached, until her lips felt raw and swollen against his.

"Your words matter," he said, nose brushing hers. "Only yours."

Her answer was to wrap her legs around his waist and draw him against her heat.

"Do you want me to fuck you?"

Her eyes gleamed, desperate, and she nodded.

"Tell me. You used words to tell me you didn't want me, now use words to say you do."

She spoke, voice low and husky, and it was the most erotic thing he'd ever heard.

"I want you to fuck me."

He kissed her again, hand going to his cock as he teased her opening. Beneath him, Persephone arched, heels digging into his ass.

"Patience, darling. I had to wait for you," he reminded her.

She paused, the pressure of her heels lessening as she offered a quiet apology.

"I'm sorry."

Then he thrust, filling her completely. He groaned as her body clenched around him, and he paused a moment, fully sheathed, head resting in the crook of her neck. When he lifted himself, he found Persephone's hand covering her mouth and removed it.

"No, let me hear this," he said, pinning her wrists over

her head.

She was tense beneath him, but after a moment, relaxed, but the pressure on his cock remained. Her sex held him in a vice-like grip, and as he started to move, he never wanted to stop. She spread her legs wider, and he pushed deeper, as if their souls might meet.

"You left me desperate," he said, pulling out until only the tip of his sex remained. She glared at him, her teeth clenched together until he thrust inside, the ridges of his cock sending pleasure straight to his brain. *This is bliss*, he thought.

"I have thought about you every night since."

He could feel her heart beating, smell the vanilla in her hair, taste her sweat on his tongue as he managed to suckle one of her breasts.

"And each time you said you didn't want me, I tasted your lies."

This is what it is to be a god.

"You are mine."

This is humbling. She let him into her body.

"Mine."

He could feel her come around his cock, a gush of warmth, a convulsion of muscles. He gripped her wrists hard, moving faster, pounding into her harder, until he began to pulse. He pulled out, finishing on her thigh before collapsing on top of her, breathing hard. For a while after, he was lost in the euphoria of the moment. His thoughts tangled with the memories of how they had gotten here—their teasing and touching, bodies coming together, the sounds of their orgasms. Then he began to feel tired, mind numbing from the high.

He met Persephone's gaze and kissed her eyes, cheeks, and lips.

"You are a test, goddess. A trial offered to me by the Fates."

He shifted to leave the bed and was surprised when Persephone reached for his hand.

A line appeared between his brows, and he leaned to

kiss her, promising, "I will come back, my darling."

He disappeared into the adjoining bathroom, cleaned himself up, and then wet a cloth for Persephone. Once she was washed, he laid down beside her again, pulling her warm body against his, and they fell into a deep sleep.

**

Hades woke instantly, his cock hard.

He groaned and rocked into Persephone's warm body, his arousal nesting against her bottom perfectly. He gripped her hips and kissed her neck, and when she turned into him, he climbed on top of her, pinning her wrists over her head so he could tease her with his teeth and lips, reveling in sounds of her breathy moans.

He parted her legs and drank her heat, using his fingers to give her pleasure until she called his name. It made him desperate to be inside her, and he loomed over her body, entering her in one swift push. He moved inside her, and the harder he thrust, the tighter her muscles gripped him.

When he felt close to coming, he switched positions, leaning back on his haunches and bringing her with him. He grasped her hips and helped her move while she held him, her breasts bouncing. Their mouths collided. It was a messy kiss, all tongue and teeth, but it was a mark of the pleasure they shared.

They did not speak, the only sounds coming from their quiet and sleepy lovemaking—breaths and moans and the keen cry of orgasm.

They collapsed, arms and legs tangled, repeating their earlier ritual of washing and burrowing into each other's warmth, and as sleep descended upon Hades, he had the thought that he would tear this world apart if anyone tried to take Persephone from him.

CHAPTER XXI – A MEMORY BRANDED

Hades woke alone.

He sat up, heart pounding in his chest. For a moment, he feared Persephone had realized her mistake and fled in the night, but once the surprise of waking by himself ebbed, he was able to focus on her and knew she remained in the Underworld, her presence as warm and right as her body against his.

With that realization, he stretched, falling back against his pillows, hands behind his head, and basked in memories from last night.

Persephone wasn't the only woman he had slept with, but she was the only one he needed. He had never felt this kind of connection before, and he preferred the intimacy. It made sex with her even better, made all the sensations more intense, the gasps of pleasure more rewarding, the aftermath more tender.

It made him even more determined to ensure their Fate wasn't unraveled, something that was still a possibility with Sisyphus on the run. At the thought of the escaped mortal, Hades sat up, manifesting a piece of cloth to cover himself. He would find that mortal today and end his beating heart. Nothing, not a mortal and not the Fates, would keep him from the euphoria that was Persephone—his lover, his queen, his goddess.

He stepped out onto the balcony and found Persephone wandering the path in the garden. She wore black, and her creamy skin was ablaze against it. He couldn't help thinking how at home she looked among the flowers of the Underworld despite her disdain for them. He knew she envied his magic, even if what he created was not real and had no true life. His flowers did not need sun or water. They did not breathe in or exhale. They simply existed as the souls did, with no purpose save beauty.

But Persephone, she had the ability to create life. Real life. He could sense it within her, the powerful core of her being, caged by disbelief. There would come a day when flowers would bloom in her presence, when her breath would call the wind, when her tears would turn to storms. She would shake the earth and build kingdoms from the rubble.

And he would stand by and watch—a husband, her king.

He headed down the stairs into the garden just in time to see Persephone step off the black stone path, bare feet touching soil, roses and peonies flourishing around her. The colors brought out the warm tones of her skin—pink skin, with red markings from lovemaking, places where his hold had been tight, and faint purple bruising from his mouth. He took in the sight of his woman ravished by his own hand and felt fire build in the bottom of his stomach.

"Are you well?"

He asked because she had not moved since stepping off the path. She twisted toward him when she heard his voice, as if he had startled her. In the early morning of the Underworld, she looked beautiful—eyes wide, wild, sun-kissed hair, parted lips. Her gaze raked down his body, and his blood surged with lust. His fingers curled, a reminder to stay where he was and not close the distance between them. She had yet to answer his question.

"Persephone?"

Her eyes lifted to his, and she smiled. She seemed peaceful, almost languid.

"I'm well," she assured.

Hades exhaled, as if those words had given him permission. He knew he feared her regret, but nothing had prepared him for the physical toll of that anxiety—the tightening in his chest and stomach, and the dread that thickened the back of his throat. He approached, cupping the underside of her jaw.

"You are not regretting our night together?"

"No!" Her quick reply banished his anxious thoughts, and as if she knew he needed to hear it again, she added quietly. "No."

His eyes fell to her lips, and he brushed them with his thumb. "I don't think I could handle your regret."

He felt strangely raw admitting what he'd been thinking moments before, and yet after what they'd shared last night, being vulnerable felt right.

He threaded his fingers through her silky hair as he pressed his lips to hers, insatiable as the desire he felt for her returned tenfold, surging through his veins, thicker than his blood, urging him to touch her, to take her, to fuck her. He didn't feel inclined to play or tease, he gripped her thighs and lifted her off the ground and guided his heavy length to her entrance, bending her backward before thrusting into her. They were close, the energy between them intimate.

For a while, they held each other's gazes, sharing breath and soft moans, but soon they were breathing harder, buried in each other's neck, and as Hades moved, he felt Persephone come. Her sex clenched around his own, and she bit into his skin, which elicited a harsh growl from deep in his throat. It made him feel feral, like a beast who wished to claim. His arms tightened, and he pumped harder, dug deeper, until he came, emptying into her.

In the aftermath, Hades remained standing, still inside

her, holding Persephone close until their breathing returned to normal. When he helped her to the ground, her fingers bit into his arms. He frowned and scooped her up, cradling her against his chest. As he did, she closed her eyes, and he frowned, wondering what she was thinking. Still, he said nothing and asked nothing, returning to his chambers.

Once inside, she opened her eyes.

"Where are we going?" she asked as he made his way to the bathroom.

"To shower," he said.

He half expected her to protest, but she didn't. She let him lower her to her feet in the shower, disrobe her, and wash her. As he worked, passing the washcloth over her calves and between her thighs and over her hips, she braced her hands on his shoulders, shivering as his lips gathered moisture from her skin.

"Hades." She spoke his name, and he stared up at her from the shower floor. "Let me please you."

Her eyes burned into his, and as she spoke, he rose to his feet. His hand came up and cupped her face, his thumb passing over her lip.

"And how would you please me?" he asked.

Her answer was to wrap her hands around his cock, thumb brushing his sensitive head, and lower to her knees.

"Persephone." Her name was rough on his tongue, and he wasn't sure why he said it—as a warning or in prayer. Either way, he didn't feel completely prepared for her mouth, even knowing the sensations she'd coaxed from him the night before. This was somehow different. This was head given in the daylight, a choice that wasn't spurred by frustration or given courage by wine. Her mouth was warm, her tongue teasing, her throat deep. He grasped her head and thrust into her until he came, and savored the sight of her licking him clean.

He helped her to her feet again and devoured her mouth until he could no longer taste the salty sweetness of his come.

They finished their shower and started to dress, when Persephone turned to him, holding the red silk of her gown to her chest.

"Do you...have something I can wear?"

He gave her an appreciative looked and answered, "What you have on will be just fine."

The look she offered was a challenge. "You'd rather I wander your palace naked? In front of Hermes and Charon—"

He'd really rather not spend the day gouging out eyes.

"On second thought..." he said, and teleported to the only place he could to find a dress—Hecate's cottage. When he arrived, the goddess sat at her table, a suite of cards spread before her. She didn't look at Hades as she spoke.

"On the bed."

He turned and found a green peplos waiting. He gathered the fabric and turned to Hecate.

"Have I told you that you're the best?"

"I will note the date and time," she said. "And remind you every chance I get."

Hades chuckled and left, returning to Persephone.

"Will you allow me to dress you?"

She stared at the peplos and then at him. Part of the reason he asked was because he was not sure how often she wore one, and wrapping it might prove difficult, but it was also an excuse to touch her. After a moment, she swallowed and nodded, and Hades thought that just as much as he was reliving the past few hours of his life, she was too.

He set to work, making slow, tedious work of the process, wrapping it around her breasts, over each shoulder. She held the fabric while he pinned, and he pressed kisses to her shoulder, neck, and jaw. As he went in to tie her belt, his mouth descended on hers, and he spent several minutes kissing her, his tongue moving languidly over hers.

Finally, he pulled away, threading his fingers with hers,

and led her to the dining room. It was a room he rarely used, save on very rare occasions when he hosted one of the Divine in his realm. Still, it was meant to impress, with diamond-encrusted chandeliers, gold dining chairs, and an ebony banquet table hewn from obsidian sourced from the Underworld.

"Do you actually eat in here?" Persephone asked. He could not place the tone of her voice, but he got the sense that she felt it was just as outrageous as he did. Still, Hades knew what it was to compete with the gods, and while he detested it, he was not above—or below—illustrating his wealth and power.

Hades smiled at her. "Yes, but not often. I usually take my breakfast to go."

Once they were seated, his staff bustled into the room, bringing trays of fruit, meat, cheese, and bread. Minthe followed. It was impossible for Hades to ignore the distinct tap of her heels against the marble floor. He didn't look at the nymph as she approached, or as she took up space between him and Persephone. He could feel her judgement and her anger, no doubt having heard how he had carried Persephone to his chambers the night before.

"My lord. You have a full schedule today."

"Clear the morning."

"It's already eleven." Her voice was tight, betraying her frustration.

He honestly could not care less about the time or his obligations at this very moment. He had just seen months' worth of agonizing fantasies come to life. This was the morning after, and what a morning it had been already. He was going to enjoy this; he would revel in it as he had reveled in war long ago.

He focused on Persephone, and as he filled his plate, asked, "Are you not hungry, darling?"

"No." She looked at him sheepishly. "I…usually only drink coffee for breakfast."

Somehow, that didn't surprise him. He thought about commenting on the nutrition, how she would need the energy after their night, but decided against it. Instead, he summoned her a cup of coffee.

"Cream? Sugar?"

"Cream," she answered with a smile that made him want to give her the sun and the moon. "Thank you."

"What are your plans today?" he asked, popping a piece of cheese into his mouth.

She was silent for a moment, glancing at Minthe with a sullen expression, but as the silence stretched, her eyes widened as she realized he was talking to her. "Oh, I need to write—"

She stopped abruptly.

"Your article?"

He tried to keep the bitterness from leaking into his voice, but it was hard. He could not deny that he felt a slight betrayal at the thought that she would continue writing, even after the night they shared.

"I will be along shortly, Minthe," he said, dismissing her, but when the nymph hesitated, he spoke firmly. "Leave us."

"As you wish, my lord." Minthe bowed and practically pranced out of the dining room. He almost snapped at her, but stopped himself, thinking, *One battle at a time.*

"So, you will continue to write about my faults?" he asked, once they were alone.

"I don't know what I'm going to write this time," she admitted. "I…"

"You what?" He hadn't meant to snap, but he could not hide his frustration on this topic, and Persephone narrowed her eyes.

"I hoped I might be able to interview a few of your souls."

"The ones on your *list?*" He would never forget that list, would never forget those names, as each one brought a different kind of pain.

"I don't want to write about the Olympian Gala or The Halcyon Project," she explained. "All the other newspapers will jump on those stories."

Of course they would, and she wanted to be unique, wanted to stand out among the crowd. Define herself as she had never been defined before. He knew what she wanted—to be good at something, but not just anything. She wanted to be good at something she *chose*, because she wasn't good at the thing she was born to be. He considered saying that aloud, the words were on the tip of his tongue, but he knew they would hurt her so he wiped his mouth and stood to leave, but Persephone followed after him.

"I thought we agreed we wouldn't leave each other when we're angry?" Her words halted him. "Didn't you request that we work through it?"

He faced her, and replied honestly, "It's just that I'm not particularly excited that my lover is continuing to write about my life."

"It's my assignment," she said defensively. "I can't just stop."

"It wouldn't have been your assignment if you had heeded my request."

She crossed her arms over her chest, and he couldn't help letting his gaze fall there, but what she said held his attention more than her breasts. "You never request anything, Hades. Everything is an order. You ordered me not to write about you. You said there would be consequences."

"And yet," he said, with as much admiration as possible. "You went through with it anyway."

She had not been afraid of him. She was a rare breed.

"I should have expected it." He tipped her head back with a finger. "You are defiant and angry with me."

"I'm not—"

He cut her off, cupping her face. "Shall I remind you that I can taste lies, darling?" He stared at her lips, brushing them with his thumb, and said in a low voice, "I could spend all day kissing you."

"No one's stopping you," she replied, her lips touching his as she spoke.

He chuckled and did as she wished—kissed her. Drawing his arm around her waist, he lifted her onto the table and stepped between her legs. He worked each nipple through her peplos until they were beaded and hard, while his hands dipped between her thighs to explore her satin flesh. Soon she was calling his name, legs spread wide on the edge of his dining table, her head thrown back, leaving her neck taut and exposed. He kissed her there, sucking the skin until it was purple in color, and when she came, he withdrew his fingers and brought them to his mouth.

Hades groaned. "You taste like you belong to me."

A smile tipped the corners of her lips, but she lowered her head and looked away.

"Do not be embarrassed," he said, guiding her chin up so she would meet his gaze. "We will speak as lovers speak."

Her eyes grew dark. "And how do lovers speak?"

He paused a moment and then answered, "Honestly."

She gazed at him, her legs still spread as if inviting him. She looked sweet and feverish.

"You want honesty?" she whispered, voice husky, shivering down his spine. "You once said you would erase the memory of Adonis from my skin. You swore it, seared your own name upon my lips. Now I will do the same. I will erase the memory of every woman from your mind."

Darling, he wanted to say. *You are the only woman in my mind.* But he kept quiet as she swore her oath, his heart and cock swelling with every single fucking word. She drew her legs around his waist, heels digging into his ass.

"I want you inside me," she said. "Fuck me, say my name as you come. Dream of me, and only me, for the rest of eternity."

"Yes," he hissed, as his hips surged forward. It was everything he'd wanted, a prayer answered by the Fates, and as he gave her exactly what she asked for, he prayed to them and threatened them.

Take her, and I will destroy this world. Take her, and I will destroy you. Take her, and I will end us all.

When they left the dining hall, he did so with a smile on his face, and his thoughts on her article aggravated him less, so he felt like that was some sort of victory. He led Persephone outside, their fingers laced, and called for Thanatos.

The God of Death appeared instantly, his pale features glared against his black robes. When he manifested, his expression was severe, and Hades imagined it was because the god had assumed he was being summoned to discuss Sisyphus. The mortal had weighed heavily on both of their minds.

But then his eyes settled on Persephone and softened.

"My lord, my lady." He bowed.

"Thanatos, Lady Persephone has a list of souls she'd like to meet. Would you mind escorting her?"

"I would be honored, my lord."

Hades used their entwined hands to draw her toward him. "I will leave you in Thanatos' care."

"Will I see you later?" she asked, and her blatant hope made him smile.

"If you wish." He brushed his lips over her knuckles, and her cheeks reddened. He chuckled quietly, thinking she had not been so quick to blush when he had lain between her thighs and drank her sweet passion.

Then, he vanished.

CHAPTER XXII – A BITTER BARGAIN

Leaving Persephone was the last thing Hades wanted to do. If Sisyphus did not still roam free, threatening his future with the beautiful Goddess of Spring, he wouldn't have, but the fact remained that the mortal was still on the run, and holding the organization's Magi prisoner had not lured Triad like he thought it might. Hades was unsure of their motives, but he did not feel good about their involvement.

It was inevitable that forces would rise to oppose the gods. They had come in all forms throughout history—scholars and naysayers and atheists and the Impious.

Hades understood the Impious' resentment of the gods. They resented them for their distance and rejected their rule when they came to Earth, and they had reason to. Very few of the gods had done their job, never offering words of prophecy or importance. Hades himself had never encouraged mortals to believe in a blissful eternity in the Underworld. Instead, they spent their time toying with mortals for their entertainment, pitting them against each other in battle.

Still, Triad was different. Triad was organized and their tactics hurt innocent people. In their early life, they had set off bombs in public places, and in the aftermath, demanded to know why the gods had not stopped them if they were all-powerful. Their goal seemed to be to continue to illustrate how the Olympians remained detached and uninterested in mortal society, and while that was true for some, it was not true for all. Something Triad was about to discover.

Hades appeared on the floor of Nevernight. His intention was to find Ilias to begin their search for Theseus, but instead, the satyr found him.

"My lord," Ilias said. "There is a man here to see you. A demi-god who calls himself Theseus."

Hades stiffened at the name, feeling uneasy that his nephew would approach willingly. What was his game?

"Show him in."

Ilias nodded and left, returning with a man who looked more like a warrior stuffed into a suit. He had dark hair, trimmed short, and a perpetual five o'clock shadow. The only thing he had retained of Poseidon's were his aquamarine eyes, which looked like two suns blazing against his brown skin. Two men also followed him. They were large and their discomfort obvious. Hades got the sense he did not need these men to protect him, that they were merely for show.

"You are a man of few words, so I will get straight to the point," Theseus said and, reaching into the pocket of his jacket, he withdrew a spindle—the one Poseidon had given Sisyphus. He held it out to Hades, but the god did not approach to take it. Ilias did, and then handed it to him.

Hades stared at the spindle. It was gold and sharp, and he could feel the Fates' magic radiate from it, distinct in its smell but hard to describe. It was the scent of life—the smell of wet grass after rain and of fresh air and wood, undercut with the odor of smoke and blood and the tinge of death.

It was a scent that triggered Hades and unearthed memories of darkness, battle, and strife. He handed the spindle back to Ilias, wondering what sort of horrors the relic had managed to pull from Sisyphus, even Theseus.

"That is a start," he replied. "But only one of two things I want."

Theseus offered a small smile. "Before we continue, I do believe you have something of mine."

Hades raised a brow at his choice of words but said nothing, summoning the magi with his magic. He appeared and instantly fell to the ground with a loud thud. He groaned, dragging himself to his hands and knees, then looked up and began to whimper.

"H-High lord," his voice quivered.

Theseus looked at one of his men, who took out a gun and shot the mortal. He fell, and his blood pooled on the floor of Nevernight. Hades suddenly understood Theseus' use for the bodyguards; they were here to do his dirty work. The god knew these types of men well—the *no blood on their hands* type. He had come to think that they believed if they did not pull the trigger or wield the knife, he could not trace their sins.

They were wrong.

Hades maintained his passive expression, but internally, he grimaced. The mortal's death was not necessary, nor was it warranted. He had given Hades no information on Triad, which was the reason Hades had detained him.

"Interesting. You did not intervene," Theseus said.

"Were you experimenting?" he asked, raising a brow.

He shrugged. "Just trying to figure out what you are about, Lord Hades."

He just stared. Perhaps Theseus thought to challenge him as Triad challenged the gods, but Hades would not bite. If Theseus and his men wanted to add to their list of sins and carve their place in Tartarus, who was he to stop them?

"Two of one, Theseus," Hades reminded, his patience wearing thin.

It was the first time Hades saw the spark of Poseidon's resentment in Theseus' eyes. He understood the mortal had come to play, had come to show the God of the Dead that he had power. But Hades was power, and he was not in the mood to entertain this man who played at being a god, even if he was semi-Divine.

Theseus nodded to one of his men, who spoke into a mic. After a moment, a third man joined them, dragging Sisyphus, and dropped him in the space between them. His mouth was taped shut, his wrists and legs bound. He looked like Hades remembered, but older—the result of using magic that did not belong to him.

Despite the gag around his mouth, Sisyphus managed a muffled scream.

"Silence," Hades said, and stole the man's voice. His eyes widened when he could no longer make sound, and he kicked and flopped on the floor, like a fish out of water.

Once there was silence, Hades lifted his gaze to Theseus. Something wasn't right about this.

"What is it you want?" Hades asked.

He was not ignorant. He could see Theseus was eager for power and hungry for control. His soul was an iron tower, strong and unshakable. It was why he had kidnapped Sisyphus—he desired something from him. Hades understood that now.

"For returning the spindle, I would like a favor." He paused, then added, "For Sisyphus, I ask for nothing."

"How generous."

He smirked, but the amusement did not touch his eyes. "How kind of you to say."

Hades considered Theseus' request. He did not feel comfortable offering him a favor, as it was an open-ended request, something Hades would be obligated to fulfill due to the binding nature of favors and immortal blood.

Yet a favor was no unfitting request for what the immortal had returned to him. He had essentially ensured his future with Persephone.

Still, Hades found that he had questions.

His eyes narrowed as he stated, "You are Divine, and yet I hear you lead Triad."

"Are you asking a question, my lord?"

"I am merely trying to suss out what you stand for."

That smile returned, and Hades knew why he disliked it so much. It was a smile that belonged to his brother.

"Freewill, freedom—"

"Not Triad," Hades said, cutting him off. "You. What do *you* stand for?"

"Can you not see?" he challenged.

Yes, Hades wanted to hiss. *I see your soul.* Corrupt. Hungry for power, just as his father but without the failure, and that made him dangerous because it made him feel invincible.

"I am merely wondering what the difference is between your rule and mine."

"There are no rulers in Triad."

Hades cocked a brow. "No? Tell me, what is your title again? High lord?"

Hades knew what was happening here. He recognized Theseus' ambition, because his brothers had shared it on the cusp of Titanomachy.

"Are the other high lords demi-gods too?" Hades tilted his head, narrowing his eyes. "Have you hope of ushering in a new legion of Divinity?"

"Feeling threatened, uncle?" Theseus asked.

Hades offered a wicked smile, and he saw Theseus' confidence wavier.

"Hubris is always punished, Theseus. If not in life, always in death."

"Rest assured, uncle, if Nemesis welcomes me upon my death, it shall not be a punishment, but confirmation that I have lived as I wished. Can you say the same? A tortured god with an eternal existence, whose chance at love hinges upon this mortal's capture?" Theseus paused. "I'll take that favor now."

Hades ground his teeth so hard, he thought they might break.

"I will grant your request," Hades said. "But it will not be Nemesis who greets you upon your death."

He would, and he would revel in the process of torturing this immortal who had used Persephone as leverage. He would separate skin from body and watch as crows feasted upon the remains.

With the promise of a favor, Theseus left. Hades' gaze fell to Sisyphus, who was trying to push himself away from the god.

"You should not have granted him such a gift," Ilias said. "You do not know what he will ask."

"I know what he will ask for," Hades said.

"And what is that?"

"Power," Hades replied. Raw power in any form, and with a favor to hang over Hades' head, he had it.

Hades' bent toward Sisyphus, and as he spoke, the mortal began to quiver.

"Welcome to Tartarus."

***

Hades teleported to Hephaestus' lab. Normally, he would arrive via the front gates and pay his respects to Aphrodite, but since La Rose, he had not wished to see her, and he did not wish for her to hear what he had come to ask for. He found the god at his forge, his large body hulked before an open-mouthed furnace that spit fire and sparks as he hammered on a flat piece of metal—a sword—gripped between a pair of tongs. Hades could tell by the set of the god's shoulders and the force with which he worked that he was angry.

The sight made him apprehensive, so he rang a bell near the door to get the god's attention. Hades was not surprised when Hephaestus twisted and threw the flat piece of metal he'd been hammering in his direction.

Hades sidestepped as it landed in the wall behind him.

There was a beat of silence, and then Hades asked, "Are you okay?"

Hephaestus' chest rose with his breath. "Yes."

The god threw his tongs down and turned fully to him. "What can I help you with, Lord Hades? Another weapon?"

"No," Hades replied. "Are you sure you don't need a minute?"

Hephaestus' stare was hard. Hades took that as a no.

"I do not wish for a weapon," he said. "I wish for a ring."

Hephaestus did not appear as if he cared, though his voice betrayed his surprise. "A ring? An engagement ring?"

"Yes," he said.

Hephaestus studied him for a long moment. Hades wondered what he was thinking. Perhaps, *Who would marry you?* Or something even more cynical. *Do not do it, it isn't worth it.*

Still, even Hades knew Hephaestus did not believe that. He knew that now more than ever, after the god had used the Chains of Truth to ask Hades if he was sleeping with Aphrodite.

"Do you have a design?"

Hades felt the unfamiliar rush of embarrassment as he withdrew a piece of paper upon which he had sketched an image. It was similar to the crown Ian had made for Persephone, only he had chosen fewer flowers and gems—tourmaline and dioptase.

He handed the drawing to Hephaestus.

"When are you planning to propose?"

"I cannot say," Hades said. He had not thought of a date or time when he would ask Persephone to be his wife. He had just felt that asking for the ring, creating the ring, was important. "There is no rush, if that is what you are asking."

"Very well," Hephaestus said. "I will summon you when it is complete."

Hades nodded and left the forge, only to find his way blocked by Hermes.

"No," Hades said immediately.

Hermes mouth opened in offense. "You don't even know what I was going to say!"

"I know why you're here. You only have two purposes, Hermes, and since you are not guiding souls to the Underworld, you must be here to tell me something I don't want to hear."

Hades pushed past him, and Hermes followed.

"I'll have you know I am offended," Hermes said. "I am not just a guide or a messenger; I'm also a thief."

"Forgive the oversight," Hades said.

"I thought you'd be in a better mood," Hermes said. "Having finally buried the weasel, got your bone honed, launched the meat missile…"

"Enough!" Hades snapped, turning to the god whose eyes sparkled with amusement. "Why are you here?"

He grinned. "We've been summoned to council in Olympia. Someone's getting in trouble for stealing Helios' cows, and guess what? It's not me this time!"

CHAPTER XXIII – OLYMPIA

Hades was not looking forward to council. He hated his fellow Olympians, and he hated the pageantry and the drama. He would much rather spend his evening with Persephone, buried inside her, exploring her body again, discovering new ways to fuck her that pleasured them both. Instead, he would be forced to sit through council, to hear his brothers argue, to hear Athena attempt peace, to hear Ares demand war, and he would have to face Demeter, knowing he'd fucked her daughter.

He sighed and materialized in the Garden of the Gods on the campus of New Athens University, using his magic to locate Persephone.

He found her faster this time, and he thought it might have something to do with the faint echo of power inside her. His darkness was drawn to that light, wanting to embrace it and foster it.

He teleported her to him. As soon as she appeared, he gripped her by the neck and kissed her. She made a sound in the back of her throat that encouraged him to part her lips and bury his tongue in her mouth. He wanted the taste of her upon his lips when he arrived in Olympia; it would be a wicked secret he would take with him.

He pulled away reluctantly, nipping at her bottom lip.

"Are you well?"

"Yes," she answered, breathless. "What are you doing here?"

He smiled, almost sad, eyes falling to her lips again. He should answer with the whole truth, even the part where he'd been thinking about fucking her in this garden.

"I came to say goodbye."

"What?" Her voice was sharp. Clearly, she had not expected that, but her surprise made him chuckle. He liked the idea that she would be disappointed in his absence. Perhaps that would mean a passionate reunion.

"I must go to Olympia for council."

"Oh." She frowned. "How long?"

"If I have anything to say about it, a day and no more."

He was not like the other Olympians, who would stay for parties and revelry.

"Why wouldn't you have a say?" she asked.

"It depends on how much Zeus and Poseidon argue," Hades replied, rolling his eyes. As he did, he caught sight of what she was holding. A copy of the *Delphi Divine* with a bold, black title that read, "God of the Underworld Credits Journalist for The Halcyon Project." Hades snatched it from her arms, where it was stacked atop her books, skimming the first few lines.

Hades, God of the Dead, astounded everyone Saturday night when he announced a new initiative, The Halcyon Project, a rehabilitation facility for mortals to be completed in the next year. The state-of-the-art facility will be located on ten acres of land and cater to a variety of mental health needs. Lord Hades went on to say his generosity was inspired by a mortal, Persephone Rosi, the journalist responsible for writing and releasing a scandalous article about the King of the Underworld. Now people are asking just how legitimate Rosi's claims were, or is the God of the Underworld merely in love?

Hades' jaw tightened. This was why he hated the media

—they could never stick to facts. They had to include speculation and commentary, and worse, he knew these words were getting to Persephone because of her question.

"Is this why you announced The Halcyon Project at the gala? So people would focus on something other than my assessment of your character?"

"You think I created The Halcyon Project for my reputation?" He tried to keep the disappointment and anger from entering his voice, but it was a challenge. She should know he of all people cared nothing for what others thought of him. She was the exception.

She shrugged her shoulder. "You didn't want me to continue writing about you. You said so yesterday."

It took him a moment to speak, a moment to relax his jaw so the words could form on his lips.

"I didn't start The Halcyon Project in hopes that the world would admire me. I started it because of you."

"Why?"

"Because I saw truth in what you said," he snapped. "Is that really so hard to believe?"

She did not answer, and Hades hated the way this made him feel. Like something heavy was sitting on his chest. Perhaps he had been wrong to come here to say goodbye, or to think their reunion would be sweet.

"My absence will not affect your ability to enter the Underworld," he said, preparing to leave. "You may come and go as you please."

Something changed in her expression, and he sensed that she suddenly felt just as desolate as he did. She stepped into him, reaching for the lapels of his jacket, her hips pressing into his. He wanted to groan, but he settled for wrapping his hands around her wrists.

"Before you go, I was thinking I'd like to throw a party in the Underworld…for the souls."

He raised a brow, eyes searching hers.

"What kind of party?"

"Thanatos tells me souls will reincarnate at the end of

the week and that Asphodel is already planning a celebration. I think we should move it to the palace."

She was referring to the Ascension. It was an event that took place about every three months, a time when souls who were ready would be reborn. The residents of Asphodel always celebrated, as it symbolized new life, a second chance.

"We?" Hades asked.

He liked the way Persephone bit her lip. "I'm asking you if I can plan a party in the Underworld."

He blinked, slightly confused. How had they gotten here? She'd just questioned his motives for The Halcyon Project, yet she was now planning to celebrate with his people in his realm.

"Hecate has already agreed to help," she added, as if that would sway him, her palms flattening on his chest.

That amused him, and his brows rose. "Has she?"

"Yes. She's thinking we should have a ball."

He was not doing a good job focusing on the words coming out of her mouth. The only one he really heard was *we*, and she kept using it. He wanted to use it, too. *We should go to bed. We should make love for hours. We should bathe together and fuck some more.*

"Are you trying to seduce me so I'll agree to your ball?" he asked.

"Is it working?"

He smirked and wrapped his arms around her waist, drawing her against him, pressing his hard length into her stomach.

"It's working," he whispered against her ear, lips brushing down the side of her neck before closing over her mouth. His hands moved over her bottom, and he cupped her ass, pressing into her. When he released her, her eyes were alight with desire, and he wondered if she would pleasure herself tonight, thinking of him inside her. He knew he would.

"Plan your ball, Lady Persephone."

"Come home soon, Lord Hades."

He smiled at her words before vanishing and held onto them as he appeared in the shadows of the golden-floored Council Chamber, where the gods were gathered. Columns lined the room in the shape of an oval, and within those columns, were twelve thrones, one for each of the Olympians. They were all distinct in creation, composed of symbols unique to the gods.

Zeus' sat at the head of the oval upon a throne made of oak, a thunderbolt and a gold scepter crossed on the back. His eagle, a golden bird, was perched upon the scepter, his name Aetos Dios. He was a spy Hades would prefer to roast on a spit, but he'd rather not be the cause of drama at council, so he refrained. Zeus looked the most like their father, a large man with wavy hair and a full beard. Upon his head, he wore a crown of oak leaves, one of his many symbols.

Beside him sat Hera. She was beautiful but rigid, and Hades always thought she looked uncomfortable beside her husband, something Hades could not really blame her for. The God of the Skies was known for fornicating across eternity, and descending to the modern world had made no difference. The Goddess of Women sat in a throne of gold, save for the back, which resembled the colorful feathers of a peacock—brilliant iridescent blue, turquoise, and green.

Next came Poseidon, whose throne looked like his weapon, the trident, made for him before the Battle of Titanomachy by the three Elder Cyclopes. Beside him was Aphrodite, whose throne mimicked a shell, pink in color and draped with pearls and blush-colored flowers. Then came Hermes, whose throne was gold, the back made to look like his herald's wand—a winged staff with two snakes intertwined.

After, was Hestia, Goddess of the Hearth, whose throne was ruby red and made in the form of flames. Ares flanked her, sitting upon a pile of skulls, some white and others yellowed from age. They were all from people—mortal and immortal—and monsters he'd killed.

Beside him was Artemis, to her great dismay, as she—no one—got along with Ares. Her throne was simple, a gold-toned half-moon. Beside her sat Apollo, whose seat mimicked the sun's rays in the form of a glimmering aureole circling behind him. Next was Demeter, whose seat looked more like a moss-covered tree, rich with white and pink flowers, and ivy spilling to the floor. Beside her, Athena, whose throne was a set of silver and gold wings. She sat, beautiful and poised, face expressionless, crowned with a gold circlet set with blue sapphires. Lastly, between the throne of Athena and Zeus, was Hades', a black obsidian seat made of lethal, jagged edges, much like his in the Underworld.

The only god who spoke was Zeus, and everyone else looked angry or bored, except Hermes. Hermes looked amused.

Probably still laughing at his joke, Hades thought.

Hades wasn't sure what Zeus was talking about, but he thought he must be telling a story because he was saying, "I mean, I am not an unreasonable god, so I said—"

Hades stepped out from his hiding spot and walked down the center of the oval. Zeus' voice boomed, echoing all around.

"Hades! Late as usual, I see."

He ignored his brother's judgement and took the seat beside him.

"You are aware of the allegations against you?" the God of the Skies asked.

Hades just stared. He wasn't going to make this easy. He knew there would be repercussions for his actions and could admit that his choice to steal Helios' cattle was petty, but Helios had prevented Hades from Divine Judgement. Wasn't the Titan only here by the grace of Zeus himself?

"He says you stole his cattle," Zeus continued. "And he is threatening to plunge the world into eternal darkness if you do not return them."

"Then we shall have to launch Apollo into the sky," Hades said.

The God of Music and the Sun glared. "Or you can give Helios' cattle back. Why take them anyway? Don't you condemn the rest of us for such...*trivial* behavior?"

"Do not be too hard on Hades. It is how he feels he must act, given he is the most dreaded among us." Those were Hera's words, and they made Hades clench his jaw.

"Not anymore!" Zeus boomed. "Our resident grump has gone and fallen in love with a mortal. He has the whole world *swooning*."

Zeus laughed, but no one else did. Hades sat, his fingers curled over the edges of his throne, the obsidian biting into his skin. He could feel the anger radiate from Demeter. None of these gods save Hermes knew Persephone's true origins. He wondered if the God of Lightening would laugh, knowing Hades had fallen in love with a goddess. There were greater implications when gods united, because it meant sharing power.

"Be kind, Father." It was Aphrodite who spoke, her voice dripped with sarcasm, her anger over Adonis still apparent. "Hades does not know the difference between attention and love."

"Do you speak from experience, Aphrodite?" Hades challenged.

Her expression turned sullen, and she crossed her arms over her chest, sinking into her seat.

His response to Aphrodite silenced the rest, because as much as they liked to make fun, they knew Hades was dangerous. Stealing Helios' cattle had been a kindness, revenge in its most basic form. If he had wanted to, he could have plunged the world into darkness himself. Helios need not threaten it.

"You will return his cattle, Hades," Zeus said.

Again, Hades said nothing. He would not argue with Zeus in front of the other gods.

"Since we are assembled. Are there any other matters you wish to bring forth?"

This was the part Hades dreaded. Council was only supposed to be four times a year, and yet Zeus would call it for a trivial reasons and then ask to hear grievances, as if he had nothing better to do than mediate arguments between Poseidon and Ares—the only two who ever spoke.

Except this time.

"Triad is being led by demi-gods," Hades said, and he looked at Poseidon as he spoke. "I have reason to believe they are planning a rebellion."

This time, Zeus was not the only one to laugh. Poseidon, Ares, Apollo, even Artemis laughed.

"If they wish for battle, I will bring it," Ares said, always eager for bloodshed. Hades hated him, hated his lust for death and destruction. He knew not one other god who wished to revel in the horror of war.

"I suppose you laugh because you think it is impossible. But our parents believed the same of us and look where we sit," Hades said.

"Do I hear fear in your voice?" Ares challenged.

"I am the God of the Dead," Hades said. "Who am I to fear battle? When you all die, you come to me and face my judges, the same as any mortal."

Silence followed his statement.

"It would take great power for these demi-gods to defeat us," Artemis said. "Where would they get it?"

From Divine favor, Hades thought but did not say.

"We are no longer living in the ancient world," Athena said. "There are weapons other than magic at their disposal."

It was true, and the longer mortals studied the magic of the gods, the more they understood how to harness it and potentially use it against them.

"I'm merely stating that it would be in our best interest to observe," Hades said. "Triad will grow in numbers and strength if their high lords are as predictable as I think."

"And who are these high lords?" Zeus asked.

Hades looked to Poseidon, and Zeus' gaze followed, eyes narrowing. "Is this some scheme of yours, brother?"

"How dare you!" Poseidon's fists clenched the arms of

his throne, cracking the shell it was made from.

"You've tried to take my throne before, you meddlesome prick!"

"Prick? Who are you calling a prick? Need I remind you, brother, just because you sit upon the throne as King of the Gods does not mean I am less powerful."

Suddenly, everyone was glaring at him, save Zeus and Poseidon, who were locked in a verbal battle. Hades just chuckled.

"Imagine this as your torture in Tartarus," he said. "For it is the sentence you'll all receive for making me sit through this fuckery."

Hours later, Hades found himself in Zeus' office. It was a traditional space, furnished with a large oak desk that sat before a set of bookcases lined with leather-bound volumes he most definitely used for show. Large windows overlooked Zeus' vast estate, where he kept a heard of bulls, cows, sheep, and swans. That was where Hades stood, while Zeus poured them a drink.

"So you stole Helios' cattle," Zeus said.

"He prevented me from carrying out Divine Judgement," Hades said. "He had to be punished."

"But you agree that his punishment has gone on long enough, yes?"

"If you are asking for confirmation that I will return his cattle, yes." Hades paused. "In due course."

Zeus sighed.

"Helios can threaten darkness all he likes, but he forgets that I am the darkness. It answers to me."

Zeus had nothing to say to that. He took a drink and swished the alcohol in his mouth before saying, "Alright, but if push comes to shove, I'm not intervening."

"I would be offended if you did," Hades replied.

He drained the drink Zeus had offered and sat the glass down with a click, preparing to leave.

"Tell me of this woman who has turned your head."

Hades froze.

"It is as I said at the gala and nothing more."

"I do not believe that is the case," he said. "If this had been any other mortal, you would have sought retribution for the things she said. Instead, you entertain her, dedicate a whole fucking building to her."

"She had valid points," Hades stated, ready to leave.

"And she has caught your eye. Admit it, brother!"

Hades did not.

"Bah! I should not expect you to be vulnerable, though I do wish you happiness."

Hades raised his brows. "Remember those words, brother."

You will not think them long, he thought.

"As such, I feel it is my duty to warn you of the deception of women, mortals in particular."

"Says the god who seduces women in the form of animals."

"That was not deception. I could not approach them in my Divine form, as it is a form mere mortals cannot truly grasp."

And yet none of us have the same issue, Hades thought.

"You disguised yourself because they had already rejected you," Hades countered. "Do not attempt to lie to me, little brother. We both know it is futile."

Zeus' lips flattened, his eyes narrowed.

"Women only want one thing, Hades, and that is power."

Hades had no doubt it was one of several things women wanted, and among them, freedom to exist without worrying about predators like Zeus.

"Perhaps you fear women in power because of the way you use your own—to rape, abuse, and torture."

This conversation had not gone the way Zeus expected, but Hades would not hear his brother speak ill of women.

He turned from him and left his office. Outside, he found himself in a courtyard that was open to the sky. A path cut through the center, flanked by marble statues of nymphs. At the center was a simple fountain in the shape of a hexagon. As Hades started down the path, he was stopped by Demeter, who stepped out from behind one of the columns lining the boundaries of the yard.

She was full of hate for him. It built in her eyes, making them murky in color, like water in a swamp. Hades knew this confrontation would come. While Demeter had been ignorant to her daughter's presence at the gala, she knew Hades spoke of her when he had given his speech, and now it haunted her. She'd probably relived it in every paper, in every magazine, on every news station. She could not even escape the knowledge at council. It was quite possibly the best torture Hades had ever doled out.

"Stay away from my daughter, Hades." Her voice was even but menacing. It was the voice she used to strike fear in the hearts of her nymphs and to curse mortals.

But it only gave Hades pleasure.

"What's the matter, Demeter?" he challenged. "Afraid of the Fates?"

His words were an acknowledgment. *I know of the prophecy*, they said.

"If you truly care for her as you so publicly claim, then walk away," Demeter said. "She stands to lose everything if you do not."

"And those are the actions of someone who cares for her?" Hades asked.

Demeter stepped toward him, her voice shaking. "I am doing this because I care! *You are not right for my daughter.*"

"I think she would disagree."

Demeter glared, and after a moment, she stepped back, laughing. "My daughter would never betray me." Hades got the feeling Demeter was only trying to convince herself of that. "She would never choose you over me."

"Then you have nothing to fear," Hades said.

Except she had everything to fear, because Persephone had already betrayed Demeter. She betrayed her every time she'd come to Nevernight, every time their lips met, every time she put her mouth on his cock, spread her legs, and let him taste her. Persephone had betrayed Demeter every time they came together, calling each other's names, and it was that thought that had him smiling as he vanished from the grounds of Olympia.

CHAPTER XXIV – THE ASCENSION BALL

Hades teleported to the Underworld. His first stop was Hecate's cottage, where he found the goddess preparing for the evening. She looked like the moon, draped in silver, her lampades weaving matching stars into her dark hair.

"Hades," Hecate said. "How was council?"

He was not often vocal, but he felt the need to recount his time at Olympia.

"Zeus will pay dearly for his commentary on women," Hecate said when Hades finished.

He had no doubt. Hecate was not afraid to punish gods. She had done so many times and in many ways, from setting traps to curses to revoking the victory of a precious hero. Her wrath was real and deadly when she was pushed.

"I worry his attention will turn to Persephone," Hades said.

Hecate's eyes glimmered like coals.

"If it does, she will be able to defend herself."

Hades looked at the goddess questioningly. "How?"

"She did not tell you? The night you had—err..." She paused, and Hades glared. He knew what she was going to say. *The night after they'd had sex.* "The day after The Olympian Gala, she sensed life for the first time. She could feel her magic."

Hades let Hecate's words sink in. Persephone *sensed* her magic. He knew it was possible that her powers would begin to awaken, but he had not expected it to happen so fast. It meant that Persephone had accepted his worship, that she had felt powerful and worthy while they had made love.

It meant that she trusted him.

The realization made his chest swell, and it made Demeter's words feel even more threatening, but when Hades expressed this to Hecate, the goddess just smiled.

"Have hope in your goddess, Hades. Has she not already chosen you?"

***

Hades did not stay long with Hecate. He was eager to see Persephone. It sounded strange, but he was curious to observe a change within her. Would her ability to sense life alter the way she thought of herself and her Divine blood? He thought of when he had met her. It was like she resented who she was, as if she felt like less of a goddess because she could not call upon her power. Power that had not arisen because she had been hidden away her whole life.

Hades clenched his fists at the thought. Demeter had let her believe she was powerless, she had watched as Persephone spiraled, putting distance between herself and her Divinity until she no longer saw herself as one.

And yet she was the most god-like of any of them.

The first thing he noticed when he manifested in the Queen's Suite—the suite that would one day belong to her —was her scent. She smelled of sweet vanilla and earthy lavender. Their eyes met in the mirror, and just as she started to turn toward him, he stopped her.

"Don't move. Let me look at you."

She froze.

It was an exercise in control, because all Hades wanted to do was be near her, and yet he maintained his distance and walked a slow circle around her, savoring every detail. She was dressed in gold, the color of power. The fabric was like water pooling on her skin and touched her in all the places Hades wished his hands could be, and beneath that thin fabric, he noted how her nipples hardened into tight peaks. As he came up behind her, he wrapped a hand around her waist and pulled her against him, meeting her gaze in the mirror.

"Drop your glamour."

Her eyes widened slightly. "Why?"

"Because I wish to see you," he said. He felt her seize beneath him. It was like the night after La Rose when she held those sheets to her chest, a shield she used to protect herself from his gaze. He reached out with his own magic, caressing hers, and he felt her open to him. He turned his mouth to her ear, still maintaining eye contact. "Let me see you."

She closed her eyes as she let go, and Hades watched as she transformed. She was everything. She was everything in any form, but there was something about watching her embrace her Divinity that was inspiring. It was beautiful. Right now, it felt intimate.

"Open your eyes," he whispered, and as she did, she didn't look at Hades but at herself. She was enchanting, and everything about her had intensified. Her skin glowed, her eyes were luminous, her horns spiraled gracefully, but perhaps she appeared like a flame because she stood before his darkness.

"Darling, you are a goddess."

He pressed his lips to her shoulder, and he felt her hand hook around his neck. She turned into his kiss, and their lips crashed together, hungry and hot. His pulse skyrocketed, and heat flooded the bottom of his stomach, filling his cock until it was hard. He made a carnal sound that came from the back of his throat, and Persephone turned in his arms. Hades pulled away, cupping her face.

"I have missed you," he said.

She smiled sheepishly and admitted, "I missed you, too."

His lips caressed hers, but Persephone was eager. She pushed up onto her toes, and their lips collided. He liked her hunger and her boldness, her hands smoothing over his chest, down his stomach, seeking his cock, but before she could reach him, he stopped her, breaking the kiss.

"I am just as eager, my darling," he said. "But if we do not leave now, I think we shall miss your party. Shall we?"

She actually hesitated, and he found himself smiling, but she took his outstretched hand. As she did, he dropped his glamour, revealing his Divine form. Unbound hair, black robes, and a crown of silver made of jagged edges that sat at the base of his horns. He could feel Persephone's gaze upon him, sinful and sweet. It touched him everywhere and sparked his hunger.

"Careful, goddess," he warned. "Or we won't leave this room."

He felt the truth of his words deep, even as he managed to lead her out of the suite into the hallway toward the ballroom. They paused behind a set of gilded doors, and Hades was glad because he wished to savor this moment—the first time he presented to his court with Persephone by his side.

Perhaps she did not even realize the significance, but from here on out, they would see her as his counterpart, as a figurehead, as a queen.

The doors opened, and silence descended. Hades' hold on Persephone's hand tightened, and he rubbed reassuring circles up and down her thumb, but the anxiety he had sensed within her seemed to lessen as soon as she saw the crowd and the smiles of those who knew her. When he glanced at her, he saw that she smiled back.

His people bowed, and he led her down the stairs, into the waiting crowd. They rose to their feet as they passed, and Persephone smiled, called each by name, showering them in compliments or asking after their day. It had never taken Hades so long to reach his throne, but watching her interact with the souls was humbling.

His eyes wandered to the faces of others in the crowd, and when he caught them staring, they looked away quickly. Part was embarrassment and part was fear, and that strange guilt returned in a fierce wave, clamping down on his heart. Then Persephone released his hand, and she broke through the crowd to embrace Hecate. Shortly after, she was surrounded by souls. Like moths drawn to flame, they descended once the darkness was gone.

He continued on, the crowd parting easily for him, and he couldn't help noticing the distance his souls placed between them. It was a stark comparison to how eager they had been to touch and embrace Persephone. He frowned, and the guilt grew heavier as he stalked to his throne where Minthe hovered. She was dressed for the occasion, in a fitted burgundy dress. It made her hair look like a sunset and her skin bloodless. He knew by the expression on her face she had things to say, and Hades hoped she understood by his expression that he wanted to hear none of them.

He sank into his chair and watched the revelry, but his shoulders were bunched and his fingers curled into the arms of his chair. He felt on edge, waiting for Minthe to say something that would only deepen the darkness inside him.

"You have taken this entirely too far," she finally spoke, her voice quivering, a hint at the storm of emotions that lay beneath her words. Hades did not look at her, but he could see her profile out of the corner of her eye and she wasn't looking at him, either.

"You forget yourself, Minthe."

"Me?" She whirled toward him, and Hades looked in her direction. "She was supposed to fall in love with *you*, not the other way around."

"If I didn't know any better, I'd say you were jealous."

"She is a game, a pawn! Here you are flaunting her as if

she were your queen."

"She *is* my queen!" Hades barked, nearly coming out of his chair.

Minthe snapped her mouth closed, her eyes widening just slightly, as if she could not believe Hades had raised his voice at her. When she spoke again, it was in a tone as icy as the air around them.

"She will *never* be enough for you. She is spring. She will need light, and all you are is darkness."

Minthe spun on her heels and left the ballroom, but her words remained, having hooked themselves in his skin. They brought his own thoughts to the surface, the ones he had buried deep, the doubt that Persephone, Goddess of Spring, could ever love him, the King of the Dead.

They could not be more different, and their entrance into this ballroom tonight had taught him that.

"Why are you sulking?" Hecate asked.

He had a feeling the goddess had been trying to sneak up on him, but as all her attempts, this one had failed too. Hades' eyes slid to hers, and he glared.

She pursed her lips. "I know that look. What did Minthe do?"

"Spoke out of turn, what else?" he grated.

"Well." Hecate's voice changed pitch, and Hades knew she was about to say something that would only add to his frustration. "She must have spoken the truth, or you would not be so angry."

"I don't want to talk about it, Hecate."

He was staring at Persephone as she danced with the children of the Underworld. They held hands and pranced in a circle. Now and then they would break away from each other to twirl or Persephone would lift them into the air, laughing as the they shrieked with delight.

"She loves the children," Hecate said.

Another pang in his chest.

Children.

It was something he could not give to Persephone, an option he had bargained away long ago. Could he really ask her to forgo being a mother to spend her eternity with him?

After a moment of silence, he spoke quietly. "I should let her go."

Hecate sighed. "You are an idiot."

Hades glared.

"She is happy!" Hecate argued. "How can you look at her and think you should let her go?"

"We are immortal, Hecate. What if she tires of me?"

"I tire of you," she said. "I'm still here."

"I knew I should not have tried to talk to you about this."

He stared harder at the dance floor when he saw Persephone turn and come face to face with Charon. He bowed to her, that damned smirk upon his lips. He asked her to dance, and she took his hand.

His knuckles turned white as he clenched the arms of his throne.

"You could not let her go," Hecate said. "You could never see her with another man."

"If that was what she wanted—"

"She doesn't want it," Hecate said, cutting him off. "You must not assume you know her mind just because you have fears. Those are your demons, Hades."

He gave her a dark look, and for a moment, Hecate's expression was just as stern, then it softened and the corner of her mouth lifted.

"Let yourself be happy, Hades. You deserve Persephone."

Then she wandered off into the crowd. Hades' gaze returned to Persephone. She drew attention like a flame, her beauty, her smile and laughter, her very presence, radiating warmth and passion and life, and despite the fact that he had disliked their earlier separation, he liked watching her. It distracted him from the fact that Minthe returned, taking up space on his left, while Thanatos appeared on his right.

"Come to apologize?" he asked her.

"Fuck you," she replied.

"He's done that," Hermes commented, sidling past them, white wings dragging the ground. He looked ridiculous, bare chested, wearing only a gold shroud over his waist. "It must not have been very good, because I don't believe he ever went back."

"Hermes," Hades growled, but the god was already parting the crowd, heading straight for Persephone. She turned as he approached, and he bowed, asking her to dance. Hades watched, frustrated, as he took her into his arms and swayed, movements exaggerated and taking up space.

It wasn't that he thought Charon or Hermes would take liberties, or that he was jealous because she danced with them. He was jealous because he felt as if he could not approach her, like the atmosphere of the room would change if he did. He should not fear it, this was his realm, but there was something so vibrant about this night. There was a life here that hadn't been here before Persephone.

As he thought her name, her gaze snagged on his and held, and he noted the longing in her eyes, as if the distance between them was a strain. It wasn't long before she broke from Hermes and approached him, eyes burning and body dripping in gold. It was something out of a fantasy, and he could not help imagining her kneeling before him to take his cock into her mouth. Already it strained, restricted by his robes.

She bowed low, the angle giving him a view of her ample breasts. As she straightened, she asked, "My lord, will you dance?"

He would do anything to touch her, anything to hold her close, anything to feel friction where he desired it most. He rose and took her hand, and did not move his eyes from hers as he led her to the dance floor. He drew her near, every hard line of his body cradled by her softness, reminding him of the way he fit against her as he collapsed atop her after release. A release he wanted now.

"Are you displeased?" she asked.

It took him a moment to detach from his thoughts and focus on her words.

"Am I displeased that you have danced with Charon and Hermes?"

She stared, a frown touching her lips. Obviously, she was concerned about his mood. He leaned into her, lips touching her ear as he spoke.

"I am displeased that I am not inside you," he whispered gruffly, and drew her earlobe between his teeth.

She shivered against him, and as she spoke, there was a smile in her voice.

"My lord, why didn't you say so?" she teased.

He drew away, eyes darkening with need, and guided her to spin before pulling her back to him. "Careful, goddess. I have no qualms taking you before my whole realm."

"You wouldn't."

Would, he thought. He would cloak this place in darkness and draw her up his body until she fit snugly on his cock. He would urge her to remain quiet but make it exceedingly hard as he coaxed her to orgasm.

The thoughts were too much, and he found himself pulling Persephone off the floor and up the stairs, his people clapping and whistling, oblivious—or perhaps not so oblivious—to his intentions.

"Where are we going?" Persephone asked, struggling to keep up with his long strides.

"To remedy my displeasure."

He took her to a balcony that overlooked the palace courtyard. She started to walk ahead of him, drawn to the edge as if she were mesmerized. He did not blame her, the view was stunning, as the whole Underworld was pitch black, save for the stars which appeared in clusters of various sizes and colors. Hecate had always said Hades' best work happened in the dark.

He was about to make that true of pleasure as he pulled Persephone back to him.

She stared, eyes searching his own.

"Why did you ask me to drop my glamour?"

He drew a golden curl behind her ear as he answered, "I told you. You will not hide here. You needed to understand what it is to be a god."

"I'm not like you."

She had said those words before, and this time, Hades smiled at them. She wasn't like him; she was better.

"No, we have only two things in common."

"And those are?" She arched a brow, and he could not tell if she liked his response, but that did not matter. Soon she would be taking pleasure from him and nothing would matter, not the world around them or their divinity.

"We are both Divine," he said as his hands traced a path down her back, over her bottom, where they settled, hooking beneath her thighs as he drew her up his body to settle against his cock. "And the space we share."

He leveraged her against the wall as his hands sought desperately to part his robes and raise her dress, exposing their most sensitive flesh to the night air until they sank into each other. Once inside, he remained still, forehead resting against hers. He wanted to linger in this moment, the initial feeling of stretching and filling, her sex clenching his to accommodate his size, and the contented sigh she offered as he slid into place.

"Is this what it's like to be a god?" she whispered.

He had one arm wrapped around her back, the other pressed into the wall beside her head, and after she spoke, he drew back to look into her eyes.

"This is what it is like to have my favor," he answered, and as he thrust into her, an electricity moved through his body, an unstoppable current that grew more intense the longer they were together. He watched her, witnessing as she was overcome with pleasure, head rolling back, exposing her creamy throat to his kisses.

"You are perfect," he whispered, cupping the back of her head to soften the impact of his movements, and when he felt close to coming, he slowed, nearly leaving her body only to slam home again.

"You are beautiful. I have never wanted like I want with you."

He had never spoken truer words, and as they burrowed into his chest, he found himself kissing her, covering her mouth with his own, teeth clanking together as he continued, hips thrusting hard. His heart was pounding in his chest, his muscles tensed, and all he could think about was the feeling of his throbbing cock and balls as they tightened and he shuddered his release, spilling into her in what felt like waves. He pressed into her, breathing hard, his horns tangling with hers.

It took him a moment to compose himself, but he finally straightened and withdrew from her, helping her to the ground. As her feet touched the floor, the sky lit up behind them with the spirit of reincarnated souls. Hades held Persephone close, and they moved toward the edge of the balcony.

"Watch."

In the distance, the sky ignited as the souls turned into light, into energy, and soared into the ether of his realm. They were leaving to reincarnate, to be born again in the world above and live a new life. Hopefully, one that was more fulfilling than the last.

"The souls are returning to the mortal world," he explained to Persephone. "This is reincarnation."

"It's beautiful," she whispered.

His people had gathered in the courtyard below, and as the last of the souls left a trail of sparks in the sky, they broke into applause. The music began again, and the celebration continued, but Hades' gaze had not moved from her face.

"What?" she asked as she looked at him, eyes glittering, and her smile made his chest feel strange and chaotic.

"Let me worship you."

Her smile changed, taking on a sensual edge, and despite how they'd come together moments ago, Hades knew he could take her again, and again and again, if she'd only answer.

"Yes."

He teleported to the baths. He had intentions of finishing where they left off the first night he had explored her body and her sweet, sensitive flesh. Except as soon as their feet touched the marble steps, Hades mouth descended upon hers and they knelt to the ground, where they made love beneath the open sky.

***

Later that night, Hades sat on the edge of his bed while Persephone slept. Her soft breaths brought comfort to his electric body. He was restless, a rare occurrence now that Persephone shared his bed. Something was wrong in his realm. He could feel it at the edge of his mind, on the fringe of his senses, like a phantom thorn in his side.

He rose, manifesting robes as he teleported to Tartarus, to his office, where he had left Sisyphus, only to find that he was gone.

CHAPTER XXV – FOR YOUR PLEASURE, A MONTAGE

Hades stood atop the precipice in his throne room, dressed in robes, glamour gone, his full form on display. His anger was acute; it vibrated throughout his limbs, eager for a violent release. It was the middle of the night, and he had called Hecate and Hermes to his side. The two bore different expressions, Hecate looked gleeful while Hermes looked sleepy.

"Could your vengeance not wait until morning?" he asked.

Hades ignored him and spoke to Hecate.

"Summon Minthe," he said.

"With pleasure," the goddess replied.

Hecate's magic surged, and Minthe appeared out of thin air, falling to the floor with a shriek, arms and legs flailing. She hit the marble with a loud smack.

"Hecate, the nymph is breakable," Hermes reminded.

"I know," she responded deviously.

Minthe groaned and pushed up onto her hands and knees, scowling as she looked at the three gods before her. Her nose was bloodied, and it coated her lips in crimson, spilling onto the ground.

Her murderous expression soon turned to fear when she looked at Hades'.

"You aided Sisyphus in his escape from the Underworld," he said. He barely kept his voice from quivering as he spoke, the rage was so acute. "Have you any idea what I sacrificed to put him in chains?"

He had granted Theseus a favor. He had given away his control, and the thought made his chest feel like a chasm, split open and oozing. It was a sacrifice he'd made that was now worthless.

"Hades, I—"

"Do not speak my name!" he roared, taking a step toward her. The whole room shook.

Minthe shuffled away, her eyes wide.

She was right to fear him. Usually, when he brought people before him for punishment, he had an idea of how he would go about the execution, but not in this moment. In this moment, anything was possible. This nymph thought she had known every emotion associated with anger and loss and grief. Hades would show her otherwise.

"I can explain—"

"Was your jealousy so severe it blinded you from your loyalty?"

"I have only ever been loyal to you!" Minthe's eyes ignited like an ethereal fire.

"Lies!" The taste was bitter, and he spat before he spoke. "You are loyal only to yourself."

"I loved you!" Her cry was guttural and real and cruel. "I loved you, and all you cared about was your imposter queen!"

Hades snarled. Persephone was no imposter. The true fraud was before him, because if she had ever loved him, she would have never helped Sisyphus escape.

"You paraded her in front of me, undermining me, berating me, taunting me. You deserve to see your Fate unravel. I hope Sisyphus pulls the thread."

There was silence.

So she had understood half of the equation, the part where the Fates had threatened to undo his future with Persephone if Sisyphus was not captured. It was information she had probably gained while spying. Well, she would spy no more. Not for him.

"If that is truly how you feel, then you have no place in the Underworld."

Minthe's mouth fell open.

"But this is my home," she said, her lips quivering.

"Not anymore." His words were cold.

The nymph swallowed. "Wh-where will I go?"

He did not know; she had never existed outside the boundaries of Hades' realm, even in the Upperworld. Her only connections were his connections, and those would evaporate the moment her exile leaked. No one would help her, because they would not wish to defy him.

"That is not my concern. Minthe, you are banished forthwith from my kingdom. If you attempt to set foot here again, I will exhibit no mercy."

Hades' magic closed in around her, and she vanished from sight. There was a beat of silence, and then he spoke.

"Hermes, spread the word that I am willing to bargain with Sisyphus. If it is eternity he wants, he has only to come to Nevernight and request a contract."

Eternal life wasn't something Hades could grant without sacrifice and required the same payment—a soul for a soul. It would mean that if he lost, the Fates would take the life of a god.

He was playing a game—a game of fate.

"I don't suppose this can wait until morning?" Hermes asked and when Hades looked at him, the god offered a nervous laugh. "I mean, on it, my lord."

He vanished.

"Don't—"

"Say I told you so?" Hecate asked. "I have waited too long for this moment. I told you to let me poison her and before that, I told you to demote her, and before that, I told you to never sleep with her."

Hades sank to his throne. Suddenly, he was exhausted, and as he spoke, his voice was tried and quiet.

"I have enough regrets, Hecate," he said.

The goddess said nothing, and after a few seconds, she quietly disappeared.

He was not alone long when Persephone entered the throne room, leaning against the door as it closed behind her.

She looked sleepy and beautiful, dressed in a white nightgown and matching sheer robe. Her hair was wild and mussed, falling in gold waves down her back. Her presence gave him the strength to straighten.

"Why are you awake, my darling?" he asked.

"You were gone," she said, approaching. She settled into his lap, her legs draped over his, her hands tangling into his robes. She took a deep breath, and burrowed into his chest.

"Why are you up?" she asked, her voice a whisper.

He considered telling her about the saga of Sisyphus—how he had cheated death twice and stolen the lives of two mortals, forever shattering their souls—but that explanation would also require divulging the Fates' threat, and with Sisyphus on the run again, he preferred to keep that to himself.

So instead he answered, "I…could not sleep."

She drew back, gazing up at him with heavy-lidded eyes.

"You could have woken me." Her voice was an erotic whisper. It promised things like throbbing lips, pounding hearts, and soft heat.

He raised a brow, and asked, "What purpose would that serve?"

Her hands dropped to his swollen sex, barely caressing it through his robes. "Would you like a demonstration?"

Hades smirked and gathered her close, teleporting to the Underworld.

***

"Any word?" Hades asked Ilias as they walked the shadows of his club. He'd been hopeful that tonight would be the night Sisyphus would take him up on the offer of a bargain.

"None," Ilias replied. "Word travels slow in the mortal underground."

Hades frowned.

The Fates had not been pleased to learn that Sisyphus had escaped.

"*Arrogant*," Lachesis had said.

"*Overconfident*," Clotho had hissed.

"*Brash*," Atropos had added.

Hades had not argued with them. It was the first time he'd gone to them and feared them, feared their vengeance, feared that they would unravel the threads they'd taken such care to weave, ready to bask in his misery.

But they hadn't. They'd merely asked who Hades was willing to trade if he lost his bargain with Sisyphus, a question he had not answered.

"He will come when he realizes he has nothing," the satyr said as they crested the stairs. "Hermes has managed to intercept several million dollars of Sisyphus' stock. What would you like to do with it?"

Hades knew how to make a mortal desperate. It was possible that Sisyphus would have remained on the run if his business was still afloat, thinking that he could survive on the lives he'd already taken, but Hades had guessed the mortal's plans and he had taken everything—would continue to take everything—until the man came begging.

By the end of this, he would wish he had died when he was supposed to.

"Burn it," he said. "And do not keep it a secret."

Ilias departed then, and Hades entered his office and halted, finding Persephone sitting on his desk, naked. Her back was straight, her legs crossed, her perfect breasts rose with her breaths, her nipples rosy. He was instantly hard, instantly thankful Sisyphus had not arrived, and that Ilias had not followed him into his office.

"Persephone," he said, closing the door and locking it.

"Hades," she said.

"You are aware that anyone could have come into this office?"

"I thought I would take a gamble," she said, a small smirk on her face.

"Hmm," he said, loosening his tie as he approached.

"Do you *use* this desk?" she asked, her hand smoothing over the obsidian.

"No," he said. "I don't. I can't sit still."

It was true—he hated to be confined.

"Pity," she said quietly. "It is a nice desk."

"I've never thought it of much use, until now," he said.

"Oh?" she asked with an innocent tilt of her head, eyes making a slow descent down his body to his cock, which strained against his trousers. She could not have made her desire more obvious.

He bent, lips hovering over hers as he spoke.

"It's the perfect height," he said in a gruff whisper, "to fuck you."

She lifted her head just a little. "Then what is taking you so long?"

He chuckled. "No one said you couldn't take what you wanted, my darling."

Her hands moved to his cock, and Hades sucked in a breath between his teeth before his mouth covered hers and his hand knitted into her hair, fingers bracing against her scalp. He drew her head back, tongue sweeping her mouth. His other hand cupped her breast, fingers teasing her nipple into a tight peak, but Persephone's hands were frenzied and they blazed a path down his chest, to the button of his pants, and as she unfastened them, his sex sprung free, his head already leaking with pleasure. Her grasp was firm, and she tugged it a few times before positioning it at her entrance.

"I burn for you," she said as Hades gripped the underside of her knees and pulled her to him, sheathing her in one slick movement. She arched against him, breasts pressing into his chest, head lulled back. He kissed her throat as he thrust into her. They moved together, uncontrolled, hands gripping, mouths caressing, tongues touching, breathings tangling. He changed positions, withdrawing from her, only to turn her on her side, and entered her with her legs pressed into her chest. Her breathing changed, her moans growing louder, and Hades continued, pumping harder, drawing her leg up to rest on his shoulder, reaching deeper.

When he withdrew again, he gathered her into his arms and sat in the chair behind his desk. With her in his lap, her back to his chest, he guided himself inside her again. His hands drifted over her body, one on her breasts, the other teasing her clit. Persephone's head fell back into the crook of his shoulder, and he kissed and licked and bit her neck and shoulder. Finally, he could take it no longer and drove into her, coming out of his chair as he did, her whole body bouncing until they came in a rush.

After, Hades cradled her body against him.

"As much as I love seeing you naked and waiting for me," he said. "I'd really rather you only treat me to this view in the Underworld. Anyone could have entered this office."

She giggled.

"And what would you have done? To anyone who saw me?"

"I don't know," he admitted, and he drew his finger beneath her chin and tilted her head up so their eyes met. He wanted to ensure she registered the weight of his words. "That should scare you."

She shivered, and he knew she understood. He could not predict how he might react. It could go one of two ways—he might understand it as the accident it was and let it go, or he would unleash the violence that lurked beneath his skin, the cruelty that had been imbued into his blood.

After a moment, he drew Persephone close and carried her before the fire, then lowered her to her feet. She lifted her hand, fingers drifting over his lips.

"What do you want?" she asked.

"You," he said. "Always you."

They kissed again, and Persephone eased Hades' jacket off. Their hands clashed as they both worked the buttons of his shirt free. Soon, he was naked, too, and together, they knelt to the floor. While on their knees before each other, Hades' hand slipped between her thighs. He teased her opening, fingers dipping into her warm, wet flesh. Another arm wrapped around her waist, and he welded their bodies together as he moved deeper inside her, using one finger, then two. He loved the feel of her, the way her breath quickened, her cries of pleasure. It wasn't long before he guided her to her back, spread her legs as wide as they would go, and licked her, sucked her, teased her. Her hands tangled in his hair, and she pressed into him, hips moving, and when she came, she arched her back, her hands dug into his scalp, and he drank her, tongue lashing to catch every bit of her sweetness. When he was finished, he climbed up her body and slid into her. Settled between her legs, he did not move immediately. He stared into her eyes, clear to her soul, seeing his life with her, their future, not just as king and queen, but as lovers.

He brushed her hair from her face. It stuck to the perspiration that glistened across her forehead before kissing her lips.

"You are beautiful," he said, and came up onto his toes, going deeper.

She sighed and let out a breath.

"So are you," she replied.

He chuckled and pulled out, the head of his cock barely inside her. "I think you are mindless with pleasure, darling."

She drew her lips between her teeth and then answered, "Yes." She gave a shuttering breath as he pushed into her again. "But I have always thought you were beautiful. More beautiful than any man I have ever seen."

He continued to move and they continued this easy

conversation, and Hades had the thought as he stared into her glittering eyes that there was something different about the way they came together this time, something deeper and darker and even more intimate.

"I will never forget how I felt when I first saw you," she said.

"Tell me," he urged.

Despite the warmth of the fire nearby and the sweat beading across their skin, she shivered.

"I felt your eyes on me, like hands touching my whole body. I had never felt so enflamed. I had never felt so afraid."

"Why afraid?" he asked. He bent closer to her lips, and she shifted, her legs spreading further apart to accommodate his movements, which had grown in tempo.

"Because..." she started, and then paused. "Because I knew I could love you, and I wasn't supposed to."

Hades' lips closed over hers, and it felt like his chest had opened up and all his thoughts and feelings were pouring into her. His pace quickened, and they were quiet after that, even their moans and sighs were quiet, until they reached their climax, coming in waves and collapsing in a heap of limbs and breaths and sweat.

Hades rolled onto his back, and Persephone pressed into him, her head on his chest.

"Your mother hates me," Hades said. "If she knew you were here, she would punish you."

Persephone rolled onto him and sat up, straddling his body. His eyes ignited as her wet and swollen center cupped his hardening flesh.

"Only if she finds out," she replied.

"Will I always be your secret?" Hades asked, doing his best to make it sound as if he were teasing, but there was a true challenge to his question because her answer would tell him about how she thought of their future.

Except, she did not answer.

"I do not wish to talk about my mother," she said, her fingers threading with his, hips rolling against his own, and

Hades didn't press. He didn't want to lose this moment—the way she guided his hands over his head and leaned over him, the way her breasts bounced as she impaled herself on his cock, the way she rode him until she was too tired to move. He had to take over then, rising into a sitting position so he could grip her body to his and continue creating that delicious friction that sent him over the edge, until his mind was blissfully blank, his concerns for their forever, forgotten.

CHAPTER XXVI – THE RIDE
OF A LIFETIME

"Why did I ask her on a date? I don't know anything about dating," Hades said, frustrated with himself. It has been a spur of the moment decision, a moment where he had felt high and happy and indulgent. He had wanted to give Persephone everything, even a touch of normal.

"Because you want to spend time with her, get to know her," Hecate said. "Outside the bedroom."

Hades glanced at her, annoyed. "I know her."

"What's her favorite color?" Hecate challenged.

"Pink," Hades said.

Hecate pursed her lips. "Favorite flower?"

"She doesn't have one," Hades replied. "She favors them all."

"What does she do in her spare time?"

"What spare time?" he asked. She was so busy; she went from class to work to him. He'd caught her in the library a few times, curled up in one of the chairs, asleep, a book on her lap.

"What does she hate most?"

Hades offered a small smile. "Our bargain."

"Do you love her?"

"Yes," Hades said without hesitation. He had known since the night after the baths.

"Have you told her?"

"No."

"*Hades.*" Hecate crossed her arms over her chest. "You must tell her."

Hades tensed immediately.

"Why?" He didn't see the need. Why expose himself to her rejection by admitting his feelings? He'd prefer to keep them to himself for now.

"She needs to know, Hades. She may be struggling with her feelings. Your admission could help her…sort them!"

"She either loves me or she doesn't, Hecate," Hades said.

The goddess' expression turned dark. "There's nothing black and white about loving you, Hades, and if you think there is, especially for Persephone, you're an idiot."

"Hecate—"

"She has been told to hate you her whole life, her existence in the Upperworld is threatened everyday she comes to your bed. She knows this, and yet she still does. She's telling you she loves you with her actions. Why do you need words to admit the same to her?"

"You allow her the option to tell me she loves me with actions. Can I not do the same?"

"No! Because she won't understand, just like *you* don't understand. I know human nature. And before you spout off about being immortal, I will tell you that love—falling in love, being in love, heartbreak—it's the same no matter your blood."

There was a short pause, and Hades looked away, frustrated. He tried to imagine how he would tell Persephone that he loved her, but when he thought of saying the words, he could hear the silence that would follow, the awful pause as she searched for something to say to ease his embarrassment.

He was certain she would reject him. While Hecate had

attempted to quiz him on his knowledge of Persephone, he knew her better than the goddess realized, because he knew her soul. He was well-aware of her thoughts when it came to how he handled mortals and their lives, how he bargained to annihilate their greatest sins. Even his work on the Halcyon Project would not erase the fact that he had roped her into one of those bargains, and it was for that reason that even if Persephone loved him, she would not say.

Still, why did it matter to hear those words? Had he not told her that actions meant more?

Because everything is different with her, he thought. *Her words matter.*

"Now," Hecate said. "If you're done sulking, let's plan this date."

***

Hades arrived outside Persephone's apartment, his stomach tangled. He felt ridiculous. He had fucked this woman, made love to her on the floor of his office, and yet he was nervous at the thought of taking her to dinner.

He blamed Hecate. If it wasn't for their earlier conversation, he wouldn't feel so uncertain or so torn over expressing his feelings. His unease worsened when he noted Persephone's expression as she left her apartment—her brows pinched, gaze distant. She was distracted.

"Is everything okay?" he asked as she approached.

"Yes," she said with a small smile. "It was just a busy day."

He wasn't satisfied with her answer, but he did not want to ruin their evening by challenging her at the start of their date, so he matched her smile and said, "Then let's get you off your feet."

He opened the rear door and took her hand as she slid into the cabin of the limo. Hades followed close as Antoni made his introductions.

"My lady," he nodded, grinning at Persephone.

"It is good to see you, Antoni," she replied with a sincerity that made Hades' heart ache. It was no wonder his people loved her. She was so genuine in her expression.

"Just press the com if you need anything."

He rolled up the privacy window, and suddenly, they were alone and the cabin was full of thick, electric air and all the unspoken things he should be telling her. It was like she knew, like she couldn't get comfortable either, because she started to fidget, crossing and uncrossing her legs.

Hades' eyes dropped to her bare thighs, eyeing her rising dress. He would much rather have his fingers, his face, his cock between those legs than think all these agonizing thoughts about admitting his love for her.

He placed his hand on her thigh, and Persephone inhaled, slowly peeking up at him.

"I want to worship you."

That, Hades thought. *I'll take that.*

"And how would you worship me, goddess?"

His voice rumbled between them, and he watched, eyes darkening as she knelt in front of him, parting his thighs as she fitted herself between his legs.

"Shall I show you?"

How the fuck did he get so lucky?

He swallowed, managing to keep the excitement from his voice. He could not say the same for his cock, which had grown full and thick.

"A demonstration would be appreciated."

She freed his sex and clasped it in both of her hands, stroking him once as she met his gaze. He fisted his hands on his thighs to keep from fitting them behind her head and taking control. She bent to him, her tongue peeking out, tasting his crown and the cum that pooled there. He groaned, seeing her mouth full of him. His whole body tightened, and as his head rolled back, the car came to a stop.

"Fuck!" Hades reached for the intercom, missing the button, distracted by Persephone's mouth as she took him deep, hitting the back of her throat.

"Antoni," he gritted out. "Drive until I say otherwise."

"Yes, sir."

He sat back, inhaling through his teeth, his hands twisted into her hair, fingers digging into her scalp. He held her there as she worked, and all he could think was that his heart felt raw and it beat hard and fast. His chest felt like the universe, expansive and full of love for this woman, this goddess, this queen. Who needed a realm of devoted souls when she would worship him like this?

Her tongue crept back up his length, her lips fastening over the head of his cock, and her hands played with his balls.

"Persephone." He hissed her name, thrusting into her. He hit the top of her mouth and the back of her throat, his hands tightening in her hair until he came, growling her name. When she let go of him, he dragged her up his body and kissed her. He pulled away, her lips catching between his teeth.

"I want you," he said, as if it were a sin he was confessing.

A smile ghosted her lips, still glistening from her work and their kiss. "How do you want me?"

"To start," he said, his hands trailing up her thighs, thumbs brushing the damp curls at her center. She straightened, hands planted on his shoulders. "I'll take you from behind on your hands and knees."

Her breath caught, and she shivered. "And then?"

His lips quirked. She was a tease, but he could play her game, parting her flesh and tickling her clit. She melted against him.

"I'll pull you on top and teach you how to ride me until you come apart."

"Hmm, I like that one."

Her hands dropped to his engorged flesh, and as she lifted herself, Hades helped her lower onto his shaft. She was warm and wet and tight; it was different from how her mouth felt because her muscles clenched around him, putting pressure on every part of his cock.

At first, he helped her move, ensuring she was seated fully before she rose up again, but after a few thrusts, he let her take over, finding her rhythm and her pleasure. Slowly, their breaths quickened and the cabin of the limo grew warm, the air thick with their lovemaking.

Her lips closed over his and traced his jaw, her teeth grazing his skin as she whispered, "Tell me how I feel."

"Like life."

She was life, his life.

His hand slipped between them, teasing that sensitive, erect nub until she came with a guttural cry. Hades' arm tightened around her waist, and he pumped into her a few more times before he, too, came. He held her for a long time, resting inside her, savoring this moment, high off the intensity they'd shared.

When she pushed away, Hades let Antoni know they were ready to arrive at The Grove—one of his restaurants. They would enter from the parking garage, from a level where only Hades and his staff had access. As much as he questioned how long he would remain Persephone's secret, he did not want Demeter finding out about their relationship via the media.

Once they arrived, Hades helped Persephone out of the limo, directing her to an elevator.

"Where are we?" she asked as the doors opened. He led her inside and pressed the button for the fourteenth floor, which led to the rooftop. The doors closed, trapping her scent. He eyed the emergency stop button, wondering how many times he could make her come before someone came to their unnecessary and unwanted rescue.

"The Grove. My restaurant," he added, because it was not common knowledge that he owned any business outside of Nevernight.

"You own The Grove? How does no one know?"

He shrugged. "I let Ilias run it and prefer that people think he owns it."

He chose to keep his assets a secret. It was better that way. No one truly knew how powerful Hades was or how much of New Greece he really owned.

The elevator stopped, and the doors opened to reveal the rooftop. It was made to look like one of the gardens in the Underworld, with beds of roses and peonies, climbing ivies and trees heavy with fruit and flora.

"This is beautiful, Hades," she said as he guided her along a dark stone path. Lights crossed over their heads, leading to an open grove where their table waited. He pulled out her chair and poured their wine.

"You said your day was busy," Hades began, sipping the wine. He did not often switch to drinking anything but whiskey, and he had to admit, he missed the smoky taste of his favorite liquor as much as he missed Persephone's mouth on his.

She hesitated, and Hades realized maybe that wasn't the question to ask. Their conversations about her work never went well. He could tell she was hiding something, even as she answered, "Yes. I had a lot...to research."

"Hmm." He took another sip of the wine. It was bitter and burned his throat, but it helped him focus on something other than his irritation about her work. What was she researching? His past? His bargains? Had she created a list of questions to ask him tonight? Or brought another list of names?

"I thought Cerberus was a three headed dog," she said suddenly. Hades was taken off-guard, and he chuckled, raising a brow.

"Is this the research you were referring to?"

"All the texts say he has three heads," she said defensively.

"He does," Hades answered, amused. "When he wants to."

"What do you mean, when he wants to?"

"Cerberus, Typhon, and Orthrus are able to shift. Sometimes, they prefer to exist as one, other times, they prefer to have their own bodies." He shrugged. "I let them do what they wish, so long as they protect the borders of my realm."

"How did you come to own him?" She paused and then corrected herself. "Them."

"He is the son of the monsters, Echidna and Typhon, who came to reside in my realm," Hades said.

"You love animals?"

He chuckled at that. "Cerberus is a monster, not an animal."

A line appeared between Persephone's brows. "But… you love him?"

He stared at her for a moment, and he sensed that this question—and her reason for asking it—meant more than he realized.

"Yes," he said at last. "I love him."

Hades was relieved when she moved on from that line of questioning to tell stories about the souls she'd spent her evening with the day before. He had begun to make it a point to walk with her, visit Asphodel, and greet the souls. She had even convinced him to play with the children, something he was far too competitive to take lightly. As they talked, they ate, and when they were finished, they walked hand in hand through the rooftop garden.

"What do you do for fun?" she asked, peering up at him sheepishly.

"What do you mean?" He had an answer, and it involved her and his bed. Actually, it just involved her. He could fuck anywhere.

She giggled. "The fact that you just asked that says everything. What are your hobbies?"

"Cards. Riding." He paused, reaching. Damn, this was harder than he thought. "Drinking."

"What about things not related to being the God of the Dead?"

"Drinking is not related to being God of the Dead."

"It also isn't a hobby. Unless you're an alcoholic."

He was probably an alcoholic.

"Then what are your hobbies?"

"Baking," she answered automatically, and he could tell

by her expression that she truly loved it.

"Baking? I feel like I should have known about this sooner."

"Well, you never asked."

He found himself wishing to experience this hobby with her. He wanted to know why it brought her such joy. What about it calmed her and smoothed the worry from her face? He frowned as they continued their walk, pausing so she would turn to look at him.

"Teach me."

Her eyes widened. "What?"

"Teach me," he said. "To bake something."

She laughed, and Hades' pout became more pronounced; he was serious. She seemed to realize this, and her expression softened.

"I'm sorry. I'm just imagining you in my kitchen."

"And that's difficult?"

"Well...yeah. You're the God of the Underworld."

"And you're the Goddess of Spring," he pointed out. "You stand in your kitchen and make cookies. Why can't I?"

She stared at him, and he wondered for a moment if he'd broken her. He reached to touch the edge of her lips, which had fallen into a frown.

"Are you well?"

His question brought a smile to her face, and yet something still seemed wrong. He noted her eyes glistening, as if she were close to tears.

"Very well," she agreed, and surprised him by pressing a kiss to his mouth and pulling away too soon.

"I'll teach you."

"Well, then," he said, hands on her waist. "Let's get started."

"Wait. You want to learn now?"

"Now is as good a time as any," he said. "I thought maybe...we could spend time at your apartment." Again, she seemed stunned, and he shrugged his shoulder, explaining, "You're always in the Underworld."

"You...want to spend time in the Upperworld? In my apartment?"

He would have to suggest this more often. It was taking entirely too long for her to get the point.

"I...have to prepare Lexa for your arrival," she said.

"Fair enough. I'll have Antoni drop you off." He looked down at his suit. "I need to change."

CHAPTER XXVII – TEACHING AN OLD GOD NEW TRICKS

Hades returned Persephone to the Lexus and teleported to the Underworld, appearing in his chambers. He took a moment to down a glass of whiskey. He hated himself for what he was about to do.

"Hermes!"

He summoned the god with a single command, and he appeared, wearing a mesh crop top and tiny leather shorts.

What the fuck had he interrupted?

"Yes, King of Death and Dark…" Hermes' voice faded away as his eyes swept the room. When he met Hades' gaze again, he seemed dazed. "Am I dreaming?"

"I need your…help," Hades said.

"I am dreaming." Hermes slapped his face.

"Hermes," Hades gritted out.

"No, no," he said, putting up his hands as if to silence him. He took a breath. "Don't ruin this for me. I might be dreaming, but I'm about to live out one of my top five fantasies—"

Hades slapped the god, who looked shocked.

"This isn't a dream, Hermes."

They stared at one another, and in the silence, Hades raised a brow. "Top five, huh?"

Hermes lifted his chin and cleared his throat. "What did you need?

"First, I think we can agree that neither one of us will disclose what goes on here tonight?"

The god's eyes widened, and his mouth fell open. "Oh my gods, I really am dreaming."

"Hermes!" Hades snapped. "I need...*fashion* advice!"

"Oh." He blinked and then broke into a grin. "Why didn't you say so?"

Hades glared at the god. He should have downed a bottle before summoning the god. After a moment, he explained. "Persephone is teaching me to bake. What do I wear?"

"She's teaching you to bake?" Surprised colored Hermes' voice. "And you're participating? Willingly?"

Hades glared.

"You must really love her."

"*Hermes*," Hades warned. If he had to say the god's name one more time, he'd send him to Tartarus for the night.

He seemed to get the hint and straightened. "Right. Casual, baking date."

He dashed to Hades' closet.

"Why do you only wear suits?" Hermes complained. "What do you sleep in?"

"Nothing," Hades answered. "What's the point?"

Clothing was hot, and it meant more layers to get to what he wanted, even when Persephone was not sleeping beside him.

Hermes sighed. "You are impossible. Hold on."

He vanished for a moment and returned with a black shirt and a pair of grey sweatpants.

"What are those?" Hades asked, voice dripping with judgement.

"*Clothes*," Hermes said. "*Casual clothes*. Not that I expect you to know the definition of casual, Mr. Suit and Tie."

He shoved them at Hades' chest. "Change."

He glowered at Hermes as he made his way to the bathroom. When he returned, Hermes clapped his hands.

"Perfect! You're ready to bake!" Then the god shook his head. "I never thought those words would come out of my mouth."

Hades pulled at the shirt, and Hermes swatted his hands away. "Stop! You don't want Sephy to know I dressed you, do you?"

"Sephy?"

"What? It's her nickname."

Hades wasn't sure how he felt about the fact that Hermes had a nickname for his lover.

"Go before Persephone thinks you changed your mind!" Hermes said. "Oh, and I'll take payment in cookies!"

He sung the last word before vanishing, and Hades had never been so glad to be rid of a god in his life.

***

Hades appeared outside Persephone's apartment door and knocked. It opened immediately, and he wondered if she had been standing on the other side, waiting for his arrival.

She offered him an appraising look, but her eyes quickly narrowed.

"Did you own those before today?" She pointed to the sweatpants.

She knew him well, and he grinned, admitting, "No."

She stepped aside, and he squeezed through the door. It reminded him of how he was not made for mortal dwellings. The doors were too short, the walkways too narrow, but he didn't mind the closeness with Persephone so near. She stared up at him, almost like she couldn't believe he had shown up.

"What?" he asked.

"Nothing."

She gave a quick smile and stepped around him, taking his hand in hers and dragging him into the living room, where her best friend, Lexa, sat on a couch with a man Hades did not know.

"Um, Hades this is Lexa, my best friend, and Jaison, her boyfriend."

Jaison waved. Hades could sense his unease and awkwardness, but he was a good enough man, gentle and unassuming—the opposite of Lexa, who was bold and energetic. She approached him fearlessly and threw her arms around his waist in a hug.

"It's nice to meet you," she said.

Hades wrapped an arm around her shoulders.

"Very few have ever spoken those words."

But he appreciated them.

"So long as you treat my best friend right, I'll continue to be happy to see you," she said with a grin.

"Noted, Lexa Sideris." He grinned and bowed. "May I say, it is a pleasure to meet you."

Lexa blushed and cleared her throat, glancing at Persephone before exclaiming, "So! Are you all going to make cookies? That's not code for something, is it?"

Hades hoped it was code for something.

Like sex.

But Persephone was quick to dash that hope by rolling her eyes. "No, Lexa, it's not code for something." She took Hades' hand and pulled him toward the kitchen. "We better get started!"

It occurred to him that she had gotten more comfortable touching him, and he wasn't sure at what point that had begun, but he liked it.

Persephone's kitchen was small and bathed in fluorescent light. She had already prepared a few things—bowls, a set of mismatched measuring cups, and a cookbook. Hades glanced at the page.

"We will be making sugar cookies?" he asked.

"My favorite," she said, pulling her bottom lip into her mouth. He really wished she wouldn't do that. It made him

296

hard, and that kept him distracted.

Maybe he should tell her.

Except she was perfectly oblivious and instructed him to retrieve a list of ingredients. Despite the lack of storage, she had everything organized and directed him easily, like she was used to getting her way.

"Why do you put everything up so high?" he asked.

"It's the only place it will fit. In case you haven't noticed, I don't live in a palace."

He was well aware, thinking that he would very much like to see her bake in the Underworld kitchens.

Once she had everything on her list, he grinned proudly.

"What would you do without me?"

"Get it myself."

Hades snorted. He would like to see that; she would have to climb the countertop, which would give him a great view of her ass.

"Well, get over here. You can't learn from there."

He pushed away from the counter where he was leaning and approached, bracing his arms on either side of her body, trapping her against the counter. He didn't lean into her, but he thought about it. His dick was hard, and it would fit perfectly against that ass he'd just fantasized about. Instead, he pressed his lips to her ear.

"Please, instruct."

It took her a moment to speak, and Hades smirked. He hoped she was just as distracted as him. What fantasies did she get lost in at night or at work while they were apart?

"The most important thing to remember when baking is that the ingredients have to be measured and mixed right or it could mean disaster."

He heard what she said, but his mind was on other things, like shoving his hand down her pants to see how wet she was. His grip tightened on the countertop, but that only kept him from acting on his thoughts. It did not prevent him from pressing his lips to her neck and letting his tongue taste her skin.

Her breath caught in her throat, and she glared at him over her shoulder. "Scratch that. The most important thing to remember is to *pay attention*."

She shoved a measuring cup into his hand.

"First, flour," she commanded, and he smirked. She took baking seriously.

He kept his arms around her as he worked. Measuring flour was like walking through ash—it clouded the air and stuck to the skin. When he had it in the bowl, he bent his head to hers, noting her rigid posture. Then he leaned in, and as his full erection pressing into her, and she laid her palms flat on the counter.

He raised a teasing brow. "Next?"

"Baking soda."

They continued like that until all the ingredients were in the bowl and mixed into a batter. Persephone took that moment to duck under his arm, freeing herself from the human cage he'd created for her. She unstacked a set of sheet pans and gave him a spoon.

"Use this to scoop the batter and make them into one-inch...balls."

She cleared her throat when she said the word *balls*.

And all he could think was how she'd teased his in the back of the limo with his cock in her mouth, and everything tightened.

Fuck.

They worked together, each of them scooping batter into a spoon and transferring it onto the baking sheet. When Hades was finished, he compared the two, and Persephone's skills were beyond his own. She'd made perfect rounds out of her batter. Hades' were misshapen and messy, like he'd slung the mixture all over the pan. He was envious of her control.

"Put this on," Persephone said, handing him a floral mitt.

"What is it?"

"It's an oven mitt," she said. "So you don't get burned when you put the cookies in the oven."

He considered telling her that he was, essentially, fireproof, but kept quiet, sliding the mitt onto his hand, only to hear Persephone giggle. His gaze snapped to hers.

"Are you...laughing at me?"

She cleared her throat quickly. "No. Of course not."

His eyes narrowed, an unspoken promise of payment for this humiliation. Once the cookies were in the oven, Hades pulled off the mitt. He had intentions of scooping her into his arms and feasting on her mouth, but she had other plans.

"Now, we make icing." She smiled, eyes alight.

He'd have liked to lick icing from every part of her body, but she handed him some type of cooking utensil with a narrow handle and wire loops.

"What am I supposed to do with this?" he asked.

"It's a whisk. You'll beat the ingredients together," she said, and poured various ingredients into a bowl, pushing it toward him when she was finished.

"Beat."

Now that was something he excelled at.

"Happily."

"That's good," Persephone said, practically snatching the bowl from Hades after he'd been whipping the mixture for a few minutes. Perhaps he's gotten carried away. There were pieces of the mixture all over the counter, his shirt, and her.

She divided the icing into a few waiting bowls and handed him a small tube of green. "Start with a few drops and mix."

They made colorful icing. Persephone worked on the bright colors—yellow and pink and lavender—while Hades made darker colors—red and green and even black, a color Persephone had helped him make. Toward the end, he caught her licking icing from her fingers.

"How does it taste?" he asked, reaching for her hand. He drew one of her fingers deep into his mouth and groaned. She was sweet and salty, and the way she looked at him while he tasted her made the fire in his stomach deepen. "Delicious."

She drew her fingers away, and there was a beat of silence. "Now what?"

Their eyes met, and the air in the room was almost unbearable.

Hades planted his hands on her waist and lifted her onto the counter. Persephone laughed and drew her legs around him, pulling him in so his cock was settled against her core. He kissed her mouth, parting her lips. She tasted like the icing she'd sucked from her fingers. He buried one hand in her hair, the other reaching between them to grip her breasts, when someone cleared their throat.

Loudly.

Persephone pulled away from his kiss while Hades' hands fell to the countertop, his head resting against her shoulder. He needed time to collect himself. If they had been in the Underworld and interrupted by one of his staff, he wouldn't have stopped.

"Lexa." Persephone cleared her throat. "What's up?"

"I was wondering if you guys wanted to watch a movie?"

"Say no," Hades whispered, teasing her ear.

Persephone slapped playfully at his chest. "What movie?"

"*Clash of the Titans?*"

Hades snorted and drew away from her, looking at Lexa. "Old or new?"

"Old."

"Fine," he agreed, and kissed Persephone on the cheek. "Going to need a minute."

Hades left the kitchen, disappearing down a hallway until he found the bathroom. He shut himself inside and leaned against the door, reaching into his pants and clasping his cock. He'd have much rather had Persephone's hand on him, her mouth around him, her sex clenching his own, but this would have to suffice until they were alone. He worked himself until he came.

When the cookies were finished, they took them out

and let them cool while they watched *Clash of the Titans*.

"Gods, I forgot this movie was so slow," Jaison said, who was the only one paying attention. With Persephone lying on top of him, her body fitting between his thighs, Hades could only think about sex. She was also giggling, and he was certain she wasn't laughing at the movie.

"I know what you're thinking," he whispered, his arm tightening around her, bodies pressing hard together.

"You can't possibly know."

"After what I put myself through this evening, I'm sure there are several things you are laughing at."

At some point, Persephone fell asleep and he carried her to her bedroom.

"Don't leave," she said sleepily when he lowered her onto the bed.

"I'm not." He kissed her forehead. "Sleep."

Hades lay beside her wide awake. Her bed was small and smelled like her. He closed his eyes, but his body felt hot and his brain was too wired, thinking about their earlier encounter in the kitchen and how he wanted to finish what they started. But Persephone was tired and he didn't want to wake her, so he rolled onto his side and closed his eyes tight. It felt like forever before he fell asleep, and it only lasted for a few seconds before he was awake again, his body on top of Persephone's, his mouth devouring her skin. She moaned and reached for him, their kisses urgent, as if they hadn't been together in weeks, months.

Hades pulled her shirt off and dumped her out of her pants before diving between her thighs. He took her slow, nipping at the inside of her legs, blowing on her hot core, sucking on her clit until she begged for his tongue. He gave her his fingers, inserting them into her heat. She was soaked, and he groaned.

"All of this for me," he said as he left her body, her come thick and dripping, and drew his fingers into his mouth before covering her body with his own. Her legs fell apart, and she arched her back, breasts filling his vision as he entered her. He paused as he loomed over her, pressing his forehead to hers.

"You are beautiful," he said.

"You feel good," she whispered. "You feel...like power."

He felt controlled at first, like maybe he could make love to her the way he had in front of the fireplace in his office. Except that the more she reacted to the invasion of his cock—gripping his arms and the blankets, and pressing her head into the mattress—he couldn't control himself. A fierce, claiming growl erupted from his throat, and he kissed her hard, teeth grazing her lips, sucking her neck, and thrusting into her, moving her entire body until they were crammed against the headboard. Hades used his hands to cushion her head while Persephone's nails scraped down his back. He didn't even feel the sting, just the ecstasy of their coupling.

The bed shook, their guttural cries filling the room, and when he came, he collapsed upon her, their bodies slick with sweat. It wasn't until he caught his breath that he realized she was crying.

"Persephone." He pushed away from her, feeling hysteria build in the bottom of his stomach. "Did I hurt you?"

"No," she whispered, covering her eyes, and he felt an immense sense of relief. "No, you didn't hurt me."

He stared down at her for a moment as she wept quietly. He knew there could be a number of reasons for her tears, but he would not speculate and he would not ask. If she wished to tell him, she could. Still, he did not wish for her to hide, no matter the reason. He pried her hands from her face, brushed the wetness from her cheeks, and kissed her forehead before moving to his side and tucking her against him. He covered their naked bodies with blankets.

"You are too perfect for me," he whispered, kissing her hair, and they fell into a peaceful slumber.

***

Hades woke instantly, and this time, it had nothing to do with desire and everything to do with the smell of Demeter's magic. It curled through the air like a bitter frost.

He rolled into a sitting position but did not manage to manifest clothes before Demeter appeared, eyes like fire, face as cold as ice.

Persephone, oblivious to her mother's arrival, rolled toward him, her hand reaching out across the sheets.

"Come back to bed."

His heart squeezed in his chest, and then her mother's voice filled the room, a sound like thunder and lightning warring in the sky.

"Get away from my daughter!"

"Mother!" Persephone sat up and paled, holding her sheets to her chest. "Get out!"

Demeter's gaze fell upon Persephone, and it took everything in Hades' power to remain where he was. He wanted to protect her from her mother, from the promise of revenge he saw written on her face. Even if he had roused Persephone in time to dress, it would have been impossible to hide what they'd been doing. Their scents clung to each other, their bodies still slick with the smell of sex.

Persephone reached for her nightshirt and shoved it over her head, covering herself as quickly as possible.

"How dare you." Demeter's voice shook, her mouth quivering with rage.

Hades remained sitting in the bed, body tense, ready to pounce at the barest hint of attack.

"How long?" Demeter demanded.

Months, Hades wanted to say, because he knew it would antagonize the Goddess of Harvest, but it was one thing to receive Demeter's anger on his own and another thing entirely to watch Persephone suffer beneath it.

"It's really none of your business, Mother," Persephone

snapped.

"You forget your place, Daughter."

"And you forget my age. I am not a child!"

"You are my child, and you have betrayed my trust."

Demeter's magic was gathering around her like a vortex. Hades knew the goddess was preparing to teleport her daughter, and while he remained on edge, he was not afraid. Demeter couldn't take Persephone from him while she was indebted to him. Still, seeing Persephone look frantically from him to her mother broke his heart.

"No, Mother!"

"You will no longer live this disgraceful, mortal life!"

Persephone closed her eyes, and he found himself torn between intervening and wishing to see how Persephone would react. *Embrace your power*, he thought. It was the perfect time, as she was protected by his mark. *I know it is fighting inside you.*

But she didn't.

Demeter's magic had culminated, and Persephone remained still, eyes closed, accepting of her mother's punishment like a pawn in a game.

Except that as Demeter snapped her fingers, nothing happened. Her face fell, wavering between shock and anger, eyes finally falling to the gold cuff Persephone wore to cover the evidence of their bargain.

Demeter snatched the bracelet from her wrist, gripping her arm. Hades felt his magic pool. He would fight the goddess for his lover. He would kill her if she left a mark.

"What did you do?" Demeter demanded, turning her fierce and hateful gaze upon him.

"Don't touch me!" Persephone tried to pull free of her mother's grip, but Demeter's nails bit into her skin and she cried out.

"Release her, Demeter." Hades spoke quietly, but his rage was acute.

"Don't you dare tell me what to do with my daughter!"

Hades snapped his fingers, and he was suddenly dressed, rising to his full height. His power gathered around him, an invisible but tangible weight he knew Demeter could sense. She released her hold on Persephone, who retreated to the other side of the room.

"Your daughter and I have a contract. She will stay until she fulfills it."

"No." Demeter looked at Persephone. "You will remove your mark. Remove it, Hades!"

"The contract must be fulfilled, Demeter. The Fates command it."

She had tried to deceive the Fates once; she could not do it again.

The Goddess of Harvest glared at Persephone. "How could you?"

"How could I? It's not like I wanted this to happen, Mother!"

He flinched, unable to hide the impact of her words. He was well-aware that she was just speaking the truth, one he already knew well. Persephone had not wanted the bargain, and while it did not mean that she did not want him, he could not help thinking that with the end of their contract, came the end of them.

"Didn't you? I warned you about him! I warned you to stay away from the gods!"

"And in doing so, you left me to this fate."

Warnings only planted the seed of intrigue, something Demeter should have learned after existing for so many years, but she, like many gods, fell victim to mortal assumptions. One of those being, she could be the exception.

"So, you blame me? When all I did was try to protect you? Well, you will see the truth very soon, Daughter."

If Demeter had been trying to protect Persephone, she wouldn't have kept her powers from manifesting. Demeter had made her daughter codependent, ensuring she would always need her—need someone—to survive. Hades hated that, and he hoped by the end of this, before their contract was said and done, her powers would manifest.

That desire intensified as he watched Demeter strip

Persephone of her favor, exposing her Divine form. The goddess was not gentle, tearing the power away with such force, Persephone fell to her knees, gasping for breath.

"When the contract is fulfilled, you will come home with me," Demeter said. "You will never return to this mortal life, and you will never see Hades again."

Demeter glared at him before vanishing, and Hades swore in that moment, the Goddess of Harvest would regret her actions.

He scooped Persephone up from the floor, cradling her against him as he sat on the edge of the bed. She couldn't seem to catch her breath.

"Shh," Hades crooned. "Everything will be okay. I promise."

She burst into tears.

"I don't regret you. I didn't mean that I regretted you."

He was glad she said it, even though he had known she hadn't meant the words.

"I know." Hades kissed her tears away.

There was a knock at the door, but before Hades or Persephone could speak, Lexa entered and halted, eyes wide as she took in Persephone's appearance.

"What the fuck?"

There was no hiding her Divinity—Persephone was the Goddess of Spring. Hades half-expected her to beg him to erase Lexa's memory, but instead, she pulled away and stood, appearing tall and regal as she spoke.

"Lexa," he heard her say. "I have something to tell you."

CHAPTER XXVIII – A PICNIC IN THE UNDERWORLD

Hades left Persephone's apartment, teleporting to Olympia. He hated that he had to return, hated that he had to go before Zeus, but it was necessary and just as he suspected, Demeter had already arrived. He could hear her voice outside Zeus' office.

"He cannot have my daughter, Zeus!" she cried. "I will starve your people if you let him keep her!"

When Hades entered, she whirled to face him. Demeter's face changed when she was in a rage. Hades imagined Persephone had seen it over and over again. Her eyes seemed to sink into her face and darken. She leaned forward, shoulders hunched, like the weight of her fury was too much to handle.

"You!"

"Kill everyone, Demeter, it only makes me more powerful."

"Hades," Zeus said, sitting behind his oak desk. "Is what Demeter says true? Have you seduced her daughter?"

"I did not seduce her," Hades said. "She came to me willingly on more than one occasion."

He glared at the Goddess of Harvest, and she glared back.

"Liar! The mark on her wrist tells me otherwise."

Zeus looked at Hades, waiting for his answer.

"She invited me to her table. The mark was fairly placed."

"It sounds as though Persephone has made her own decisions, Demeter," Zeus said.

"She is my daughter, Hades! I have a right to decide her fate!"

Hades did not look at the goddess, but at his brother.

"She is Demeter's daughter," Hades said, "But she is destined to be my wife. The Fates have woven her into my future, and Demeter has interfered."

There were few things that scared Zeus, but the Fates were one.

"Is this true, Demeter?" He looked to the goddess for her answer, but Hades responded instead. He was ready for this to be over.

"It was what the Fates demanded in exchange for giving her a daughter."

"I will never believe that she came to you willingly!" Demeter seethed. "The Fates be damned."

"I am sure Hecate would be happy to testify on my behalf," Hades added.

"That will not be necessary," Zeus said, and he knew his brother did not want to appear as if he were questioning the Goddess of Witchcraft. Theirs was an old friendship, a strange one, and just as Hades relied on her for advice, so did Zeus. "Demeter, I will not grant your request. It seems your wishes are not in line with the will of the Fates."

Demeter's fury gathered, and massive roots broke through Zeus' marble floor. Hades cast his magic like a net, enveloping the entire place in shadow, blinding the goddess and Zeus. Their battle was short-lived, however, as a bolt of Zeus' lightning separated the two. With their concentration lost, their magic faded.

"I will not mediate childish fights between you two," Zeus said. "My word is law, and you will both abide."

Hades glared. *Childish fights?* There was nothing childish about his love of Persephone, nothing childish about the wrath of Demeter. Still, he was thankful Zeus had sided with him, not that it meant a lot in the end. Persephone was her own person, she had free will. If she wanted, she could leave him.

"There is another matter we must discuss," Zeus said. Hades did not think it was possible, but the mood of the room darkened. "A goddess has not been born in centuries. Has she any power?"

"None to speak of," Demeter answered quickly. Hades glared at her. She answered too fast.

Zeus looked to Hades. He would have to respond truthfully. "Her power is dormant. She has shown no ability to wield it."

"Hmm." Zeus was quiet, ever suspicious of new gods. It was only fair that he feared a rebellion like the one he had led against their father. "I wish to meet her."

"No." The two said instantly.

Zeus' eyes flashed.

"Persephone has no desire to embrace her Divinity as of yet," Hades explained. "Introducing her to Olympia too soon may scare her away. We would never know how truly powerful she was then."

His brother studied him.

"Let her remain where she is," Hades said. "Hecate will train her, and when her powers start to surface...I will bring her to you myself."

It was the only way he'd allow the meeting to take place. It was inevitable, but it would be inevitable with him by her side.

Zeus' eyes narrowed, and then he chuckled. "Ever the protector, brother. Very well, as soon as she shows her power, you will bring her to me." He paused a moment, his hand resting on his stomach, and shook his head. "A goddess, masquerading as a mortal journalist. No wonder you fell in love, Hades."

Once they were outside Zeus' office, Demeter turned to him.

"Your life may be woven with my daughter's, but that does not mean you were meant to love one another."

"I will always love her," Hades said. It was the only thing he could promise. "And I care for what I love."

"If you cared, you would have never touched her. She is a Daughter of Spring!"

"And a Queen of Darkness," Hades countered. "If you wish to be angry with anyone, be angry with yourself. It was you who planted the seed of her betrayal, you who pushed her further away with your tyranny, you who left her powerless and afraid. She deserves loyalty and freedom and power."

"And you think you can give her that? King of Death and Darkness?"

"I think she can take it for herself," he replied and vanished, leaving Demeter alone with her fury.

***

In the weeks that followed, Hades tried to distract Persephone from her mother's wrath, but she seemed to grow more morose. He saw it most when she thought he was not looking—in the moments before he surprised her by appearing in the library while she read, or just before she left the palace for a walk, or in the early mornings when she rose before him to shower and dress.

She was creating distance between them. He could feel it growing, pulling at the threads that bound them for eternity, and it hurt.

He found her standing in front of her still desolate garden. He hated to find her here, staring at this patch of land that had come to mean so much to the both of them.

He wrapped his arms around her waist and pulled her back against him.

"Are you well?" he asked, his head falling against her

shoulder.

She did not answer, and the weight in his stomach felt sharp and acute. She turned in his arms, staring up at him, and he got the sense that she wanted to ask him something. Instead, she answered him.

"I'm just stressed. Finals."

He studied her, eyes searching. "Persephone, you can tell me anything."

She frowned, as if she did not believe him, and Hades felt the inside of his chest wilt, like a flower exposed to too much sun.

He closed his hand over her wrist, where the mark covered her skin.

"Are you worried about the contract?" he asked.

She looked away.

He didn't know what to say; the contract was binding. The terms had to be fulfilled. He could not comfort her with promises that everything would be okay when he knew what she wanted—the ability to move between worlds. It was a reality he was coming to terms with, that his love for her would never be enough. She would need her freedom, too.

"Come," he said. "I have a surprise for you."

He guided her hand to his, threading their fingers together, and tugged her toward the open field outside the garden. They walked for a while, entering the forest on the other side of the field. He did not follow a set path, navigating between trees to a meadow where a blanket was spread and a basket of food waited.

"What's this?" Persephone asked, looking up at Hades.

"I thought we might have dinner," he said. "A picnic in the Underworld."

She raised a brow, suspicious. "Did you pack the basket?"

"I…helped," he said. "I even made cookies."

Persephone grinned. "You made cookies?"

"You are far too excited," he said. "Lower your expectations."

But she was already racing to the blanket. She fell to her knees and opened the basket, digging inside until she located what she was looking for—a small bag of chocolate chip cookies. Hades had slaved over them. It had taken hours in the kitchen last night, and he had made a mess Milan, the head chef, had been very unhappy about.

Persephone sat cross legged and opened the bag.

"You know those are for dessert," Hades said as he lowered himself to the blanket.

"And? I'm an adult. I can have dessert for dinner if I want."

Hades chuckled and fished out the remaining items he had packed—meats and cheeses, fruits and breads. Last, a bottle of wine and his flask. He wasn't keen on another evening spent drinking fermented grapes.

He popped a cube of cheese in his mouth and took a drink from his flask as Persephone bit into a cookie. It crunched loudly, and Hades flinched. They were not at all like the cookies they had made together. Hers were soft, chewy, melt-in-your-mouth delicious. His were hard and kind of burnt.

"You don't have to eat those," Hades assured her as she continued to crunch.

"No, they are the best cookies I have ever had."

Hades raised a brow. "You don't have to lie."

"I'm not."

She wasn't, but he didn't understand. He knew those cookies were terrible.

"They're the best because you made them."

Hades snorted.

"I'm serious," she said. "No one's ever made anything for me before."

Hades stared at her for a moment, and suddenly, he was the one who felt ridiculous for not taking her words for granted.

"I'm glad you like them," he said, his voice quiet.

They sat in silence. Persephone continued to eat his cookies, and he continued to drink. After a moment, she rose to her knees.

"Do you want one?"

She came toward him and held out her hand, a cookie clasped between her fingers. Hades grasped her wrist and bit into the cookie. It was exactly what he expected, hard and bland, only slightly sugary. Still, he loved it if she loved it. As he chewed, her eyes dropped to his lips, and he raised a brow.

"Hungry, darling?"

He wasn't sure how she would answer, given her earlier sadness, but when she lifted her eyes to his, he could see her longing.

"Yes," she answered.

He leaned in to press his mouth to hers. For a while, they maintained their distance as they kissed. Hades enjoyed this, the feeling of desire building up inside him, resisting the urge to take her into his arms and touch her. He ran his tongue along her mouth, and just as he was about to pull her to him, he pushed her away as a ball flew between them, followed by Cerberus, Typhon, and Orthrus.

"Sorry!" Hecate's voice came from the trees beyond.

Hades sighed, and Persephone giggled.

"Oh, a picnic!" Hecate said as she appeared in the clearing.

"Hades made cookies!" Persephone said. "Would you like one?"

Hecate did not hide her obvious surprise and looked at him. "You…baked?"

He glowered, and Persephone, who was either oblivious to his obvious discomfort or did not care, said, "I taught him!"

Hecate laughed and took a cookie. Hades was a little relieved. Maybe she would leave, and he and Persephone could get back to kissing.

Except that Persephone had other ideas. "Sit with us!"

"Oh, I don't want to intrude—"

No, you don't, Hades thought.

"There is more food in the basket, and Hades brought wine!"

The two looked at him, and he sighed, relenting. "Yes, join us, Hecate."

Persephone dug around in the basket, handing Hecate a variety of foods, while Hades poured the goddess a glass of wine.

Cerberus, Typhon, and Orthrus returned, the three fighting over their red ball.

They weren't there long when Hades sensed Hermes' magic.

"Fucking Fates," he mumbled, drawing the attention of Persephone and Hecate.

"Oh, Hades!" Hermes sung as he appeared in the clearing. "Oh, a picnic!"

"Did you need something, Hermes?" Hades asked, his jaw tightening, frustrated that the evening he had planned for him and Persephone had turned into this…circus.

"Nothing that can't wait," he said. "Are those cookies?"

"Hades made them!" Persephone said.

Hermes sank to his knees on the blanket, and Hades watched Persephone offer food and wine, and smile and laugh, and his frustration at having their evening interrupted lessened because she was happy. He also found that he did not mind the company so much, though he could do without Hermes' teasing.

They spent a long time in the woods together, until the Underworld's light faded and Hades' night lit the sky. When they left, he and Persephone walked side by side back to the palace. They did not touch.

"Thank you for tonight. I know it did not go as planned."

Hades chuckled. "It was nothing like I had imagined."

They came to a stop, shrouded by the garden just outside Hades' fortress, and faced each other.

"If Hecate had not thrown that ball at our faces, I would have kept kissing you," he said, and his hand came up to cup her face.

"Is it too late?" she asked. "To have it all?"

Hades stared at her for a moment, thumb brushing her cheek. He stepped closer.

"What are you asking for, my darling?"

"I'm not sorry Hecate interrupted us," she said. "But I still want that kiss and everything that comes after."

"I'm only sorry you didn't ask me sooner," he said, obliging her request. His mouth touched hers, and he drew her against him, making love to her beneath the stars in the garden outside his home.

CHAPTER XXIX – A TORTURE
LIKE NO OTHER

It was a week later when Aphrodite arrived to see him unexpectedly. Granted, she never arrived with notice, but Hades thought she would come closer to the end of their six-month deadline, which was now weeks away.

Hades sat behind his desk at The Cypress Foundation, finalizing a few small details for the Halcyon Project before handing it over to Katerina. He had a hard time concentrating, thinking that the last time he had been stuck behind a desk, he had been more preferably engaged with Persephone.

He'd have liked to have her here now and chuckled at the thought of teleporting her to him. Would she be in the middle of writing a story or in an important meeting? Would she be angry for long when he took her mouth in a searing kiss? When his hands skimmed up her thighs, when his fingers teased her opening and he finally gave her what she begged for—release.

"You win," Aphrodite said. She looked more severe than usual. Even when she was angry, she didn't have this...look. It was hard for Hades to place at first, but he soon recognized it for what it was because he had felt the same thing multiple times in the last six months.

Hysteria.

"She loves you."

Hades' brows knitted together.

"What are you talking about?"

"I visited her today, your little love," the goddess explained.

His stomach suddenly felt endless. He rose from his chair, his anger coiled like a snake.

"What did you do, Aphrodite?" His voice shook as dread descended, cloaking his body. He felt as if he were trying to breath with no air.

"I only meant to gauge her affection for you. I—"

"What did you do?" he snarled.

"I told her about the bargain."

"Fuck!"

Hades slammed his fists on his pristine table. This time, it shattered. Aphrodite's eyes widened, but she stood her ground and did not flinch at his outburst.

"Why?" he demanded. "Is this revenge for Adonis?"

"It began that way," she admitted, looking surprisingly devastated.

"And how did it end, Aphrodite?"

"I broke her heart."

***

"Where is she?" Hades demanded as he teleported to the Underworld. He was not calm enough to sense her yet. He appeared in the middle of his palace, where his staff were meandering, oblivious to his agony, his fear, the potential end to the happiest he had ever been.

He had known this would be a possibility, but he had been grossly unprepared, because at the end of it all, he loved her.

"Persephone! Where is she?"

"Sh-She went for a walk, my lord," a nymph said.

"She was following Cerberus," another added.

"Toward Tartarus."

Fuck.

He vanished and appeared on the outskirts of Tartarus. This part of his realm was vast and covered hundreds upon hundreds of acres. *Why would she come here?* he thought as he attempted to focus on finding her, rather than his racing heart and the dread boiling in the pit of his stomach.

He'd told her from the beginning he did not want her to know the path to Tartarus, that her curiosity would get the best of her. Had she heard Aphrodite's words and sought to prove herself right about him? Perhaps she had come in hopes that she would find something to prove he was just as cruel and calculated as she thought.

Well, she would find it here.

It wasn't long before he felt her—a faint pull at the edge of his senses.

She was in The Cavern, the oldest part of Tartarus. When he appeared there, he felt her presence strengthen and he knew where he'd find her.

In Tantalus' cave.

Disgust curled in Hades gut.

Tantalus was a king, a demi-god born of Zeus, and among the first generation of mortals to populate the Earth. Gifted with Zeus' particular brand of arrogance, he thought to test the gods by committing filicide. The wicked king killed his son, Pelops, ground him to a pulp and attempted to feed him to the Olympians. Hades remembered the smell of burnt flesh wafting through the Great Hall. The merriment had ended immediately, and their wrath had been swift. Hades had stood, pointed at Tantalus, and sent him straight to Tartarus, while the others attempted to assemble Pelops again.

That had not been the end of Tantalus' punishment, either, as Zeus had cursed his legacy, the impact of which was still felt to this day.

Hades made his way into the darkness that blanketed

the cave, where Tantalus had lived and suffered for an eternity. He saw Persephone race toward him, terror written across her beautiful face. She slammed into him, and he grabbed her shoulders to steady her.

"No! Please—" Her voice broke, full of fear and his emotions raged.

"Persephone," Hades said quickly, trying to calm her.

When she looked at him, recognition and relief descended upon her face.

"Hades!"

Her arms tightened around his waist. She buried her head in his chest and sobbed.

"Shh." He kissed her hair, thankful that she still touched him, that she still found comfort in his presence. "What are you doing here?"

Then he heard Tantalus' voice cut through the dark and Hades' blood turned to ice.

"Where are you, little bitch?"

Hades set Persephone aside and approached the grotto where Tantalus was imprisoned, snapping his fingers so that the pillar where Tantalus was chained turned. The man was a sack of bones, loose skin sagging over sharp angles. He was pale and withered, his hair scraggly and matted, like wire coming out of his face and head.

He had not looked upon the prisoner in years, as his method of torture tended to take care of itself, starvation and thirst while always being within reach of food and water. Except that Hades knew he had partaken of drink because his lips, drained of color, glistened.

Hades flung his hand toward Tantalus, and the mortal's knees gave out, pulling the manacles that held his arms overhead tight, and he cried out.

"My goddess was kind to you," Hades hissed. "And this is how you repay her?"

Hades closed his fist, and Tantalus heaved, spitting up the water Persephone had given him until there was nothing left to vomit. Then he parted the water in the grotto, creating a dry path straight to the prisoner. The wicked king struggled to find his footing, pressing his feet flat against the column to which he was chained. Hades enjoyed watching him struggle. It eased the burden of his anger and his wish to see this mortal meet a violent end.

"You deserve to feel as I have felt—desperate and starved and alone!" Tantalus spit out as Hades approached.

Hades' hand closed over the man's neck.

"How do you know I haven't felt like that for centuries, mortal?" he said quietly, his voice deadly in its tone. It promised punishment and pain, it promised all of the things Tantalus claimed he felt now, but worse.

His glamour melted away, and he stood before his prisoner in his Divine form as he had in the past.

"You are an ignorant mortal," Hades said, his magic bubbling under the surface. "Before, I was merely your jailor, but now I shall be your punisher, and I think my judges were too merciful. I'll curse you with an unquenchable hunger and thirst. I'll even put you within reach of food and water, but everything you partake of will be fire in your throat."

Hades dropped Tantalus, and he hit the stone pillar with an audible thud. It did nothing to deter the mortal, who growled like an animal and attempted to lunge for him, snapping his teeth. The feral attempt at an attack only amused Hades, and earned him a slot on his own victim's list.

Hades snapped his fingers, sending the prisoner to wait in his office. After, he turned to Persephone.

He had never seen her look like this before—wide-eyed, small, shaky. She took a step away from him and slipped. Hades lunged forward to catch her before she could hit the ground, free of water since he still stood in the middle of the parted lake.

"Persephone." Saying her name hurt his chest. "Please don't fear me. Not you."

Her eyes watered, and she broke, crying into his robes. His grip on her tightened, and yet, though he held her close, he felt that she was far away, and he realized that this was what it was to be on the brink of losing everything.

Still, he thought, *if I hold her long enough, if I give her long enough, maybe I could hold her together, maybe I could hold us together.*

He teleported to his room, where he sat near the fire, hoping she would warm enough to stop shivering, but she didn't. He grew frustrated and gathered her against him, heading to the baths.

When they arrived, he lowered her to the floor. He drew her finger beneath her chin and tilted her head to meet his gaze. He wanted her to speak, to say something—anything—but she remained quiet. The only thing that gave him hope was that she did not protest as he undressed her or as he cradled her against him and carried her into the water.

"You are unwell," he said after he could no longer stand the silence between them. "Did he…hurt you?"

He asked because he had to be sure.

Her answer was to squeeze her eyes shut, something he never knew could hurt his heart so badly.

"Tell me," he whispered, brushing his lips across her forehead. "Please."

She opened her eyes, glistening with tears.

"I know about Aphrodite, Hades," she said. "I'm no more than a game to you."

Those words made him angry. She had never been a game. In truth, he had rarely thought of the bargain with Aphrodite since it had begun. No, it had always been more than that. It had become a quest to see her power, to show her what it meant to be Divine, to convince her that she could be a queen.

"I have never considered you a game, Persephone."

"The contract—"

"This has nothing to do with the contract!"

He released her, and as Persephone struggled to straighten, her reply was venomous.

"This has everything to do with the contract! Gods, I was so stupid! I let myself think you were good, even with the possibility of being your prisoner."

"Prisoner? You would think yourself a prisoner here? Have I treated you so poorly?"

"A kind jailor is still a jailor," Persephone snapped.

"If you considered me your warden, why did you fuck me?"

"It was you who foretold this." Her voice shook. "And you were right—I did enjoy it, and now that it's done, we can move on."

"Move on?" He was rage incarnate, and his whole body shook. Was she speaking like this because her mother had caught them? "Is that what you want?"

"We both know it's for the best."

"I'm beginning to think you don't know anything," he said, stalking toward her. "I'm beginning to understand that you don't even think for yourself."

How had they gotten here? Where was the woman who had grown confident among his people? The woman who had waited for him, naked, in his office? The woman who had made a home in his heart?

"How dare you—"

"How dare I what, Persephone? Call out your bullshit? You act so powerless, but you've never made a damn decision for yourself. Will you let your mother determine who you fuck now?"

"Shut up!"

"Tell me what you want." He cornered her, pinning her against the edge of the pool.

She didn't look at him.

"Tell me!" Hades commanded.

"Fuck you!"

She was fierce, and her eyes were alight. She leveraged herself against him, legs around his waist. She kissed him hard, and he took every bit of it. He held her in place, hands spanning her back and bottom. He sat her on the edge of the pool, intending to go down on her, to taste her anger and her desire raging between her legs, but she clawed at him.

"No, I want your cock inside me," she said. "Now."

He obliged, practically jumping out of the pool. She pushed him on his back, wrapped her hand around his sex, and guided him inside her, filling herself full of him until her bottom touched his balls. He groaned, hands digging into her skin.

"Move fucking faster," he commanded. They were both angry and goading the other, and inside, Hades felt his magic rising. It was calling to hers, the darkness teasing the light.

"Shut up," she snapped, glaring down at him.

Hades responded by squeezing her breasts, rising to suck her nipples. Persephone moaned, and held him to her, legs tightening around his waist. He could barely catch his breath, but he encouraged her. He would lose his mind to her.

"Yes," he hissed. "Use me. Harder. Faster."

He came with a roar and covered her mouth with his, but the ecstasy was short-lived as she pushed him away and stood, leaving him sitting on the cold marble. She gathered her belongings and hurried up the stairs. Hades followed after her.

"Persephone!"

As she walked, she pulled on her clothes. He hurried to catch up with her, exposed in the hallway outside the baths.

"Fuck!"

When he reached her, he grabbed her arm and pulled her into the throne room. He shut the door, and pushed her into it, caging her with his arms. She pushed against his chest, but he didn't budge.

"I want to know why!" she demanded, her voice was thick with tears, and Hades hated that he had caused this pain. Hated that he was the reason she was broken, but he sensed something else inside her, something powerful waking the angrier she became. "Was I an easy target? Did you look at my soul and see someone who was desperate for love, for worship? Did you choose me because you knew I couldn't fulfill the terms of your bargain?"

"It wasn't like that."

It was something so completely different. If he could only explain, but he didn't want to start with the Fates because even though they had woven her into his future, he would have still wanted her. When he looked at her, he saw her power, he saw her compassion, he saw his queen.

"Then tell me what it was!"

"Yes, Aphrodite and I have a contract, but the bargain I struck with you had nothing to do with it. I offered you terms based on what I saw in your soul—a woman caged by her own mind." He knew what he said next would piss her off, but she needed to hear it. "You are the one who called the contract impossible, but you are powerful, Persephone."

"Do *not* mock me."

"I would never."

She snarled, "Liar."

There were few things he hated more than that word.

"I am many things, but a liar I am not."

"Not a liar then, but a self-admitted deceiver."

"I have only ever given you answers," he said, growing angrier by the second. "I have helped you reclaim your power, and yet you haven't used it. I have given you a way to walk out from underneath your mother, and yet you will not claim it."

"How? What did you do to help me?"

"I worshipped you!" he snapped. "I gave you what your mother withheld—*worshippers*."

If Demeter had introduced Persephone to society upon her birth, her powers would have blossomed, she would have had altars built and temples erected in her name, she would have risen in the ranks, surpassing Olympians in popularity. Of that, he was certain.

She blinked up at him.

"You mean to tell me you forced me into a contract when you could have just told me I needed worshippers to gain my powers?"

It was not that simple, and she knew it. She had rejected Divinity as if it were the plague. He did not believe she would have done anything with that knowledge but hide, fearing the unknown.

"It's not about powers, Persephone! It's never been about magic or illusion or glamour. It's about confidence. It's about believing in yourself!"

"That's twisted, Hades—"

"Is it?" he said, cutting her off. He did not wish to hear her tell him how terrible he was, how deceptive he was, how much of a liar he was. "Tell me, if you'd known, what would you have done? Announced your Divinity to the whole world so that you might gain a following and consequently, your power?" She knew the answer, and so did he. "No, you've never been able to decide what you want, because you value your mother's happiness over your own!"

"I had freedom until you, Hades."

"You thought you were free before me?" he asked, leaning toward her. "You just traded glass walls for another kind of prison when you came to New Athens."

"Why don't you keep telling me how pathetic I am?" she spat.

"That's not what I—"

"Isn't it? Let me tell you what else makes me pathetic. I fell for you."

Fuck. Fuck. Fuck. His heart felt like it was suffocating in his chest. She looked as devastated as he felt, and he wanted to touch her, but she pushed away vehemently, putting distance between them. "Don't!"

He did as she asked, though his whole body wanted to deny her request. The only thing he wanted to do was be near her, because she loved him. Because he loved her.

He should tell her.

But she was so angry and hurt.

"What would Aphrodite have gotten if you had failed?"

He did not want to answer, because he knew what she would think. At this moment, she felt as if everything

Demeter had taught her was true. She would think that Hades would do anything to keep his people in his realm, even deceive her, but he answered anyway.

"She asked that one of her heroes be returned to the living."

A request he would happily grant if it meant she would stay.

"Well, you won. I love you," she said, and he wanted to collapse. "Was it worth it?"

"It wasn't like that, Persephone!" he said, desperate for her to understand, and as she turned from him, he asked, "You would believe Aphrodite's words over my actions?"

She paused and faced him, and he could see that her body shook, could feel her power racing in her blood. He could smell her magic, and it was heavenly, a scent so unlike anything he had experienced. It was distinctly her—a warm mix of vanilla and sunshine and fresh spring air. But she said nothing, and he shook his head, disappointed in her inability to understand this situation, her worth, her power.

"You are your own prisoner."

Those words broke her open. He saw it the moment the last syllable fell. There was a loud rushing in his ears akin to a scream, and great, black vines shot through the floor, tangling around his arms and wrists like restraints. He was shocked; her power had come to life and it had been directed at him.

She had created life.

In the aftermath, she breathed deep, chest heaving. He would have liked to commend her, celebrate her, love her. This was her potential, a taste of the magic inside her, but it had taken her anger to unleash it.

He tested the restraints; they were strong and tightened as he pulled, as vengeful as she was in her anger. He met her gaze and laughed humorlessly. Looking at her was like seeing his death, a day he thought would never come.

"Well, Lady Persephone. It looks like you won."

CHAPTER XXX – CHEATER

A day later, Hades stood before Tantalus, bident in hand. Since Hades had appeared in his office, the soul had glared at him. He showed no remorse for his treatment of Persephone, though Hades was not surprised. After years of dealing with true evil, he had come to understand that not everyone who experienced eternal torture would change.

Sometimes, it only made them worse.

"You wished for me to feel desperate and starved and alone," he said, twisting the bident in his hand. "Shall I tell you how I feel at this very moment?"

Hades leveled the pointed ends at the soul, one aimed at his breastbone and the other at his navel.

"I feel numb," he hissed. "Do you know what it is to feel this way, mortal king?"

There was a glint in Tantalus' eyes and a tick to his mouth as he started to smirk.

Yes, Hades thought. *Smile at my pain. Your torture will be sweet.*

"In the last week, I have felt things I have never felt before. Me, an eternal god. I pleaded for the love of my life to stay. I am starved for sleep without her beside me. I am alone. I feel as you claim, Tantalus."

The mortal began to laugh, and it was a terrifying cackle, raspy and broken.

Hades pushed on the bident, and the sharpened edges sunk into his skin. The man was still laughing when he began to gurgle and cough, spattering blood upon Hades' face.

The God of the Dead did not blink.

"Do you know how I know you have never felt this way?" Hades continued. "Because no man would laugh in the face of this pain, even you, bastard that you are."

Hades shoved the bident clear through Tantalus' body, and it lodged in the wall behind him.

"My lord."

Hades turned to find Ilias standing in the doorway. The satyr glanced passively at the dead mortal pinned to Hades' wall. This was not an unusual display for either of them.

"Sisyphus has arrived. He awaits you in the Diamond Suite."

It had taken weeks, but Hades' promise of a bargain had finally lured the mortal to Nevernight.

"Shall I call in a crew?" he asked, looking at Tantalus again.

Hades frowned. He had made a mess.

"No," he said. "I'll bring him back after he rots and torture him again."

Hades started to shift when Ilias stopped him again.

"Perhaps it's the look you're going for," he said, "but you do appear to have just murdered someone."

Hades stared down at his clothes, spattered with fresh blood. He could leave it, perhaps it would serve as a warning to Sisyphus, except that Hades knew there was little that could scare the mortal now. He had, after all, run from Hades twice. The god snapped his fingers, restoring his pristine appearance, before teleporting to the Diamond Suite.

Like the other suites, it boasted luxury. The windowless walls were decorated with modern, monochrome art. A chandelier dripping with glimmering crystals hung at the center of the room, and beneath that, a set of black leather couches faced each other, a slab of marble made into a table separated the two.

A man occupied one of the sofas. He looked a little rough, his beard not nearly as neat, his suit not nearly as tailored, the gold that had weighted down his fingers gone, and the odor of fish and salt clung to his skin.

In previous weeks, Hades had imagined this moment feeling quite different. There had been more momentum behind his wish to see the mortal imprisoned in his realm, because he was in danger of losing Persephone. He had felt desperate and determined, and he saw capturing Sisyphus as claiming his future.

And he guessed, in a way, that was still true.

This was his future. He was the God of the Dead, a punisher.

"Tell me, mortal," Hades said. Sisyphus' head snapped toward him, and he sprang to his feet. "What convinced you to come?"

"My lord, I did not know you had arrived."

Hades moved to the bar and poured himself a drink. He turned to Sisyphus, whose eyes had not moved from him.

"Well?" he asked.

The man gave a breathy chuckle. "Well, you offered immortality."

Hades downed his drink and poured another, saying nothing else.

He took a seat across from Sisyphus, who sank into the cushions. Hades manifested a deck of cards. All the cards used here were the same, black and gold, the picture on the back an image of the Fates, spinning, measuring, and cutting the Thread of Fate.

It was a fitting image for the pair.

Sisyphus sat on the edge of the couch, knees spread out, hands dangling between them.

"Blackjack," he said as he cut the deck and shuffled the

cards. He could tell the sound of the cards flicking made the mortal nervous. His fingers were twitching. "One hand, Sisyphus. You have already wasted enough of my time."

"A fifty-fifty chance," the mortal responded. "Are you so confident?"

Hades did not reply as he dealt them each two cards. Sisyphus dragged them with his chubby fingers, but just as he started to pry up the edge, Hades stopped him.

"Before you reveal your hand," he said. "I would like to know why."

"Why, what?"

"Why did you run from death?"

"You can hardly blame me when presented with the opportunity," he said.

Hades knew he referred to the spindle Poseidon had given him.

"That is not an answer, Sisyphus," Hades said. "What hope did you have in extending your pathetic life?"

"Pathetic?" Sisyphus' face turned red. "I was on the cusp of an empire, and then you came and took it all. Why not defy you? What could it possibly mean in my afterlife? You had already sentenced me to Tartarus."

"Hmm." Hades' eyes fell to the cards before him, fingers poised to flip.

"Why did you ask?" Sisyphus questioned, a note of hysteria in his voice. "Why demand an answer?"

Hades considered remaining quiet, but Sisyphus' passive fear of Tartarus angered him, so he answered. "Because, Sisyphus, your existence in Tartarus will be everything you've ever feared, everything that ever angered you. You will obtain your empire and then you will lose it, over and over and over again."

Hades turned over his cards—a king and an ace, twenty-one. A perfect hand.

His eyes lifted to Sisyphus'.

"Turn your cards, mortal."

There was a beat of silence, and the mortal moved, not

to flip his cards, but to draw a weapon, a gun.

Normally, Hades found displays like this amusing, but coming from Sisyphus, it enraged him. His eyes darkened, and the gun melted in the mortal's hand, coating his skin in burning metal. His screams filled the room, piercing and agonizing. He fell to his knees, holding his hand aloft, eyes bulging out of his head.

Hades sighed and leaned forward, turning the mortal's cards.

A five of clubs and a nine of hearts—fourteen.

Hades stood, drained his glass, and straightened his jacket. Sisyphus cupped his arm against his chest, sweaty and breathing hard. He looked up at Hades, hatred in his eyes.

"Cheater," he accused.

Hades smirked. "Takes one to know one."

He snapped his fingers, sending Sisyphus to Tartarus, and strolled out of the suite.

***

A week later, Hades found himself in Hephaestus' lab. He had put this off for as long as possible, dreading his return to the God of Fire after what he had asked him to make only a few weeks ago.

When the god handed him a small box, Hades peered inside. The ring he had commissioned sat on a pillow of black velvet. It was a beautiful, delicate thing, despite the numerous flowers and gems decorating the band, and it brought with it the pain and embarrassment he felt at losing Persephone. Perhaps if he had not been so presumptuous, perhaps if he had not had this ring made, he would have her now.

"It is beautiful," Hades said, snapping the box closed. "But I no longer require it."

Hades met Hephaestus' gaze, and the god raised his brows.

"I will pay you handsomely for your work," Hades

continued, holding out his hand. He returned the ring to Hephaestus.

"You will not take it?"

Hades shook his head. It was a symbol of what he might have had, of a future that was no longer on the horizon, and he could not bear to see it or know that it existed in the same realm as he did.

"I will not ask you why you no longer want the ring. I can guess well enough," The God of Fire said. "But I will not accept payment for something you do not wish to keep."

"Would you rather I take it?"

"No." Hephaestus smiled. "I have a feeling it would end up in the ocean, and I have doubts about you asking Poseidon to retrieve it when you want it again."

CHAPTER XXXI – TO CLAIM A QUEEN

Hades watched from a distance as Persephone walked across the grand stage at her graduation. She looked beautiful, her honeyed hair gleaming beneath the bright sun, her skin glistening like gold, and a smile curving her perfect lips.

"She looks so...happy," Hades said, more to himself than anyone else, but Hecate was there to answer.

"Of course she's happy. She just spent four years in purgatory."

"College, Hecate," Hermes corrected. "I think you mean college."

"Same thing," she shot back.

"She invited me to the afterparty," Hermes said with a grin, and Hades tried not to smirk when Hecate elbowed him in the ribs.

"Ouch! Stop!"

He tracked Persephone as she left the stage, holding onto her hat as the wind blew. It picked up her scent and carried it to him, leaving him feeling hollow. It was then she paused and looked in their direction.

"Oh, oh! I think she sees us!" Hermes waved.

"She can't see us, we're invisible!" Hecate said, elbowing him in the ribs again.

"Watch it, Hecate! I'll turn you into a goat!"

"Just try, feather feet!"

Hades sighed and rolled his eyes at the two, but quickly focused on Persephone again. She seemed troubled, a line forming between her brows and the corners of her mouth dropping. It was in that moment he thought he saw the truth of her heart—she was just as devastated as he was. It was almost unbearable, and the thread that still connected them throbbed in his chest.

He ached for her, wanted her, loved her.

"Go to her," Hecate encouraged.

"She would deny me," Hades said.

"Maybe," Hermes replied.

Hecate raised her arm again, and the god flinched, shuffling a few feet away. She turned back to Hades and argued.

"She would welcome you. She loves you."

"She *loved* me," Hades said.

"Do you want me to call you an idiot again?"

Hades glared.

"At least she told you she loved you," Hecate said, hands on her hips. "She still hasn't heard those words from *you*."

He frowned and felt ashamed. Hecate was right, he should have told her he loved her the moment he realized it. All this time, he had gone on about how she was his goddess and queen, and he had not even managed to say the three words that would illustrate the truth of how he felt because he feared her rejection.

Persephone's attention turned from them as Lexa's name was called. She cheered for her best friend as she walked across the stage, and the two embraced before they returned to their seats. Despite his painful thoughts, Hades found himself smiling as he watched her continue living.

He had few regrets in his long life, but one of them

would always be never telling her how much he loved her.

***

Hecate flung open the door to Hades' chambers. It was noon, and he was still in bed, exhausted from a night of bitter bargains at Nevernight.

"Get up!" she said, and threw open the curtains, letting in daylight. Hades groaned and rolled over, covering his head.

"Go away, Hecate."

There was a pause, and then his blanket was torn away.

"Hecate!" Hades sat up, frustrated.

"Why are you naked?" she demanded, as if she had just seen something horrifying.

"Because," he said, gesturing to his room, "I'm in bed!"

She tossed the blanket back to him.

"What are you doing?" he demanded.

"We're going to get Persephone," she said. "Well, *you're* going to get her. I'm going to help."

"We've been through this, Hecate—"

"Shut up," she snapped. "I miss her, the souls miss her, you miss her. Why are we spending all this time missing her when we can just…get her back?"

Hades laughed, mostly from disbelief. "If it were that easy—"

"It *is* that easy!" Hecate threw up her hands, frustrated. "You've spent all this time waiting for the Fates to take her away, but they didn't. *You* did."

"She left, Hecate. Not me."

"So? It doesn't mean you cannot go get her. It doesn't mean you can't still tell her you love her. It doesn't mean you can't still fight for her. You're the one who always talks about actions. *Why don't you live by your words?*"

"Fine," Hades gritted out. "We'll go, and then you'll see once and for all that she does not want me."

He threw off the blanket Hecate had thrown back at him.

"For Fates' sake, put some clothes on!" she snapped.

"If you did not wish to see me naked, Hecate, then you should not have come to me when I was in bed."

"Forgive me for assuming you'd be clothed," she snapped, rolling her eyes.

Hades sighed, frustrated as he disappeared into the bathroom, splashing water on his face. He was tired. He had not slept well since Persephone had left, and his mood had changed. He was quick tempered, fighting more with everyone, even Hecate. It had to stop, and maybe this would put an end to it, or make it all worse.

He glamoured up and returned to his room, where Hecate waited.

"I've been thinking," she said, rubbing her hands together. "We should make this a bet. If she runs into your arms like I think she will, then I require more room for my pois—plants. For my plants."

Hades raised a brow. "Fine. You want a bargain?" he said. "If I win, then I never want to hear another word about Persephone again."

Hecate rolled her eyes. "Deal," she said, then added, "For someone who can taste lies, you sure spout a lot of them. You had better get ready to give up a fourth of your realm, lover boy."

***

Hades paced the length of his chamber, waiting for Hecate to give him the signal—a burst of magic she would send when she located his goddess. He had not been able to concentrate since she left. As much as he hated to admit it, Hecate had given him hope.

He paused, frowning at himself in the mirror, realizing for the first time just how much Persephone had changed him. She had made him want things he'd never wanted before, like a life that offered a little more simplicity. He wanted walks and picnics and burnt cookies. He wanted to laugh and to never go to bed alone again.

This was the first time in his life he hoped to lose a bet.

He felt the pulse of Hecate's magic, and something rock-hard settled in his stomach as he followed it, appearing outside The Coffee House. When he saw Persephone, his whole chest ached. *Fuck, she is beautiful.* She'd pulled her hair up, away from her graceful neck, but golden ringlets had worked their way free. She wore white, the straps of her dress thin, exposing her lithe, freckled shoulders.

Hecate sat beside her as the two spoke, and he caught part of the conversation.

"So, go to him. Tell him why you hurt, tell him how to fix it. Isn't that what you're good at?"

Hades wanted to laugh.

Persephone did and rubbed her eyes, and he thought that maybe she was trying hard not to cry. His chest ached.

"Oh, Hecate. He doesn't want to see me."

She was wrong, so wrong. It struck him that perhaps they had both made assumptions about the other. Maybe they had wanted to see each other this whole time. Maybe if he had just done what he had wanted to all along, go to her, see her, hold her, he would not have felt this agony.

"How do you know?" Hecate asked.

"Don't you think if he wanted me, he would have come for me?"

Oh, darling, Hades thought. *I will spend the rest of my life showing you how much I want you.*

"Perhaps he was just giving you time," Hecate replied, and lifted her head to meet his gaze.

Persephone followed her stare, and when their eyes met, she rose from her chair and broke into a run. Their bodies collided in a familiar way as Hades lifted her off the ground and her legs found their home around his waist. Their bodies sealed together tightly.

"I missed you," he said, his head buried in her hair.

"I missed you, too."

He would never let her go again.

"I'm sorry," she whispered. Her fingers brushed his

cheek and his lips, and her touch ignited a fire within him so acute, he thought he might turn to ash. He had missed this—burning for her.

"Me, too," he said. "I love you. I should have told you sooner. I should have told you that night in the baths. I knew then."

Her smile was beautiful, and it was something he wanted to win every day of his life.

"I love you, too."

Their lips touched, and that fire inside him grew, heady and molten. His grip tightened, his hands pressing into her lower back. He wanted her to feel how much he missed her, how hard he was for her. He wanted her to understand what awaited her once they left this place. They would spend the weekend in bed, sequestered to his bedroom. He would have her in ways he had never had her before, and she would come, screaming his name, left in no doubt of his love for her.

The claws of her passion reached deep, but before they could commence their weekend of bliss, he had one more thing to claim. As he broke their kiss, Persephone gave a frustrated growl and tried to regain their connection. Hades chuckled at her eagerness, holding her just a little tighter, grinding his cock into her softness, a promise that he would soon be inside her.

"I wish to claim my favor, goddess," he said. For a moment, her eyes widened, so he spoke quickly, hoping to ease her anxiety. "Come to the Underworld with me."

She opened her mouth, but Hades claimed it in a kiss, and when he pulled away, he rested his forehead against hers.

"Live between worlds," he begged. "But do not leave us forever. My people, your people, me."

She gave a breathy laugh, her eyes watering, and nodded. "Of course."

Hades returned her smile. It was like she had just given him the world, and he would treasure her gift forever. After a moment, Persephone's grin became impish, and she smoothed her hands across his chest.

"I'm eager for a game of cards."

He tilted his head. He did not think it was possible, but his cock grew harder at her request, his mind running wild with the possibilities—hours of foreplay, erotic words, and amazing sex.

"Poker?" he asked.

"Yes."

"The stakes?"

"Your clothes," she answered, already unbuttoning his shirt.

Who was he to deny a queen?

BONUS CONTENT

BONUS CHAPTER - MINTHE
THE MINT PLANT

Hades looked up as Persephone entered his office, and he immediately felt his cock twitch. She was dressed s in red, and the fabric clung to her body and dipped at her breasts, welcoming his gaze. Her expression was impish, and his eyes narrowed, suspicious. He hoped she had come to seduce him. The thought made his sex grow thick and heavy, and he rested his hands on the arms of his chair to keep himself seated as she approached.

"So the desk is not just for show," she teased, a smile curling her inviting lips.

That depends on what you consider work, Hades thought, raising a brow. He had definitely labored over her upon its pristine surface and he could tell by the flush on the apples of her cheeks that she was thinking the same thing.

"I can be very productive when I wish," he said.

"Oh?"

"Yes, as you are aware, darling, I am a great multitasker."

He could kiss her, knead her breasts, and fuck her.

"Hmm. I seem to have forgotten you possessed that particular skill. Perhaps you can enlighten me?"

He narrowed his gaze, taking her banter as a challenge. Perhaps he had not branded her skin or fucked her hard enough. He considered how he might surprise her—vanishing from this spot to her in seconds, he would take her hair in his hands, and pull her head back to devour her mouth before settling her on his cock. He would take her against the windows overlooking the club.

Except that he now noticed that she held something in her arms—a plant in a red pot.

"Have you brought me something?"

Persephone pulled her lip into her mouth, and his gaze burned. She placed the pot on the edge of his desk and suddenly all he could smell was sweet spearmint—it was a mint plant. He did not like it because it covered up Persephone's aroma.

"Actually, I'm returning what was already yours," she said.

Hades raised a brow. "I think I would remember leaving a mint plant at your home, Persephone."

"Well, you see, this...plant wasn't always a plant."

He waited.

"She was a nymph. Minthe."

His brows knitted together, and he pointed at the plant. "You're saying that. Is my assistant?"

"Yes."

It took more control to not laugh then it had to stay seated when he wanted to fuck her.

He could tell she was anxious about admitting what she had done. Hades had never told her that he had dismissed Minthe and exiled her from the Underworld. There were a few reasons, among them, that he had not really thought about the nymph since he had captured Sisyphus.

Still, as he looked at Persephone, he was curious. How has this come to be?

"And why is my assistant a plant, Persephone?"

"Because," she answered, averting her eyes. "She upset me."

Ah.

Well, he could guess how Minthe had gone from being a nymph to a plant—whatever she'd said—and he was certain Minthe had *said* something because her only power was her words—had pissed Persephone off to the point her power had manifested. If it was anything like he'd experienced, it had probably exploded from her.

Still, he knew she was not telling the whole truth. He waited, thinking that she might cave and tell him on her own, but he knew better—Persephone never felt pressure to expound on anything, and usually only did so when they sat on opposite sides of the table, playing a game of cards.

"What did Minthe do to upset you?" He asked carefully.

"That doesn't matter anymore," she answered, and shrugged a shoulder. "I took care of it."

Clearly, he thought.

"I thought I would give you the option of returning her to her true form."

Hades had no wish to see Minthe returned to her natural form, but it amused him that Persephone was offering, if not made him a little suspicious. If he had to guess, she was feeling guilty.

He raised a brow.

"You wish for me to make that decision?"

"She is your assistant."

Hades rose from his chair and came around the desk, taking Persephone's hand, he pulled her to him, lifting her chin with his fingers. As he stared into her eyes, green as raw emeralds, he asked in a low voice, "How shall I convince you to tell me the truth?"

Her gaze fell to his lips. "Are you asking to play?"

The corners of his lips tipped, and he pressed a kiss to the hollow of her throat. Persephone's grip on him tightened as he traced along her jaw to the edge of her lush lips—but he did not kiss her. Just as she was about to give a frustrated growl, he gripped her hips and guided her to the edge of his desk.

"No," he said, as he slid his hands up her thighs and under her dress. "I'm multitasking."

Their mouths collided, his tongue diving to meet hers as his fingers hooked around her panties. He broke from her mouth long enough to slide them from her legs and took his place between her legs, spreading her wide, exposing her sensitive core. Hunger coiled low in his stomach, and he drew his tongue over his bottom lip in anticipating of his feast, fingers trailing her slick heat.

Persephone's breath escaped in a harsh stream and Hades noted how her body tightened with anticipation—and then he entered her, parting her warm flesh, using one finger then two, then reaching deep inside her until his fingers curled, stroking until she moaned his name.

"Do you like that?" He mumbled, leaning over her, he pressed a kiss between her breasts, then drew his tongue over the skin.

"Yes," she breathed.

"Tell me what you want," he said.

"More. Harder. Faster." It was a wish and a command they had both given, and often. Normally, Hades was more than happy to oblige, but not this time.

This time he withdrew, a stream of liquid heat came with it.

Fuck.

He wanted nothing more than to taste her come, but he refrained. This was his game—he would pleasure her to the point of pain until she offered up the answers he wanted, but as he met Persephone's gaze, he wondered if this was the right decision.

She was furious, her eyes ablaze with a combination of passion and fury.

"Why did you stop?" she demanded.

"Tell me why you snapped," he said. "What did she say to upset you?"

"*This* is your game?" she snapped, still reclined before

him, legs open, tempting.

Hades said nothing, and Persephone started to sit up, but he caged her against the desk, and he kissed her again. She had not answered his question, so she would face another bout of pleasure. He would bring her close to orgasm this time and he would do so with his tongue. A thrill of anticipating went through him, and his cock throbbed.

Persephone seemed even more eager, her hands going to the buttons of his shirt, her palms smoothing over his chest and abs until she reached his engorged sex. When she freed his cock, he groaned.

Perhaps she wasn't as angry as he thought.

Her hand closed over his shaft, and she pushed into him. Hades allowed himself to be guided back, into a standing position, and Persephone followed.

She stroked him, her thumb toying with the head of his cock and his mind was so clouded with arousal, he didn't feel her magic gathering until it was too late—until they were already in the Underworld, in the garden outside his palace, weeping wisteria growing overhead.

"Persephone—"

Hades wasn't sure what he was about to say or warn again, he just had the feeling he was in trouble. Then, she snapped her fingers, and vines sprouted from the ground, winding their way around Hades' wrists and ankles.

Where had she learned that trick, he wondered?

He didn't have to guess long, he knew—*Hecate*. His eyes darkened; his jaw tightened.

"Persephone." He said her name again, and he wasn't sure why—this was hot, though he would much rather see her restrained and pleasured.

"Yes, my lord?" She asked, looking up at him with her hand still around his cock. How could she sound so innocent and look so sinful?

"What are you doing?" he asked through gritted teeth.

She stroked him, and his chest heaved. This was the time when he wanted to have his hands in her hair as her mouth closed over him.

"What does it look like?" she asked, continuing to stroke him.

She rose onto the tips of her toes, her mouth devouring his own, her tongue sliding against his. When she kissed down his neck, he nipped at her lips, wishing to recapture them and make love to her mouth—and yet she continued, blazing a path along his skin.

"Tell me what you want," she whispered as she sucked on his earlobe and he growled, his muscles rippling as he attempted to free himself from her restraints.

"You, Goddess."

She smiled lips passing over his stomach and to the dark curls around his cock. She took him into her mouth then, and he bucked against her, groaning at the heat and the pressure. She held him at the root as she worked him up and down, as her tongue slide over his crown. Her other hand cupped his balls, and he swore at one point, she took those into her mouth. When he came, he did so in waves, and he felt like a puppet, attached to strings, his body heavy with release.

In the aftermath, she stood apart, and he missed her warmth.

"Is it torturous?" she challenged, something akin to evil in her eyes, and he had the fleeting though that perhaps she should assign torture in Tartarus. "To take pleasure from me, and not give it in return?"

This is her revenge, he realized. This is why her magic had worked so well.

She undressed and stood naked before him. She was perfection—beautifully sculpted with large breasts and wide hips. She was everything he never knew he wanted and seeing her like this made him even more desperate to be free. He wanted to put his hands on every inch of her skin.

"What do you want, Hades?"

The question roared through him, and the vines that restrained him finally snapped and Hades descended upon her, a predator after his pray. He lifted her with ease and brought her down upon his cock. He felt violent and wild as he leveraged her body against the jagged rock wall, pounding into her. Persephone responded just as fiercely, he heels dug into his ass and her nails scraped down his back. Her sex clenched around him, and her orgasm coaxed him to come.

When he finished, he could no longer hold himself up and knelt to the ground, holding Persephone close. As they caught their breath, his goddess pulled away, meeting his gaze, her eyes as fierce as they were before their coupling.

"You will not use sex to get what you want, do you understand?"

A smile curled the edges of his lips as he answered. "Yes, my queen, but I will tell you what I want—an answer when I ask for it."

"Do you not trust me?"

"I could ask the same of you," he countered.

He did not think this was about trust in the end—he believed she didn't answer because she was afraid—of what, he was unsure. Perhaps judgement?

Persephone looked away, "It is not so easy to answer you."

His brows drew together as he asked, "Why?"

She pressed her lips together and Hades touched her chin, drawing her eyes back to his. "Are you ashamed?"

She sighed. "I was angry and rash in my decision, but she questioned my power and I thought to teach her just how powerful I was."

It did not surprise him that Minthe had pushed Persephone to this point.

"If you had not punished her, I would have for leading you to Tartarus."

He had assumed from the beginning that Minthe was the one to encourage Persephone to wander to Tartarus, leading to her unfortunate encounter with Tantalus.

Persephone looked at him, surprised.

"You knew?"

"I suspected," he said and then smiled. "You just confirmed."

She swatted his arm. "That is deceptive."

Hades chuckled and kissed her nose before growing serious again. "Still, why protect her when she put you in danger?"

"I wasn't *protecting* her...I was handling her on my own. I don't want you to fight my battles, Hades."

"My lady, it is very clear to me that you do not need my helping fighting your battles."

Especially if she got angry enough—still, that was something they would need to work on. Persephone need to be able to call upon her power even when she was calm.

They dressed and with their appearances were restored, Hades snapped his fingers, summoning Minthe the Mint Plant from where they'd left her in his office at Nevernight.

"Now, what shall we do with her?"

"I have not completely forgiven her," Persephone admitted. "But I should like to provide her with at least one comfort, and that is to be returned to the Underworld."

She was far more kind than him. Hades had chosen to deprive her of that comfort after her abhorrent betrayal. Still, if that is what his goddess wanted, he would agree. Though, as he observed a few wilted leaves, he said, "Is that because you have neglected her in the Upperworld?"

"No!" Persephone huffed.

Hades laughed.

"If you must know, I spend more time here anyway which means Lexa's responsible for watering her and that doesn't seem fair. Plus...I'd rather not be responsible for her death."

Hades, still smiling, kissed the top of her head. "As you wish, darling."

Together, they transplanted Minthe into Underworld soil.

After, they went for a stroll. Hades guided their walk—passing through the Asphodel Fields heading for a part of the Underworld he created especially for Persephone. A thrill of excitement shot through him at the thought of revealing this portion of his realm to her. It was a feeling he was getting used to as he experienced it more and more.

Their fingers were laced, and the air was warm, and Hades took pleasure in this peace.

"Hades." He heard the hesitation in her voice as she spoke. "I wish to ask that you not call me my—"

"Lady?"

"Queen," she said corrected.

He stopped and turned to face her. He was not surprised by her request, as she'd been making it since they had met. Still, he would make the same argument. Persephone was a goddess—her title was lady, and when they wed, her title would be queen.

She explained quickly. "I recognize you spoke in a moment of passion—"

He had spoken in a moment of passion, but that did not mean the words were not sincere.

"I meant it," he said. "You are my queen. Only you hold sway over me."

"Hades—"

"Why do you fear it? The title?"

"It's not fear...it's..." she trailed off, unable to find words. "Your people already call me their queen, don't you think it's a little...too early?"

"So it is fear," he said. "Fear that you and I will not work."

Perhaps it was not so much fear that they wouldn't work as much as someone driving them apart—an all-to-real possibility given that the Fates would unravel their future, or that Demeter would continue to rage against them—not to mention when Zeus discovered Persephone's Divinity, an inevitability, he was certain the Olympians would have their opinions.

"My people will always see you as their mistress

because of how you have treated them whether you choose to love me or not," he said. "As for me, well—you will always be the ruler of my heart."

"You cannot know that," she whispered.

You cannot know my heart, he wanted to say.

"I have waited lifetimes for you," he said fiercely. "I know it."

He turned from her then, their fingers unraveling. He did not like the emptiness as it reminded him of the same void he'd felt over the ages—a hollow ache he wanted filled with desire and passion and love.

What would it take for her to trust that this would work?

She has burdens just like you, he reminded himself, and the thing about burdens was that there were none greater or heavier—they just were.

After some time walking in silence, they came to the edge of a cliff. At their feet, acres of silver trees flourished beneath a darkening, starry sky.

"This is beautiful." Persephone said.

Hades looked at her and spoke. "I am glad you think so because it is yours. Welcome to the Grove of Persephone."

Her eyes snapped to his, widening. "But—"

"I thought you might like to have a place to yourself—somewhere to practice your magic. A place that doesn't...remind you of our beginning."

He felt shame flood his body at the reminder of how he'd marked her. Looking back, there was a better way to coax her power to fruition, but he'd made his decision from a place of fear and the consequences had been painful.

He was surprised when Persephone touched his cheek and said, "Hades, I love our beginning."

He did not believe her, and his expression was wry.

"It is true I haven't always *loved* it, but I could never hate anything that brought me to you."

He covered her hand with his own and pressed his lips to her palm before drawing her close and he marveled at her presence—at how beautiful and warm and solid she was. Then he kissed her, and unlike their other kisses, this one was gentle and sweet and slow—a savory exploration of her mouth and their tongues and their taste.

When he pulled away, Persephone was breathless, her body warmed beneath his hands, her eyes alight with desire. It was the first time he knew he had been right to grant Theseus his favor, no matter the consequences, because it meant that this woman would be by his side for the rest of his eternal life—and she was power, raw and terrible power—not only for what she would soon be capable of, but for what she inspired inside him.

"You will be my queen," he swore to the moon and the stars and the sky—and all the gods who had ever lived and died. "I do not need the Fates to tell me that."

BONUS SCENE - COMPASSION

Hades appeared on the sidewalk outside a bar called Tyche's—though, it was not owned by the goddess herself —it was known for live, local music. It was also where Orpheus played, and when Hades manifested there, he did so in front of the mortal.

Orpheus stopped in his tracks, staring wide-eyed at Hades, dressed in a red and black flannel shirt and jeans, his guitar slung on his back, the strap cut across his chest.

Neither said anything for a beat, and then Orpheus spoke.

"Are you here to kill me?"

Hades just stared, peeling back layer after layer of Orpheus's soul, and beneath the grief and the longing and the love, he finally found what he was looking for—the guilt. It was a weight upon the mortal, it kept shackles around his wrists and ankles, kept him submerged under water, unable to breath, unable to open his eyes, unable to live.

"Your soul is bent with guilt," Hades said. "Why?"

He'd seen this before from men and women who had cheated, or lied, or kept secrets from their partners, and Hades could not reconcile why they begged him to return their love if this was how they treated them while they lived—but Orpheus' guilt wasn't the same, and it bothered Hades that he could not see the root of it, so he had come to ask.

The mortal man stared hard at Hades, his eyes watering. Then, he looked down at his feet and said. "I don't know. I just feel…guilt for not telling Eurydice I loved her more, for not spending more time with her. I feel guilty for living—not just existing but for doing everyday things like watching television or hanging out with friends. I feel guilty for smiling or laughing or feeling anything other than sadness in her absence."

As he spoke, his glistening eyes welled over, and tears spilled down his cheeks.

"I just feel guilty for everything."

Shame descended, sitting heavily on Hades' shoulders. He'd been wrong about this man. He had assumed Orpheus' guilt was because he had betrayed his wife, he had never considered that he would feel such an emotion because she no longer lived.

Hades knew what it was to feel guilty, but he did not know this guilt—nor would he ever. He and Persephone were immortal, and despite the fact that they we not together at the moment, Hades did not want to imagine what it would be like to continue existing without her in the world.

He placed a hand on the mortal's shoulder and Hades was surprised when he did not startle.

"Come, I have something to show you."

Orpheus' brows drew together, but after a moment, he nodded. Hades wondered why this man was so comfortable around him—or was it that he could not bring himself to care? Whatever the reason, Hades vanished with the mortal.

They appeared in Asphodel, in the meadow where the souls had built houses, planted gardens, and setup shops. Today, as they did most weekends, they were setting up for a festival. Colorful flags hung between the homes, children ran with baskets full of flowers, tossing them in the road, and the smell of sweets wafted from open windows as they prepared food for the evening.

"Where are we?" Orpheus asked.

"This is the Underworld," Hades said. "Asphodel."

Orpheus met Hades' gaze, eyes wide.

"But it's…" his voice trailed away, and a smile touched Hades' lips. He knew what the mortal would say—it was not what he expected. It was not what anyone expected.

"Why bring me here?" He said at last.

"You asked to take Eurydice's place," he said.

"Yes," the mortal breathed, and Hades felt his hope rise. It wasn't something he actually expected. He'd thought, when faced with this, the mortal might recant—but he didn't.

"And while I cannot allow that. I would like to offer something else."

He had thought long and hard about Orpheus, about the ways he might have helped him. He heard Persephone's words in his head now and remembered her frustration: *Would it have been relinquishing your control to offer him even a glimpse of his wife, safe and happy in the Underworld?*

He would do one better.

"I'm giving you an evening," Hades said. "Use your time well, mortal."

"Orpheus?" His name slipped from the mouth of a beautiful young woman. Her hair was thick, black and wavy, her skin a rich brown. The combination made her eyes look like green fire, and her lips as red as an imperial rose. She was vibrant and full of life, even in death.

"Eurydice."

They ran to each other and embraced, and when their lips met, Hades turned away. The scene only reminded him of what he no longer had, and his stomach tightened with loneliness.

He missed Persephone.

He missed kissing her and tasting her and fucking her. He missed her breathy moans and her voice and her laugh. He missed feeling her presence in the Underworld, he missed hearing the souls talk about how she had come to visit them, had tea with them, danced with them. He missed not being able to convince Cerberus, Typhon, Orthrus to play fetch because they wanted to trot along after her. He missed smelling her, and knew it was only a matter of time before her scent no longer clung to his sheets.

He missed every single thing about her.

"My lord."

Hades paused at Orpheus' voice, turning toward him. "Thank you. I shall tell all who will listen of your kindness."

Hades turned fully to the man. "Do not speak of my kindness, speak of Persephone's kindness. It is she who deserves your worship, for it was she who changed my mind."

Orpheus' eyes widened slightly, and Eurydice placed a hand on his face, guiding his gaze back to hers as they kissed again.

Hades left, returning to his palace—and while it felt empty without Persephone, he was content in the knowledge that after tonight, Orpheus would start the spread of his goddess's earth-bound worship.

THANK YOU FOR READING!

I sincerely hope you enjoyed reading this book as much as I enjoyed writing it. If you did, I would appreciate a short review on Amazon or your favorite book website. Reviews are crucial for any author, and even just a line or two can make a huge difference.

AUTHOR'S NOTE

A Game of Fate is a book for my readers. When I started writing A Touch of Darkness, I knew I was writing Persephone's story and it could not be any other way. In truth, I thought that Hades' POV would be too difficult to explore—he was not talkative, and he often gave one-word replies when questioned. It sounds insane, but this is how I write. I tell the story I'm told. As I sat with this idea of writing ATOD from Hades POV and read more about how the Olympians came to power, I began to understand something about our beloved God of the Dead: he was born into a ten-year war. For some reason, this knowledge really hit home for me. I started to understand why Hades felt so dark, why he was so quiet, why he was so impatient and eager for control and eventually, I made my way through A Game of Fate.

So thank you so much, readers—without **you**, this book would not exist!

As with all my books, I pulled from a variety of myths and I want to go into those details now.

Of course, the major myth I play upon in this book is that of Sisyphus (de Ephyra in my book, which just means *of Ephyra*, another name for *Corinth*), the King of Corinth who cheated death twice. There are a few variations of this myth, but the main points are that the first time Sisyphus cheated death, he tricked Thanatos into chains (which is so ridiculous but this is an absurd story so stick with me) and escaped from the Underworld (see where I got the chain idea?). As a result, no one died because Thanatos was not free to reap souls—and guess who got mad? Ares. So, Ares freed Thanatos. So, Sisyphus lived a little while and died again and this time, made a plea to Persephone—could he return to the living and instruct his wife on how to properly bury him? See, prior to his death, Sisyphus had advised his wife NOT to bury him. This guy just did not want to die. Of course, compassionate Persephone agrees. After this, Sisyphus lived to be quite old (because… apparently Hades…no one…really cared that he had escaped the Underworld???), and when he died again, he was sentenced to roll a boulder up a hill only to have it roll back down once he reached the top which doesn't seem like that horrible of a punishment. I mean, literally other people get their livers eaten out by vultures on the daily. But, it's very fitting for Sisyphus because he has, essentially, been sentence to struggle for eternity—to obtain success only to watch it unravel before his very eyes. If you think about it long enough (don't), you'll see that Hades journey mirrors this same fate…except with a positive outcome.

A few other things to note about Sisyphus: He was known for violating Zeus's Law of Xenia, which was basically showing hospitality to guests (how nice and ironic that this is Zeus's SACRED law). Sisyphus would do the opposite and kill his guests because he's a man and wanted to show his ruthlessness as a king. I also talk about how Sisyphus helped protect Poseidon's granddaughter from Zeus. This is a play on a similar myth where Sisyphus tells the river god, Asopus where Zeus had taken his daughter, Aegina after he kidnapped her. In some myths, Asopus is the son of Poseidon. In the first instance, Sisyphus incurred the anger of Zeus. As for the second, Zeus ordered Thanatos to chain Sisyphus in Tartarus…and we all know what happened next.

You will also notice the introduction of Helios, God of the Sun. I reference several myths with him. One was the death of his son, Phaethon, who asked to drive Helios' chariot, lost control, and had to be killed by Zeus before he set the whole world on fire. The other myth I reference is Helios' sacred cattle. They pop up a few times in mythology—once when they were stolen by the giant Alcyoneus and when they were slain by Odysseus' men. Both times, Helios took revenge but something I noticed is that he always takes his revenge through other people. For instance, in the case of Alcyoneus, Hercules is the one who defeated the giant and in the case of Odysseus, Zeus helped Helios by sinking the king's ship, so when it came to Helios being angry with Hades, he goes to Zeus for help first. While I do not directly reference this, in my mind, Helios also told Demeter when Hades was in bed with Persephone. I think there's irony to the fact that Helios has consistently NOT shown his power—the worst he's done is threaten to take the sun to the Underworld (in mythology) and plunge the world into darkness (in my book).

Next, Adonis. In Mythology, Adonis was a handsome mortal Aphrodite found as a child. The Goddess of Love asks Persephone to raise him. Aphrodite returns when Adonis is grown but Persephone refuses to give him back as she has fallen in love with him. Now, I like to think that maybe Aphrodite was romantically in love and Persephone saw Adonis as a son, but the myth suggests they are both romantically in love with Adonis (eww). Either way, Zeus got involved and declared that Adonis had to spend a third of the year with Persephone, then with Aphrodite, and for the remaining third, he got to choose (idk why Zeus is all about solving these custody settlements by dividing up the year but whatever). Anyway, Adonis chooses to spend the remaining third with Aphrodite. In the end, Adonis was killed by a wild boar (who knows, maybe Sephy sent it). As he died in Aphrodite's arms, her tears mixed with his blood, creating the anemone flower. Of course, in my books, I could not accept that Persephone would love anyone else but Hades, so I wanted Adonis to be a villain of sorts—and we know how that turned out.

I will not go into too many details on Aphrodite and Hephaestus, as they will have their own book once the Hades x Persephone Saga is finished, but I just have to say that I think Hephaestus is an intriguing god—I mean, he has created some really powerful weapons and a HUMAN (Pandora). I had a lot of fun imagining how he/his interests would evolve with the modern world and I cannot wait until he and Aphrodite have their own book!

Finally, I just want to say a word about Hermes. I was so excited to play upon his title as God of Thieves. In case you don't know, Hermes' title comes from the fact that he stole Apollo's sacred cattle (I know, he and Helios BOTH have sacred cattle but it's likely because these two gods are sometimes thought to be one and the same). Anyways, did I mention that Hermes is a BABY when he does this? He was literally born and then the next day he steals this cattle BECAUSE HE IS HUNGRY. Apollo is, obviously, not happy and confronts Baby Hermes. The two end up reconciling (because Zeus) and Hermes gives Apollo a lyre and Apollo gives Hermes his golden staff. The end.

Thanks for coming to my TED Talk! I hope you all enjoyed A Game of Fate. I'm so appreciative of your support. It means the world to me. Don't forget to leave a review and tell all your friends how awesome I am so we can have a Netflix series one day!

Love,
Scarlett

ABOUT THE AUTHOR

© Photo: Ashli Amador

Scarlett St. Clair lives in Oklahoma with her husband. She has a Master's degree in Library Science and Information Studies. She is obsessed with Greek Mythology, murder mysteries, love, and the afterlife. If you are obsessed with these things, then you'll like her books.

For information on books, tour dates, and content, please visit www.ScarlettStClair.com or check out her social media

  @AuthorScarlettStClair

 @ScarlettStClai1

CPSIA information can be obtained
at www.ICGtesting.com
Printed in the USA
LVHW110751100821
693143LV00009B/14

9 781735 771915